Jan. 1[illegible] 2015

Dear Rose,

Best wishes and enjoy the story.

Norman Gaudrault

Topsfield, Massachusetts

U.S.A.

and

Georges Idier

Grenoble / Nantes

France

Norman Gaudrault – Georges Idier

Two Years in America

The Discoveries of a French Family

Société des Écrivains

Sur simple demande adressée à la Société des Écrivains,
14, rue des Volontaires – 75015 Paris,
vous recevrez gratuitement notre catalogue
qui vous informera de nos dernières publications.

Texte intégral

We dedicate this book to our families
and particularly to our spouses, Evelyn and Marie-Thérèse.

N.G. and G.I.

Acknowledgments

Many people contributed to this work by offering their opinions and through their suggestions. In winding my way throughout the United States and Canada, I received a warm welcome wherever I traveled.

I wish to particularly thank my friend Thomas Kelly who introduced me to the computer; Jack Driscoll, former editor of the *Boston Globe*, for his ongoing encouragement; Bill Lewis; Sherry Kenney; Joseph Thibodeau; Carol and Lawrence Essember; Chuck Davis; Roger Montgomery; Greg and Harry Carpenter; Nancy and Neil Morrissey; Patti and Ron Siegemund; Judith and Normand Paulhus; Gail Cole; Donna, Gerry and Irene McAfee; and Benoit and Michele Pilon.

The French version of the baseball chapter was written with the help of Jean-François Bégin of *La Presse* of Montreal.

I wish especially to thank Jacqueline Williams, Principal of the Woodrow Wilson High School; Rory Pullens, Principal of the Duke Ellington School of the Arts and the Administration of the *Musée du Fort* of Quebec.

Judith Connelly, Sibyl Hezlett, Carol McGrath, Tracy Berenson and Noelle Martignetti of the Topsfield, Massachusetts Library assisted me in my research. Katia Hale-Mason and Stephen Lais guided me in the electronic transmission of the manuscript.

I am also grateful to Anne Idier and to Michele and Suzanne Gaudrault who were of significant help in a number of ways in realizing this work. Evelyn Gaudrault and Judith Lais read the translated version of the story and made a number of invaluable corrections and suggestions.

I finally recognize both wives who encouraged us throughout this project.

N.G.

Introduction

This story was originally written in French under the title of *Deux ans en Amérique* for a French-speaking audience. Its purpose was to give these readers, and especially those from France, a sense for life in America from a variety of perspectives in an entertaining manner.

Over time, many English speakers expressed a desire to read this novel and its translation was accordingly undertaken.

It is hoped that the reader of this English version will consider these original objectives, allowing for *nuances* that would be of particular interest to French speakers.

With these thoughts in mind, we hope that all who read this novel will enjoy the story and that nothing will have been lost in the translation!

Chapter 1.
July 2000 – Nice-Paris
The Departure

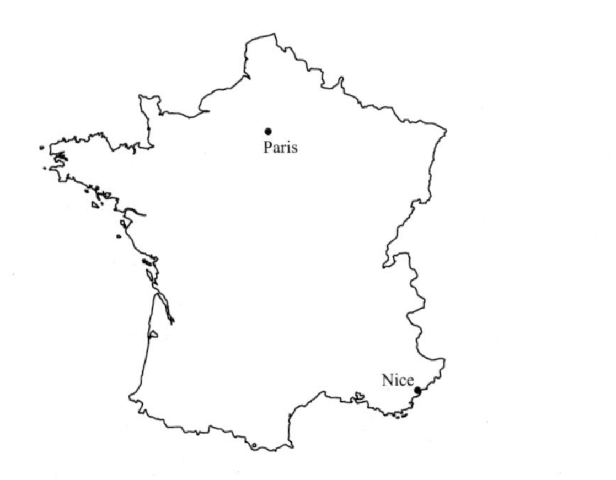

Go West!

After a year of discussions and many apprehensions, the Benoits have decided to leave Nice and to go to the United States for two years.

Pierre, a biologist-immunologist of international renown, celebrated for his research in contagious diseases and vaccines, has accepted an invitation from the National Institutes of Health (NIH) to come and work for this period of time in its laboratories near Washington, D.C.

Dominique intends to seek employment, in teaching if possible. After marrying and with a master's degree in the classics, she has taught in private schools on the outskirts of Paris, then in Tunis, and finally in Nice.

The most challenging issue has been that of the children's schooling: Julie, sixteen, having brilliantly completed her third year of lycée studies and particularly Philippe, fourteen, who, in spite of having satisfactorily finished his first year, is a mediocre student who doesn't apply himself in his studies.

Their apartment in Nice has been rented and it is time now to finish packing before leaving. Julie would like to bring all of her CDs, but she will need to leave most of them with her paternal grandparents in Cannes. She adores all the popular singers. She is leaving her friends with some reluctance, but she nonetheless feels that she will learn much in the United States. Her English is far from perfect and she still hesitates to speak it but, hey, she will learn to get by. In fact, these three days before their departure seem an eternity to her. She is eager to get to America.

For several weeks, Dominique has been organizing for this event. She has often felt alone in her preparations. There has been so much to do: details surrounding the apartment, insurances, not to speak of the necessary shopping. She has felt frazzled these past several days. Fortunately, with her computer skills, she has been able to make all the reservations online.

"We are leaving in three days. I could use a bit of help. Julie, supper is for you to prepare this evening. And you, Philippe, you are not an invalid. If you want to come along, shut off the TV and get off the couch. Please go pick up your room and finish your packing."

"I would prefer to stay home. I am old enough to be with grand-mère and grand-père. All of these plans bug me."

* * *

The day of departure has arrived. The suitcases are ready. Reservations for a cab were made yesterday evening.

Breakfast is eaten in silence. All are wondering if the right decision has been made to leave this city which they love so much. Will Pierre benefit from this experience? Will Dominique find any kind of work? Will she be accepted in her new environment? How will she be able to help the children in their adjustment? Philippe and Julie ask themselves with some trepidation if they will be able to make new friends.

Ah, but it is no longer time to reflect. The die is cast. All angles have been studied and considered over these past few months. The time has come to leave, quickly and without regrets, and especially to not forget the tickets, passports, and other documents.

It is a cool morning with bright sunshine and a clear blue sky. The city is slowly awakening. The streets are practically deserted when the taxi arrives.

"The front seat is mine," declares Philippe.

"If you wish. I'll sit out back with the ladies," answers his Dad.

Pierre then addresses the driver. "Good morning, I think that we will fill your trunk with all our suitcases. How are you this morning? "

"As usual. You know, life is not easy. We rely on good tips. The days are long and driving in this city is not easy. And besides, foreigners around here drive like fools. It is well known: only the French know how to drive! By morning's end, you might just imagine, it will be total gridlock and traffic will come to a standstill."

During the ride, Dominique sensed that they might cover all the world's problems were the trip to be any longer. Fortunately, the train station is upon them and each person is responsible for his or her own luggage. Pierre pays the fare and, previously well advised, adds a generous tip.

The station is crowded. It would appear that everyone is traveling by train this morning. Departure time is in thirty minutes.

"How about a hot chocolate?" asks Philippe.

"Okay," answers Pierre. "Buy me *Le Monde*. There will be ample reading time during the trip. Purchase *L'Equipe* for yourself and you can let me know if we will win the World Cup in 2002."

"Papa, of course we will win. Unfortunately, I won't be around for the finals."

"We might have returned by then. In any event, we aren't going to the ends of the earth. They do have TV in the United States."

As the train leaves, Dominique takes a deep breath. All her recent efforts have been directed toward this moment. She has done all that needed to be done and often with no help. She did not get to bed until after midnight, but she will have a chance to nap during the trip.

Julie immerses herself in a novel. An avid reader, she is a literary person and is strong in languages. Her hope is to make much progress in English and in Spanish. Philippe, more scientifically oriented, is not as good a student as his sister. For the moment, his gaze is directed out the window and he has nothing to say. As his tears well up, it is clear that he is upset.

Apprehension and fatigue dominate during the northward excursion. A 4 p.m. arrival at the Gare de Lyon becomes a new discovery for the children. They have been to Paris before, but when they were much younger and they have long since forgotten what they previously experienced. They will have two days to see as many sights as possible.

The parents are well acquainted with Paris, the place where they first met. Dominique hails from the Parisian outskirts and she completed her studies at the *Sorbonne*. Pierre was born in Toulon. His work brings him frequently to the capital.

The departure from Paris is scheduled for the fifteenth of the month. The family will stay with Dominique's retired parents who live outside the city at Vésinet. While Pierre attends to a few administrative details at the *Institut Pasteur* and at the Ministry of Foreign Affairs, Dominique and the children will be able to visit Paris.

Pierre hails a taxi. "Please, no discussions with the cabbie this time," implores Dominique.

* * *

Alma accompanies her daughter and grandchildren to the *Musée d'Orsay* this first morning. Dominique is particularly fond of the Impressionists. She recalls her visits to Monet's home and studio in Giverny: his gardens, the Japanese bridge, the blue and yellow decor of his fabulous kitchen. She lingered there on more than one occasion and took in the weeping willows hovering over the pond lilies that the artist brought to life in so many of his paintings. She can now be mesmerized by these creations before which she stands but she does not dare to become overly engrossed for too long as Philippe is easily bored and distracted by all this culture.

Dominique and Julie quickly glance at works by Renoir, Manet, and Caillebotte. The mother and daughter agree that they could easily spend the entire day in this museum and still not even come close to appreciating everything that there is to see.

The afternoon is spent on the hill of Montmartre. The panorama of the city from outside the basilica impresses the children. Dominique points out the most important monuments. The grandmother finds the interior of Sacré-Cœur to be austere compared to Notre-Dame but beautiful nonetheless.

On the Place du Tertre are gathered a number of artists, one of whom approaches Julie for a portrait. "May I, mother? Here is my chance for fame and recognition."

"How about with Philippe? A painting of the two of you together would make a nice gift for your Benoit grandparents."

Passersby have been drawn into the experience. After a brief sitting, the work is completed and all are pleased. Dominique congratulates the artist who signs in the lower right hand corner "Jean D."

* * *

Pierre accompanies his wife and children the following day. "Why don't we start with the Eiffel Tower?" a plan that does not exactly thrill Dominique, forever anguished from having been stuck in an elevator for a half hour in a hotel in Tunis.

Following a quick lunch on the Champs-Elysées, "and certainly not at McDonald's," says the father, the Benoits find their way to Place de la Concorde. "We will eat American soon enough."

Dominique insists. "Turn around and look closely. Focus on the Arc de Triomphe off in the distance. It is said that this is the most beautiful thoroughfare in the entire world! Let us be like all these tourists and take a few pictures that you will be able to show your new American friends!"

"If I find some."

"Don't worry, Philippe; you will find some."

From the banks of the Seine, the group crosses the Pont Saint-Michel. For Dominique and Pierre it is almost a pilgrimage to stroll up the Boul 'Mich' up to the Rue Soufflot.

"Heavens! Le Capoulade and Le Dupont have disappeared, replaced by a MacDo and a Quick! How can that be? Could this already be America?"

The parents ask themselves how to spend this last evening on French soil. A Tunisian restaurant is the consensus choice. The waiter is from the island of Djerba. When he discovers that Dominique and Pierre have spent two years in Tunisia, he speaks to them of his life in Paris over these past four years. He is happy here but he still yearns for the life that he left behind and he is impatiently awaiting the vacation that will bring him back home later this summer.

* * *

"Your tickets and passports, please," requests the smiling Air France representative. The formalities are quickly handled. The luggage allowances have not been exceeded.

Julie is held up at security. Her metallic belt buckle has sounded the alarm. Removing her belt, she passes through a second time without incident.

It is the first flying experience for the children. Philippe's cracking voice betrays the feelings that he cannot suppress. The brother and sister look attentively at these enormous planes that are taking off and landing. They examine the arrival and departure board in amazement. Flights are coming in from Rome, Cairo, Tel Aviv, Munich, Sydney, Beijing, Montreal, Istanbul. They are leaving for Tunis, Johannesburg, Hong Kong, Dar as Salaam, Khartoum, Chicago, and Jakarta. It would take a world map to situate all these cities.

"For the time being, Washington will suffice," says Philippe. "With all these people," adds the mother, "how will we ever be able to retrieve our luggage at the other end?"

"No problem. They are not frequently lost."

Before being seated, Philippe would love to have visited the cockpit. He is immediately impressed as he glances at all the gadgetry through the open door on the way down the aisle. After takeoff and following the flight attendant's instructions, the pilot indicates the transatlantic route to be followed and the weather patterns that are expected. "It should be a smooth flight for the most part. We will run into a bit of bumpiness along the way but nothing too significant. Our time in the air will be seven hours and twelve minutes. It will be hot and hazy in Washington. In the meantime, relax and enjoy your flight."

* * *

"We will be crossing six time zones and we can reset our watches accordingly." Julie challenges her brother to a game of Mille Bornes "… and I will whip you without mercy."

"We should have time for a movie as well."

Dominique and Pierre stare at each other and exchange a forced smile. Dominique is not comfortable flying and her expression betrays her anxiety. They both seem to be wondering. What will they encounter at the other end? Have they made the right decision in all of this? What will the long-term consequences be for them and for their children?

But the decision has been made. The Air Bus takes off. All four have butterflies in their stomach. Dominique squeezes Pierre's hand. "Off we go."

"No turning back. America awaits us. Go West the Benoits", whispers Pierre in his wife's ear.

As the sight of Paris fades in the distance, he hums the familiar tune that Dominique recognizes. *America, America, I want to see her*!

Chapter 2.
July 2000 – Washington, D.C.

We hold these truths to be self evident... That all men are created equal... Life, liberty and the pursuit of happiness.

Thomas Jefferson,
Author of the Declaration of Independence

At Washington-Dulles Airport, the immigration procedures offer the Benoits their first surprise. Contrary to what they had been told and what they had anticipated, the entry takes place without a single problem: the officer barely looks at their passports, stamps them officially, and greets them with a warm welcome.

Having waited quite long for their baggage, they pass through immigration and the female officer, in full conversation with her colleague, takes the entry form that Pierre had meticulously filled out during the flight with hardly a glance. “We are being run through the mill,” thinks the father.

The doors open automatically. “What do you know? We are in the country.”

A representative from the National Institutes of Health (NIH) holds a sign with their name. He introduces himself, welcomes them, and takes Dominique’s suitcase. “We will go to the parking garage and I will show you to your car. Here is a map of the city that should help you during these first few days. Also, you have my business card with my phone number. Should you encounter any kind of problem, by all means, call me. This is the vehicle that the NIH has put at your disposal. Follow me and I will show you to your house."

"What a huge car!" exclaims Philippe.

"Get used to it," replies the father. "You won't see many of our small cars from this time onward." Forty minutes later, Dominique can hardly believe her eyes when they pull into the driveway. "The house looks beautiful and to think that, for the next two years, it will be our home."

The family will live in this dwelling in the northwest part of the city. It is a substantial home that reveals itself to be comfortable and is comprised of seven furnished rooms on two levels. The first floor consists of the kitchen that includes a good-sized refrigerator, a stove, microwave, dishwasher, and the usual cooking paraphernalia. The dining room, living room, and den/office space complete the downstairs. The bedrooms are on the second floor. There are two full baths. The room dimensions are generous by French standards. Julie and Philippe are happy to each have their own bedroom. The outside is painted a pale green with a darker green trim. The two-car garage on the right-hand side contains a garden hose, lawnmower, three bicycles, and sufficient shelving for handyman storage of assorted kinds.

Dominique compliments Pierre on his choice. He had made his selection the previous month when he had briefly visited the National Institutes of Health to finalize his arrangements. Philippe discovers an ample lawn in the backyard. "I will be able to practice my soccer. Hopefully, there will be boys my age in the neighborhood who will be able to join me."

"And, hopefully, girlfriends for me as well," muses Julie.

"Most certainly," says Pierre. "One finds especially young families in this neighborhood. I inquired at the NIH and was assured that we would be living in a section of town with a mixed population. You will discover the melting pot of the United States around you. That won't be such a bad thing. But I doubt that there will be many French people in our immediate surroundings. We shall see."

Dominique is solicitous toward Philippe who is still out of sorts. "Don't worry. All will be well. You may find it difficult at the outset, but we will manage. You will get accustomed to the place and you will certainly come to like it."

Pierre adds his own comments. "We have the next two weeks before I start my work. As your mother indicates, we will progress slowly day-by-day."

"Yes, Papa; easy for you to say," replies Philippe.

"Do you like your room, Julie?"

"Yes, Maman. I can already see how I would like to furnish it. I brought my favorite pictures to hang on the walls. The bed will go in the corner and my desk will be by the window. I enjoy looking outside while I am studying. On the other side will be a futon for reading. I will need a stereo very quickly."

Philippe hasn't a clue as to what to do with his room. Dominique promises that she will assist him. For the moment, there is no way to console him.

* * *

The following day at breakfast, Pierre proposes the schedule for the day. "We will run our errands this morning. After all, we have to eat and there is no food in the house. So, Philippe, relax. We will fill the refrigerator for you."

Julie asks where the post office, the school, and the shopping mall might be. "You, Philippe, might be on the lookout for a football field."

"We first need to find a bank," implores Dominique. "We have but a few dollars left. How nice that the NIH should have greeted us and have provided us with wheels. Now we need to change some money. Then we can head for the supermarket."

"Agreed. And then we will need to present ourselves at the embassy in order to register."

"What for?"

"To be listed among the French who are living in the United States. It could be useful. Besides, we might find some cultural programs that might be of interest to us. Visiting the city can wait for another time."

"But, Papa, we could pay a quick visit to see the major areas and high points that we studied before leaving."

"Okay, Julie, if you insist."

Thanks to some excellent directions provided by a policeman, they make their way to a branch of the Riggs Bank.

"Is it possible to change 5,000 francs into dollars?

"Of course."

"While we are here," asks Dominique, "could we open a checking account? We will need to pay some bills before long."

"You need only fill out this form and I will give you a dozen checks while you await those with your printed names that you will receive shortly."

"Perfect."

"Your accent is charming. Good luck and welcome to the United States."

"Many thanks and good-bye."

Safeway is part of a commercial center. Julie recites the names: Walmart, Staples, CVS Pharmacy. There is a Chinese restaurant, a dry cleaner, and, of course, an obligatory McDonald's. Pierre finds a parking space but is cut off by an SUV. "I guess I will need to be more aggressive the next time around."

The supermarket is enormous. The Benoits are certainly not alone. Dominique consults her list. "We will buy just the necessities and that will leave us time for the rest of our errands. Choose two items apiece that might appeal to you. Remember that our meals will be simple at first. Philippe, don't wander away. Let's stick together."

At the first counter, Philippe points to a pastry and acknowledges the clerk with a timid *thank you*. "For a first experience, that wasn't too bad. It might be more complicated the next time." A bit more confident, he stops at the bakery section and requests a "loaf of bread" and, to his great surprise, he is served accordingly. "Phew, that will do it for me today."

Julie goes up and down the aisles methodically and studies the labels very carefully. "It isn't that different from back home. There is Nestle's and *La vache qui ri*." She finds Evian bottled water, *eau de sources naturelles des Alpes françaises*. "But what about this Brie from Vermont? Is it possible? This is outrageous. Only we can put out a real Brie." Having satisfied her curiosity, she selects a pizza and a jar of Skippy Peanut Butter.

Dominique and Pierre fill their shopping cart. Making an inventory of their purchases, they agree that nobody will die of starvation.

Pulling up to the checkout counter, they empty their cart. The white, African-American and Asian cashiers are very efficient. "You are French? I am Haitian. Welcome to the country. Did you find everything that you were seeking? That will be $120.43."

The retirees with their green aprons, supplementing their social-security benefits, bag the groceries. The full containers are put back into the shopping cart and Philippe pushes it to the car.

"Next, let us find our way to the post office," says Pierre." We will spend just a few minutes there. We will need to provide our address and we could use a few stamps. For our first outing, we have not fared too badly."

Dominique notices that Philippe is still not happy. "We have been well-received and these folks have gone out of their way to ease our purchases. Feeling strange is bound to last a few weeks, but we will manage. We knew this culture shock was bound to occur, but we will make our way through the experience."

The fridge is filled and Pierre will attempt to lift everyone's mood. He suggests a ride around town. "Julie, your idea is a good one."

Pierre studies the map of the city, one that appears to be very geometrical. They begin on Massachusetts Avenue which leads to Dupont Circle. "Yes, Dupont had been a revolutionary who left France. It is his son who started the chemical company, Dupont de Nemours. In a few minutes, we will be at Lafayette Square, another good French name."

Staying on the same avenue, he makes his way toward Union Station. Taking a right onto Delaware Avenue, they are impressed by the Capitol building. Turning right again onto Constitution Avenue, Pierre heads toward the Washington Monument. They stop briefly next to the Mall so that the children can stretch their legs. "Do you know that cows pastured here as late as 1826?" The national museums occupy the other side of the Mall. The Washington Monument recalls the obelisk at the Place de la Concorde, but is much taller. The Vietnam and Korean War Memorials are observed from a distance. The White House is visible on the right and, further down toward the south, the Lincoln Memorial. Behind the Washington Monument is the reflecting pool, another reminder of the circular body of water at the Place de la Concorde.

Having crossed the Potomac River over the Arlington Memorial Bridge, they come to the Arlington National Cemetery. From a distance and on the other side of the Potomac, they can see the Jefferson Memorial. Pierre crosses the Potomac in the opposite direction toward the impressive Kennedy Center. He takes Virginia Avenue, then Wisconsin Avenue. Having detoured to see Georgetown University, he heads toward the Naval Observatory and regains Massachusetts Avenue to complete the circuit.

"I have the impression of a city that is incomplete."

"I agree, Pierre. The architect Pierre L'Enfant, a Frenchman who had participated in the American Revolution, did not have time to complete his work," replies Dominique.

Pierre adds. "The site for the Capital had been hotly contested after the American Revolution. The northern states naturally preferred the North and, the southern ones, the South. A compromise was reached by Alexander Hamilton and Thomas Jefferson and, on July 16, 1790, an act of Congress established an area… *not to exceed 260 km2* in the region of the Potomac. President Washington and the men who would participate in the construction of the city chose the exact site."

The melancholy has lifted. "I told you that your spirits would improve. We will return for more leisurely strolls to see the city in much greater detail in the coming weeks and months."

* * *

"Julie, go see who is at the door."

"It is a young boy. He is asking for Philippe."

"Show him in and call your brother."

The visitor introduces himself. "My name is Ross Appleton." He gives the reason for his visit. His soccer team is playing in Alexandria, approximately six miles outside of the city. His mother will be bringing him along with two of his friends. Would Philippe like to come along? "I saw you playing alone behind your house. I live on Cleveland St. We are neighbors."

Dominique encourages her son. "Philippe, you have nothing to do. Here is a good chance for you to make a few friends."

Philippe seems interested. "Ross, when do you expect to return?"

"Around four or five o'clock."

"OK, Maman. I will go."

His new friend is fourteen years old, as is he. Jim and Manuel are fourteen and fifteen. Ross's mother seeks to put Philippe at ease. Philippe offers a few words and asks especially that everyone speak slowly. It is the first time that he is really put to the test. In the course of the trip, he begins to make himself understood. He explains with some difficulty that he is from Nice, that he will spend two years in the United States, that his father is a biologist, that his mother is a teacher and that he has one sister. He will be a freshman in high school. His companions enjoy his French accent.

Manuel explains that he and his buddies are teammates on the Jaguar soccer team. They are in the midst of a summer competition and today's match, if they win, will allow them to qualify for the next round. The championship itself will occur on Labor Day, just before the beginning of the school year. There are sixteen teams from the Capital and the suburbs that are participating in the tournament.

The Jaguars carry the day in a tightly played 2 to1 contest. The coach is thrilled by the team's play and is effusive in his remarks at the conclusion of the game.

The return home is interrupted by an ice cream and soda break. Everyone is excited and most engage Philippe in conversation. He feels that he is already accepted by these new friends.

Pierre greets Philippe at the door. "Well, how about it? Did the match go well?"

"It wasn't easy talking to all these people but I kicked the ball around a bit and everyone was very friendly."

"When the conversation becomes easier for you, you can explain to them how we trounced Brazil in 1998, 3-0, and how we defeated Italy this year."

* * *

During the following days, Dominique organizes the house. She adapts easily enough to American food. Breakfast is quite similar to back home but the family accommodates to a simple sandwich for lunch. The evening meal, eaten earlier than in Nice, becomes a special family time. Dominique sticks to the French ways with its leisurely approach and its several courses. It is the time for the family to gather and to speak of the experiences of the day which, increasingly as the days go by, are more easily negotiated. English is also becoming more manageable.

* * *

During the second week, Julie meets a girl of her age at the pharmacy while shopping for cosmetics. Not knowing the brands, she inquires. “Excuse me; what kinds of soaps and shampoos do you recommend?”

They introduce themselves and discover that they live in the same neighborhood. “My name is Juanita Mendez and I live on Garfield Street. I am learning a bit of French at the Woodrow Wilson High School.”

“Oh, I will also be going to that school in September. I am from Nice, France, on the *Côte d’Azur*.”

They decide to see each other again. Juanita adds: “We could find more interesting products that are much cheaper at the mall.”

True to her word, Juanita calls the following Saturday and Philippe answers. “Julie, it’s for you.”

“Hello, Julie. Do you remember me? This is Juanita Mendez. Would you care to have lunch at my house and are you free to go to the shopping center with my mother and me?”

“Let me ask my mother.”

Dominique agrees and Julie is ready in a jiffy. Like most girls of her age, she is very fashion-conscious. She can spend an entire evening reading the issue of *Seventeen* that she recently purchased at the supermarket. Also, and much to the annoyance of the other family members, she can tie up the bathroom for an inordinate amount of time while fixing her hair and filing her fingernails.

It is a fifteen minute walk to Juanita’s house. Washington is hot at the beginning of summer and, after the recent rains, there has been an explosion of nature with an abundance of flowers in front and back yards. Julie is impressed by the number of homes that fly the American flag and by so many basketball hoops that are attached to adjoining garages, findings which for her are so much different from back home.

"Hello, Juanita."

Juanita introduces Julie to her mother who in turn welcomes her graciously. "My mother is preparing subs for us. Let me show you my room, but only briefly because I really want to get to the mall. My mom also has some shopping to do and she will join us."

"My afternoon is free, so whatever you decide. I have a bit of money of my own to purchase a few items."

Inspecting the room, Julie exclaims: "I love your posters. Jennifer Lopez and Ben Affleck are among my favorites. Do you have any of Jennifer's CDs?"

Juanita is very hospitable. She doesn't take herself too seriously and her room is a bit of a mess. The house itself is comfortable, although not pretentious.

* * *

"Well?" asks Dominique.

"Yes, Maman, the afternoon went well. Juanita is very friendly and her mother is charming. But they can really go at each other and they are so demonstrative in their mannerisms."

"Have you forgotten the Italian ladies from Nice with their own flamboyant ways?"

"Right. We should have Juanita and her mother over some day. In any case, the shopping center is not that different from our French ones. For the most part, I just looked, but I did buy this sweater. I also found some earrings. They are a bit flashy, but they were not too expensive. I'll save them for a special occasion."

"Your brother and you have not needed that much time to find new friends. All in all, you are making significant progress and I am proud of you."

Chapter 3.
July 2000 – Washington, D.C.

Not for the faint of heart

Pierre makes his way to the NIH in Bethesda, located in the northwest outskirts of the Capital. Driving away from the city is fairly easy for the morning commute finds most of the traffic heading in the opposite direction. That will spare him the inevitable tie-ups that regularly occur as the mass of governmental bureaucrats wind their way toward their offices. He pulls in at his destination after twenty-five minutes.

The NIH reminds him of the Orsay Faculty in Paris where he had done part of his training. Located in a hilly neighborhood, he has the feeling of being on a university campus. It pleases him to be able to work in this collegial atmosphere. Having been here the previous month, he remembers the way. He parks next to what will be his future laboratory and finds the corridor that brings him to the office. His appointment is for 10 a.m.

"Good morning. I am Pierre Benoit. You are expecting me, I believe."

"Yes, I am Karen Miller. I am pleased to meet you. Has your trip gone well?"

"We are settled in and we like the neighborhood. The children have established a few friendships. We are getting accustomed to this country and we are confident that we will spend two good years here in Washington."

"You will have a chance to meet your colleagues a bit later this morning."

Karen Miller impresses him immediately. A native of Minnesota, she has worked at the Institute for the past twenty years. "I will show you to your office. Ah, call me Karen."

"Okay, Karen. I am dependent upon you, particularly during the early going."

"Here is your office. You are lucky. Many do not have access to seeing the outdoors. We are pleased to have you among us. Feel free to settle in slowly and pace yourself. You will find your schedule filling in soon enough. Already, your services are being requested in a few parts of the country."

Pierre is left alone and he quickly assesses his office. It is comfortable and well-equipped. Dominique will help him with some of the details. There is ample shelf space for his books. A screen and projector will come in handy for his abundant collection of slides. There is sufficient space for him to receive his colleagues.

A short while later, Karen introduces Pierre to the other members of his team. They are not totally unknown to him as he has had the opportunity to review their files beforehand.

Harvey Kantrowicz, from Cincinnati, is a graduate of the University of Tel Aviv and is a specialist in infectious diseases. Larry Winship, from Rockland, Maine, is an immunologist and is renowned for his work in bacteriology. He studied at Dalhousie University in Nova Scotia. Cynthia Cousins, from Omaha, Nebraska, is a graduate of Stanford.

She is a mathematician with a specialty in statistics. Abby Murphy, from Phoenix, Arizona, did her graduate studies at MIT and is a virologist.

The meeting is very cordial. Pierre will begin his work next week. He will receive a salary of $7,250 per month in addition to his housing and car expenses. As he prepares to leave, Karen presents him with a letter that she has received this very morning.

"Dear Professor Benoit,

> I am pleased to welcome you to the United States. I hope that you and your family are settled in to your satisfaction.
>
> You will surely be well received at the NIH and your work will be appreciated.
>
> I am grateful that you have accepted this position.
>
> Kindly receive my best wishes for success in all your undertakings. I recall with warm feelings my previous visits to France. I look forward to meeting you soon.
>
> Very truly yours,
>
> Thomas Regan,
> *Secretary of Health and Human Services*"

"Hey, this is the very first time that I have received a letter signed by a cabinet member," thinks Pierre.

"Thank you, Karen; I will see you in a few days. If you need me before then, you know how to reach me. So long until next Monday."

* * *

Seeing the need for a few projects around the house, Pierre and Philippe make their way to a Home Depot to find the necessary equipment. The interior of this home goods store is as big as a football field.

"Our football is their soccer, Papa."

"Okay! You're right! As big as a soccer field, but I doubt that I can get used to that term."

"Will we find any French products here?"

"I see here a saw with instructions in French and translation in English: *Power motor, carbon teeth, capable of cutting the hardest materials*."

"Yes, but made in Taiwan."

"Here are ceramic tiles for walls, Italian-style."

"These are from Thailand and those are from Mexico."

Air conditioners, paints, lamps and innumerable other products, all appear to be manufactured in Taiwan or China, although still a few in the U.S.

"OK. Let us ask for help. Otherwise, we will be here all day."

Yet again, Pierre and Philippe are struck by the graciousness of the workers who give the requested information without a trace of annoyance. *Thank you's* are always followed by *you're welcome.*

The walls of the kitchen are done over with a fresh coat of sage green paint. The woodwork is covered with semi-gloss white. After the two-day project, Dominique is impressed with the results. "I will prepare you a special meal on Sunday."

* * *

The children will soon be in school. Six weeks remain before opening day. While here, Julie will need to prepare for her baccalaureate exams upon her return to France. Philippe has fortunately passed the *Brevet des Collèges*. Before leaving home, there had been interminable discussions regarding which educational direction to take. The French Embassy in Washington had been consulted regarding the possibilities *à la française*. "Yes, it would be possible." But would there be any advantages to following an American curriculum? The family had been divided. Pierre's father, Frédéric, a retired engineer, leaned toward a French lycée. Dominique agreed with her father-in-law. On the other hand, Pierre preferred an American school. "They will never have an opportunity like this one. We will be there for two years; we need a total immersion in the culture and in the education."

The debate had gone on for weeks. Julie had asked if anyone would consult her. Her grandfather had replied with an emphatic *non*. Philippe had indicated that his schooling was a good reason to leave him in Cannes with his grandparents.

With Pierre's argument prevailing, a school had to be found. The Woodrow Wilson High School was contacted in May.

Julie, a good student, would pose no problem. She will study English literature, American history, chemistry, advanced algebra and a foreign language: Spanish, German or Russian. She can also enroll in a photography course or theater and she will be expected to engage in one or more sports. In addition, she will be encouraged to participate in a social awareness activity. During the second semester, she may be placed in an honors program.

Philippe's situation will be quite different. He will need some special assistance as subjects in English will be difficult for him, at least at the outset. He will need a tutor for his course in English composition, western civilization, history and earth science. He will have two sessions per week in the computer lab. Like his sister, he will study a foreign language. Sports are obligatory for all students.

Julie and Philippe will accordingly be enrolled at the Woodrow Wilson High School, Julie as a junior and Philippe as a freshman. At the insistence of their grandfather, they will also keep up with their requirements back home on weekends via the internet.

For her part, having found a notice in the *Washington Post* for a French teacher in the Foreign Languages Department, Dominique has submitted her resume to the Duke Ellington School of the Arts. She has taught classical French in private schools in Paris, Tunis and Nice. She interrupted her career seventeen years ago to tend to her children. They are older now. Why not pick up from where she left off so long ago? Her teaching hours and vacations would coincide with those of the children. Each family member has approved her decision.

* * *

Having received a call for an interview, Dominique finds her way to the administration office of the Duke Ellington School of the Arts on Reservoir Street, not far from Georgetown University and near the French Embassy. Upon arriving, she notices that it is a big school with a white facade, located in the middle of a busy section of the city. It appears to be well-maintained from the outside. She is greeted by the principal, Dr. Clark.

"I received your CV. You have taught in France and in Tunisia at the secondary level and you undoubtedly had the experience in Tunisia of dealing with non-French speaking students."

"Well, yes, but many of the Tunisian students had received a bilingual education at the primary level. For those students, French was not totally alien to them. Also, foreseeing this Washington experience, I took courses in teaching

French as a foreign language. As you can see from my documents, I taught for eight years before my children were born. I have been at home since then, but I would very much like to pick up anew this work which I have loved in the past."

"Your credentials are fine and you have excellent references. While I cannot give you an immediate response, I can say that I will present this folder to the School Committee which meets monthly. At the next meeting in two weeks, we will examine your papers along with those of any other candidates and you may be called for another interview. Suffice it to say that I will speak favorably on your behalf. In the meantime, I might introduce you to the chairperson of our Department of Foreign Languages. He can provide you with more details that might be of interest to you."

"May I present Mr. Hornung."

"Pleased to meet you, Mrs. Benoit. Dr. Clark showed me your CV. Can I answer any questions?"

Somewhat intimidated at the outset, Dominique regains her composure. "How many students do you have in this school?"

"There are 468 young people in our four years of high school, a modest number. It is a diverse population of students: whites, African-Americans, Hispanics and, recently, more and more Asians; a few Native Americans round out the list. The academic level of the student body is quite variable, but I can say that, if selected, you would have a very good class of students who have chosen to study French. Your other classes would consist of young people who are obliged to study a foreign language. Let me just say that they might not be as passionate about the French that you would be presenting to them and, as a result, they probably would not overextend themselves. Some students might also have any number of social problems at home.

"Having said that, I think you would find the atmosphere here to be cordial and pleasant. Also, as the name of the school suggests, we encourage the arts: music, theater, and even visits to the museums of the city which are readily accessible."

"Thank you for your overview. I hope the School Committee will look favorably upon my application and that we will see each other again in September."

Exiting the school, she reflects upon these meetings and feels that she had been at her best. Teaching French would not necessarily be all that difficult. Her only concern might be that of discipline, especially among the less-motivated students. Alas, those are the issues that one finds everywhere and this is no different from back home in France.

Turning around and taking final stock of the Duke Ellington School of the Arts, Dominique is impressed that it is an inner-city public high school with a mixed population of students deriving from the lower middle class. It is certainly a melting pot of sorts. What an opportunity this would provide her! Teaching here would certainly entail a good deal of work but the experience would undoubtedly be a good one.

* * *

The following Sunday during dinner *à la française*, the conversation naturally revolves around the events of the past two weeks.

"I am still embarrassed by my English," admits Julie. "I always seem to be translating word for word from French and it requires so much effort. Juanita's friends are always making me repeat what I have just said. Time also seems to go by so slowly. People are friendly but, at the same time, I feel almost strange, so out of place."

"But that is part of our charm."

"Cool it, Pierre," shoots back Dominique. "For once, please be serious. And what about you, son?"

Philippe shrugs his shoulders. "I feel completely lost. Everything and everyone that were in my life are missing here: my house, my friends, my bed, and even, with few exceptions, your cooking."

"But you have made some friends, you are making good progress in your English, and you are even receiving a few phone calls. You have been introduced to the Jaguars. See how they play foot… excuse me, soccer here as well."

"I guess you are right, Maman. Maybe in a few more weeks."

The meal continues in silence. After a time, Pierre interjects. "We arrived in Washington in mid-July. We are now at the end of the month and I will start my work tomorrow. For you, and we hope for your mother, school will begin early in September. Between now and then, we should have time for a short trip.

"We will be ready to get out of the city. My contacts suggest that we should consider going to Maine, known as *Vacationland*. That state is not too far away; certainly within driving distance and particularly if we have an overnight in Massachusetts. We will bypass Baltimore and New York and will save them for later.

"Okay, take courage! All is possible for those who are not faint of heart."

Chapter 4.
August 2000 - Maine

The rocky ledge runs far into the sea,
And on its outer point, some miles away,
The lighthouse lifts its massive masonry,
A pillar of fire by night, of cloud by day.

Henry Wadsworth Longfellow
The Lighthouse

The first month behind them and the settling-in more or less in place, the Benoits have decided to vacation in Maine this week on the recommendation of Larry Winship whose brother, Louis, is a lobsterman in Rockland.

Following *Route I-95*, their first evening is spent in Topsfield, a charming small colonial village twenty-five miles north of Boston in Massachusetts. A sleepy community for the most part, the town comes alive every year in early October when the *Topsfield Fair* attracts visitors from the entire area. Dating back to 1818, it is the longest continuous county fair in the country. Preceded by a parade down Main St. on opening day, the fair prides itself on its prize winning giant pumpkin, its flower presentations, its animal exhibits, children's rides, cotton candy, and Anna's fried dough.

The family is received, American-style to be sure, by a colleague of Harvey Kantrowicz. Following a barbecue that is very much to Philippe's liking, there is the obligatory tour of the village: Proctor School, town hall, library, Congregational Church, all surrounding the village green. Nearby, the Parson Capen House is recognized as one of the oldest buildings in the country. Across from the Fairgrounds, they are impressed by a small colonial cemetery that is so much different from the ornate ones that they have experienced in France; simple small tombstones with the names of the deceased: Towle, Bradsteet, Smith, Balch.

Topsfield is home to 7,000 residents. The community is located on the outskirts of Boston where many of its residents work. One has the feeling of really being in the country.

Julie will sleep in Kristen's room. She too is sixteen years old. They establish an immediate connection and compare their summer activities while listening to her favorite CDs before going to sleep.

"I baby-sit a neighbor's child three mornings a week. I attended a Girl Scout camp for a week earlier this month," says Kristen.

"Do you play any sports, as do so many of the girls in Washington?"

"I play soccer. My mother is a *soccer mom*. She shares the driving with other mothers to bring my teammates and me to neighboring communities such as Danvers, Rowley and Byfield for our games. Starting my school year shortly, I will be in my third year of high school. The summer vacations go by much too quickly."

"We saw your school, Masconomet Regional High School."

"It is an Indian name. Masconomo was the chief of the Agawam tribe which occupied this area in the sixteen hundreds. He signed a friendship treaty with the English in 1644. Within a century, however, the tribe was decimated by subsequent factions and the infectious diseases that Europeans brought to this country. Ours is a regional school that serves three communities: Middleton, Boxford and Topsfield, with an enrollment of 2,200 students."

A few CDs later, Julie has made herself a new friend.

Following this relaxing overnight visit, they undertake the second phase of their trip, crossing a narrow strip of New Hampshire before arriving in Maine, a vast state but sparsely populated with only 1.5 million inhabitants. While briefly in New Hampshire, Pierre is struck by the State Liquor Store and wonders if the state controls the sale of alcohol there. "We will stop on our way back to see if they carry any good French wines."

Julie has read that Maine established itself as the 23rd state of the Union upon separating from Massachusetts in 1820. The name was given in honor of the French province of Maine, once a possession of the King of England, Henri II Plantagenêt.

* * *

Millinocket, on the banks of the Penobscot River, is situated in the center of the state, fifty-five miles north of Bangor, at the foot of Mount Katahdin[1]. "It is the last summit in the northern part of the Appalachians that extend over 2,200 miles from their origin in Georgia. Every year, hun-

[1] *The Most Majestic Mountain* in Indian.

dreds of hikers of all ages make their way northward to this point, leaving in April or May and arriving here triumphantly in early fall."

"Those who make it," remarks Pierre.

"Many do," answers a bystander.

The Benoits obtain the keys to their cabin at the office of the Maine Timberlands Company. "Here is the map of the property. You should have no trouble finding your unit. Have you brought all that you need?"

"I believe so. We followed the directions that you sent us in your guidebook."

The log cabin is in the middle of the forest near Millinocket Lake which reflects Mount Katahdin located on the opposite side.

Julie is the first to enter. "The cabin is furnished for six people, Maman. Two of the three bedrooms have bunk beds. I will lay claim to an upper berth."

Dominique quickly eyeballs the quarters. "The unit is rustic but comfortable. All appears very basic and neat. I think we will be able to settle in nicely. Screens seem firmly attached to all windows."

"Winship is from Maine and he warned me. In the evening and night, the place is overrun by mosquitoes and they are formidable! We can go for a jaunt immediately after supper before they make their appearance."

The main room is large and bright. The furnishings are simple and solid. Philippe notices that there is no TV set. Dominique inspects the kitchen and finds all that she will need to prepare adequate meals. Outside one of the bedroom windows is a canoe that will provide some excursions on the lake.

After dinner, the family wanders toward the edge of the lake. Dominique exclaims: “Shhh… listen; listen to the birds as they prepare to turn in. We are really alone and we have not experienced any quiet like this since we have been in this country. It is great to leave the city behind. Our time here should go a long way toward recharging our batteries.”

Returning to the cabin, the family meets a gent who is out for an evening stroll. “Ah, you are the French people that I heard were coming. My name is Léon Villette. I will be spending a few days here. Welcome to our beautiful state of Maine.”

“Would you care to join us for a drink tomorrow evening?” asks Pierre.

“It would be a pleasure.”

“6 p.m.?”

“Okay.”

They reach the cabin at dusk following a few mosquito bites. “Winship was right. Those bugs sure are ferocious.”

Julie challenges Philippe to a game of *Scrabble*: horizontally in English and vertically in French. “Julie, you could get some kind of recognition for that way of playing the game.”

Philippe is no match for his sister. *Quiz* on a triple word puts her over the top.

Pierre presents a tentative schedule for the following day. “Rest and relaxation for everyone. Sleep as late as you want; reading, canoeing, swimming; Julie, you can work on your tan. And, Monday, white-water rafting.”

Philippe isn’t about to waste the day. “I’m going fishing tomorrow. Anyone care to join me?”

* * *

As planned the previous day, Léon Villette presents himself and is impressed by Pierre’s French Sauvignon Blanc. He is not timid in recounting his story. "I am eighty-six years old and I hail from the northern part of the state, Aroostook County as it is called. Presque Isle is where I have spent most of my time, but I actually was brought up ten miles further north in Caribou. I am of Acadian descent. Many in the region have grandparents like mine and we still speak a few words of French. Names like Villette, Lalumière, Larosière and Saulnier dot the landscape and give witness to our background.

"Aroostook County is potato country. The harvesting of this product is important enough to close the schools for three weeks in the fall so that the children can help in the fields."

"In France at the outset of the last century, before the First World War, rural schools were similarly closed for harvesting purposes."

"I started picking potatoes when I was five. The work then was done by hand. Today, the entire process is mechanized and fourteen-year olds are allowed to drive the heavy equipment. Considering that I could not afford to continue my education beyond high school, I worked as a telegrapher at the post office. I became aware of the buying and selling prices for our potatoes and it occurred to me that I might be able to intervene on behalf of the farmers. For one thing, this position was much less physically demanding than the picking was. Imagine, forty-five to fifty bushels per day from sunup to sundown at ten cents per bushel! We were certainly dirty and exhausted by the end of the day."

"Did you have a farm?"

"Later, I did. During the war, I even had twelve German prisoners. There were several Germans in Maine, many housed in Houlton. They were happy to be on this side of the Atlantic where they were certainly better off than in Europe. I must say too that they were good workers.

"After the war, I traveled the northeastern part of the country from my home area to as far south as Washington and as far west as Pittsburgh. Supermarkets were becoming popular at that time. In 1958, I founded the Maine Farmers Exchange which received then, and still does now, orders for our potatoes from throughout the country. We are vigilant with regard to the quality of our product. Today, we have 600,000 acres under cultivation. I am presently retired from the day-to-day operation of the *Exchange*, but I still offer my advice… even when it is not requested!"

"So you must be the supplier for McDonald's?"

"I was."

Léon Villette could have gone on all evening, but the next day's rafting required a good night's sleep. Before leaving, he invites the Benoits to come to Presque Isle to participate in the harvest. "Philippe, you could lend us a hand. You could even drive the potato picker with its conveyors that transport the potatoes from the field to the workers who sort them according to size and quality."

"I would enjoy that," says Philippe, "but it will be for another time, thank you."

* * *

Monday is devoted to negotiating the Penobscot River. The Benoits share a boat with the Sinclairs from Des Moines, Iowa. The children, Emma and Derek, occupy the front with Julie and Philippe. Victor introduces himself and will be their guide. Dominique and Pierre are reminded of their trips along the Verdo River in France in kayaks. This will certainly be a different experience. Helmets and safety vests are mandatory for all, blue and yellow for the tourists and red for the guides.

At the last moment, Dominique, apprehensive of what lies ahead, declares that she prefers to remain behind. “I will meet you back at the starting point.”

“No way, Maman; you need to be with us. You can’t back out on us now,” offers Julie.

“Come, don’t be timid. I have been organizing these excursions for six years and I know the Penobscot like the back of my hand.”

“If I must; but I have to tell you that this is not my kind of thing.”

The morning journey along the upper river is tranquil and Victor is able to describe their surroundings. “Quiet, look at that deer who is standing still over there. Yes, I have hiked the Appalachian Trail. No, I am not much of a hunter, but I have friends who are. By the way, be careful of moose when driving along our back roads and even along the Maine Turnpike. They are the cause of serious accidents from time to time.”

The ladies are reassured that the trip has been quite pleasurable to this point. A light picnic lunch is the dividing point to the next phase.

The rapids of the Reporgimus Gorge offer the big challenge. Victor hollers to hold on. “We are going to get wet, but hang in there. Here we go!”

As the current gets stronger, the raft picks up speed and is briskly buffeted up and down and from side to side. Victor maneuvers from behind with a quick jerk to avoid an ominous looking boulder.

“Maman, what are we doing here? We’ll never make it back alive.”

Victor yells out instructions to Derek and Philippe. “Keep on paddling. Rest assured; these are not the Niagara Falls.”

No sooner said, the bow is briefly submerged and everyone gets soaked. Emma shrieks as she tries unsuccessfully to dry her eyes. The ordeal goes on for another twenty minutes that seem more like two hours.

Finally, water calmness is restored and everyone arrives safely at the final destination, tired, wet and mentally exhausted, but elated at having passed the test.

"Looking at you, Dominique," says Pierre, "I was thinking of Marilyn Monroe in *River of No Return.*"

"I assure you that I was not thinking of Robert Mitchum!"

Sporting a huge smile, Victor asks if anyone would like to join him again tomorrow. There are no volunteers.

Pierre offers a possibility for the following day. "We could consider going to Mount Desert Island to visit the home of Marguerite Yourcenar."[2]

"The children are tired and so am I. Better to have one more quiet day before heading to Rockland."

* * *

After this well-deserved day of rest, the clan reaches, by way of Bangor, the rocky coast which they follow to Rockland. "Having seen the interior, time now for views of the ocean, and to the celebrated lobsters of which we have heard so much. But let us not confuse these lobsters with our *langoustines*."

The Rockland Lobster Festival, by a happy coincidence, is celebrated during the month of August. An improvised stage has been set up in the center of the commercial section of the city, not far from the port. A nearby carousel is an attraction

[2] Marguerite Yourcenar (1903-1987), French writer and author of *Mémoires d'Hadrien.*

for the children and their parents. Blaring music is no hindrance to napping infants in their strollers. Clowns, magicians and jugglers entertain the crowds that gather around them. A floral display adds color to the event. Children feed the animals in attendance. And, in the midst of all of this, people eat lobsters in its many forms. But, before eating them, one needs to catch them!

"Does anyone care for a ride on the carousel?" asks Pierre.

Julie drags everyone along. "Then, we should find Louis' house."

At seven o'clock on this Thursday morning, the Benoits join Louis on his boat. He plies his trade by himself. He too speaks a few French words which he learned in Quebec during his childhood. He has been fishing for thirty years and he sells his catch to the restaurants in and around Rockland. He is the owner of 250 traps, each of which on a good day might collect four or five lobsters. It is hard work, particularly during the winter.

Once at the site, Louis raises his traps which rest between ten and twenty meters below the surface: three lobsters in the first trap.

Louis instructs his audience. "I begin by attaching these elastics to the claws and I then measure the lobsters for, if they are too small, I need to throw them back. The rules are very strict in order to maintain the reserves. We are tightly controlled and we do our own policing to a point. We are also obliged to throw back females that are swollen with eggs. If we violate these rules which we have accepted, we are severely penalized."

"Where do these lobsters originate?" asks Philippe.

"Some are born here and many are transported to this location by the currents from Canada and the northern part of this state. Many larvae are devoured by fish. Those that survive hide along the ocean floor among the rocks and stones. It takes six to eight years for them to grow to 700 grams, 11/4 to 11/2 lbs., the weight of those that I generally catch. On rare occasions, a much older and larger lobster might be caught, such as the one that found its way into one of my traps and that I estimated to have survived seventy years."

The morning passes quickly. The Benoits participate in the activity, raising the traps and rebaiting them with scraps of fish after collecting the lobsters. Julie impresses her parents and brother by attaching the elastics to a few claws. "You see, Philippe, I am not as much of a sissy as you make me out to be."

Dinner at the Winships on Vinalhaven Island consists of steamed clams, potato salad, corn on the cob and, of course, boiled lobsters. It is the traditional American clambake. Dominique can't help mentally calculating the price of a comparable meal in Nice. Pierre has purchased two bottles of Meursault for the occasion. Philippe attacks a second lobster with his nutcracker, drawing raised eyebrows from his mother. "But, they are really delicious, Maman."

The setting sun reddens the sky above Rockland which is readily visible from the island. Several sailboats are seen to be returning to Penobscot Bay as dusk sets in.

"A wonderful evening," comments Pierre, "and such hospitality. This view reminds me of our summer place on the Island of Noirmoutier off the coast of Nantes in France."

Before heading back to Washington the next day, the Benoits visit the Farnsworth Museum. Louis has suggested a brief visit to get a flavor for the works of local painters, the most recognized of whom is Andrew Wyeth. Several of his paintings capture the tranquillity of the rural countryside and the simplicity of its lifestyle. "*Turkey Pond* and *French Twist* remind me of Caillebotte, one of our impressionist painters," offers Dominique, the expert of the family.

* * *

The visit of this state ends in Freeport by way of the mythical Route 1. "Be sure to spend some time at L.L. Bean," had mentioned the Winship brothers. "Otherwise, you will have totally failed the experience of Maine."

"Our friends probably exaggerate," intones Pierre, "but we will stop briefly."

The main store that is mostly on one level dominates the center of this typical small New England town: bank, coffee shops, boutiques, post office, library, and, inevitably, a number of wooden churches of various denominations.

Many shoppers make their way up and down the aisles, most of whom are out-of-towners, for L.L. Bean is known throughout the United States and beyond. It is a model of the American success story.

The history of the store is unparalleled, given its very modest beginnings. L.L. Bean, its founder, opened his first establishment in a basement in 1912 to sell a particular hunting boot that became legendary thanks to a polar expedition of Admiral Donald MacMillan in 1921. Subsequently, L.L. Bean added clothing and sporting goods to his collection. He then published a catalogue in 1925 and equipped the army in 1942.

Satellite stores were established, initially in New Hampshire, Virginia and Maryland and later even in Japan in 1992.

When L.L. died in 1967 at the age of ninety-four, 50,000 condolence letters were received from throughout the United States and abroad.

There are now 4,000 employees who serve the public in one capacity or another and the annual gross sales exceed one billion dollars. Shopping by way of the L.L. Bean catalogue remains immensely popular and total customer satisfaction is guaranteed. The main store in Freeport never closes. It is open 24/7 all year round.

"This is a far cry from our thirty-five hours per week back home," whispers Pierre in Dominique's ear.

"These Americans just don't know how to relax."

The Benoits succumb by buying boots and winter clothing for themselves. "While we are only in August, we could consider doing some skiing at holiday time."

"And it occasionally gets cold and it may even snow in Washington."

Philippe, holding a polo shirt with the L.L. Bean logo on the pocket up to his chest, asks to purchase it. "I'll be able to say that I bought it on the premises. It will really impress my friends when I get back to France. What do you think, Julie?"

"You are so cool!"

* * *

On the trip back to Washington, comments are made along the way. "By the ocean," voices the mother, "I was reminded of being in Brittany, except that these houses are made of wood. Also, New England is very different from Washington."

"Harvey Kantrowicz had warned me. The Rockland people have a particular accent. They say *lobstah* instead of *lobster* and *ayea* instead of *yes*. It is the lingo of the Downeasters. For that matter, we pick up Larry Winship on the very subject of his accent all the time."

Louis had explained that the Downeaster term derived from the prevailing winds at the backs of vessels that sail up the coast of Maine from locations such as Long Island and Newport, Rhode Island. Skippers would be sailing *downeast*, pushed as it were, as opposed to being challenged by head-winds when sailing in the opposite direction.

"Now, children, no more fun and games. Time for the school opening. Monday is Labor Day and Tuesday will be the start of classes. As for me, I will be on the road shortly and Maman will assume her teaching position."

Pierre stops at the Kittery Bridge for a last snapshot before leaving Maine. "We are coming to that short stretch in New Hampshire and I would like to check out that State Liquor Store for a bottle or two of wine."

* * *

Early Labor Day morning, Ross Appleton appears and explains the situation. "The Jaguars are playing in the finals today. If you would like, Philippe, you might want to come and watch the game."

"Maman, may I go?"

"By all means. You have nothing better to do and it will give you another chance to improve your English with a *French touch.*"

"Okay, Ross. Just give me a few minutes to get ready."

He comes down from his room wearing his red and black Nice soccer shirt. At the field, Philippe participates in the Jaguar warm-up. He realizes that soccer is quite international and that it is easier for him to communicate with his feet than with his tongue. Toward the end of the practice session, the coach, Mr. Caldwell, speaks to Ross and they both approach Philippe. "We are short one player. Would you care to join us?"

"Are you serious?"

"Yes, but you will need to change your shirt."

He feels up to the task. The Jaguars are being opposed by the Greyhounds. The green shirt that he is given carries the number 12. "I would have preferred Zidane's number 10," says he to himself. He takes off his red and black shirt and gives it to Mrs. Appleton. He will be a defender at the beginning of the match.

Right from the outset, Philippe gives the team his entire effort and he feels an immediate acceptance by his new teammates. Everyone calls him *Phil*, a nickname that surprises him initially, but to which he becomes rapidly accustomed, hardly realizing that it will stick for the entire time that he will be in this country.

As the first half unfolds, Philippe attends to his defensive position. He is smaller than most of the other players, but he is among the fastest on the field. He succeeds in intercepting several errant Greyhound passes and making precise kicks to his green-shirted teammates. During most of the first half, neither team can seem to overcome the other's defense. At one point before halftime, Philippe electrifies the fans by deflecting, while fully extended in a slide, a shot that was headed toward the right corner of the goal.

During the intermission, Coach Caldwell claps his hands and rallies his troops. He puts his hand on Phil's shoulder and explains his second-half strategy. "I'm going to play you up front as a striker and I want you to take advantage of your speed. Don't hesitate to attack and shoot if you get the opportunity."

Both teams remain even during most of the second half, one that is played at a frantic pace. Parents on the sidelines enthusiastically encourage the participants. In the final minutes, Philippe sees an opening between two Greyhound defenders and kicks the ball to a streaking Ross Appleton who, without breaking stride, launches a missile beyond the outstretched arms of the opposing goaltender into the left far corner of the net.

The goal clinches the match for the Jaguars. Amidst an avalanche of screeches and high-fives, Philippe is ecstatic with joy and cannot help yelling: "a touch of soccer French-style, *à la Zidane!*"

Ross congratulates him. "We are the champs!"

At home that evening, Phil gives a full account at the dinner table. Pierre asks if he reminded his teammates that "we won the World Cup in 1998 and the European Championships this year."

"I did, but they did not seem that impressed. Moreover, nobody knows who Zidane is. All the same, I did not embarrass myself."

"That is worth celebrating," as Pierre clinks his wine glass to Philippe's Pepsi can.

Chapter 5.
September 2000 – San Francisco, California

I left my heart in San Francisco, high on a hill. It calls to me where little cable cars climb half way to the stars. I think the morning sun will fill the air. I don't care; my heart waits there in San Francisco.

Tony Bennett

Two days before Pierre's departure for San Francisco, he and Dominique are invited to dine at the home of the Cousins. There, they are introduced to Ken McCabe, a journalist from the *Washington Post*, and to his wife, Rosemary, an employee at the Senegal Embassy.

The discussion around the table covers a variety of subjects: the weather in Washington: "The heat is so oppressive", the baseball season: "I must admit that the fine points of the game are beyond me," the NIH, the fashion world, French wines: "Do you like this Meursault?" Inevitably, as always in the Capital, the political landscape becomes part of the conversation.

"Clinton is intelligent," affirms Rosemary; "unfortunately, his personal conduct… At any rate, with Hillary, we may get our first female president."

“My dear,” responds her husband, “that is not a foregone conclusion. For the time being, we need to see if it will be Bush or Gore. The polls at the moment make it a toss-up. We need to hang in there for another six weeks. The victory for either candidate from all appearances would appear to hinge on either Ohio or Florida.”

“You have many polls.”

“We have too many polls. In Washington, we seek out your opinion on everything and everyone; especially on the president, his advisors and on Congress.”

McCabe continues by informing the Benoits on the subtleties of the federal government. “I have been a member of the Press Corps attached to the White House since Nixon and the Watergate scandal. There is much that I have seen, both good and bad, during my career. At this point, nothing surprises me. Washington is a very partisan and political city.”

“Do you sense any differences between presidents?”

“To be sure! Each president has his own style. Since Clinton defeated Bush, Sr. in 1992, he has brought in his own people and there is a vast difference. The Donkeys have replaced the Elephants. When there is a change of administrations, there is great flux throughout the city and one feature of which one can be certain is that the apartment rentals always rise. Everyone around the president also seeks to position himself or herself to exert the greatest influence.”

Pierre adds, “You also exert a certain influence.”

“Yes, but we try to remain objective; we realize that public opinion still carries a certain amount of weight. Since my arrival in Washington, I have cultivated my sources and I try not to leave any stone unturned in my articles. You might discover along the way that even the NIH has its politics and it necessarily seeks to cozy up to the administration of the day for its own budget depends upon the good will of the team in power. You will find that I am by nature a bit skeptical."

"We will read your articles with great interest."

* * *

Pierre will leave for San Francisco to attend the Annual Meeting of the American Academy of Infectious Diseases. He is scheduled to deliver a talk relating to the flu vaccine on the second day.

This year's vaccine is ready and will be administered in the fall. The NIH is preparing itself for next year, given that antigenic mutations of the organism require annual adjustments to the vaccine. He will discuss this issue. The other talks on a variety of infectious disease topics will enable him to hear other experts in his specialty. In spite of natural apprehensions on his part, he feels assured that these days will be useful for the continuation of his work in this country. He indeed should have no serious concerns for he has researched this vaccine for the past fifteen years at the Pasteur Institute in Paris and he has gained an international reputation among his colleagues for his expertise on the subject.

* * *

"Well, Karen?"

"Here are your airline tickets. You will be traveling in first class. Be at Dulles Airport around eleven o'clock on Wednesday. Your departure is scheduled for 12:45 p.m. with an arrival in San Francisco of 3:55. You will gain three hours on your flight."

"That's right. I had forgotten the time zone changes."

"You will be returning at 7:45 on Saturday, arriving in Washington at 4:15 p.m., losing the three hours that you will have gained on the way out."

"Always the time zones; four in this country, I believe."

"If you don't count Hawaii. The seminars begin at 7:30 a.m. and finish after lunch at 1:00 p.m. Thereafter, you are free to visit the city. The conference will take place at the Moscone Center, not far from your hotel, the Westin St. Francis. You will like this hotel. It has a very good reputation. As for the Moscone Center, you will find that it is an enormous complex. I attended a conference there some time back and I nearly got lost in the building."

"Thank you, Karen. As usual, that sounds perfect. I will try not to forget the text for my Friday morning presentation… and a compass to not get lost! I will take advantage of my free time to appreciate the city."

"Your laptop and slides are on the table in the reception room."

There are a few details for Pierre to complete at home. It will be his first absence from the family since his arrival in the United States, but that should not be a problem. The children will be in school and Dominique has just started in her teaching position. He will return over the weekend and he has no concerns; he is even eager to visit the West Coast.

At the airport, Pierre is surprised this time by the increased security. He has the impression that his passport is examined more closely. "Where are you going? Why? Where will you be staying?" His responses must be satisfactory for his bags are not opened. "Why all this fuss? Is it because of my accent and my Mediterranean complexion, or does this reflect a certain paranoia on my part? Our arrival in July was so much easier."

Pierre is barely seated when the flight attendant offers him a beverage. "An orange juice, please." Once settled, he reviews his notes quickly. He has but to stretch out and relax. He looks over the *Washington Post* that another attendant presents him. In his reflection, he realizes that he has of necessity distanced himself from the French political scene and from world affairs since leaving his own country. He barely has a chance to buy *Le Monde* once a week at most. Although there isn't much on France in this edition, he now has time to catch up on what is going on elsewhere.

Pierre notices an article on the front page by Ken McCabe that is questioning issues surrounding campaign finances. Candidates this year will be restricted to receive no more than $1,000 from any one donor. "A question of influence, no doubt," thinks he. Also on the front page are two photos of Bush and Gore who will go head-to-head in the first presidential debate this evening. On the inside, he reads an article on the adaptation of Europe to the euro, another on the Common Market and a third on the position of the State Department regarding the status of NATO. The Middle East is well covered in the Foreign Affairs section. He smiles while thinking that some of his friends back home, geography students to be sure, speak of the Middle East as the Near East, Europe being the true reference point. An editorial questions some of the subsidies being given to farmers. Tax credits being taken by certain corporations are being investigated by the office of the Attorney-General. "Hey, that sort of thing is not unique to us in France!" On the sports pages, a significant amount of space is devoted to baseball. The Red Sox defeated the Orioles, 6-4, and the Phillies beat the Cardinals, 7-2. "Actually, it is the Cardinals who should be wearing red socks. These Americans have it all wrong!" A very small article is devoted to football (soccer, Papa!), indicative of the little interest of the readers for this sport compared to baseball, American football, basketball and hockey. The American soccer team is gearing up to take on Venezuela. "That is true; at the laboratory, nobody has alluded to our winning the European Championships and Philippe mentioned that nobody has heard of our Zidane."

As he is presented with his meal, the passenger in the adjoining seat, a woman in her forties, chimes in. "For a Frenchman, this isn't exactly the Tour d'Argent!"

"To be sure, although this steak and fries looks quite good. The Tour d'Argent is a five-star restaurant in Paris where I have never eaten. It is far beyond my means. But I eat well at home."

"Lucky you. My name is Christine Hogan."

The conversation gains momentum. Pierre explains the reason for his trip. Christine works in Silicon Valley. She is returning from Philadelphia and Washington where she engaged in significant business matters for her dot.com company located in San Jose. Following a fantastic decade of growth, her employers may fall on harder times as a bursting of the net economy bubble could be looming on the horizon. If that were to occur, many will lose their jobs or will experience reductions in salaries. The owners may receive smaller bonuses at the end of the year, but they will feel less pain than the salaried-workers. As a matter of fact, compensation packages are even now being increasingly scrutinized. This will probably be Ms. Hogan's last experience in first class. "The next time, I will fly coach with the rest of the crowd."

They compare their respective cultures, French and American. Pierre has been introduced to the American private enterprise system and has noted that companies that fail to meet their profit expectations, what they refer to as the bottom line, are liquidated and the employees invariably suffer. That strikes him as the 'American way of life', which seems cruel toward those at the bottom of the economic ladder. "We are better protected, I believe, with our social programs and, moreover, we only work thirty-five hours per week. We also benefit from more vacation time than you do."

"We are approaching our destination where the temperature is seventy-two degrees under clear skies. Kindly fasten your seat belts. We thank you for choosing American Airlines and we wish you a pleasant stay in San Francisco. We realize that you have choices in your airline selections and we hope to be able to serve you again soon."

Following a smooth flight, a landing without incident and a quick retrieval of their bags, Ms. Hogan and Pierre wish each other well and go their separate ways.

* * *

The Moscone Center is named for the former mayor of the city who was assassinated in 1978 for having been sympathetic toward the gay movement. It consists of large reception and conference rooms, a sports complex and an exhibition center. Pierre is immediately in agreement with his secretary. "It really is an immense building that can easily accommodate the eight hundred people who are enrolled in the conference." He makes his way to the welcoming table where the hostess, very elegant in her dark blue outfit, welcomes him, presents him with his identity badge and the program of activities for the next two days. Over breakfast, he notices in this booklet that he is scheduled to deliver his talk tomorrow at 10:30 a.m. He smiles as he notices his picture, a mug shot of sorts, and a brief description of his background and career. Also indicated is the table number to which he has been assigned for his lunches and the roundtable discussions for which he will be responsible. The designated topics each day should allow for lively interchanges among the participants. Pierre will be the expert moderator for table #17 on Thursday and Friday.

While his talk will deal with the flu vaccine, the program indicates his expertise on vaccines in general. That suits him well; questions will be much more varied. For this first morning, he is free to attend lectures that most appeal to him among the dozens that are listed.

Pierre initially selects a lecture on the reappearance of tuberculosis, especially in the third world. The infection is often linked to AIDS and the organism is increasingly resistant to the usual antibiotics. According to the World Health Organization, the number of cases is diminishing in Western Europe but is increasing in Eastern Europe and in Africa. The third world problem is of greater concern and is one for which there are no easy solutions. In any case, massive financial outlays would appear to be inevitable.

After a second presentation on the excessive use of antibiotics and the resulting development of resistant organisms, Pierre allows himself a break before approaching his assigned table. In spite of the huge crowd, the Moscone Center retains a relaxing charm.

Having been seated, the physicians introduce themselves and comment on the talks that they have attended. Pierre directs the conversation toward the assigned vaccine topic and he responds to a number of questions. He quickly senses that the participants are intent upon learning about the French medical system. In a few words, Pierre describes his *Sécurité Sociale*. "Basically, we see our physician and we are reimbursed for his or her services. There are no problems. The *Sécurité Sociale* is financed through employer and employee contributions. We fear, however, that we may soon encounter a serious problem as the costs of medical care are exploding in my country."

Pierre is given an earful on Health Maintenance Organizations (HMOs). These health care organizations have expanded exponentially throughout the country since 1985, having as objective a decrease in the cost of health care. Physicians sign contracts with any number of HMOs which in turn direct their subscribers to them. Hospitals also are involved and they often negotiate fee schedules that may or may not be beneficial to each party. In many instances, a competitive climate is established among hospitals and physicians. The results can be contentious. Patients can find themselves limited in their choices of physicians and they may be directed to medical facilities that are not of their choosing. Physicians are encouraged to prescribe generic medications. Those that are not vigilant in containing the numbers of tests that they order may not have their contracts renewed.

While there has been some containment in medical costs, there have been occasional abuses within the system. Some HMOs and their directors have been accused of generating scandalous profits and patients oftentimes have been denied benefits for care that has been considered either unnecessary or experimental. The duration of hospitalizations has been tightly monitored to avoid stays that would be considered excessive.

* * *

After the meal, Pierre engages one of the participants in conversation, Dr. Frank Mitchell, from Phoenix, Arizona. He too is in San Francisco for the first time. Their heads are full of statistics and they agree that it is time to visit the city and that they might perhaps do it together. They are eager to see the Golden Gate Bridge. “My colleagues at the NIH have advised me that it is from the bridge that we have the best view of the bay. We could leave after a short nap, for you must agree that we have not relaxed since early this morning.”

The sun is warm, but there is a breeze emanating from the bay. They rent a car. Pierre offers his French license that is ‘good for life’ and discovers that those in the U.S. must be renewed every two years. “That is okay; I have an international permit as well.”

After making their way to their destination, Pierre parks at the northern entry to the bridge. The sign indicates that it is 2.7 kilometers long and the suspended portion measures 1.9 kilometers. Considered an engineering marvel, the work occurred from 1933 to 1937 under the direction of the well-known Joseph Strauss.

The corrosive salty atmosphere demands continual upkeep. The maroon paint is adapted to the surrounding conditions. Frank points to two laborers who are working in the center at the highest point. “They sure are courageous to climb to that height. I have read that Strauss, concerned over the well-being of his workers, had installed a safety net to protect them during the construction of the bridge. Nineteen of them did fall and they became known as the ‘Halfway-to-Hell Club’. Unfortunately, fifteen or so workers perished at one point as the staging on which they found themselves fell through the net.”

“Truly, this view is great and deserves its reputation. Note this bit of fog in the middle of the bay, a meteorological phenomenon which is a characteristic of that site, even on the clearest of days. San Francisco is noted for the thickness of its fogs which have contributed to a good number of navigation disasters down through the centuries."

The two acquaintances walk onto the bridge. Pierre thinks back to the earthquake of 1906, pictures that he has seen and with which he is quite familiar. He and Frank are part of a significant crowd which includes joggers, cyclists and rollerbladers, all in a variety of flashy outfits; also many families and, of course, tourists among whom are assorted Asians with their obligatory cameras. In the midst of this population is a young mother on rollerblades wearing a baseball cap and a jogging outfit while pushing her infant in a stroller. Returning to Vista Park, Frank and Pierre purchase T-shirts that appropriately show the Golden Gate Bridge in all its magnificence. "Philippe will be able to add to the collection that he started at L.L. Bean."

* * *

It is 6:00 p.m. Frank suggests a tour of the bay by boat. "We can embark at Fisherman's Wharf. We will get another view of the bridge and, from the other side of the bay, we will have a good angle on the Oakland Bridge. The cruise leaves from Pier 39."

Fisherman's Wharf, as the name suggests, was formerly the place from which fishermen left to earn their living. It is now more of a tourist area from where visitors are relieved of their dollars. One might occasionally find a fisherman, but that would require arriving early in the morning. From Ghiradelli Square at Pier 39, Pierre and his new friend stroll in front of many shops and restaurants before boarding the cruise boat.

Alcatraz is situated on an island in the middle of the bay. Formerly a prison, it is known to have precluded any chance of escape. Now, it is a museum but, from 1931 to 1963, the most violent and most hardened criminals were detained there. The prison was abandoned in 1963 because of the logistics of confining people on this site with its attendant costs. Al Capone and Machine-Gun Kelly were among the most notorious of these prisoners.

To Frank's surprise, Pierre is aware of the prison's history. "Oh, yes; once along the banks of the Seine, I found a book about J. Edgar Hoover that described the lives of some of these famous gangsters. I remember the Machine Gun Kelly character. There is also the story of a woman, Ma Baxter, and of her sons, all hardened criminals, that were investigated by the FBI."

"J. Edgar Hoover is known in France?"

"Absolutely. I once found comic books in my father's attic describing the *Secret Agent X-9* from the FBI that preceded the Second World War. He even had comics of *The Phantom*, *The Lone Ranger* and *Mandrake the Magician!* I also saw the movie entitled *The Escape from Alcatraz* starring Clint Eastwood."

"You know more about this prison than I do. You speak of *The Phantom* and *The Lone Ranger*. How about *Tarzan*, *Flash Gordon* and *Buck Rogers?* Do they mean anything to you?"

"I am quite acquainted with American comic books. We, of course, have well-known comics also. *Tintin and Spirou* is typically Belgian and we claim *Astérix le Gaulois* as our own."

"I have never been a big fan of comic books, but I have read some translations of Camus and Stendhal. We studied *The Three Musketeers*, *Around the World in 80 Days* and *20,000 Leagues under the Sea* in school. I have also seen the movies that were based on these stories."

* * *

The setting sun reddens the sky in the west. “Tomorrow will be a hot one,” predicts the skipper as everyone disembarks.

“I would suggest a restaurant along Fisherman’s Wharf,” says Frank.

“That sounds fine. According to the guide, The Boulevard Restaurant would be a good choice. It is at the other end of the Wharf.”

“I take it that all these restaurants are known for their fish specialties.”

Walking along the Wharf gives them another perspective of the bay. They now really feel part of the tourist crowd and they eventually arrive at the restaurant.

The waiter spells out the specials of the day. Pierre is intrigued by the choices. “The Egg ravioli with spinach looks good for starters and I will then go with the Sea bass with sundried tomatoes.”

“For me, truffles followed by the grilled salmon.”

“Truffles in San Francisco?”

“Here they are on the menu!”

While waiting to be served, the two diners compare some of their traveling experiences.

Frank has vacationed in Italy and attended a seminar in Dubrovnik, Yugoslavia, but he has never been to Paris.

“Ah, Paris. You must come. For me, it is the most beautiful city in the world and it is there that I met my wife.”

“How did you meet?”

“Well, you will never believe this, but it was at *Les Deux Magots* on the Boulevard Saint-Germain. I bumped into her table and spilled her glass of wine. I excused myself, of course, and offered to buy her another glass. With an engaging smile, she replied. ‘Better yet, how about a new dress?’ I laughed. She accepted my offer and we chatted. We saw each other again… and there you have it. I learned later that she was the daughter of two teachers."

Frank reviews his background in the Southwest. "I did my undergraduate studies at the University of Arizona and then I attended the University of New Mexico School of Medicine in Albuquerque. I subsequently specialized in pediatrics in Los Angeles hospitals for three years. I returned to Phoenix where I established my practice. I attend courses like this one to keep myself up-to-date. Last year, I went to the American Academy of Pediatrics meetings in Miami, Florida. I miss the vacations that I had become accustomed to taking at my uncle's ranch in Montana. Nowadays, it is my son, Scott, who goes there during the summer. He loves that place as much as I did when I was growing up."

Pierre reciprocates with an account of his own training and of his years at the *Institut Pasteur* in Paris. He too had been strong in sciences from his days at the lycée level and he particularly took a liking to biology. He earned his doctorate from the Sorbonne, having written his thesis on the complications of toxoplasmosis in infants. After his wedding in Paris, he spent two years in Tunisia where Dominique taught in private schools while he had a position at the *Institut Pasteur* branch in Tunis. Following his return to France, he worked initially in Paris and then in Nice where he became affiliated with the university and where he is now close to his aging parents. He continues to travel regularly to the *Institut* in the capital. He has long been involved in research on vaccines and he finds himself lecturing frequently on the subject of his expertise everywhere in France and occasionally abroad.

"But how is it that you have come to Washington?"

"Two years ago, I was contacted by colleagues at the NIH with whom we collaborate. An accord exists between the two institutions that provides for an exchange of high-level personnel. An American and a German are currently working at our laboratory in Paris. I hesitated initially when I received this offer because of the children… their education, the foreign language and the issue of finding employment for my wife. My son was not at all enthused over moving here. At his age, I would have jumped at the opportunity. In the end, we decided to come. Dominique might find a teaching position after all. Julie would adapt to her new circumstances easily enough and Philippe, reluctant as he was, would undoubtedly benefit from the experience. Traveling to this country would be no problem for me. I think I could do my work just about anywhere. All things considered, and my parents being sufficiently healthy, it seemed like an opportunity to not turn down."

"How is your son coming along?"

"It was difficult for him at the outset, but he is making steady progress. He has made a few friends and he receives an occasional invitation, especially to play foot… excuse me, soccer. He is even asked to play baseball from time to time. We bought him a glove. I must admit that I don't understand much about that game."

Frank comes back to his uncle's ranch. "Scott will be spending some time there next summer. Do you think that Philippe would like to join him in Montana? I could speak to my uncle. He certainly would not refuse. Scott is fifteen years old. Your son and he could become good friends on the Crooked Cactus Ranch."

"It is an idea worth pursuing. I will mention it to Philippe."

"Have your wife and daughter adapted to American life?"

"Julie has a number of friends and she is enrolled in our local high school. The transition for her has gone smoothly so far. It is only three weeks since she started attending classes. My wife, it turns out, was hired and she has been teaching for the same amount of time. She seems to be adjusting to her new environment."

"And you?"

"My work situation is very interesting. I have been received cordially by the members of the team to which I have been assigned. The laboratory conditions are superb. I am happy to be here and I am looking forward to addressing an American audience tomorrow."

* * *

Pierre begins his talk by describing the influenza epidemic of 1918 and the attendant mortality that resulted from this outbreak at the end of the First World War. He then describes his own research on the highly effective flu vaccine that he has helped develop. The yearly preparation of the vaccine has necessitated the assimilation of data from around the world. He anticipates that the results of this year's vaccine will be good provided that an adequate supply is available for the general public. His own data suggest that modifications will be forthcoming for next year's version.

Following his talk, Pierre rejoins Frank Mitchell in the vestibule. "Your lecture was excellent. Do you intend to publish your findings? If so, would you be kind enough to give me an autographed copy?"

"I finished in a total sweat. I hope that my English was understandable."

"You were well-applauded and everyone seemed to enjoy your accent. In listening to you, I was thinking of the old movie, *The Merry Widow*, with Maurice Chevalier."

"Is that a compliment?"

"Absolutely. There may have been a bit too many statistics, but don't discard them in case you decide to submit an article to the *New England Journal of Medicine*."

"For those of us who are involved in research, statistics can be a trap. The next time, I will simplify a few of the charts."

At lunch, Pierre introduces himself to the seven new physicians at table #17. The subject of a number of vaccines is discussed at greater length, particularly those against poliomyelitis and chicken pox. Dr Graham, who works on an Indian reservation, has seen any number of complications of chicken pox among these people. "While we think of chicken pox as being a benign infection, it can actually be quite devastating. The varicella vaccine as it is called is very effective."

In the course of the discussion, Pierre learns that the Rotary Club in the United States has raised enormous sums of money with the goal of eradicating polio on a worldwide basis.

Pierre answers a number of questions relating to the vaccine against varicella zoster, shingles as it is called. The meal concludes and the crowd disperses. Pierre feels that he has been up to the task as the moderator of his group and that the exercise has certainly not been a waste of time.

* * *

Pierre meets Frank at the reception desk. "Enough science and medicine. There is still much to discover in San Francisco. We barely touched upon what there is to see yesterday."

"But what we did see was well worth it."

"What do you propose for today?"

Frank does not hesitate. “We will ride the cable car, a noted feature that will give us a good view of the hills of the city.”

This afternoon is warmer than the previous one. It is the height of the tourist season. There is a considerable line to board on the car that is driven by a man dressed in his traditional uniform. As the name suggests, the car is attached to a cable, similar to that of a cog railway, and travels at a speed of fifteen kilometers per hour. Reaching the summit of one of the hills, Pierre and Frank have a sense that the descent will plunge them into the bay. While the speed remains the same, the illusion is that of descending much more rapidly. “Have no fear,” says the conductor, “the cable is firmly attached.”

Pierre is reminded of the television series that he has seen back home, *The Streets of San Francisco*, and he half expects Michael Douglas and Karl Malden to appear suddenly in the pursuit of one or several gangsters. “It is surprising in a way to see these places where I had never set foot and yet I do not feel totally disoriented.”

The cable car brings them to Nob Hill, a high-end residential site before the 1906 earthquake and now known for its expensive hotels. “We saw this area yesterday from Vista Park.” The cable car is increasingly crowded to the point of some passengers hanging on from the outside as did Buster Keaton in *The Cameraman*. The conductor asks that passengers push in to allow more people to board.

Toward the end of the line, a tour through Haight-Ashbury shows the new friends the diversity of the city’s population, some of it considered countercultural. One has the impression of being in a different world where mixed groups appear to exist side by side in full tolerance of one another.

Then it is onto Chinatown. A stroll along California Street and, from there, onto Kearney and Stockton Streets and finally Grant Avenue make evident the bustle of the area. The elderly Chinese ladies go about their shopping in their traditional clothing, carrying their baskets from store to store. They cast disapproving looks upon young Sino-Americans in revealing halter-tops and shorts. Pierre tells his companion that there is also a Chinatown in Paris. "The reactions are the same everywhere. It is not unlike what we experienced in Tunisia where older women in veils looked threateningly upon the young girls dressed European-style."

* * *

The formal dinner at the conclusion of the two-day event takes place at the Monaco Hotel next to Union Square. Pierre naps for twenty minutes before donning his tuxedo. The organizing committee has reserved the main ballroom for the occasion. Pierre is to be seated at the head table with the other specialists who have addressed the 800 participants. "This is no longer a celebrity status for me. It rivals the glory of all of France!"

During the meal, Pierre is introduced to Dr. Grace Ward. "I was very impressed by your lecture. My research takes place at the Centers for Disease Control, the CDC, in Atlanta, Georgia. I hope that the NIH and the CDC will have the chance to collaborate while you are here and that we will be able to work together on one or another project."

The president of the Academy of Infectious Diseases thanks all of the attendees and he is particularly complimentary toward those who delivered talks to the many physicians and other health care professionals. "Our conference will take place in Philadelphia next year and we hope that many of you will join us there."

After the meal and as planned, Pierre and Frank meet next to the elevator. "Would you consider a beer at Fisherman's Wharf to conclude this experience?"

"Good idea, but you probably should change. You might raise a few eyebrows if you go there in your tux. And try not to spill your beer all over me."

"I can be ready in ten minutes."

* * *

"The next time, we should bring our wives."

"I thought of your ranch proposal for next summer. But even before then, we are planning a vacation in Colorado at Christmas time. Would you consider having our families meet there to do some skiing?"

Frank raises his glass. "That sounds like a great idea. We should stay in touch."

Pierre reciprocates by clinking his glass to Frank's. "To San Francisco! To all the vaccines! And to Johnny!"

"Johnny?

"Johnny Hallyday, our national rock star!"

As they sip their beer, they listen to Tony Bennett's *I Left My Heart in San Francisco.* "That is for sure," says Pierre. "Everyone who comes to San Francisco leaves his heart here."

* * *

Pierre has the last word. "We just need to find an excuse to return."

Chapter 6.
October 2000 – Boston, Massachusetts

Give me liberty or give me death.

Patrick Henry

Julie's class has come to Boston for a three-day field trip. They will visit the city where the American Revolution began. They are accompanied by their English teachers, Mrs. Cooper and Mrs. Hébert.

Julie's father and grandfather, both diehard republicans, frequently immerse themselves in passionate discussions of their own French Revolution. Julie will be attentive to the American counterpart in order to compare the two historical events. She will then certainly be able to impress all the members of the family with her newly-acquired knowledge.

* * *

The English Parliament in March of 1765 promulgated the Stamp Act which imposed a tax on legal documents, almanacs, newspapers and almost all other paper products. This decision angered the population of New England as the Stamp Act followed the Sugar Act of the previous year that had in turn taxed sugar, coffee, wine, molasses and cloth. These levies were a burden on commerce and they had been imposed without the consent of the colonists.

An assembly in Rhode Island declared the Stamp Act to be unconstitutional. Representatives from nine colonies gathered in New York proclaimed that Parliament in London had no right to impose these taxes on the people who were not represented there. The population rose up defiantly and assembled under the name of the Sons of Liberty to obtain the repeal of this set of taxes.

Boston remained a center of discontent and agitation during the following years, and John and Sam Adams became leading figures in the movement toward independence. Many other citizens joined them in their efforts.

In 1773, London granted a monopoly on tea to the East India Company in all of the British colonies. Many ports refused to accept deliveries of this product and, on the 16th of December of that year, a group of patriots dressed in Indian costumes threw 10,000 pounds of tea into the waters of the Port of Boston.

The first phase of their visit is precisely on the pier where the famous Boston Tea Party took place. The guide, in an Indian costume as in December 1773, invites the students to throw the boxes of tea, empty of course, into the harbor. "Don't be concerned. We will retrieve them tonight after all of you have left and well before the arrival of tomorrow's tourists."

Five minutes later, the group finds itself at Quincy Market. It is Indian summer and the leaves are resplendent in their magnificent colors.

"Do you realize," says Mrs. Hébert, "that Alfred Hitchcock produced a film here in barely a few days because the theme depended on the vivid colors of this very fleeting season?"

The cobblestone pavements are crowded. The students separate for lunch. "Stay at least in groups of three."

After a meal taken on the run, Julie, Karen Johnson and Juanita Mendez saunter through the three buildings of the marketplace, casting glances at the abundance of boys. Engaging some of them in conversation, they are nearly late for the next part of the tour.

Gathering in front of Faneuil Hall, they are told that this building was the site of The Cradle of Liberty. Completed in 1742, Pierre Faneuil was instrumental in allowing the use of this building to foster the patriots' cause. He had made a personal fortune in commerce and notably had been involved in the slave trade of the time from the West Indies. The lower floor had been used in his commercial ventures. The floor above became a civic center.

Before the revolution, Faneuil Hall had been a place of assembly and a site from where many inflammatory speeches had been made. The students imagine the orators addressing the sometimes rowdy crowds and Julie thinks of the Jacobins from the time of the French Revolution and of Robespierre, her grandfather's hero.

They then follow the Freedom Trail, a red brick line along the sidewalks and roadways that brings them to the Italian section in the North End of the city. They quickly visit the home of Paul Revere, the silversmith made famous for his night ride to Lexington and Concord to alert the Minutemen of the coming of the British Redcoats. He had discovered that the royal troops under General Gage were to march from Boston to these communities northwest of the city where weapons were stored. Forewarned by Revere, the Minutemen, farmers for the most part, armed with muskets and hidden behind trees and stone walls, responded by inflicting significant casualties on the largely unsuspecting Redcoats. This in effect was the first armed conflict of the revolution. Julie will learn subsequently of the important French involvement at Yorktown, Virginia on October 19, 1781. Generals Rochambeau and Lafayette availed themselves well alongside General Washington in the decisive battle against General Cornwallis to seal the Patriot cause. Admiral de Grasse's fleet of eighteen vessels also arrived from the West Indies to prevent General Howe's naval force from becoming a factor in the skirmish.

"It is in Boston that the hostilities began. In spite of his noncombatant status, Paul Revere is one of the heroes of our revolution," says Mrs. Cooper to the group. "Even he was of French descent," adds Mrs. Hébert. "His name in fact had been anglicized from *Rivoire*."

Julie smiles demurely upon receiving the grateful compliments of her classmates.

* * *

"We will now take the subway, the 'T' as it is called, to make our way to the Boston Common. Stay together. You may have heard of the hit tune of the 70s, 'The Man on the MTA', lost under the streets of Boston and never to have found his way back to the surface. We don't need any of you to suffer that fate."

Julie is reminded of the *Black Mic-Mac* film in which the *marabout* wandered aimlessly and endlessly throughout the corridors of the Paris Metro.

Leaving Park Street Station, they are startled by the golden dome of the Massachusetts State House. Turning around, they notice the Park Street Church where the first anti-slavery speech was pronounced on July 4, 1829, and where was first sung on July 4, 1832, *My Country 'Tis of Thee, Sweet Land of Liberty*.

Directly in front is the King's Chapel, the first Anglican church of Boston. This was the site where the king's representative solicited a plot of land for a cemetery. The Puritans on their part refused such a sale to those who had persecuted them back in England. In an adjoining cemetery is buried a majority of the first generation of colonists: in particular, Mary Chilton, who had been the first person to disembark from the *Mayflower* in Plymouth in 1620. A bit further on is the Granary Burying Ground where Paul Revere, Peter Faneuil and the parents of Benjamin Franklin are buried. John Hancock, Samuel Adams and Robert Treat Paine who affixed their signatures to the *Declaration of Independence* are also included. The Granary, an ugly building of the eighteenth century, served as a warehouse for wheat and other items that were distributed to the destitute.

The walk concludes with a visit to the present day financial district where the Boston Massacre occurred. Mrs. Hébert relates how the Redcoats had most probably been provoked by the people of the city during this March 5th incident in 1770. Five colonists died when fired upon by the British militia. A widely circulated Paul Revere engraving subsequently inflamed the other colonies and served as one of the rallying points around the revolution. *Five dead*, thinks Julie. *Not exactly of the magnitude of Verdun, Stalingrad or Normandy, but a dramatic event nonetheless.*

Entering the Boston Common, the class senses a certain relaxation from the hubbub of the city. Very quickly, however, they come upon a scruffy-looking man who has drawn a crowd as he harangues anyone who will listen on the imminent end of the world. "Prepare yourselves…" He continues his speech and is goaded by hecklers; others just silently walk away. “This is what is called freedom of speech, the foundation of our democracy, as in London’s Hyde Park,” says Mrs Cooper. “I have been to Hyde Park on a number of occasions.”

Further away, a mother and father are having a picnic with their two children. The twenty students spend fifteen minutes playing frisbee. Four musicians are giving an impromptu performance before dancing toddlers and their approving parents.

The Swan Boats are a well-known Boston attraction. There is always a line and there is a half hour wait to embark. The swan likenesses grace the bow as two young college students paddle the vessel with their feet from the stern. Julie cannot help commenting to Juanita, “It is refreshing to see this form of locomotion in this high-tech country of yours.”

It is time to savor the warmth of the sun, the gentle breeze and the fragrance of flowers as four or five boats carrying some thirty passengers each slowly navigate around the pond that is no more than one meter deep.

The group then wanders through the Public Gardens on the other side of Charles Street and Julie is reminded of the *Marché aux Fleurs* in Nice.

Having returned to the hotel, the students enjoy a swim in the indoor pool before dinner. In his role as the clown of the group, Randy threatens to throw the girls in the water. “You had better not,” screams Sarah Johnson. A spirited game of water polo has everyone famished and ready for the buffet that follows.

* * *

The second day begins with a visit to the Museum of Science. The floor to ceiling windows of the entryway offer a panoramic view of the Charles River with the Back Bay skyline to the left and Cambridge to the right. Julie is told that Harvard University and Massachusetts Institute of Technology are both on the Cambridge side. "Your MIT is the equivalent of our *Polytechnique*," she says. Rowers from the two universities are practicing for an upcoming regatta on the river.

Tickets purchased, the students are encouraged to separate. Julie and Juanita are inclined toward the Hayden Planetarium for a lesson in astronomy. A video explains the mechanism of the seasons, provoked by the 23-degree inclination of the earth on its axis in relation to the sun. Julie recalls a conversation that she had with her father who had given her an amateurish description of this phenomenon using a football, pardon me, a soccer ball, and a yellow balloon, and which turned out to be completely incomprehensible. "I would suggest that he come here to get a better idea of this phenomenon."

The Mugar Imax theater has Julie seated next to Randy who scares her out of her wits while watching all manner of animals prancing through the Serengeti National Park.

* * *

Mrs. Cooper gathers her squealing students around her. "Let me have your attention. We could easily stay here all day but there is more to see. We will ride the subway once again on our way to Cambridge. We will buy sandwiches in Harvard Square. Let us hurry before the rains descend upon us."

Mrs. Hébert fills in the details of the landmarks facing them. "Before hopping on the 'T' at Lechmere Station, notice the Zakim Bridge which was built within the framework of the Big Dig, a massive project that placed the roadway from north to south under the city, thereby alleviating the daily commuting bottlenecks. The bridge and three tunnels took more than ten years to build at a cost of some sixteen billion dollars. Time and cost overruns were hallmarks of the construction, still considered a civil engineering marvel and the most gigantic of its kind in the entire world."

"A marvel it might well be," muses Julie, "but hardly anything compared to our tunnel under the Channel."

Harvard Square is permeated by a cosmopolitan atmosphere. Students are clearly from every continent. Harvard University is the oldest in the United States, belonging with seven other universities in the northeastern part of the country to the Ivy League[3]. Twenty thousand candidates apply to Harvard each year, of whom two thousand are accepted.

The teachers enter the campus with the students through the Massachusetts Avenue gate. "The steps of the library will be the perfect place to take photos and to eat your sandwiches. But first, let us wander toward the statue on the left."

Harvard Yard is generally rectangular in shape with the lawn being surrounded by residence halls, administrative buildings and the library. The so-called statue of John Harvard with a 1638 inscription on its base is a necessary gathering point. Mrs. Cooper explains why it is called the statue of the three lies. "First lie, John Harvard is not the father of the university. It was actually founded by the Massachusetts Bay Colony General Court. Second lie, the school opened in 1636 and not 1638. Third lie, this statue is not a representation of John Harvard as no portrait of him was in existence at the time when it was sculpted. The artist, Daniel French, randomly chose a student, Sherman Hoar, to sit for him in 1884."

---

[3] Harvard, Yale, Brown, Dartmouth, Columbia, Cornell, Princeton and Pennsylvania.

The library with its columns impresses these young people. The appearance is that of a Greek temple. In its collection are three to four million volumes of which 3,500 can be considered to be rare or unique. One of the ten copies of the Gutenberg Bible in existence at the time was received by the library in 1944.

Mrs. Hébert approaches a student. "Excuse me, would you be kind enough to take a photo of this group of vagabonds?"

"It will be my pleasure. Everyone smile for the camera." *Click*. "One more time." *Click*. "Perfect!"

Julie asks to be allowed to check out the newspaper kiosk.

"OK, we will meet you there."

She buys a copy of *Paris Match* and one of *Le Monde*. Out of the corner of her eye, she notices a white T-shirt. *I pa'k my ca' in Ha'va'd Ya'd*. "Philippe will appreciate this Harvardian humor."

* * *

The John F. Kennedy Library offers a great view of the Boston skyline from the other side of the bay. Columbia Point is also an ideal site from which to see the takeoffs and landings of airplanes from Logan Airport. More than five million visitors from around the world have made their way to this site to appreciate that brief moment in history when JFK made his presence felt on the world stage.

The vestibule, designed by the American architect of Chinese origin, I.M. Pei, reminds Julie of the metallic tube and glass pyramid of the Louvre that he also created. As she looks at the city from the south through the glass wall, she is moved by the building's simplicity, its brightness and its beauty.

Julie wanders through the many rooms with Sarah and Randy Thompson. "Be serious now, Randy," says Sarah. In one of the displays, Julie comes upon pictures of the Kennedys with General de Gaulle. Knowing the impression that his wife had made among the French, the president had offered memorable remarks upon arriving in France by declaring, "I am the lucky person to be accompanying Jacqueline Kennedy to Paris."

Julie's interest next shifts to the history of the Peace Corps that JFK founded in 1961, since her father had met a number of American volunteers in Tunis while he worked there. More than 180,000 individuals have volunteered in a variety of third world settings to this point, lending assistance in such areas as agriculture, teaching and medicine. Currently, 6,800 volunteers are serving in approximately sixty countries.

In the auditorium, a guide comments on a film that describes the Cuban Missile Crisis. "You perhaps are not aware of that moment in history back in the 60s when this dispute over nuclear arms in Cuba nearly brought the Americans and Soviets to the brink of a nuclear confrontation. Kennedy's firm dealings with Khrushchev averted a potential catastrophic nuclear war as a tense world watched on television. Nuclear weapons bound for Cuba were seen to turn around and to head back home."

A video of the Kennedy speech '*Ich bin ein Berliner*' is projected in an alcove. Several photos of the assassination in Dallas on November 22, 1963, are reviewed on the walls of a corridor. A film of this tragic event shows 'John John' saluting the horse-drawn casket carrying his father. Julie recognizes several Washington buildings in the background. She remembers as well many of these scenes that she has experienced previously on French television and recalls having been touched on each occasion. She has moreover visited the gravesites of the president and his brother Bob with her parents at Arlington National Cemetery.

Sarah, Julie and Randy leave the Kennedy Library in total silence.

* * *

"We will be attending the Boston Pops this evening. I would ask that you dress well and that you act appropriately."

Symphony Hall is home to the Boston Symphony Orchestra and the Boston Pops. The Symphony, under the direction of Seiji Ozawa for the past twenty-nine years, is one of the best orchestras in the country. Keith Lockhart is the director of the Pops which plays a lighter and less formal fare of music. Before Lockhart, Arthur Fiedler had been the maestro of the Pops for fifty years.

Juanita, Sarah and Julie are stunning in their long dresses while the boys, wearing sports jackets and ties, are unaccustomedly sharp. Lively Broadway show tunes have the audience clapping. The *Saber Dance* and *76 Trombones* excite the crowd. Julie appreciates two French titles: *Claire de lune* and *Rhapsodie norvégienne*.

The evening is delightful for all the young people and they all return to the hotel in the highest of spirits.

* * *

Mrs. Cooper rallies the troops early the following day. "Our last stop this morning before returning to Washington will be the Museum of Fine Arts for the Monet Exhibition. The curator will give us a private tour before opening the museum to the public. Julie, you who are French, you must be familiar with Monet's work."

"A bit. I saw some of his paintings at the Musée d'Orsay in Paris, but my brother was not all that enthused and so we did not stay for any great length of time. My mother is especially knowledgeable about the Impressionists in general and Monet in particular."

The group is greeted by Mr. Seaver. "There is much to experience here, but the occasion for your visit today is to see this Monet exhibit, the most popular one of its kind in the history of this museum. In the past 2½ months, more than 100,000 visitors have passed through our doors. After the closure here, the exhibit will travel to the Royal Academy of Arts in London."

"How have you assembled such a collection?"

"Good question. Monet created nearly two thousand paintings during his prolific career. Most of his works were acquired by individuals or large museums throughout the world. Your French classmate saw a few of them in Paris. Our exhibit of inestimable value brings together some ninety of the paintings that he created after 1900. This collection has been obtained from just about everywhere. That accounts for the increased security that you cannot help but notice."

Julie raises her hand. "My mother mentioned to me that this museum has in its own collection the *Portrait of Madame Monet* dressed as a Japanese lady."

"You are quite right and, in your honor, we will conclude your visit here by examining this famous masterpiece."

A portion of the exhibit, forty-eight paintings, is devoted to the *Nymphéas*, the water lilies which Monet created in Giverny between 1903 and 1908. Julie recognizes the Japanese bridge and the willow trees on the banks of the pond that she saw at the Musée d'Orsay. Scenes of Venice are noted in the last halls through which the students pass.

Julie is struck by the irony of admiring all these works of a famous French painter in a foreign country and, to be sure, she feels a certain pride at the same time. “France and French culture are beautiful, even in Boston!”

Mr. Seaver leads the group to a different location in the museum. “Here you have the *Portrait of Madame Monet* of which your French classmate spoke. When this work was created, there was an interest in Japanese culture that was emerging in France. This is one of our most renowned paintings. Notice the details: the tilt to Madame Monet’s head and her amusing smile; also the samurai seeking to escape from her vivid red kimono.

“I leave you now that you have experienced that for which we take great pride. Have a safe and pleasant journey back to Washington.”

* * *

This brings the visit of Boston to a close. Fortunately, nobody has been lost on the MTA. Julie approaches Sarah while boarding the bus. “This trip to Boston offered me a great lesson in your history. But, so many dates to remember and what happened here was the first of this and the first of that.”

“*Mon amie*, it is here where it all began! Well, almost.”

Chapter 7.
November 2000 – Washington, D.C.

Actually, if you don't count the murders, the level of criminal activity in Washington is very low.

Marion Barry,
African-American mayor
of Washington. 1979-1991
and 1995-1999.

Dominique finds her way to the teachers' room. She is finishing the corrections of an assignment that she has given to her best class. Those students do not hesitate to speak French.

She has been teaching at the Duke Ellington School of the Arts since the beginning of the school year and, after nearly two months, she feels quite at ease. She was chosen from among five candidates after a second practice-teaching experience during which she thought she had made a good impression. She received an acceptance letter one week later from the principal, Dr. Clark. Included were her teaching schedule and her class assignments. She would have three classes of eighteen to twenty-two students three days per week: Monday, Wednesday and Friday. The Honors Class would have a duration of seventy-five minutes and the two others would meet for fifty minutes.

* * *

Dominique has befriended a young African-American instructor, Tracey Robinson, who has been teaching social studies for two years at the Duke Ellington. It is her first teaching experience. She and Dominique share several students and they frequently meet before their classes. Tracey and her colleagues have 'adopted' Dominique who communicates with them in a mixture of French and English. A few of the teachers have a passing knowledge of French and welcome the opportunity to practice with a native Parisian.

"Ah, Paris; the museums, the chateaux of the Loire… the cuisine, the wines. But how do you manage to stay so thin with all this wonderful food?"

"A cassoulet diet washed down with a good Bordeaux."

"A cassoulet diet?"

"Too hard to explain. I'll cook it for you one of these days"

Last Tuesday's election results are today's main topic of conversation. "Tracey, you don't have the results yet?"

"There is this problem in Florida of hanging chads, all these ballots that are equivocal and impossible to tabulate. Who would have thought with all our technology that it would be so complicated? We will need to wait several days or even several weeks before we learn who the winner is."

Dominique looks at Tracey quizzically. "I noticed a sign in front of my neighbor's house that offered the name of a candidate for the post of Sheriff."

"We did not only vote for the president. We elected or reelected all the members of the House of Representatives and a third of the senators at the federal level. At the state and local levels, we expressed our preferences for any number of officials: governors, mayors and assorted tax collectors among others. My ballot had some twenty candidates listed.

Our midterm elections will take place two years from now on the first Tuesday of November. Campaigning in this country is a never-ending phenomenon."

"It all seems so complicated. But, then again, our system has its own set of rules that can baffle the most sophisticated voters among us."

* * *

Tracey brings the conversation back to the students. "How are your corrections going?"

"I am nearly finished. These last assignments are from my two best students. Amy speaks well. For André, this exercise is not that difficult. Creole is his native language as he was born in Haiti, but he has also studied French in school."

Miguel Chavez joins his two colleagues. He is one of the pillars of the institution, having taught mathematics for twenty-eight years and having been the baseball coach for the past ten. He is recognized as a very devoted teacher. He is also the teacher representative before the School Committee. This committee is comprised of three professional people, two educators, a small business owner and a merchant. Dominique is intrigued by this group for its function seems so different from anything to which she is accustomed in France. She learns that it is responsible for the physical maintenance of the school, the recruiting of the principal and the establishment of the annual budget, which in turn must be approved by the local government. Taxes paid by the citizens ultimately finance all expenditures.

Miguel addresses Tracey and Dominique. "I hope that you will attend tomorrow evening's meeting. The School Committee will be addressing teacher contracts for the next three years and we could certainly use your support. May I count on you?"

Dominique had sensed from the beginning that she would need to participate actively in the life of this inner-city public school. "I am merely passing through here in my two-year commitment, but I will gladly attend the meeting. Are there salary issues that will be discussed?"

"There are always salary issues. We also need to negotiate our retirement and medical insurance benefits. We are proposing significant increases in medical benefits to offset the inflationary spiral that affects all of us in this area."

"These are often serious issues in France as well. Teachers in public schools are employees of the national government and they frequently go on strike. Hopefully, that will not be the case here."

"Demonstrations occasionally do occur. Rarely are there strikes, but instructors carrying placards *Better Salaries for Teachers* will sometimes parade in circles in front of schools."

The library, which Dominique visits regularly, is near the teachers' room. She would like to recommend reference books and novels for the French section that has clearly been neglected.

"And you, Tracey, what are your plans for today's class?"

"We will speak of the segregation issues that arose back in the 60s and 70s. I am told that there had been problems even here at those times. We will obviously recall Martin Luther King's influence in all of this. We live in a more relaxed atmosphere now and you can appreciate that this school functions in a certain quiet harmony, but that has not always been the case."

"Will you speak of the Black Muslims and of Angela Davis?"

"Another time. We will watch a video of the MLK 'I Have a Dream' speech as a lead into a discussion of any personal experiences that the students have had."

"And you, have you suffered any racist problems?"

"Not especially here in Washington and certainly not in this school. The mayor of the city is black. We have made a good deal of progress since the days of M.L. King, although equality is still not a reality of our times. My grandparents did experience any number of indignities. My grandmother did domestic work and my grandfather was a porter. They recall the days when they were obliged to sit in the backs of buses and when they could only use toilets 'For Negroes Only'."

"That reminds me of our soccer team's World Cup victory in 1998. We had four or five black players and one from North Africa. As they paraded down the Champs Elysées, the crowd hollered, 'Black, Brown, White.' My students seem to get along well, but I notice that they tend to stick together according to their race and their place of origin. I suppose that that is normal. In Tunis, in a Catholic school taught by French nuns, I had mostly Muslims as students along with a few of Jewish background. In France, my students belonged to the *bonne bourgeoisie*. They tended to be of a higher class. As I think about it, with this experience, I will be able to say that I have covered a broad sociological spectrum in my teaching."

"We need to get beyond these cultural barriers."

"'A gargantuan project,' would have said de Gaulle!"

"Yet, the school setting would be the most logical place where this integration would take place, and it does occur to some extent in the sports setting. But, even in a school of this fairly small size, many students do not find their way onto one of the teams."

"We could talk about this phenomenon all day, but my students are awaiting the wisdom that I am about to impart to them."

* * *

"Good morning, everyone."

"Good morning, Madame."

Thus begins today's class. Leaning over her desk, Dominique takes in those in attendance before her: eighteen students of whom seven are girls and eleven are boys. Among them are three Hispanics, one Asian and six blacks. The classroom is in the oldest section of the school. It is very clean, but a coat of paint would do no harm. The teacher's desk is raised above the floor. A chalkboard covers two walls. Posters on the back wall encourage students to not smoke and to avoid drugs. The schoolyard and sports fields are visible from the windows of the fourth wall and the door opens to a corridor along which student lockers are aligned. Turning around, Dominique encounters the American flag in the corner. She recalls the crucifix at her school in Nice but none is to be found in this building. A prayer was recited before class back home, but that is not the case here. She is reminded of the constitutional separation of Church and State in this country.

Dominique recalls the first time that she had entered the class to introduce herself to her students. She had been understandably apprehensive and had asked herself how she would manage before these gangling teenagers. "Hello, my name is Dominique Benoit. I am from France, born near Paris. I am married and I have two children, a boy and a girl. I hope that we will spend a good year together." She had spoken slowly in French and had articulated distinctly. She had noted from the beginning that some students expressed themselves well and others less so. She had found the first conversation amusing. "I have two other names as well, Louise and Françoise, that are used only on official documents; on my passport for example, and on my identity card." She had been asked what an identity card was and she had responded that it was a document with a photo that proved that she is French. She had even removed this card from her pocketbook in order to show them.

"Ah, yes, a photo ID. We are requiring them more and more in this country as well."

There had been many other questions. "What are the names of your children? Have you been to the top of the Eiffel Tower? Do you like Picasso?"

"My children's names are Julie and Philippe. I have been to the Eiffel Tower several times, but never to the summit. I am afraid of heights. I prefer the Impressionists."

Her eighteen students had introduced themselves: first and last names, date and place of birth and occupation of parents. Among them were children of government officials, bank employees and construction workers. One father was employed by the FBI, another a conductor on the Metro. Some parents spoke primarily Spanish.

This lesson is designed to improve the students' oral expression. They will be encouraged to speak of their future plans. Now in their senior year, more than half intend to pursue their studies at the college level. Most of this group have already visited and applied to a number of schools and they are eager and somewhat apprehensive to hear the results of their efforts. This Honors Class is comprised of serious students. One would like to study archeology, another pre-medicine, another pre-law. "Not unlike in France," thinks their teacher.

Marsha is interested in theater and would like to become an actress on Broadway. "Madame, I will be playing the role of Julie Andrews in *The Sound of Music* next week."

"I will attend with my children."

Joanne dreams of studying French and of traveling to France. "Like everyone, I will visit the Eiffel Tower and, unlike you, I will go to the summit."

Dominique seizes the opening. "Let me tell you a story. An important American businessman asked a cab driver in Paris to quickly show him some of the principal monuments of the city between two appointments. The driver parked in front of Notre-Dame Cathedral.

"How long did it take to build this church?"

"A century!"

"A century? Back home, it would have taken us ten years."

Along the rue de Rivoli, the cabbie drives the several blocks of the Louvre. "How many years for this palace?"

"A number of centuries, but in several stages."

"Back home, it might have taken us twenty years."

Place de la Concorde, Trocadéro and the driver points out the Eiffel Tower. "How long?"

"I'm not sure. It wasn't there when I drove by this morning!"

Joanne and the students laugh. Joanne vows to tell that story to her folks that evening.

Dominique concludes this pleasant encounter. "I need to tease you Americans a bit. You are in such a hurry to get things done and you are so intent upon efficiency. Paris has been around for a long while and those of you who will go there will find that its history extends in time well beyond the founding of your own country."

The bell rings and time to change classes. "Continue to read *Le tour du monde en quatre-vingts jours* or, as you would say, *Around the World in Eighty Days*. We will discuss this work by Jules Verne the next time we meet. Any questions? No questions? Okay, I will see you the day after tomorrow."

* * *

"Madame Benoit, you have a project that you would like to discuss?"

"Dr. Clark, more of a proposal. I spoke to the chairman of the department, Mr. Hornung. I would like to organize a *Cercle français*, a French Club. We could meet in the cafeteria at lunchtime. I had thought initially of meeting in the evening during the week, but, for a number of reasons, I don't think that that would be possible."

"That seems to be a good idea. How often would you meet and what are some of the details?"

"Initially, we could meet once a week. Students would agree to speak only in French during this meal. We would keep it informal and would have no specific agenda."

"I will speak to the cafeteria personnel and you can start next week. Keep me informed."

Tracey and Dominique meet over lunch. "Well, how was your idea of the French Club received by Dr. Clark?"

"He was very receptive."

"I am not surprised. He is generally supportive of proposals that can improve the climate within the school. He helped me last year to organize a group of my students who were experiencing social problems of one kind or another. Good luck; I'm sure that you will succeed."

"Changing the subject, how would you like to attend a volleyball match with me tomorrow? Our girls team is hosting the girls from the Woodrow Wilson High School."

"Agreed. Actually, I was planning to attend. You see, my daughter coincidentally is on the Woodrow Wilson team."

* * *

Miguel Chavez meets Dominique in the teachers' room and thanks her for having attended the School Committee meeting. "It is not easy to get my colleagues out for these evening sessions." He gives an update to the other teachers in the room who missed the meeting. "We negotiated our contracts for the next three years, without total satisfaction of course, but with a modest increase in salaries. Classroom teaching materials are being taken into consideration. While we will not get everything that we would like, I believe that, on balance, we did quite well." He reassures Dominique. "Additions for the French section of the library are being included in the budget. Your presence at the meeting did not hurt your cause."

* * *

The *Cercle francais* has met with surprising success over the past three weeks as participation has increased from seven to thirteen students. Dominique is delighted, and particularly so since five of the students come from her less motivated classes. The subject arises at home. "Well, Maman, what about this French Club of yours?"

"It isn't perfect yet, but we are making progress. The students are still struggling to maintain their conversations in French, but the effort is certainly there. A few words in English are inevitable of course. There is joking and laughter and, even now, I can sense some more sophisticated give-and-take. It is a good beginning."

"So there is still some attraction to speaking French?"

"Unless that attraction comes from my own personal charm."

Pierre comes back at her quickly. "Please, Dominique, at your age?"

* * *

Entering the classroom, Dominique comes across the clown of the class who is standing on the riser and giving his best impersonation of the teacher. She immediately senses what is taking place and smiles discreetly. Jose Santiago motions her toward an empty seat. "Kindly sit down, Madame, and try not to disturb my students." He engages his classmates on *Around the World in Eighty Days* and suggests that everyone receive an 'A' for their reports. He concludes by endorsing a moratorium on homework for the remainder of the term.

All the students and Dominique applaud as Jose takes a bow and returns to his seat. The teacher corrects a few of his mistakes and commends him for his effort. "With Jose around, you hardly need me. But, just in case, let us continue with our most recent lesson on a few of the grammatical rules. I am especially intent upon having you speak, but you will eventually find that French has its rules and exceptions. We will cover some of these along the way."

Increasing student participation is developing along all these fronts. The classes are animated and with only a few disruptions, and the time goes by all too quickly!

Chapter 8.
December 2000 – Vail, Colorado

The La Tour Restaurant invites you.
The best Franco-American cuisine
of *Vail Valley.*

It is a continuous hundred-mile ascent from Denver, Colorado to Vail on Interstate 80. The Eisenhower Tunnel, itself two miles long, gives way to Mounts Breckenridge, Keystone and Copper.

At an altitude of 2,400 meters and dominated by the Wildwood Summit at 3,600 meters, Vail can receive upwards of eight meters of snow over the course of a winter. The storms originate in the Pacific, they travel across California, Nevada and Utah, and they cover the mountains of Colorado with a dry, powdery snow. Vail has developed its reputation and is host to a skiing community from throughout the United States, Canada and even Europe. Reservations are made long in advance and especially for the weeks surrounding the holidays. Much like everyplace else, this small city has been transformed and the flyers invite the tourists to enjoy lodging at Antlers at Vail, Christiana's at Vail, and many more. One can even eat *à la française* at La Tour and Chez Mirabelle.

The Benoits had decided to spend the Christmas holiday with the Mitchells and Pierre rented a chalet for the occasion back in early October.

* * *

Philippe, impatient to show off his skiing prowess, has arisen at six o'clock this Wednesday morning and has encouraged others to hasten. He is already wearing the hat that will later cover his ears. He takes it upon himself to fasten the skis to the roof of the car. "Julie, hurry. The mountain is waiting for us."

"It will still be there whenever."

"Stop poking and let's get on with it."

The meeting place with the Mitchells had been agreed upon the previous evening, "…in the center of town beneath the Clock Tower which rises above the Orehouse Restaurant." Pierre is reminded of a monument at the Saint-Lazare train station. The two families get acquainted. Scott, fifteen, is taller than Philippe. After the initial handshake, they compare their equipment. "Oh, Philippe, Rossignol parabolic skis. I like your style."

Scott breaks up the conversation between Julie and his sister. "This is Katherine and she is ten years old."

Frank's wife, Estelle, describes the surroundings with which she is familiar to Dominique and Pierre. An immense Christmas tree graces the foot of the Clock Tower. Ice sculptures are noted in front of many stores, almost all of which are devoted to winter sports: skiing, snowboarding, ice skating. One senses at every turn the exploitation of the throngs of tourists, apparent even at this early hour.

* * *

Skiing is obviously on the agenda of the first day. The two boys head directly to Lion's Head summit, the point of departure of the most difficult trails: Powerline Glade and Gandy Dancer. They are struck by the beauty of the view.

"It is our good fortune that our fathers met each other in San Francisco. Otherwise, I would have been obliged to watch over Katherine and she would have refused to come this high up on the mountain."

"We can skip Look Ma for now. Those two black diamonds would probably be beyond my skiing level. Let's begin with a somewhat easier trail."

This twenty-minute descent is a time of pure joy. The two new friends are able to demonstrate their considerable skills. Philippe is faster but his companion has better form. Scott glides from side-to-side whereas Philippe heads more or less straight down the mountain. At the base, he congratulates Scott. "You are no amateur at this sport. Do you ski often?"

"Living in Arizona as we do, we are obliged to travel to the snow. I get to ski two or three times each year. We went to Utah in November. Last year, we took a trip to Vermont. The snow there was different; less powdery. I enjoyed Mount Mansfield and Smuggler's Notch. We stayed at the Trapp Family Lodge, an Austrian-style chalet in the village of Stowe. I would love to visit France someday where the Winter Olympics took place. My father has spoken to me of your champion, Jean-Claude Killy."

"I have skied twice in Grenoble. It is a neat place. It would be a treat if you were able to come."

"Why don't you suggest it to my parents?"

"Okay, I will mention it at the restaurant this evening."

The girls and the parents have made their way to the top of Gold Peak where they are able to choose less challenging trails. They too are impressed by the beauty that surrounds them. The mothers are content to ski for an hour before returning to the lodge to warm themselves and to chat. Julie and Katherine sign up for a lesson while Frank and Pierre rejoin the boys for the rest of the morning.

The two fathers and four children come together at the end of the day for a last descent on the Blue Ox trail. The morning wind has subsided. The girls have progressed as a result of their lesson. The six 'experts' form a line and glide slowly down the mountain for this last run as the sun sets before them.

After dining at Chez Mirabelle, the families gather at the Mitchell compound where they are able to better get to know each other. They inevitably compare their work experiences and their lifestyles. "Who would have thought," asks Pierre, "that a chance meeting in San Francisco would have led to this trip to Colorado?"

The following day, the children continue their skiing adventures on the Beaver Creek side of the mountain. Julie, contrary to what she would have done the previous day, joins Scott and 'Phil' at the Discovery Overlook peak. They slowly descend The Wild Side. Philippe offers Katherine another lesson. The adults show a preference for shopping in the area.

* * *

After another intense day of skiing, Philippe complains, "Maman, I have a bellyache and I feel like throwing up."

"Did you fall or bump into anything?"

"I took a few spills, but I was able to get up immediately and to go on with my skiing. There were no problems."

"Show me where it hurts."

Philippe points to the middle of his abdomen.

"Lie down. I will prepare some tea and lemon for you; it should pass."

Around midnight, while everyone is asleep, Philippe arises and vomits a second time. He awakens his father. "Is the pain similar to what it had been earlier?"

"Yes, but now it does not go away."

"Still in the same location?"

"Now, more on the right."

"That does not sound so good. Let me call Dr. Mitchell."

Frank is accustomed to this type of early-morning phone call. "You are not disturbing me. Your description of Philippe's symptoms may not indicate anything serious, but he may be showing signs of an appendicitis. I would suggest that you head to the Emergency Room and I will meet you there."

The hospital is six miles from the chalet. The pain is becoming more intense during the car ride and each bump in the road provokes more discomfort. Upon arriving at the Emergency Room, Pierre presents himself at the reception desk. He briefly recounts his son's story. There are four sick patients ahead of Philippe, but, seeing him doubled up in pain, a nurse is called and he is quickly wheeled into one of the examining rooms.

Dominique asks if her son could receive some pain medication.

"Let us wait a bit. The doctor will be with you shortly."

Passing by other rooms, Dominique had noted a small child receiving treatment for a respiratory illness, a young man being sutured for a chin wound and an older man attached to a cardiac monitor.

Pierre fills out the necessary information. No, the patient has no allergies and has not had any previous surgery. Yes, he was hospitalized once at seven years of age for observation after having lost consciousness following a soccer injury. Apart from that incident, he has been in good health.

The nurse, Mrs. Fletcher, reassures the frightened teenager. She takes his temperature and blood pressure.

Pierre and Frank rejoin the uncomfortable patient.

"Good evening, my friends; or rather, good morning. My name is Dr. Wilson. So, things are not going very well?"

Dr. Wilson, an emergency specialist, has been treating sick patients at this hospital in Vail for the past six years. He deals frequently with fractures of one kind or another and is one of a group of five physicians who are on duty 24/24 and 7/7. He arrived at 7 p.m. yesterday evening and he will be relieved at 7 a.m. later this morning. It is approaching 2 a.m. now and he has not had a break since his arrival.

Dominique provides the details of Philippe's story. "We called our friend, Dr. Mitchell, who suggested that we come here."

"My dear colleague, have you examined this young man?"

"No, we talked over the phone and we met here."

Dr. Wilson listens to the patient's heart. Philippe winces when his abdomen is palpated. The doctor comments to Dr. Mitchell. "It is probably an acute appendicitis. We will do a blood test and a urinalysis. Do you agree?"

"Absolutely."

"I will see my other sick patients while awaiting the results. In the meantime, I will leave you with Mrs. Fletcher and we will start an intravenous drip of Ringer's lactate."

The laboratory reports are consistent with the diagnosis. "It is most probably an acute appendicitis. I will call one of our surgeons."

Dr. Mitchell is not surprised.

Dominique consoles her son. "Doctor, do whatever is necessary."

* * *

Dr. Wilson informs the family that Dr. Richardson did his medical studies at the University of Pennsylvania and his surgical residency at the Boston Medical Center. He has been in practice for some thirty years and he is the Chief of Surgery at this hospital of one hundred beds, the Vail Valley Medical Center.

It is approximately 4 a.m. when the surgeon arrives. Very distinguished-looking, he is dressed in shirt and tie and a sports jacket. He seems to have slept all night. This is the beginning of his day and he is scheduled to perform three more operations later in the morning. For the moment, his undivided attention is directed toward Philippe, who grimaces once again when his abdomen is palpated. "I agree with Dr. Wilson. I need to remove your appendix."

"As we mentioned to Dr. Wilson, do whatever is necessary."

"Everything is ready. The anesthesiologist is on her way. We will not delay."

The surgeon explains the procedure to the parents in the corridor. The operation is straightforward enough, but any operation carries certain risks. "Your son is in good shape and I do not foresee any problems. There are a few papers that you will be asked to sign at the reception desk. Dr. Mitchell is aware of all these formalities."

After an injection, Philippe falls asleep in the elevator that brings him to the surgical suite. Julie is at his side when he awakens. "You are in the same kind of gown that George Clooney's patients wear on *ER*"

The parents have returned to the chalet to rest after a sleepless night. Dr. Richardson spoke to the family immediately after the operation. "It was indeed an acute appendicitis but with no rupture." That evening, he revisited the post-operative patient. "My friend, you will be back in good form in a few days, but your skiing time for the rest of this vacation is over. At least, you will be back at the chalet for New Year's Day. We will offer you something to drink tomorrow morning and something to eat later in the day. If all goes well, you can be discharged tomorrow evening or the day after tomorrow."

Following his last visit, Dr. Richardson commented to the parents, "I have a colleague who practices at the George Washington University in D.C. I will speak to him about Philippe. Here is his telephone number. I would advise that you call for an appointment with him in a week. I will be more at ease if I know that a follow-up visit has been scheduled."

"We thank you for your kindness."

They shake hands a last time. Pierre makes a final comment, "If you ever have the opportunity to visit France, let us know. Here is my card. Our Alps lend themselves to very pleasant vacations."

* * *

The hospital charges will be paid by the insurance program to which the NIH subscribes. As a salaried federal employee, Pierre will have no medical expenses. Before coming to the United States, he had often asked himself how the American system would respond to a medical problem. He knew that the care would be above reproach. He had learned through the discussions in San Francisco that the HMOs could be complicated. As a matter of fact, the boy in Philippe's neighboring bed with a leg fracture would be discharged as soon as possible within the guidelines set by his HMO. Dr. Mitchell explained that all these regulations required a considerable administrative workforce to assure adequate medical care, but without superfluous treatment.

Philippe will also be discharged as soon as possible. "Our *Sécu* is so much simpler," thinks Dominique. "We don't have all of these constraints."

* * *

The telephone rings. "It is for you, Philippe. It is Scott."

"Hello, Scott. Yes, I am better, but my skiing is finished for the moment. For this last day, I would ask you to coach my sister who apparently has made good progress. I have a copy of your *Sports Illustrated* with a picture of Mia Hamm on the cover. I will be interested to read about her soccer prowess. I will see you this evening. You will surely have a number of stories to tell me."

* * *

The two families have gathered at the chalet to calmly celebrate New Year's Eve. Pierre has purchased a bottle of champagne for the occasion. Scott consoles Philippe. "Our sisters have improved their skills on the slopes. Oh, by the way, what do you think of the possibility of spending time on my granduncle's ranch next summer? You could live like a real cowboy for three weeks!"

"I could consider that and will discuss it further with my family."

* * *

American football is one of the topics of conversation during the evening. The Benoits are intrigued by the tradition of watching Bowl games over the New Year's Day holiday. Frank explains the complicated system by which schools are invited to participate in the different Bowl games. "The Sugar Bowl in Miami, the Cotton Bowl in New Orleans and the Rose Bowl in Pasadena, California are among the most popular. We could watch games on television continuously tomorrow from noontime until after midnight. I will be content to watch portions of the University of Arizona contest."

* * *

At the stroke of midnight, Pierre lifts his glass. Everyone wishes Philippe a "*Happy New Year*." Frank salutes his audience. "Let us drink to our fun on the slopes."

Pierre responds. "But next time, Philippe, avoid the distraction of the hospital… even though you were well treated there."

Chapter 9.
January 2001 – Vancouver, British Columbia, Canada

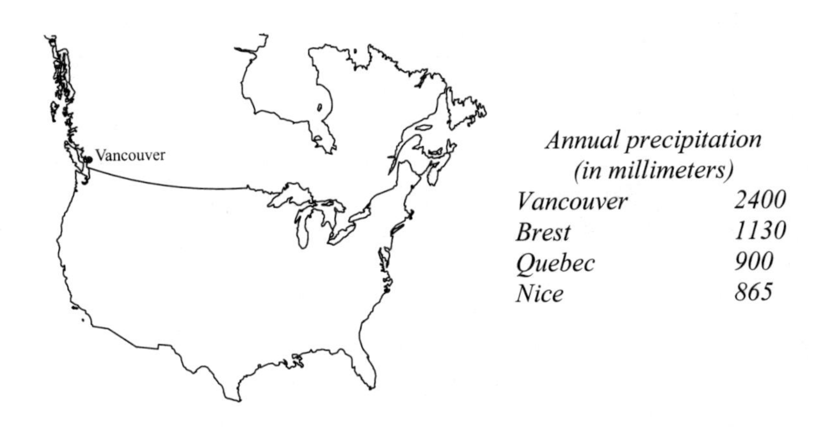

Annual precipitation (in millimeters)

Vancouver	*2400*
Brest	*1130*
Quebec	*900*
Nice	*865*

At the request of the Canadian government, the NIH has sent a team of experts to Vancouver to participate in a conference on Mad Cow Disease. Three cases were discovered in Washington State last week and the source has been traced to British Columbia. The Canadian Minister of Public Health, Raoul Lafontaine, and his American counterpart, Thomas Regan, met in Ottawa. This conference was subsequently organized in five days after intervention from the White House itself, now occupied by the new president, George W. Bush[4].

---

[4] Declared victor in Florida by 537 votes out of 5,963,110 votes cast!

Karen Miller gives the details of the trip which she has carefully orchestrated. “We will be joined in Vancouver by Dr. Grace Ward from the Centers for Disease Control of Atlanta, Dr. Wayne Grabowski, virologist from the University of Toronto and Dr. John Casey, epidemiologist from the Dalhousie School of Medicine in Nova Scotia. The conference will be hosted by Dr. Ichiro Hoy from the University of Vancouver and it is his secretary, Susan Maynard, who is charged with the on-site arrangements. We will be staying at the Fairmont Hotel.”

“Have you seen the article in this morning’s edition of the *Washington Post*?” asks Harvey Kantrowicz. It mentioned that 40,000 tons of meat from cows that were to be exported to Japan and other countries have been blocked in several ports. Fewer hamburgers are being sold at McDonald’s.

“Is that a problem?” Pierre’s attempt at a bit of humor falls flat.

The results of the conference will be transmitted as quickly as possible to the White House. “It is the president himself who will make the final decision.”

* * *

Dr. Hoy welcomes the participants this Friday morning and he introduces Pierre, who will be the first speaker.

“The animal that is affected by this infection that we refer to as Mad Cow Disease is incapable of standing. The consumption of infected meat can affect man, albeit rarely, after several years and gives rise to an entity referred to as Creutzfeldt-Jakob disease that is characterized by a combination of dementia and paralysis.

“In 1986, hundreds of thousands of suspected cows were sacrificed. Few humans were affected, actually fewer than twenty cases, but the economic consequences were disastrous."

Dr. Casey continues: "Analyses are performed on each cow older than thirty months in Europe and every animal regardless of age in Japan. While the number of cases may not be great, inspections should be carried out more rigorously, a reality that must lead to more cooperation between Canada and the United States."

* * *

Following this first session and before meeting at a local restaurant, Pierre decides to explore the city with Harvey and Dr. Grace Ward. They hail a taxi driven by a Chinese driver who has a wealth of information that he is able to share with his passengers. "My name is Ram Lu." He opens and closes the doors somewhat ceremoniously before beginning.

"The city takes its name from a captain of the Royal Navy, George Vancouver, who in 1792 discovered this bay, which later was developed into a port. Between 1850 and 1860, Chinese immigrants searching for gold appeared on the scene. They gave this province the name of *Gun-shaw*, the Gold Mountain. A short while later in 1867, a legendary figure by the name of Jack Deighton made his presence felt in this neighborhood. An English seaman, he arrived by canoe at the site of the Hasting Sawmill. He was accompanied by a native wife and a yellow dog. His possessions consisted of a minimum of provisions, a barrel of whiskey and six dollars in his pocket. He met workers from the sawmill who were obliged to travel three miles by boat and ten more by foot to reach New Westminster if they wanted to drink something stronger than tap water. In exchange for his whiskey, thirty of these workers built a bar, the Globe Saloon, in twenty-four hours. It soon became known as the 'Home of Perdition' within the village that at the time was called Granville Townsite. Several other bars were constructed subsequently, but 'Gassy Jack's' saloon remained the most popular. He made a habit of throwing the workers out at 10:30 in the evening for they still had to work the following day. He raised the Canadian flag above his bar when British Columbia joined the Canadian Confederation in 1871. Deighton became fabulously wealthy, but he died penniless at the age of forty-five."

"Does the sawmill still function?"

"The lumber industry flourished until the end of the nineteenth century. The story is told that our wood had no equal and that beams without a single knot measuring thirty-four meters were transported from our mills of Burrard Inlet to the Imperial Palace of Beijing.

"Maximillian Michaud traveled by foot from Montreal to Vancouver in 1869. Here, he purchased a hotel that housed our first post office, which consisted of a simple slab of wood tucked away in the kitchen.

"Ewing Buchan composed our first national anthem, 'O Canada', here in Vancouver in 1880, but it is the Quebec version that we sing today. For many years, the Canadian Club of Vancouver began its meetings by singing Buchan's hymn."

"And what can you tell us about the railroad?" asks Pierre.

"The Canadian Pacific built its transcontinental railroad in 1885 with Granville Townsite as its western terminus. The first train departed from the Atlantic coast and arrived here one minute late on July 4, 1886, after a trip of five days and nineteen hours. The city became larger after that event and became known as Vancouver.

"Three weeks before the maiden train voyage, a fire destroyed one thousand buildings here in less than one hour. An office worker reported that many houses simply melted under the intense heat. 'The fire followed the sidewalk of Hastings Road near our establishment and spread from there more quickly than a person could run!'

"The city was rebuilt around Gastown under the direction of Mayor David Oppenheimer and became a major commercial center following the arrival of the first transcontinental train."

Harvey relates a story that he has heard from a Canadian friend. "A Toronto physician who grew up in Vancouver told me of a boatload of tea that arrived here at English Bay from Yokohama, Japan in 1887 after a journey of thirteen days and then left for New York on the Canadian Pacific. The tea was then transported from New York to London on the *City of Rome* vessel, arriving at its final destination after a total of twenty-nine days. The comparable maritime journey around Cape Horn would have taken forty-five days. The transcontinental railroad was a huge commercial success and solidified Vancouver's position as a leading port in North America."

Ram Lu continues his narrative. "Electricity was installed this same year. By the end of the century, Vancouver was one of the largest cities on the continent. The commercial role of Gastown diminished by the middle of the twentieth century, but its historical importance remained intact and accounts for the renewal that we are witnessing today. Apartments in this area are very desirable because of the old charm that has been recaptured."

Grace Ward points to a few vintage buildings that their driver is describing. At the corner of Water and Carroll Streets, Ram Lu points out the Byrnes Block, the site of Jack Deighton's second bar, built after the great fire of 1886. A statue of 'Gassy Jack' is noted in the vicinity. The first hotel, The Alhambra, "...with clean rooms containing one or two beds and costing only one dollar" is also nearby.

From there, it is onto Chinatown. "This is where I live. My neighborhood preceded the arrival of Jack Deighton. Chinese immigration had already begun and reached its peak in 1880 during the construction of the transcontinental railroad. Ten thousand Chinese workers were recruited for this backbreaking and dangerous work. The story is told that explosions in the Rocky Mountains while laying down the roadbed would have seriously injured or killed on average one of my compatriots for every mile of track.

"One of my ancestors, Yip Sang, appeared on the scene in 1881. He began his career by delivering sacks of coal on foot. Later, he founded an import/export establishment here on East Pender Street and gave it the name of *Wing Sang*. It is the oldest building in Chinatown. After 1900, he was employed by the Canadian Pacific and he successfully recruited many Chinese workers who were needed here and in Alberta. Yip Sang married four times and he fathered nineteen sons and four daughters.

"In 1907, anti-Asian demonstrations occurred and heavy taxes were imposed to discourage further Chinese immigration. The result was a fifty-year period of hardly any new influx of my people into this country. It is only recently that there has been a reawakening in this neighborhood, influenced largely by investments originating in Hong Kong. The architecture that you see here is inspired particularly from Canton."

"Are there any concerns over racism toward the Chinese today?" asks Harvey Kantrowicz.

"No, we are accepted now. We represent a very large community and we get along well with the Canadians of European extraction. I have many friends among them."

* * *

Dr. Grabowski showed a great interest in Pierre's presentation and he has further read of his work. That evening over dinner, he approaches Pierre and proposes, if he has any interest, a series of lectures at the University of Toronto. "Harvey Kantrowicz visits us annually for two or three weeks at our Medical School. Your expertise in virology and epidemiology would be very useful to our students. Think about it and let me know."

"That presents all kinds of possibilities. My colleague tells me that Toronto is a very nice city and I would like to see it before returning to France. I will approach the NIH administration to see if this proposal would be feasible."

* * *

Saturday is devoted to the prevention and spread of Mad Cow Disease.

"Is it necessary to test every animal as they do in Japan or can we get by with doing analyses on just those over thirty months of age as they do in Europe? It is primarily the older cows that are affected. Should we also concentrate on other means of prevention?"

Dr. Casey feels that more attention needs to be given to what these animals are fed. "You have no idea what finds its way into the food chains of these cows. Inspectors need to be particularly vigilant and they should prohibit the entry of the brain and spinal cord of these cows into our own food supply."

Further, Grace Ward thinks that there should be better coordination among the twelve governmental agencies in the United States that have a voice in dealing with the problem. "I doubt that there is any communication among all these people."

"Not unlike in France," thinks Pierre. The irony only heightens his false sense of security.

Dr. Grabowski adds to the discussion. "The sanitary measures that are taken to prevent Hepatitis A, salmonellosis and other dysenteries are not that difficult to implement and yet, it is impossible to watch over vegetable pickers and kitchen chefs to see if they wash their hands before every food-handling encounter."

Dr. Hoy makes some concluding remarks. "Your presentations and comments are very relevant to the problem and I am sure that our governments will be able to intervene to curtail the spread of the problem. Now it is time to liberate you so that you can enjoy the city."

* * *

Pierre is struck by the beauty of the snow-covered mountains and thinks of Grenoble, which he has visited several times. Before arriving at the *Jardin chinois du Dr Sun Yat-Sen*, the group --Karen, Harvey and Pierre-- chauffered by Susan Maynard, stops in front of the Freemason Building, known for its two facades, one Victorian and the other Cantonese. Then, there is the insurance building, *Sam Kee*, which houses the narrowest commercial company in the world with an inside width of only five feet. "Usually, tourists do not enter, but my friend will make an exception. As you can see, customers remain outside and transactions take place through one of these several windows."

At the Chinese garden, the group is received by a smiling young lady in traditional clothing, a black and blue gown and a shiny high-collared blouse. "The garden was built in 1986 by fifty-two artisans who came here from Suzhou, 'the city of gardens'. Note the craftsmanship; the techniques are those of the fifteenth century. Only materials from China were used here and no modern tools were employed: no glue, no nuts and no bolts."

The dominant tree species are the ginkgo and the fir, also from China. The group is shown into the main pavilion. "It is here that the *Erudit*, the 'Learned One', received his guests. As owner of the property, he also came here to listen to music and poetry."

Arriving at a second pavilion, they are struck by a multiplicity of flowers of every type and color. "Just to name a few, we have here many types of orchids, chrysanthemums, prunuses and lotuses. One has the impression of floating on the *Bassin de Jades*. The soft green of the Jades of China symbolized peace and tranquility. In every authentic Chinese garden, you will find a mountain and a body of water."

Pierre experiences a sense of calm as he and the others are invited to sit for fifteen minutes. "This must be how the Garden of Eden felt before the Fall."

"Chinese philosophy is all well and good. But I am starving," says Susan Maynard. "Why don't we go out for a few hamburgers?"

"Better yet a pizza. No Mad Cow," offers Pierre with a laugh.

* * *

Named after a former governor of Canada in 1888 and having functioned as a military camp in times gone by, Stanley Park is a busy refuge for the population during the warm-weather months. Susan continues the tour by visiting the Pacific Railway Museum on Granville Island. As mentioned previously by Ram Lu, the Canadian Pacific played an important role in the development of the western part of the country. "Today, the railroad is paralleled by a highway that also sees an abundance of traffic. As you might surmise,

Canada is a vast country. A story may illustrate this for you. One day, two friends heading to Ottawa from here came upon a detour sign which they dutifully followed. After five hundred miles, they found themselves near Hudson Bay where they were forced to spend an overnight in a motel. You see that detours can take you further afield than you might expect in this country."

The museum includes the original locomotives that had been built in Montreal after 1880 and registered numerically from *371* to *378*. The *371* transported the first passengers from the Atlantic to the Pacific in 1886 and remained in service until 1914. The *374* was restored that very year and continued to operate for another thirty years, becoming a historical monument as of 1945.

The afternoon is devoted to a visit of the Public Market at the northwest tip of the island. Pierre finds a few souvenirs for the family: a sweater with a maple leaf logo for Philippe, a necklace for Dominique and perfume for Julie.

The two delegations meet for dinner on the 50th floor of the Harbour Center. This rotating restaurant makes a revolution in one hour and offers breathtaking views of the illuminated city, of the bay and of Stanley Park. Pierre points out the tour boat that will be leaving for Alaska this evening. "We had a good view of it from our hotel this morning."

In the course of the meal, Pierre observes that the people appear more relaxed in Vancouver than they do in Washington, "…a bit like in San Francisco. Would it be due to the Asian influence?"

"That is very true," says Susan, "and this Asian influence extends to where my family lives and where I grew up. I am from Victoria, the capital of British Columbia, which is located forty-five miles from here at the southern tip of

Vancouver Island, the longest island in all of Canada and extending 325 miles from north to south. There, as is the case here in Vancouver, we are blessed with an excellent quality of life. It is only too bad that it rains so much. Vancouver is the city in North America that receives the most rain."

"Back in my country, Brest has that distinction and, for this, it holds the unsavory title of the chamber pot of France."

"It is the ocean effect in both places, of course."

* * *

At the time of separation, Dr. Casey approaches Pierre. "You who are French, be sure to visit the eastern part of the country as well. That is where I was born and where the so-called maritime provinces consisting of Nova Scotia, New Brunswick and Prince Edward Island are located. They are also well worth a detour and you will not end up near Hudson Bay. And, of course, there is always Quebec, la *Belle Province*."

"I am certainly considering it. Thank you for your invitation."

* * *

The team returns to Washington the following day. As they descend from the plane, Pierre and Harvey are greeted by the cameras and microphones of three local television stations. A reporter and a photographer from the *Washington Post* are also on hand for a front-page story on Mad Cow Disease and a photo of the two experts that will appear in tomorrow's edition.

"You are really a celebrity now, Pierre," says Dominique. "If only your mother could see you."

Chapter 10.
February 2001 – New Orleans, Louisiana

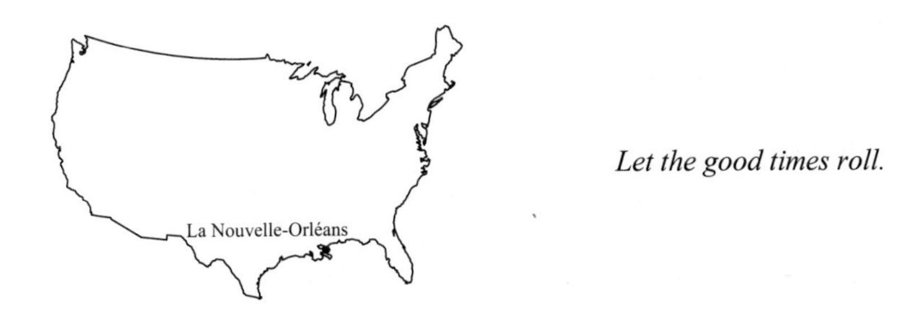

Let the good times roll.

"The School of Epidemiology at Tulane University is among the most recognized in the entire country," declares Karen Miller. "You have good fortune for New Orleans, along with Boston and San Francisco, is one of the most picturesque cities in our country and you will likely experience a bit of French history that is bound to please you."

"I am sure, Karen", answers our biologist. Pierre had represented the NIH two weeks earlier before a congressional commission, senators and representatives, investigating the problem of the West Nile virus which caused 129 deaths the preceding year and is beginning to concern the American local and national press. The members of Congress, having no reassuring comments for their constituents, had decided upon the creation of this commission. Pierre had been designated by the head of the NIH to represent him before these investigators.

"Who, me? A total stranger?"

"You see that we are not racists! Besides, you have been here long enough to no longer be a stranger."

"Yes, but my accent betrays me."

* * *

With two physicians from the Centers for Disease Control, Pierre had answered the questions from the members of Congress for an entire day. At the end of this grueling inquiry, the five congressmen and the three experts had agreed that the priority of prevention should lie in the control of the mosquito population, the vector of the infection. "If the number of cases increases substantially, one would need to consider other control measures as well."

A press conference was organized after the discussions. Herbert Longval, senator from Louisiana, had taken advantage of the situation to address Pierre. "Do you realize that we have an excellent university in New Orleans and the epidemiology section is already dealing with the problem. A collaboration with the NIH could have significant advantages for both organizations. You could perhaps speak to your director whom, for that matter, I will also contact to see if this would be feasible."

"That makes sense. We should stay in touch."

"Let's have a picture taken. You can never tell. A good photo below a front-page headline back home could garner votes in the next election. There is also the issue of funding and federal contributions could double the research money of the university. In my position, one always must consider public opinion. Governing to a large extent is anticipating the next election. You remember that last November's presidential results in Florida were decided by very few votes."

* * *

Karen handles the final details before Pierre's departure. "Do you have everything that you will need for the trip?"

"I will need very little. It is not like my trips to San Francisco and Vancouver where I had presentations to make. I am going primarily to hear what the people from Tulane have to say."

"I will give you a folder that has the most up-to-date national statistics with regard to the West Nile virus."

"Because you doubt that the laboratories at Tulane don't have them? It would be surprising if epidemiologists stopped at the limits of their own state. Contagious diseases do not recognize administrative boundaries. It is not like the cloud of Chernobyl that was said by some to not extend beyond its own departmental limits. I will tell you that story some other time."

"I insist that you have the big picture in all of this. One never knows. The people from Tulane could have a very narrow view of the problem."

"Thank you. I will read your folder during the flight."

"So, you will arrive in New Orleans on Friday and you will have the weekend to get settled. The working sessions are scheduled for Monday and Tuesday and you will return on Wednesday."

"We will be there for *Mardi Gras*. How fortunate."

* * *

Dominique found her way to the principal's office before also leaving for New Orleans. "The two weaker classes are slowly progressing. But my Honor's Class is excellent and is moving along rapidly. Some students are beginning to hear from a few universities. Harry Rubin will attend Stanford where he will study nuclear physics. Young Marsha Bingle, Julie Andrews in *The Sound of Music*, has been accepted at the University of Florida to pursue her interest in theater."

"Those acceptances motivate us as educators. This time of the year is very exciting. More responses will certainly be forthcoming over the next two months."

"You had asked me to attend this teachers' conference in New Orleans during the winter break. Pierre and I will be leaving on Friday. He was able to have his dates coincide with mine."

"And the children?"

"They will also be on vacation. Julie and Philippe will stay with one of Pierre's colleagues. They will find many opportunities to amuse themselves."

"You will be accompanied by our Spanish teacher, Ramon Espinosa. The two of you can file a report with me upon your return."

"I will take copious notes."

"You will be reimbursed for your expenses. Save your receipts and *bon voyage*."

* * *

In their search for a route to the Pacific in 1673, Louis Joliet and the Jesuit priest Jacques Marquette had succeeded in exploring the superior part of the Mississippi River. René-Robert Cavelier de La Salle followed the river to its delta that empties into the Gulf of Mexico nine years later. He had planted a cross and had taken possession of this land on both shores in the name of Louis XIV after a voyage of one month. Shortly thereafter, he nailed the bottom of a cooking pot on which had been engraved the coat of arms of the King of France to the trunk of a tree.

La Salle would attempt a second voyage by way of the Gulf of Mexico but he would miss the entry to the Mississippi and one of his vessels would be damaged beyond repair in the process. Confrontational issues with the Native Americans complicated affairs and, eventually, some of his own companions would revolt and kill him one night in 1687.

The site was called New Orleans in 1721 and it became the capital of the colony in 1722. The name was given in honor of Philippe, the duke of Orleans, regent of France during the childhood of Louis XV. The development of the colony was made possible by Pierre Le Moyne Sieur de Bienville, who originated from Canada. The expansion of the colony was somewhat curtailed by events in Europe and the little interest of the French government at the time. The territory subsequently encompassed the vast expanse of land extending from the Mississippi River to as far as the Rocky Mountains.

In those early years, France, England and Spain vied for control over the area and interest was also shown by the Indians and, after their independence, by the United States themselves. The Treaty of Paris that brought the Seven Years War to an end in 1763 gave England all of Canada and the part of Louisiana east of the Mississippi. The land to the west of the river would be bought from France by Spain. It is particularly from this point that the French renewed their interest in New Orleans and its extensive territory, regaining control of much of the area over time.

* * *

Dominique and Pierre arrive Friday evening and are staying at the Quarterhouse Hotel on the edge of the French Quarter. They venture forth this Saturday morning on Chartres Street. They are immediately impressed by the charm of the homes with their wrought-iron balconies and abundant overhanging roses. They are told that Adrien de Panger began the construction of the city in 1718 and imparted this style to the French Quarter. The commission of this enclave is strict in maintaining this mixture of French and Spanish influences.

The streets have unmistakable French names: Royale, Bourbon, Dauphine and Toulouse, but the architectural style is distinctly Spanish, the result of a reconstruction of the city that took place in 1788. The French Quarter must be visited on foot and Dominique and Pierre follow Chartres Street to Jackson Square after a five-minute walk. It is in this former public square that the French flag was replaced by the Star Spangled Banner on December 20, 1803 in an event that doubled the land area of the United States. Old-World charm remains a feature of the area. The Saint Louis Cathedral is located on the edge of the Square and is flanked by the Cabildo Museum and the *Presbytère*. At one time, the Cabildo was the administrative center for the entire Mississippi Valley and is now the site where the sale documents that relinquished Louisiana to the United States by Napoleon for 15 million dollars can be found. Much of this money was used to finance his imperial coronation, which took place in Paris on December 2, 1804.

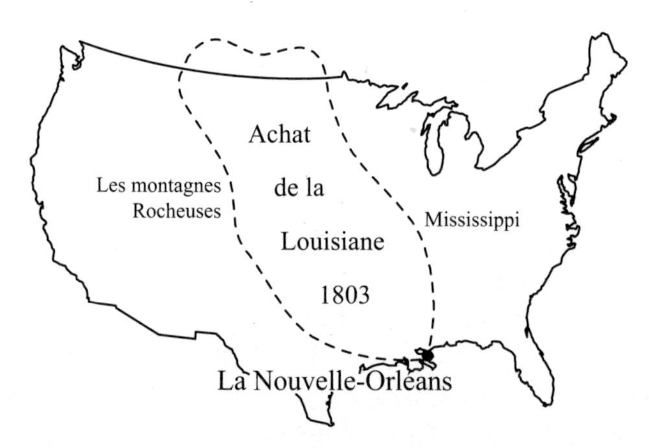

The Benoits become aware while lingering through the

rooms of the Cabildo that the French influence had been profound in the heart of America. Mark Twain, in fact, had stated that his country was indebted to the French for the exploration of the shores of the Mississippi. It was they who had traveled 3,200 miles from Cape Breton in Quebec to the Gulf of Mexico by way of the Saint Lawrence River, the Great Lakes and the Mississippi River. It was the French who put their stamp on the region, exchanging necklaces, hatchets, firewater and guns with the Indians. French religious orders --Recollet, Jesuit and Sulpician-- educated the natives and spread Christianity. It is the French who established a string of forts: Louisbourg, Chartres, Duquesne. It is the hardy explorers, the *coureurs de bois* who, a century before the birth of the country, established rudimentary roads along and between the many rivers across the Great Plains as far as the Rocky Mountains. They had named these byways: *Portage des Chênes*, *Portage des Perches*, *Portage Talon* and *Portage de la Roche Fendue*[5]. These trails were the forerunners of the railroads and the paved roads that followed and that allowed for the construction of factories that in turn gave rise to the cities: Saint Louis, Saint Joseph, Detroit, Duluth and many others. These adventurers were the first to discover the richness of the Mississippi Valley. Far from their beloved homeland, they also encountered conflicts with Indians and they contracted diseases, often fatal, to which they were to become susceptible.

---

[5] *Portage* indicates locations along rivers and streams where explorers encountered rapids and waterfalls that required them to carry their canoes in order to bypass these hazards.

Portage des Chênes	= Portage of Oaks
Portage des Perches	= Portage of Perch
Portage Talon	= Portage of Heels
Portage de la Roche Fendue	= Portage of the Split or Clefted Rock

* * *

Before leaving the museum, Dominique takes a photo of the sale document signed by Robert Livingston, James Munroe and the Marquis de Barbé-Marbois and another of the molded mask of Napoleon's face after his death. Crossing the square and passing by the equestrian statue of Andrew Jackson, they arrive at the *Café du Monde* where they each delight in three *beignets* covered with powdered sugar and an excellent cup of chicory coffee.

Then, it is onto Decatur Street where the *Marché Français*, the French Market, remains an important commercial center after 150 years and from where one has an imposing view of the Mississippi River. Ursulines Street leads to the oldest building of the valley, the Old Convent of the Ursulines, sole vestige of the original colonial-French period, and a structure which, according to Dominique, housed these French religious teachers who were 'saintly women in an ocean of perdition'. The building served as an orphanage and as a girls' school. Dominique and Pierre walk through the schoolyard and imagine the young students playing there during recess periods. Having wandered through the *Chapelle des Archevêques*, the Archbishops' Chapel, Pierre is ready to head toward Bourbon Street for, as he puts it, "a change of atmosphere."

"No, my friend. There will be time for Bourbon Street later. We will return to our hotel the same way that we came here and pass in front of the Saint Louis Cathedral once again."

"Okay, if you insist. We will rest this afternoon and Bourbon Street will be for this evening."

* * *

There are many attractions of course in New Orleans, not

the least of which is jazz. Jazz is headlined everywhere in the city and the king of jazz is none other than Louis Armstrong.

Dominique and Pierre make their way on this Saturday evening to Maxwell's Toulouse Cabaret in the middle of the French Quarter where the Dukes of Dixieland are playing. Pierre, a longstanding jazz fan, recognizes 'Someday You'll Be Sorry'.

The hall is packed. Onlookers are smoking and drinking. A few are dancing. Most are just listening. Dominique and Pierre wind their way through the crowd and find two empty chairs at a table occupied by another couple. They are invited to sit down. Introductions are dutifully carried out and the conversation begins.

The Sangers live in the city and they often come to these jazz establishments. They have more than a passing knowledge of the history of this music and they have been to every club in the French Quarter on several occasions. Pierre also knows many of the names: King Oliver, Louis Armstrong, of course, and Sidney Bechet whom he saw during his youth at the *Festival d'Antibes*.

Larry Sanger relates Satchmo's history. "He was born here on July 4, 1900 into a poor family that had been the descendants of slaves. He was passionate for this type of music from a very young age. He adored King Oliver, one of the first giants of jazz.

"At the age of twelve, on New Year's Eve in 1913, he was arrested for having shot six blanks from a revolver on a local street corner. In the aftermath, he was brought before the children's tribunal and was committed to the Colored Waif's Home for Boys, a school for young delinquents.

"Louis learned to play the trumpet there. It was a happy coincidence that he received lessons at this 'school' from Peter Davis, another great jazz musician. The orchestra of boarders paraded through the neighborhood where Louis had lived… Liberty and Perdido Streets. The spectators threw money to them, enough to purchase new instruments. Louis left after eighteen months with a perfect command of his horn.

"At seventeen, Louis played in bars owned by Henry Ponce and Matranga where fights regularly broke out. It is said that, one Sunday morning, Ponce had 'taken out' three or four men who were stone-drunk. In this environment, Armstrong needed to protect himself. He was advised to duck when bullets whistled by him. The police often intervened. They would throw the rabble-rousers in the Black Maria, the so-called 'salad basket' of the time, that was pulled by horses, and they were carted to the Parish Prison, from where they were released two or three days later after the necessary fines had been paid by Henry Ponce.

"Louis Armstrong's talent was quickly recognized. He played with Kid Ory on the riverboats of the Mississippi. King Oliver encouraged him and became a mentor for him. Papa Joe Oliver went off to Chicago and invited Satchmo to join him. They played together at the Lincoln Gardens in King Oliver's Creole Jazz Band. A popular group consisted of the Dodds brothers, Honoré Dutrey and Papa Joe. Their fame surpassed that of all other groups. Through all this, Armstrong became the great star of jazz, the realization for him of his wildest dream."

Pierre mentions that Louis and King Oliver loved to improvise. "While other musicians rested during breaks, they often did their own thing and they regularly brought down the house. On the trumpet, they had no equal. They recorded together 'Just Gone', 'Canal Street Blues', 'Dippermouth Blues' and many others."

Larry agrees and continues, "Armstrong later struck out on

his own. He traveled to New York and then California with an orchestra that he had brought together. He eventually returned to New Orleans in 1931 after these wanderings and was acclaimed the 'New King from Perdido'. He made numerous trips to Paris and everywhere in Europe. He was especially known for his guttural voice and the ten to twenty well-ironed handkerchiefs that he used to wipe his brow in the course of his performances."

"Some of my favorites," adds Pierre, "include 'Jazz Hot', 'Saint Louis Blues', 'Tiger Rag' and 'Ol' Man River'."

Pierre continues: "In 1956, Louis found his way to Africa. He was greeted by fifty thousand fans in Ghana, but he was not allowed to go to South Africa because of the system of Apartheid."

Cindy Sanger nods approvingly. "He became one of the world's most celebrated musicians, giving concerts on every continent."

"And, don't forget," interjects Dominique, "that he played with all the giants of swing, men like Artie Shaw, Benny Goodman and Count Basie. I teach at the Duke Ellington School of the Arts and I have been introduced to all these names. Duke Ellington was a famous jazz musician in his own right. He came from Washington and his group, the Washingtonians, also traveled to Europe on a number of occasions. Much like Armstrong, he was a man of great personal charm and a strong presence before an audience."

Pierre and Dominique are invited to visit a few more clubs. "The evening is just beginning. We are in the 'Big Easy'. The musicians never stop before three o'clock in the morning. You must see Preservation Hall. It is among the most famous establishments in the city. It is here on Saint Peter Street."

It turns out that Preservation Hall is nondescript in appearance, but the music does not disappoint. Lit merely by a few exposed lightbulbs, spectators sit on three or four wooden benches while most stand on the sides and in the back of the room. Three black and three white musicians have the audience swaying and clapping to their lively numbers.

After Preservation Hall, it is onto the Fritzel European Bar on Bourbon Street. There is hardly space to move. The revelers are crammed in the street and on the sidewalks. Many have had too much to drink. Total strangers yell out to one another from the wrought-iron balconies above to the street below. At the bar, Pierre and Dominique drink the specialty of the house, a strawberry daiquiri, as they listen to still another group.

* * *

After much too little sleep and on the recommendation of the receptionist, Dominique and Pierre make their way to the Oak Alley Plantation, well-known for its oak trees that had been planted in the seventeenth century. The van with six passengers heads in the direction of Baton Rouge, the capital of the state. It follows the levees that were constructed to prevent the floods that formerly ravaged the countryside. The passengers are impressed by the enormous fields of sugarcane, the growth of which is favored by the hot and humid semi-tropical climate.

In the mid-nineteenth century, the plantation had been inhabited by Jacques Télesphore Roman, a Creole planter, who had made a fortune growing sugarcane. He had acquired the property to offer it to his young wife. Two centuries earlier, twenty-eight oak trees had been planted by the first owner. More than fifty slaves worked in these fields to grow and harvest the sugarcane. Today, most of the labor is done by machine and the 600 acres of land require but a few paid workers.

The visit shows graphically the extent to which the life of slaves was miserable. By contrast, the homes of the masters displayed the utmost in luxury.

The antebellum[6] manor is surrounded on three sides by a porch. The ground floor consists of two small parlors and two other spacious rooms: a dining room for grand receptions and a ballroom for the accompanying festivities. In the upstairs bedrooms, the tradition holds that a pineapple wished a visitor a warm welcome. A second pineapple a few days or weeks later indicated the time of departure. It was time to leave! From the balcony, there is still the magnificent view of the 28 Oak Alley and, beyond, of the Mississippi River itself.

* * *

Back in the city, they spend the afternoon on a river cruise aboard the *Natchez*, one of the five riverboats that take tourists up and down the river.

The Mississippi, which the Indians called *Meschab*, flows into the Gulf of Mexico by way of a vast delta whose arms are continuously modified by their flooding and their sedimentation. A depth of sixty meters allows for a maritime traffic that makes New Orleans the second most important port in the country, being surpassed in commercial terms only by New York City. Chemical and refining products are exported from this port. A short distance up the river, one appreciates the enormous Domino Sugar plant where sugar is refined from cane.

The captain explains that the Mississippi and its tributaries were the great means of transportation in the country before

[6] The architectural style from before the Civil War.

the arrival of the railroads and highways "…but the river even in this day plays an important transport role as far upstream from here as St. Louis." The flow of the river is very complicated, often turbulent, and altogether different from its tranquil appearance. The sediment, constantly deposited, continuously changes the bed of the river. Its mouth, which formerly often was no more than two or three meters deep, caused any number of explorer and trader shipwrecks. The problem was partially resolved by dredging and by constructing levees[7] that eventually allowed today's commercial development.

The captain points out the factories, where barges were built that were used in the Normandy landings and in those of the Pacific Islands.

"The city finds itself at an average of 1½ meters below sea level. You will find the consequences of this phenomenon when visiting the Saint Louis 1 and 2 cemeteries, for it is impossible to bury the dead. You will notice above-ground funeral chapels of various styles."

Dominique and Pierre stroll to the stern of the *Natchez*. The paddlewheels whip up the water with monotonous regularity. They listen to still another group lamenting the Blues of the slaves. Dominique proves herself very observant. "Hey, we saw that pianist at Preservation Hall late last night. I wonder if he had any sleep."

* * *

Pierre arrives at Tulane University on Saint Charles Avenue this Monday morning. It is a beautiful campus and he is reminded of his own years of schooling back home. The students seem so young and casual. T-shirts and baggy pants are

---

[7] Written before *Hurricane Katrina*.

the style for both sexes.

He is shown to the Department of Epidemiology where he is introduced to Dr. Mark Chase. "It is a pleasure to meet you and I welcome the opportunity to cooperate with the NIH on this West Nile problem. Let me show you my laboratory. We have several projects in progress."

Pierre tells the story of his meetings at the Capitol. "First of all, those of us representing the NIH and the CDC explained what you already know about the infection. The West Nile virus is similar to those that cause Saint Louis encephalitis, Japanese encephalitis and Yellow Fever. The virus is transmitted to man by the female mosquito. Birds and horses are also affected. There is no transmission between humans. The illness did not exist on this continent before 1999 although it was well described in Africa, Eastern Europe, the Middle East and Asia. In 1999, sixty-two cases were discovered in New York, seven of which were fatal. You have the figures for last year."

"Yes, we have. I hope you impressed upon these members of Congress the importance of mosquito control."

"Of course. The presence of the virus in this country is now without question and, while the number of cases to this point is not large, it is likely to grow. Epidemiologists like you and agencies such as the one that I represent will be called upon to allay the fears of a concerned American population."

"At the moment, AIDS is a much greater problem, but the press has a way of giving exaggerated importance to the West Nile situation. We are already considering a vaccine. The CDC, NIH and our university could easily combine our resources hopefully to eradicate the infection but much research will be required and it will probably take a number of years."

"This is the point of my being here and I am due back at the Capitol in two weeks to report the results of our encounter."

"It is one of the points of your being here. Another point relates to eating *à la Créole* this evening and I will show you where we can find the best turtle soup and a real great chicken gumbo. We can continue our discussion at the Galatoire Restaurant."

* * *

Pierre inquires about Dominique's activities when they meet again at the hotel. "Tell me about your language seminar."

"It was very interesting, my dear. Being the only native French person, I was put in charge of our group. I took notes for our small group and gave a summary of our recommendations. Everyone seems to be dealing with the same basic issue of making a foreign language relevant to a group of students for whom speaking a second language is not a high priority. My colleagues were interested in my experience in this country to this point. And you?"

"I dealt with Dr. Chase, a very amiable scientist. We will attempt to put together some type of collaboration that allows state and federal funding for the types of studies that we both feel need to be carried out to avert greater problems from the West Nile virus. But, beforehand, we are meeting him and his wife this evening at a restaurant on Bourbon Street. We will conclude our discussions tomorrow, *Mardi Gras*, at noon. He has invited us to attend one of the masked balls with his wife and himself tomorrow evening. They will be our guides."

"My conference also concludes at noon. We will need costumes."

* * *

Promptly at twelve o'clock, work is set aside! It is *Mardi Gras*, the biggest and most important holiday of the city, the preparations for which started way back on the feast of the Epiphany.

New Orleans has been celebrating the eve of Ash Wednesday since 1872 and this city attracts tourists for the occasion from everywhere in the country and beyond. To hide one's identity, to dress in the most extravagant costume, to behave according to one's wildest fantasy and to make that fantasy one's reality for the day, that is *Mardi Gras*. The rules of the rest of the year are suspended on this day.

We meet once again on Bourbon Street. Dominique and Pierre join Mark and Harriet Chase on the second floor balcony of the Royal Sonesta Hotel, offering a perfect view of the festivities below.

Dr. Chase points out that the approaching orchestra in green trousers is that of King Zulu. The musicians are almost all black; the few whites have blackened their faces and are playing to an African beat while singing:

> I have my ticket in my hand
> And I am going to New Orleans.
> I am going to the *Mardi Gras*
> And I will meet King Zulu.

Mark Chase yells to Dominique above the noise. "They are tossing coconuts into the crowd that will bring happiness to those who catch one. I am not sure that any will reach up this high but see if anyone in the orchestra will throw one up to you."

From the balconies, spectators toss colored necklaces to one another. The two couples watch several more orchestras before making their way to the street level and they meander toward the intersection of Saint Charles and Canal Streets. "This is where the real carnival will take place. The streets of the French Quarter are too narrow to accommodate the platformed vehicles that we will see here. Formerly pulled by mules and lit at night by torches, these floats are now towed by tractors. Rex, the King of the carnival in a gaudy red, blue and gold costume over a shiny satin shirt, has solemnly arrived by boat this morning and he ceremoniously occupies the lead float of the parade."

By now, Dominique is decked out in a dozen multicolored necklaces that have either been thrown at her or that have been given to her by Mark Chase and his wife. "Look, Pierre, at these extravagant floats. The flower displays are so different and all are magnificent."

"They really are extraordinary."

> Oh when the saints come marching in.
> Oh when the saints come marching in.
> I want to be there in that number.
> When the saints come marching in.

Pierre waves to Miss Louisiana as she passes by. "I think she noticed me and blew me a kiss."

Dominique won't let him get carried away. "There are thousands of people here. How would she ever focus on you?"

"Why not on me? I'm not bad-looking and, in all modesty, I think I stand out in a crowd. That was probably meant to be my *Mardi Gras* moment."

After three hours of spectacle, they return to the hotel. "We will leave for the masked ball at 8 p.m. Mark Chase has arranged for the four of us to be transported by limousine to accommodate you and Harriet in your hooped skirts."

* * *

The limousine passes across the *bayous*, the marshes of the Mississippi. The evening is spent at the Laura Plantation manor where one discovers the Old South. Pierre thinks back to *Gone With the Wind* which he has seen several times and to Scarlett O'Hara and Rhett Butler from Atlanta. Pierre presents himself as Louis XIV and Dominique as Marie Antoinette. "They lived at opposite ends of the eighteenth century, to be sure, but anything is acceptable on *Mardi Gras*."

Dancing goes on throughout the evening and the costumes are all impressive. Highlighted are a musketeer, a cowboy, an Arab emir, a Spanish nobleman in a huge sombrero, a mustachioed Mongolian warrior, a dainty Japanese lady in her kimono and many others.

The buffet is elegant and the bar is amply stocked. Both are honored by the guests and the bar is, in many instances, frequented on multiple occasions.

Dominique and Pierre dance several times together, but Dominique is also asked to dance by a cleverly masked *hombre* and an Arab sheik for other numbers. Pierre observes a few dances from the sidelines and is keen to invite a few partners of his own. Dominique and Pierre arrange to dance the last waltzes together, floating around the ballroom fluidly and effortlessly and smiling at each other lovingly.

Mardi Gras ends precisely at the strike of midnight.

* * *

Lent has begun.

Chapter 11.
March 2001 – New York, New York

Give me your tired, your poor, your huddled masses, yearning to breathe free.

Inscription on the Statue of Liberty.

"Harvey's sister is really kind to loan us her apartment. He and his wife, Rachel, will join us during our visit."

The Benoits are spending a long weekend in New York, "…Woody Allen's city." They will be content to visit Manhattan, one of its five boroughs. New York was founded by the Dutch in 1626 and was named New Amsterdam. Before the Dutch, Native Americans had occupied the area.

While here, Pierre will call upon a colleague in infectious diseases from Mount Sinai Hospital whose office is in one of the Twin Towers.

* * *

Battery Park, from where cruises that circle Manhattan leave, is the destination for this Saturday morning. "This ride will give us an overall perspective of the 'Big Apple'. It is cool but the sun is shining brightly."

Going up the East River, the boat travels under the Brooklyn, Manhattan and Queensboro Bridges, passing in front of the United Nations Building. The Chinese and Italian sections are seen from a distance. The Harlem River that separates Manhattan from the Bronx is entered. A crew hand indicates to Philippe that Yankee Stadium is located in the Bronx. "You should be wearing a Yankees cap."

"We just arrived yesterday. I will shop for one before our stay in New York is over."

Gaining the Hudson River, the cruise descends to the point of embarkation, passing the site where the Twin Towers stand.

The parents are impressed by the line of skyscrapers, among which is the Empire State Building, which for a long time had been the tallest building in the world. Julie and Philippe are overwhelmed and can only speak in superlatives. "Wow! This is all so immense. These buildings are so tall."

"That is why it is called the 'Big Apple'," responds Philippe's crew person. "Let me give you a list of the places that you should visit while you are here."

"Do you realize," says Pierre, "that our little excursion around the island of Manhattan has logged almost fifty kilometers?"

* * *

"We are in the financial district. Let's follow Wall Street and pass by the New York Stock Exchange, the center and symbol of American capitalism."

The family starts on Vesey Street before reaching the Twin Towers. Dominique suggests a cup of coffee in the atrium of the South Tower while Pierre takes the elevator to the eighty-third floor. He will have a preliminary meeting with Dr. Abraham Schwartz at that level. He is scheduled to return next month for a work session with a group of physicians who, along with the NIH, are doing research on AIDS, a serious problem in the city.

The Twin Towers are part of the World Trade Center which was conceived in the early 1960s to replace what had been a run-down neighborhood. The Downtown Lower Manhattan Development Association spearheaded the project with the help of the Chase Manhattan Bank and the leadership of David and Nelson Rockefeller. The site occupies sixteen acres and, during its construction, the project employed ten thousand workers, sixty of whom died accidentally before its completion. The Towers were the tallest buildings in the world when finished in 1972, only to be surpassed by the Sears Tower in Chicago one year later.

Dr. Schwartz remarks that fifty thousand people work within the Towers and 200,000 visitors enter these buildings on any given day.

While Dominique is engaged in conversation with a New York businesswoman, the children decide to visit a gift shop on the seventh floor. "Ross Appleton asked me to bring him a souvenir from New York."

"I could also find something for Juanita and Dawn."

After considering the options, Philippe picks out a New York Giants sweatshirt and Julie selects two coffee table picture books of New York with a color photograph of the Twin Towers on the cover.

* * *

Rockefeller Center, situated below street level, features an ice skating rink that interests Philippe who rents the necessary equipment for a half hour.

Radio City Music Hall is also in the area. They learn that the Hall is the home of the famous Rockettes. Formerly called the Roxiettes, the troupe debuted at Radio City Music Hall in 1932. This group consists of two hundred women dancers who are known for their precision routines and flawless execution. While based here in New York, members tour throughout the country and delight audiences wherever they go. "They even dance the *French Can-Can*."

Lunch is enjoyed next to the rink while watching the world pass by.

* * *

After a power nap at the apartment, the Benoits take the subway to Central Park. They come upon a carousel that attracts young and old alike. Much like the Boston Common, immediate relaxation is experienced as the walkways are full of rollerbladers and joggers. A lady wearing sunglasses is walking her leashed dogs, nine of them, who are pulling her in as many directions. Two mounted policemen keep an eye on the area, assuring the tranquility that people seek. Girls are playing jump-rope. Boys are tossing a football.

While the parents rest on a park bench, Philippe takes Julie on a rowboat ride on the lake which reflects Midtown Manhattan. The family then leaves by way of the Dakota Apartments where John Lennon was assassinated in 1980. On the other side of Central Park is the Metropolitan Museum of Art that Julie and her mother visit while Philippe and Pierre make their way to Greenwich Village.

The museum is featuring the private collection of Janice Levin, a Fifth Avenue collector. The 'Met' has acquired thirty-five of her impressionist paintings for three months, among which are Monet's *Le Jardin d'Argenteuil* and others by Boudin, Morisot, Pissaro and Renoir.

Rejoining the men, Dominique sings the praises of what she has seen. "The Metropolitan is a wonderful museum that easily rivals those of ours in Paris. As for this collection, I never tire of the Impressionists. This art collector has brought together a significant group of paintings of enormous value."

Julie cannot contain herself. "As magnificent as this group of paintings is, it does not approach what I saw of Monet in Boston."

Pierre is quick to add. "French culture, you see, can be appreciated anywhere!"

* * *

The family returns to Battery Park the next day for a ferry ride to the Statue of Liberty. On October 26, 1886, more than one million spectators witnessed the unfurling of the French flag, revealing the head and torch of the Statue. For many immigrants, this landmark has been the very symbol of liberty and the hope of a new life. Some of Dominique's colleagues have shared stories with her of their grandparents or great-grandparents. She and her family will next revisit the journeys of those brave people on neighboring Ellis Island.

The museum recreates the experience and fate of twelve million immigrants who arrived here between 1892 and 1938. The medical personnel and police processed thousands of prospective citizens on a daily basis. Each candidate had a sticker pinned to his or her clothing. The process took up to five hours and required many interpreters. The most common condition that resulted in a quarantine and occasional outright rejection was trachoma, an eye infection that was prevalent in Eastern and Southern Europe. The officers charged with the uncomfortable task of retracting the eyelids to detect this infection were among the most dreaded. A single physician could examine as many as 450 'patients' in a single day.

The center operated ten hours each and every day. Two percent of the candidates were returned to their country of origin. Those who were accepted might sleep in huge dormitories for days or weeks. Diphtheria and measles were common. In order to enter into the country, women needed to be accompanied by a man. Many who were traveling alone often found an uncle or a cousin of convenience. Some were married on site.

Unfortunately, 3,500 died during these fifty years. During this same period, some 350 births were also recorded.

Those who were accepted passed through swing doors that opened new lives for them. These immigrants provided the labor that would help in the development of this young country. It is estimated that one hundred million citizens are able to trace their origin to these European adventurers. Immigration laws were stiffened in 1920 and the center was closed in 1954, becoming a museum to the memory of those who had arrived with barely the clothes on their backs and their possessions in a suitcase or in a sack flung over their shoulders.

* * *

The afternoon is devoted to shopping. "We have already acquired quite a bit and so we should restrain ourselves," says Pierre. "Dominique and Julie might consider some shoes. Philippe, you probably want another T-shirt. You won't be the one to break the bank."

"And for you?" asks Dominique.

"I hesitate between a Rolls Royce and a high-end three-piece suit."

The first stop is at Bergdorf-Goodman on Fifth Avenue… to look around, no doubt. "The prices are sure to be beyond our means," says Pierre. As planned, Philippe buys a Yankee

T-shirt and cap to add to his collection. "Maybe I can turn some of my friends from Nice into baseball fans."

Julie has a comment of her own. "This is hardly L.L. Bean."

* * *

The Orpheum on Broadway is the theater where *Les Misérables* is playing. "We shall see if the English version compares favorably with the one that has been playing back home." They hop into one of the thirteen thousand yellow cabs of New York. As planned, the Benoits meet Harvey and his wife in front of the theater. Julie is wearing the new dress that she managed to purchase earlier in the day and her mother notices that she is attracting a few stares. Dominique advises her husband to be watchful of his daughter instead of paying so much attention to the female stars who are being surrounded by a crowd.

They had earlier read favorable reviews of the play in the *New York Times* and are not disappointed. "Do you realize that this play has had a run of more than ten years in London?"

"And here as well, my dear Dominique," replies Rachel.

Julie particularly appreciated the role of Eponyme. "The young girl who played her role is about my age. She was so authentic in her acting and she has a beautiful voice."

Dominique agrees. "The program also mentioned that she was selected from among some four hundred contestants in a singing and acting audition for which she was allowed less than two minutes."

Harvey notices that Philippe is getting restless as they reach the lobby following the performance. "I will now show you parts of New York that are familiar to me and that you must see. You probably are aware of the New Year's Eve celebration that takes place in Times Square on television. We should go to where that crowd assembles.

"It wasn't so long ago that the area was really dirty and was bordered by any number of disreputable establishments. One passed through here at one's own risk. The place has been cleaned up and you can be at ease now. This is the Sears Tower from where the huge ball descends during the last minute of the year as the crowd counts down the last seconds and then yells out 'Happy New Year'. Fireworks are set off as everyone sings 'Auld Lang Syne'."

Pierre recalls the millennium celebration. "Some American friends called us when they witnessed our illuminated Eiffel Tower extravaganza on television at midnight. We in turn woke up six hours later to view your celebration here and we called them in return with our best wishes."

According to Harvey, there are still homeless people who sleep on the sidewalks and in the alleys of the area. "Unfortunately, it is a problem in New York and in most of our large cities. The mayor of Boston does an annual survey to quantify the number of those who are either on the streets or in shelters across his city. Recently, there were six thousand in shelters and two hundred on sidewalks. There may be even more here, although the recent building of low-income housing in the Bronx has alleviated the problem significantly."

Julie is sensitive to these social problems. "It is a sad reality in our country," says Harvey. "I hope the mayor and our new president will really address the problem."

"To see Times Square has always been a dream of mine since my childhood," admits Dominique. "This has been wonderful."

"To see Times Square and die," concludes Rachel.

* * *

Harvey and Rachel Kantrowicz await the family at 10:30 at the entrance of the Empire State Building at the intersection of Fifth Avenue and West 34th Street this Monday morning. The elevator transports them to the observation deck on the eighty-sixth floor from where they have a panoramic view of the city. They go even higher to the 102nd floor from which point Central Park is seen to the north and the Statue of Liberty to the southwest. The amount of boat activity that is visible on the East and Hudson Rivers gives proof that New York is the most important port in the country.

The guide gives a history of the building. "Your French countryman, Pierre Dupont, had helped finance the construction of this skyscraper that employed, among others, hundreds of Mohawk ironworkers from Montreal."

Pierre recalls that a Canadian tribe of Indians had the distinction of not being affected by heights with any signs of vertigo.

"It may well have been this group of workers."

The guide continues. "The project was completed in a little more than a year at the peak of the depression in 1931. As a result, much of the office space remained vacant and the building was not profitable until 1950. You may have seen pictures of construction workers having their lunch while seated on iron beams of upper floors, the city visible far below."

Dominique comments on the impressive illumination of the top of this skyscraper that she noticed last evening. "I was struck by the orange, blue and white colors and wondered if there were any significance to that combination."

"Those are the colors of our basketball team, the Knicks, who were playing at the Madison Square Garden. The colors this evening will undoubtedly be red, white and blue since our hockey team, the Rangers, is scheduled to compete against the Vancouver Canucks."

Pierre mentions that he was in Vancouver two months ago. "The people there are passionate over their hockey team."

"Different colors are chosen to match other calendar events: St. Patrick's Day, Independence Day and even Bastille Day."

Sensing everyone's hunger, Rachel decides that it is time for lunch. "I know every Jewish deli in the city. It isn't cold. Let us buy a sandwich and join the crowd on the steps of the New York Public Library. It is one of our customs here to gather at this location to engage in conversation and to observe the hustle and bustle of the city."

Between bites, Dominique breaks the news of an offer that she has received from her principal. "He asked me last week if I might be interested in teaching a weekly two-hour course in French literature at Georgetown University starting next fall. A colleague of his indicated that a position was about to open and I might want to submit an application. We spoke about it at home. It is a position that is worth considering."

* * *

A visit to the United Nations is on the agenda for this afternoon. The guided portion lasts one hour and includes entries into the General Assembly Hall and that of the Security Council.

Julie recalls the Cuban Missile Crisis film that she saw at the Kennedy Library. "It is here that Adlai Stevenson, while representing the United States, had challenged the Russian delegate. 'Do you or do you not have these nuclear weapons? No need to wait for the translation. I am prepared to wait for your answer until hell freezes over if necessary.'"

Harvey adds with a smile. "There is a photo of Stevenson that made the rounds on television and in the newspapers that pictured him with a huge hole in the sole of one of his shoes. The poor guy couldn't even afford decent footwear."

Julie is impressed by the photos of Hiroshima and Nagasaki. As the one who invariably espouses conflict resolution through negotiations, her response to Rachel is predictable. "We talk about this at home frequently and it seems to me that we cannot allow this sort of thing to happen again. I hope that we can achieve peaceful settlements to our differences."

Pierre agrees, but cannot help adding, "Another huge program, would have said de Gaulle."

Rachel relates the experiences of an older man who had been a neighbor in the days of her youth. "He is in his eighties now, but I recall when he came back from the war in 1945. Everyone gathered at the home of his parents to welcome him after he had been discharged. He served in the Pacific and he told his story. He talked of the places that have become all too familiar to us: Pearl Harbor of course, Midway, Wake, Okinawa and Iwo Jima. His plane had crashed in the Pacific and he had somehow not been killed. He was a POW in awful places like Ofuna, Omori and Naoetsu. He was sure that he would not have survived had those two bombs not been dropped. He was convinced that the *Enola Gay* plane that had been piloted by Paul Tibbetts on August 6, 1945, in the secret attack on Hiroshima and the subsequent attack three days later on Nagasaki turned the war around."

"Tokyo was also severely bombed, as these pictures show," intones Pierre.

"Wilfred was his name. He went on with his life from that day and he apparently never talked about those experiences again."

Philippe shows particular interest in the replica of the Russian Sputnik before leaving.

Outside once again, Harvey recalls that the design of the building was made possible through the combined efforts of a number of architects from around the world, symbolic of international peaceful cooperation.

* * *

Times Square is revisited before returning to Washington by Amtrak. Jim McCabe from the *Washington Post* had been able to organize a meeting with Peter Jennings of *ABC News*.

While the children are shown around the studio, Pierre and Dominique engage Jennings in conversation. "Are you responsible for the content of your reporting?"

"Yes, I am. I select from among the events that are presented to me by a very competent staff. I am surrounded by a group of professionals who provide me with much from which to choose. In the final analysis, I write my own script."

"You are in competition with the other networks."

"Absolutely. McCabe and I talk about this all the time. Whether it be newspaper or television journalism, we need a substantial audience to attract the necessary advertising revenue."

"What will be the subject matter of this evening's broadcast?"

"This edition of *World News Tonight* will devote a significant segment to the relations between the mayor of New York and the unions that represent the police, the firefighters and the sanitation workers. The city's expenditures are forever increasing and risk exceeding the receipts. I will interview Mayor Giuliani on the subject."

"You know the mayor?"

“Yes, he always has something to say about the problems of the city and is opinionated about most everything.

“I will also talk about the reception that President Bush gave to President Kim Dae Jung of South Korea earlier today. Both leaders are seeking trade agreements that could be mutually beneficial.

“It might also interest you to know that English is increasingly becoming the language of diplomacy at the United Nations, although French and Spanish remain important, and I will comment on that phenomenon.

“As always, there will be a sports segment. This is a sports-crazed city and the Yankees command a great deal of attention. Spring training in Florida is nearing its completion. The long baseball season will begin in ten days.”

* * *

At 6:30 sharp, the camera is fixed on Jennings. “Good evening, America…”

Chapter 12.
April 2011 - *Camden Yards* Baltimore, Maryland

If you do not understand baseball, you do not understand America.

Bud Selig, Commissioner of Major League Baseball

Pierre and Philippe have been invited by Larry Winship and his son Andrew to attend the opening-day game between the Baltimore Orioles and the New York Yankees. Larry was able to obtain these highly-prized tickets online well in advance of this special event. Camden Yards, with a capacity of 48,000, is reputed to be one of the most beautiful stadiums in the country and this foursome will be part of the sellout crowd to pack into the park.

The Yankees are always a big draw and are favored once again to win the American League pennant. Today's game initiates the long 162-game season that will conclude at the end of September and will then be followed by a string of playoff series among the four top teams in each of the American and National Leagues. The winning team in each league will then compete in the final series, the World Series, the winner of which will be acclaimed champion toward the end of October.

* * *

During the 45-mile ride from Washington to Baltimore, Larry gave some of the historical highlights of the game. "Baseball lore has it that the game was born in 1839 in a small community called Cooperstown in upstate New York. The game is said to have been invented by Abner Doubleday who conceived of the diamond around which run players who hit a thrown ball with a bat. A point is scored when a player completes the tour of the four *bases*, returning to the point of origin, *home plate*. Many feel, perhaps more accurately, that Alexander Cartwright was the real pioneer of the game when he fielded a team of New York firefighters known as the Knickerbockers in the 1840s. They played their games against teams in the New York and New Jersey area. The new sport spread to surrounding communities and, from there, it gained popularity throughout the country, eventually becoming the 'National Pastime'."

From their seats on the third-base side, the fathers and sons have a view beyond the outfield of the Baltimore skyline. The stadium reverberates with a carnival atmosphere. Fans yell and scream, eat and drink. Hot dogs are the principal item on the menu. For those who are old enough, beer is the main beverage. Pierre and Philippe become quickly aware of the good-natured conversation among the spectators. Loud music contributes to the electric feeling.

The pre-game festivities include a recall of the two Oriole championship teams of the 60s. Andrew, a long-time baseball card collector, shows Philippe those of Brooks Robinson, Frank Robinson and Cal Ripken, Jr., explaining that Frank

Robinson holds the distinction of having been the only person to be voted the Most Valuable Player in both the American and National Leagues.

* * *

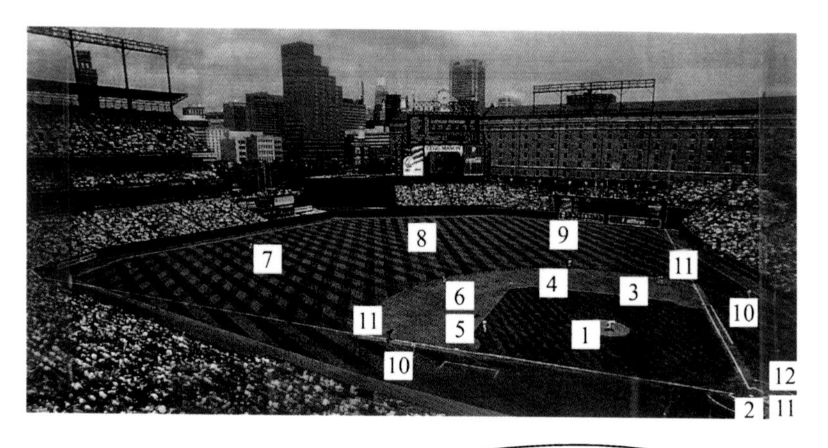

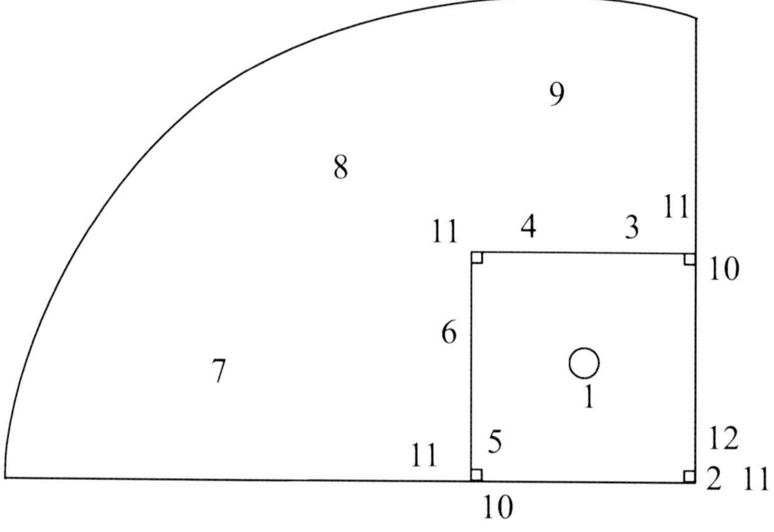

1 – Pitcher
2 – Catcher
3 – First baseman
4 – Second baseman
5 – Third baseman
6 – Shortstop
7 – Leftfielder
8 – Centerfielder
9 – Rightfielder
10 – Coaches
11 – Umpires
12 – Batter

Pierre asks Larry to explain the rules.

"In a nutshell, the batter must hit the ball as far as possible to allow his teammates to score points by running from base to base. These bases represent the four angles of the diamond. The ultimate hit is the one that reaches the stands on the fly in fair territory, a hit that is called a home run. These home runs occur on average three or four times per game. Runs can also be produced with lesser hits --singles, doubles and triples-- that allow players to circle the bases in stages, crossing the base of origin, home plate, to register the score. Much depends on the speed of runners offensively and the position of fielders defensively. Actually, the most important player for the defense is the pitcher whose thrown balls to the batter are more or less difficult to hit. The defense is successful in recording *outs* by catching struck balls on the fly or by throwing balls that have been hit on the ground to a baseman more quickly than the batter or baserunner can reach the base in question. The batter can also be eliminated on strikes if he misses or *fouls off* three pitched balls.

These are the general principles, but the explanations will become clearer when I point out exactly what is happening as the game progresses. First, we should have our hot dogs before we stand for the National Anthem."

The game begins and the Yankees strike first in the second inning on a home run by Bernie Williams. Andy Pettitte is the Yankee starting pitcher and he seems overpowering, fanning two batters in each of the first three innings. The Orioles get on the board in the bottom of the fourth, however, to take a 2-1 lead on consecutive doubles by Brian Roberts and Jerry Hairston, an infield out and a sacrifice fly. An unearned run in the fifth inning extends their lead to 3-1. The Yankees rally for three runs of their own in the top of the seventh.

Philippe and Andrew buy ice cream bars from an orange-shirted vendor during the seventh-inning stretch. The Orioles proceed to erase the Yankee 4-3 lead with two runs in the bottom of the eighth inning to regain the advantage, 5-4.

Manager Mike Hargrove goes to his bullpen for the third time to start the top of the ninth. The Yankees counter with a left-handed pinch hitter who triples. With the infield drawn in, Derek Jeter bloops a single to right and he scores after a walk, an infield out and a fielding error by the Oriole third baseman.

Mariano Rivera is then summoned as the closer for New York to save his team's 6-5 lead. He retires the first two batters with his cut fastball, but he walks the next hitter. With the crowd on its feet, David Segui, the designated hitter, smashes Rivera's second pitch over the right field wall for a *walkoff* home run that sends the delighted fans home with an exciting 7-6 victory and the early hopes for a successful season.

Larry had ample time to elaborate on his explanations during the 3½ hour game, one that seemed interminable to the two French spectators. More accustomed to the continuous play of soccer, they found that there were many interruptions between innings and even between pitches. Those in attendance did not seem to mind, however, as they chatted with each other and ate and drank abundantly. In spite of the slow pace, Pierre and Philippe found that there still were several exciting moments. For one, the Yankee centerfielder, Bernie Williams, made a highlight sliding catch while fully extended to take an extra base hit away from the Oriole catcher and Ken Singleton of the Orioles reached into the stands to 'rob' Jorge Posada of a home run. There was even a bench-clearing brawl that held up the game momentarily when the Oriole cleanup hitter was struck by a pitch. B.J. Ryan, an Oriole relief pitcher, was subsequently ejected when he sought retribution by hitting the Yankee second baseman the following inning.

* * *

Baseball is a game laden with statistics and rabid fans can cite so many of them in their unending trivia contests. Newspapers highlight every detail through box scores and the Sunday editions capture each team's up-to-date summaries at any given point in the season.

Larry explained to Pierre and Philippe that the Hall of Fame located in Cooperstown, New York brings together the best players to have participated in the game since its inception. Only three or four players are voted into this shrine each year and the induction ceremony that takes place in August is one of the highlights of the entire baseball season.

"You, the French, have certainly heard of Joe DiMaggio in the context of marrying Marilyn Monroe, but here he is better known for having hit safely in fifty-six consecutive games, a record that many feel will never be broken. Jackie Robinson became the first African-American to play in the major leagues in 1947. There is always talk of Don Larsen's perfect World Series game while pitching for the Yankees against the Brooklyn Dodgers in 1956, recording twenty-seven outs without yielding a hit or a base-on-balls. This is still recognized as a remarkable feat by a player whose career was otherwise quite ordinary.

Many other statistical achievements continue to be revered. Among these are Mark McGwire's seventy home runs in 1999[8] and Ted Williams' .406 batting average in 1941. To give you an idea, a .300 average would be considered very good; .350, superb; and .375, extraordinary. Nobody has been able to maintain an average over .400 for an entire season since Ted Williams did, although a few players have flirted with this accomplishment until late in the season."

"Are these players well paid?" interjects Pierre.

"Baseball players can earn enormous salaries. A slugger, one who hits many home runs, can command twelve to fifteen million dollars for a season. Alex Rodriguez signed a ten-year contract with the Texas Rangers for 252 million dollars!"[9]

Pierre is overwhelmed. "When will researchers like us be equally compensated?"

"Don't hold your breath. That may be scandalous, but the sport needs to deal with occasional other scandals as well, the most notable of which was the intentional losing of the World Series by the infamous Chicago Black Sox in 1919 following an arrangement between players and a gambling syndicate. In our day, baseball is threatened by performance-enhancing drugs, a problem in other sports as well."

* * *

"Well, are you completely converted to our baseball?" asks Larry.

"To be perfectly honest," answers Pierre, "I still prefer our rugby and soccer. I enjoyed this game, but there are too many interruptions. Our sports by contrast are so much more continuous."

---

[8] Barry Bonds from the San Francisco Giants will hit seventy-three home runs this very year.

[9] Rodriguez was subsequently traded to the New York Yankees in exchange for other players.

"And you, Philippe?"

"I will always be more taken up by our football; what you call soccer. But, now that I am playing baseball, I am understanding the sport better and I definitely enjoy it. I like the glove with which I catch the ball."

Andrew chips in. "Had you caught that foul ball that landed two rows behind us, you would have a real Camden Yards trophy."

"I will settle for this pennant souvenir that I bought. It's cool."

On the way back home, Larry reviews some of the finer points of the game that he tried to highlight during the contest. "As you saw, a fast runner can attempt to steal a base. The defense can position itself to reduce the likelihood of a base hit or an extra base hit. A player who is replaced during the game cannot return in the same game. The batting order is established in such a way as to capitalize on the particular talents of each player. Starting pitchers are part of a five-person rotation, returning on average to pitch every fifth day and resting their arms between assignments. Consider how different your soccer game would be if five goaltenders shared the task on a rotating basis. Also, remember the duration of the regular baseball season… 162 games."

"Ah, yes," says Pierre. "But still less empty time in our sports."

Larry gets the last word. "You Frenchmen are all alike. But we can still toast our baseball with your French wine and our Coca-Cola when we arrive home. The entire season lies ahead of us. We will convert the both of you to the sport well before playoff time!"

Chapter 13.
May 2001 – Phoenix, Arizona

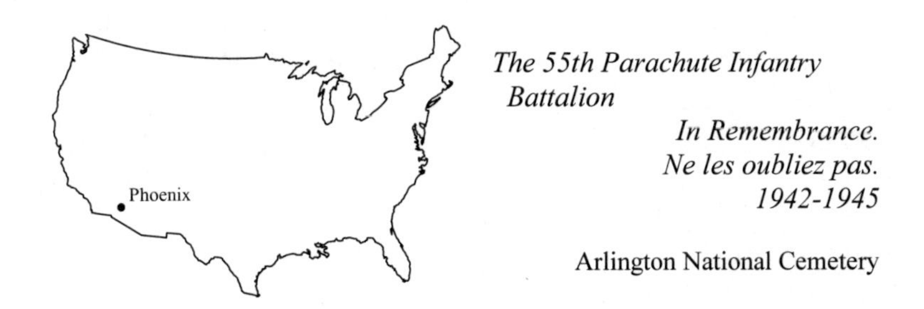

The 55th Parachute Infantry Battalion

In Remembrance.
Ne les oubliez pas.
1942-1945

Arlington National Cemetery

Philippe and Julie have been invited to Phoenix by the Mitchells for Memorial Day, celebrated in the United States on the last Monday of May, in memory of all the American veterans who have died in the several conflicts around the world. “Look at the lights of the city, Julie. Seen from above, they seem to be forming a grid.”

In the middle of the desert, Phoenix has experienced a striking demographic explosion during these recent years and ranks as the fourth most populous city in the country behind Los Angeles, New York and Houston. Known as the Sun City, it is located in the midst of the Sun Belt which extends from Florida to California.

During the flight, Julie and Philippe have compared notes on their stay in the United States to this point. They are within three weeks of the summer vacations. Time has gone by more quickly than they had imagined shortly after their arrival. For Julie, the success that she has experienced in her studies has been but a continuation of her good results in France. She particularly likes her history and American literature courses. She had a role in *West Side Story* in March. Rehearsals took up her after-school hours three afternoons a week. The performances themselves were met with a great deal of success. She has made several friends among the girls and boys at school, most notably Juanita Mendez, Sarah Johnson and Dawn Walker.

Philippe on the other hand has felt at ease only within the past two months. He was forced to cease all sporting activities for six weeks following his appendicitis. He has resumed soccer and has contributed to the success of the Woodrow Wilson team. Now, and particularly since attending the game at Camden Yards, he is increasingly interested in baseball. Like his sister, he has established several friendships, among whom are Ross Appleton and Felipe Torres, not to forget Scott whom he is about to meet once again in a few minutes at the airport after the landing of this Boeing 727.

* * *

After a warm American-style welcome and a good night's sleep, Julie and Philippe are awakened at 6 a.m. The excursion that they are about to undertake will be long and rigorous under a blazing hot sun. Mrs. Mitchell has suggested shorts and T-shirts "... for, by noontime, it will be at least 100 degrees. And bring lots of water."

Julie goes outside. It is already hot. There is no lawn around the stucco house. The property is surrounded by white stones. "Grass would require too much watering. Our supply comes to us from the Colorado River and its tributaries through a system of canals. These sources provide several states of the Southwest with their water needs, needs which are continuously increasing because of the ever larger population numbers. Hispanics form the majority in the area," Mrs Mitchell informs them.

* * *

Dr. Mitchell passes several large shopping malls as he drives beyond the city limits. "These neighborhoods did not exist when we arrived here twelve years ago. They appear to grow like mushrooms. The city itself owes its name to a gold seeker, recalling the legendary bird of a bygone era."

"How is that?" asks Philippe.

"Perhaps because Phoenix, burnt by the scorching sun and with the help of irrigation, has risen in the desert like the mythical bird that also rose from its ashes to live another five hundred years."

Julie comments on the flatness of the terrain. "There is only a cactus here and there."

"We are in the Sonora Desert. The climate is hot and dry and there is very little vegetation, apart from these occasional cacti."

Scott interjects, "We study the cactus extensively in our natural science classes. The scientific name for this kind of growth is the *Seguaro* which can have a lifespan of two to three hundred years."

"My father, who spent a fair amount of time in Tunisia, indicated that the Island of Djerba off the southern coast of the country has olive trees that go back to the time of Christ."

"Given its extensive root system, these cacti can hold up to five or six thousand liters of water. This phenomenon accounts for their ability to resist a dry climate such as ours. They are more susceptible to freezing temperatures, however, and our nights can sometimes get quite cold."

"Like in the Sahara."

Dr. Mitchell continues toward the mountains northeast of Phoenix. “It rarely rains here, often less than 250 mm in a year, but when it does rain, we can experience some terrible flooding.”

Julie is reminded of similar occurrences back home. “This happens in France as well, particularly in the southern part, close to the Mediterranean. North Africa also experiences these torrential rains on occasion. Our grandparents tell the story of friends of theirs who nearly drowned during such a storm while living in Gabès, a city in southern Tunisia.”

Scott continues to impress with his fund of knowledge. “It is said that Indians used the water from cactus trees while crossing this desert that covers a large portion of Arizona, New Mexico and the southern part of California. The *Seguaros* are identified by their different flowers. Some are barrel-shaped and are quite tall while others are very small and may look like a pin cushion. You have probably seen those around the house.”

* * *

To get to the Superstition Mountains, Doctor Mitchell follows the Apache Trail to the Weaver’s Needle. “Now we will walk. Don’t forget your canteens. It is already 90 degrees. We are going to sweat. Caps and sunglasses are obligatory. Scott can lead the way and I will bring up the rear. We are looking at a two-hour climb to the top and we will take a break every half hour.”

The last hundred yards of the ascent are the steepest and there is a need to catch one’s breath upon reaching the summit. “We are overlooking the Sonora Desert, a real desert as you can see. The air in the distance seems to be trembling. Offsetting the blue sky is the brown of the mountains and the distant plains.”

Julie mops her brow. "I feel as though I am stuck in a furnace; but it is a dry heat."

"I warned you that it would be hot, well over 100 at this point. Before leaving this mountaintop, take in this view. Hot or not, you must admit that it is spectacular. It will be easier heading down. We will make our way to Goldfield Ghost Town for lunch and for a long fresh drink."

Katherine cautions Julie not to slip on the stones during the descent. They meet a group heading upwards. "Take courage; you are within thirty minutes of the top."

Having reached the base of the mountain, Philippe empties his canteen in three huge swallows.

Dr. Mitchell congratulates the expeditioners. "We should be at the Goldfield Ghost Town in ten minutes. I will tell you the story of the Superstition Mountains. The Goldfield Village is very much a part of the story. As you can see, we have a real western atmosphere here."

Julie turns around to gaze upon the Superstition Mountains. "To think that we were there at the summit two hours ago."

Philippe has the feeling of being in the village of the *Hangman's Treasure* with Richard Widmark and Robert Taylor. He points his finger in Scott's direction. "Bang, bang." Scott plays the role and falls to the ground, motionless on his back. Julie cracks up and attempts unsuccessfully to rouse him. "Philippe, what did you do to him?

"I think there are bandits around here."

* * *

The Apache Junction Restaurant is mercifully air-conditioned and allows Dr. Mitchell to throw himself into his story.

"Why the name Superstition Mountains?" asks Philippe.

"It is the story of the *Lost Dutchman's Mine of Jacob Waltz*. While lost, some to this day continue to look for this mine.

"The saga starts with a Mexican, Don Miguel Peralta, who originally discovered this mine around 1830. A certain Jacob Weiser then came into the picture by saving Don Miguel's life during a fight in the course of a botched-up poker game. As a result, Weiser was invited to exploit the mine and to share in its profits with Peralta. Weiser in turn had a German partner named Jacob Waltz, mistakenly nicknamed *Dutchman* rather than *Deutchman*. Together, the two Jacobs went into these mountains that we just climbed and that you can see from this window. They became separated at some point and Weiser was killed; we do not know to this day how or by whom. It was not a rarity for people to die while mining here. Apaches could have murdered him. There were often conflicts between Redskins and Whiteskins, the two races always competing for the riches that these mountains harbored.

"With Weiser out of the picture, Waltz sought to cash in on the fortune. He had always been a gold seeker, first in South Carolina, then in Georgia and subsequently in California. It may surprise you to know that gold was struck in the Southeast before the Goldrush in California occurred.

"Apart from his relationship with Weiser, Waltz was an inveterate loner. He worked the mine by himself and he split the take with Peralta. He spent part of the year in Phoenix and paid his expenses in gold. He never married and he led a reclusive life. His work in the mine extended from November to May. After his death in 1891, a stash of gold worth 4,500 dollars was found under his bed, an enormous sum in those days.

"The year before his death, Waltz, in poor health, sought to share the secrets of the mine with a number of his acquaintances, but those whom he contacted refused to get involved for one reason or another.

"At this point, it is difficult to separate legend from reality. I will give you a version; there are certainly others.

"Waltz died in the presence of two other miners, Dick Holmes and Gideon Roberts, who accepted the offer of succession and to whom Waltz had provided the necessary information. While they were not exactly friends, they could have been considered colleagues of sorts. On his death bed, Waltz confessed to having personally killed seven people.

"There are several legends surrounding Holmes, his son, George, and any number of other characters who sought the fortunes that gold could bring them. Many thought that Dick was a fraud who sought to profit from Waltz's death by recovering the gold hidden under his bed, but without having received any kind of mine information."

Scott interrupts. "But, Dad, is there or is there not a mine in these mountains? According to your story, there must be a ton of gold up there. It might well be a legend, but where did the gold of Waltz and Peralta come from?"

"That indeed is the question. You can cross the street and merchants in any number of those stores will sell you 'authentic' maps that will identify the precise location of the mine. Just realize that, like everyone else, you will find nothing. If the mine of Jacob Waltz exists, its entrance is undoubtedly closed and inaccessible and the reference points are no longer to be found. Just imagine that, for one hundred years, the mine thumbs its nose at all those who go into the mountains, only to leave with empty pockets. What's more, some don't even manage to leave, these mountains being particularly dangerous."

"As we have experienced, the heat of summer can be brutal."

"Yes, Julie, and there are other risks as well. In the winter a freezing rain can transform these mountains into a sheet of ice. With the treacherous slopes and the rocky terrain, it would not be easy to find one's way out."

"We did not see any animals, but I have read that wild beasts live in these desert regions."

"Absolutely. One can on occasion encounter cougars and wild boar along one's path and they can be ferocious toward those who encroach on their territory. Then again, scorpions and snakes may not be very hospitable. One needs to be very prudent. Ah! Phoenix's baseball team, the Diamondbacks, carries the name of one of these particularly venomous creatures that one can encounter there."

The doctor concludes his tale. "This legend is symbolic of the origins of Phoenix and of the majority of places in the southwestern states of this country. It is the story of the Wild West of the nineteenth century, a history of the search for and the discovery of gold, but, more often, of failures, of sweat, of blood and tears."

Philippe is wide-eyed at this juncture in the narrative. "Was Goldfield Ghost Town a haven for bandits?"

The doctor agrees. "The conquest of the West was a story of courage and sacrifices, but also of theft, crime and murder. Living in this area was not for the faint of heart; it was the law of the jungle and often it was only the fittest who survived. These Superstition Mountains hide a mineful of these stories."

* * *

Mrs. Mitchell is preparing dinner when the adventurers return. "You all strike me as being tired and weary."

Katherine answers. "You have no idea of what we have done today."

"Did you find any gold during your expedition?"

* * *

Dr. Mitchell and Scott are the first to awaken the following morning. This year in 2001, Memorial Day falls on the 29th. It will be celebrated here and everywhere throughout the country with a parade which will end at the main cemetery where the graves of so many veterans of foreign engagements are draped with flowers and graced with a small American flag. The father and son leave early to participate in the festivities. Scott will play the trumpet in his school band and his father will be among the veterans, for he spent two years in Vietnam, and he retrieves his uniform once a year to march with those who served there as well as in Korea and in the Gulf. He is proud to have served his country and he is motivated to honor those less fortunate who died in battle far from the homeland. There are still a few survivors of World War II, but each year their number diminishes, the youngest among them being now in their eighties. Philippe and the women will view the parade in town at the intersection of MacDowell Road and Central Avenue.

In spite of the solemnity of the occasion, a carnival atmosphere prevails. Our friends witness the strutting of marching bands from many schools and organizations, between which are floats depicting any number of scenes, including those that were experienced in the mountains yesterday. Military music abounds, but popular tunes are also included.

Julie catches Philippe's attention. "This is hardly like back home on November 11th. Our events are much more serious."

Cowboys on horseback throw candy to the children seated on the shoulders of their fathers. Scouts march behind their troupe banners as well as behind the Stars and Stripes. Costumed pioneers and an array of government officials strut along the parade route and wave to the crowd. A group of jazz musicians enlivens the festivities. A simulated U.S. Cavalry draws a round of applause. Philippe thinks of John Wayne, one of his father's movie heroes. "This is a bit like New Orleans on *Mardi Gras* judging by the photos that our parents took."

Mrs. Mitchell notices her son and gestures toward him. The trumpet at his mouth, he is unable to respond. Scott is part of the Phoenix High School Marching Band, students numbering 120 strong. Dressed in white pants, green jackets with gold buttons and darker green top hats sporting a yellow feather, they are flawless in their presentation.

Interspersed are the veterans. Most are in their uniforms representing the different military branches in which they served. A few that have put on weight are content to wear their caps. All, uniformed or not, proudly wear the decorations that they have earned. They respond smilingly to the grateful acknowledgments of the crowd. The parade concludes with three convertible cars carrying the oldest soldiers who are no longer able to keep up with the marchers, but who are no less appreciated.

Philippe is the first to see Dr. Mitchell who responds with a salute. Most of the veterans have turned grey and are not as spry as the students. A good number of women are represented within the ranks.

The parade route extends over 2½ miles. The spectators are estimated to exceed one million every year. While it is a recognized holiday, many watch from open business windows above street level in the middle of the city.

The parade goes on for nearly two hours and ends at the cemetery where speeches are delivered. The prevailing mood becomes much more solemn. A twenty-one gun salute and taps bring tears to many eyes and the reality of war becomes manifest. The Mitchells and their guests find their way to the Tomb of the Unknown Soldier, where the mayor lays a wreath and delivers the concluding remarks. “It is thanks to those who are dead that we can celebrate this event today. To you veterans as well, we are appreciative. Through your sacrifices and through the sacrifices of those who are buried here, we are able to live these lives that we cherish, to live happily, freely and peacefully. We will always be grateful and we will never forget.”

Mrs. Mitchell congratulates her son. “You played well. Your director must be proud of his band.”

“It is always a thrill to perform before this audience. Julie, what do you think of my uniform?”

“Magnificent. Put your hat on and go under the American flag with your father so that I may take a photo.”

Philippe asks Katherine if she has considered joining a marching band.

“I still have four years to go before reaching high school. I would like to be a drum majorette when I am old enough. I will twirl my baton and be a real high stepper.”

Dr. Mitchell catches the eye of one of the World War II veterans and takes his two guests by the hand. “Julie and Philippe, I would like to introduce you to an old friend who participated in the Normandy invasion on June 6, 1944.”

Lieutenant Schaeffer, wearing the uniform that still fits him, albeit snugly, has the 82nd Airborne insignia on his cap. Along with his colleagues, he parachuted behind the enemy lines during the night of June 5th into the morning of the 6th at Sainte-Mère-Eglise. “It always pleases me to meet French friends like you.”

Julie becomes the historian at the slightest provocation. "Our grandfather has spoken to us of these events on a number of occasions. He was a member of the Resistance, the so-called *Vengeance*. He never forgot the sacrifices of the Allies in Normandy and he participated in a number of ceremonies on the beaches of the *Débarquement*. We are grateful to you."

Philippe asks the Lieutenant what his role had been.

"I was a parachusist in the 82nd Airborne outfit and our mission was to jump behind the German defenses, behind the Wall of the Atlantic as it was called. We were charged with cutting the German communications in order to prevent the arrival of reinforcements. With the first light of day, I found myself in Sainte-Mère-Eglise with two of our battalions. Bullets were whistling by from all sides. One of my buddies was suspended from the tower of the church, dead at the end of his parachute. It was an awful scene. We incurred many losses, but the townspeople helped us by guiding us between the houses. When the hostilities ended, what a reception! What joy! I drank a strongly-fermented apple cider."

"It is called *Calva*, after the name of the region that produces it, *Calvados*."

"We otherwise only had water and so you can imagine that many of us drank too much. The officers got angry at us, but we didn't care. The following morning, the people gathered and sang *La Marseillaise*. Since that time, I am always touched when I hear it. I think of Humphrey Bogart saying 'play it, Sam.' I'm not sure why, but it is just the way it is.

"The Germans were defeated after a tenacious resistance. The American flag was raised and replaced the German one that had flown in the town square for an interminable four years. It was the first town liberated by the Allies.

"It is impossible to tell you the whole story. I would simply say that the losses in this Operation Overlord were staggering on our American side, especially on the Omaha and Utah beaches. The English also saw major battles on other beaches, Gold, Juno and Sword, after they had fought with the Canadians and the Polish in Caen; and not to forget French civilians who pitched in significantly along the way. We need to think finally of the Russians who fought in the East, without whom the Normandy invasion would never have occurred. I say again that your grandfather and his friends helped us tremendously. They were brave people and you certainly can be proud of them."

The doctor points to his watch. "We must move along. Our friends have a plane to catch in two hours. They are returning to Washington."

Julie has lost herself in the soldier's story. "Thanks to you and thanks to all who did not survive. We have seen the movie *The Longest Day* several times. I learned by heart the coded message that served to alert my grandfather and his friends: '*Il y a le feu à l'agence de voyage; inutile de s'y rendre*[10]*. Demain la mélasse deviendra du cognac*[11]*. Jean a de longues moustaches*[12]*. Les sanglots longs des violons de l'automne blessent mon cœur d'une langueur monotone.' »* [13]

"Doctor, allow me to give this young lady a kiss on the cheek; it will remind me of Sainte-Mère-Eglise. My children, speaking of movies, if you have a chance, watch *Casablanca* and you can think of me and my friends, dead and alive, while listening to *La Marseillaise*. 'Play it, Sam.'"

---

[10] *There is a fire at the travel agency; no use going there.*

[11] *Tomorrow the molasses will turn into cognac.*

[12] *Jean has long mustaches.*

[13] *The sounds of the violins of autumn touch my heart with a monotonous languor.*

Dr. Mitchell gives the last eulogy. “This gentleman and your grandfather are symbols of an event which truly changed the course of history. Tom Brokaw, news reporter and author, spoke of these people as being members of ‘The Greatest Generation’.”

* * *

Philippe leans over and whispers in Scott’s ear. “I went to the Weaver’s Needle early this morning while you were all sleeping and I found the lost mine of the Dutchman Jacob Waltz. Before leaving, I will need to retrieve the sack of gold that I hid under your bed.”

Chapter 14.
June 2001 – Jackson Hole, Wyoming

The Last and the Best of the Old West.

Philippe and Pierre arrived at Jackson Hole by plane. They rented a car and now find themselves in the midst of the Grand Teton National Park. Four million tourists are attracted each year to this picturesque area and to the town itself, a Western town that could still serve as the scene for a John Ford movie! The national park covers an area of more than 2½ million acres within which are found a number of camping locations with very colorful names: Colter Bay, Jenny Lake, Lizard Creek, Signal Mountain and *Gros Ventre*[14]. Dominique had reserved a site in this last location for no other reason than for its 'French touch'. As usual, she had found a promotion in a wilderness magazine offering good rates for a fresh air adventure that could not be refused.

"Well, then, let's do it. Everyone speaks of the American national parks that just should be seen."

---

[14] *Gros Ventre = Big Belly.*

Philippe completed his school year last week at the Woodrow Wilson. He is thrilled to be on vacation. "Papa, we will need to fend for ourselves during these few days."

"No need to worry. I was a scout in my youth. Let's start by unpacking our bags and putting up the tent."

They are in the middle of the forest, far away from civilization. They are separated from their closest neighbors by more than fifty yards. A picnic table and fireplace are found at each site. Water must be fetched from over two hundred yards away. The blue tent, made in Taiwan, is top of the line and will resist all manner of natural disasters.

Philippe lights a fire while his father looks for the lantern. "We have one hour of daylight left. Let's sit down at the table and have something to eat. A can of beans will not make us forget your mother's cooking, but we will survive. It has been a long day and I believe that I will sleep like a baby within twenty minutes of having eaten."

Before zipping the flap that closes the tent, Pierre admires the cloudless star-filled sky. Philippe listens to the sounds of the night while bundled up in his sleeping bag. Pierre reassures him. They are both quickly fast asleep.

* * *

Taking a stroll through the Grand Teton National Park allows the pair to discover a geology that exceeds 2½ billion years. Pierre reads one of the panels that explains this phenomenon. Over time, compression of the earth's crust formed the Rocky Mountains from Mexico to Alaska, "at about the time when the Alps were formed," thinks Pierre, and forming the peaks of the Grand Teton chain. These are among the most impressive heights of the Rocky Mountains, with a vertical movement that exceeds thirteen thousand feet. The western part that includes the Tetons is the more elevated while the eastern part, lower in altitude, extends to Gros Ventre. An enormous valley that is called Jackson Hole extends between the two chains, the southernmost point being the location of the city of Jackson. The French names --Grand Tetons, Gros Ventre, Rivière de la Belle Fourche[15]-- were given by the first explorers to arrive on the scene, French-Canadian trappers, of whom the father and the son will soon learn.

An abundance of moose, deer, antelope, bear and buffalo inhabit the valley and the national park occupies most of it. A few ranches that attract hardy individuals for a week at a time can also be found. The city is named after a certain Davey Jackson who apparently distinguished himself by claiming ancestral roots all the way back to Charlemagne! Sure enough, a descendant of the Emperor, a lady named Ursula, had married Richard Jackson from Yorkshire in England, the distant ancestor of the family! General Stonewall Jackson, famous for his role during the Civil War, was also a member of this family.

Born in 1788, Davey Jackson excelled as a sharpshooter, hunter and trapper. He discovered the South Passage of the Rocky Mountains leading to the Pacific in 1824 as well as the famous Oregon Trail. He also drew precise maps of the area that helped open the West and later the Southwest of the fledgling country.

Philippe notices on another panel that dinosaurs inhabited the area in times gone by. "Look, Papa, Triceratops bones were found here; what if we were to come face to face with one of these animals?"

"I think that would be unlikely. This is not Jurassic Park."

---

[15] *Rivière de la Belle Fourche = River with the Pretty or Beautiful Fork.*

* * *

Bicycles are rented the second day. Other signs indicate that the park was preserved through the efforts of John Rockefeller and that the region was rediscovered by Beaver Dick Leigh who settled in the area with Jenny, his Shoshone Indian wife. Philippe and Pierre ride along Lake Leigh and Lake Jenny that have been named after them and along whose surfaces is reflected the chain of the Tetons.

During a pause at the Transfiguration Chapel, they see the Cathedral Group of peaks from one of the windows, the highest of which is the Grand Teton that rises to fourteen thousand feet and which is flanked by Mount Owen and Teewinot.

The father and son come to a waterfall a bit further from there. Boots and socks are removed and feet are soaked in the refreshing, albeit surprisingly frigid water. Pierre dozes briefly while Philippe wanders among the wonders of nature.

Returning to their campsite, they hurriedly have a cold lunch before hopping into their rented car. They head north to Yellowstone National Park. "We will not stay long, but we will go as far as the Old Faithful geyser which gushes up to 130 feet for forty seconds every 78 minutes."

The guide explains. "Old Faithful is the most famous geyser in Yellowstone National Park and is the result of at least three volcanic catastrophes over the past two million years. Thermal forces are responsible for the spouting that you see, but we still are unable to explain the regularity of this phenomenon."

Returning from this brief visit, Philippe and Pierre cross the Continental Divide three times. The guide had mentioned earlier that this is the point that separates the flow of water: to one side, water flows eastward and to the other side, westward.

* * *

They sleep late the following morning for the bicycle ride had left them exhausted. But the day still has a major activity scheduled. Luke will guide them on a fishing expedition. "I am pleased that you are not late for there are three activities in Wyoming for which you must always be on time: work, church and fishing."

The Snake River is calm as they begin their journey by canoe with four other couples. Philippe recalls their Maine experience. "I hope that we will not be jostled about as we were on the Penobscot."

Luke identifies a few birds and the columbine flowers which are seen in great abundance. He astutely points out three elk that are hiding in the underbrush.

The five canoes travel two miles before reaching their fishing destination. "Gather around me for a lesson in fly fishing. I have more than enough flies and I will demonstrate the art of casting these lines that I am providing you."

Questions are answered and the group then separates. Luke finds Philippe and offers a few suggestions. "I notice that you have a strong arm, but you need to establish a certain rhythm. Move a bit further into the water so that you will not catch your line on those tree branches behind you. The river is shallow here. When you cast your line, relax your wrist. Notice the small rainbow produced by the refracted water around your line."

The initial awkwardness overcome, Philippe reels in several trout and drops them in the basket hanging over his right hip.

Pierre is set up one hundred yards downstream. Alone in his thoughts after Luke's attention, he is reminded of the scouting days of his youth when he had camped on the banks of the Loire. Fishing there consisted of a simple baited line that was dropped from the side of a rowboat. What he is doing here, he realizes, is more of a challenge. He admits inwardly that this experience represents real fishing.

The catch for both is sufficiently bountiful to bring about a sense of satisfaction. "No need to be embarrassed," says the father to his son. Luke congratulates the participants who clean their take before going their separate ways.

Returned to their campsite, Philippe cooks a half dozen trout on the grill as Pierre opens a bottle of Merlot. "Maman would have made a fancier meal out of this, but I find that what we have cooked here might be even more to our liking."

"She and Julie will be impressed when we describe the success of our cuisine."

* * *

The last day is spent in Jackson. "We are not that far from Montana which I will visit next month. There must be a rodeo here to amuse all the people."

The history of Wyoming is discovered by the campers at a nearby museum. Although vast in surface area, Wyoming is the least populated state in the country. The Indians arrived here well before the white man. Two French brothers in fact, François and Louis-Joseph Vérendrye, first established themselves in 1742. The state was included in the Louisiana Purchase from the French in 1803. During the 'Beaver Fever', mountain men like Davey Jackson hunted beavers for their skins, used to make the hats that were popular in Canada and Europe. Mountain men also explored the area, either alone or in small groups. They would come down from the mountains for the *rendez-vous* that brought together so many of the hunters, the Indians and the merchants from St. Louis.

While assembled for a week, they exchanged the pelts for the provisions that they would require for the following year. Later, when silk hats became more fashionable and replaced the beaver hats, these hardy individuals became guides for a new generation of pioneers. In fact, two waves of such groups were to follow: those who came west as settlers and those as cowboys to tend to the herds of buffalo and other animals. The Indians on the other hand were unceremoniously displaced and confined to reservations in the Dakotas.

Wyoming, they discover, was the first state where women obtained the right to vote in local elections. This prerogative was established in 1869, long before the 19th amendment of 1920 which granted women's suffrage throughout the country. The municipal council of Jackson in fact had once been composed entirely of women. They, in turn, had been responsible for creating a surplus in the budget, improving the quality of the drinking water, clearing the roads of garbage, constructing streets and beautifying the cemetery.

Pierre sums up their accomplishments. "This is all quite impressive. Three cheers for the women!"

* * *

"And tomorrow, it is finished. Philippe, you will still be on vacation, but I must get back to the laboratory. I could stay here for an additional two weeks, but Karen Miller will have planned my schedule for the next few months. Bernard Shaw once said that man is not really put on earth to work. 'The proof is that work tires him!' "

* * *

Father and son have grown closer during this brief trip. Pierre senses that Philippe has matured and is interested in more than just sports. Philippe in turn realizes that he will need to devote some time to his studies, particularly science and math, between this trip and the one to Montana next month. His mother will hold him to at least two hours per day. His sister and he will enroll in courses via the internet to keep up with requirements back home, particularly those that Julie will need to pass her baccalaureate exams and those that he will need to be at the third year lycée level. Of course, they will still attend to the curriculum of the Woodrow Wilson High School.

Pierre reflects with Philippe on the accomplishments of his first year. He is well-satisfied with his work. Guided by his secretary, he may spend more time in the laboratory over the next few weeks. He foresees collaborating with members of the CDC of Atlanta on the flu vaccine for next year. He knows his way around Washington now and he is a regular visitor to the Capitol.

Weary from their long days in the fresh air of Wyoming, they each nap during the return flight to Washington. Awakening before landing, Philippe recognizes the Washington Monument and the White House.

"Your mother and sister will be at the airport to greet us."

"Seeing our photos, they will be envious of what we will have seen and done."

Chapter 15.
June 2001 – Walt Disney World
Orlando, Florida

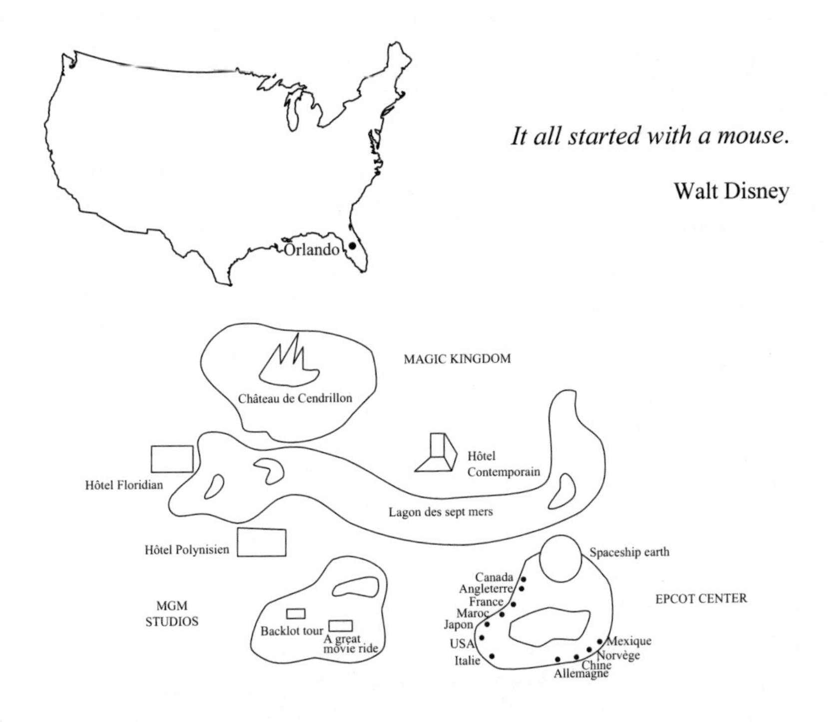

It all started with a mouse.

Walt Disney

"Welcome to the Contemporary Hotel; I wish you a pleasant stay among us." The doorman, disguised as Donald Duck, greets Julie, Dominique, Juanita Mendez and her mother, Maria, after a van ride from Orlando Airport. Philippe and Pierre having returned from Wyoming, the women will have their turn to get away for three days at this popular resort. "Mickey and Minnie Mouse, Goofy, the Seven Dwarfs and I will be at your disposal. Go straight to the reception desk. I will take care of your luggage."

Dominique and Maria started planning for this vacation in March, looking for special rates and knowing that this would be the height of the tourist season since the children would not be in school. Their adjoining rooms are on the tenth floor of this hotel, built in the form of a pyramid and located within the resort itself. Julie is reminded of the pyramid-styled suites of Villeneuve-Loubet near Nice. Her mother cannot help but remark, "You are so French; always comparing."

According to Dominique, the monorail which transports the tourists around the park is like a futuristic metro. In fact, one of the monorail's stops is within the hotel itself at the fourth floor level. Reaching their rooms, Dominique peers through her window and sees the Magic Kingdom and Cinderella's Castle in the distance. The room is typically American and spacious by French standards. The green and purple colors are bright. The furniture is top of the line. The air conditioner had been turned on prior to their arrival. Julie comments that it is hot outside, but very comfortable inside. "We are not that far away from the tropics."

While the mothers unpack, Julie and Juanita take the elevator down to the ground floor where a game room for adolescents is located. The two friends stroll among the electronic games. "We have these kinds of games back home as well, but this room is much larger than ours," says Julie.

They play a game of air hockey which Julie wins handily. Juanita gets her revenge at basketball, scoring twelve hoops in thirty seconds while Julie is successful only three times.

* * *

Dominique suggests a monorail tour of the park. "We have studied the map, but this ride will give us a better sense for what we should see. We can then outline our plan for the next three days."

The elevator stops at the fourth floor. The wide-eyed teens gaze in all directions. Julie looks up and counts to the tenth level to find her room. Several multicolored flags are suspended from the ceiling. "There must be a thousand rooms in this hotel." One still cannot help but be surprised when the train arrives inside the hotel. Dominique imagines the Metro stops in Paris, but this one is so much more spacious. Below the level of the monorail are a number of shops and restaurants. "It is a Frenchman, an engineer by the name of Bertin, who had the idea of a kind of monorail, really a train on an air cushion. President Pompidou had supported him and had constructed an experimental line of about twelve miles that one can still see near Orléans. The early trials had been promising, but Giscard D'Estaing let the project languish and it was eventually suspended. Later, the Japanese picked up the idea and made a real success of it. I believe they have a number of lines in operation now."

Several tired-looking passengers disembark. Julie and Juanita are invited into the conductor's section of the lead car. Traveling outside of the hotel, they immediately come upon the Magic Kingdom and see Cinderella's Castle once again. They stop at a number of stations as they ride around a lake: Magic Kingdom and Floridian Hotel from where they have a view of the Contemporary Hotel which they just left. They change lines at the Polynesian Hotel and make their way to Epcot Center where the train circles the ball representing the earth, in miniature to be sure.

"What are your first impressions?" asks the conductor.

"Such a crowd," answers Juanita.

"Our system must function perfectly to transport all these people. Is this your first time here?"

"Yes."

Julie is impressed by the neatness of everything that they have seen thus far.

"It could be a problem because the tourists are not always attentive. You will notice many workers who immediately pick up any rubbish that is discarded. Otherwise, the grounds would be a mess."

"Your cleanliness issues are not so different from ours in France."

The conductor adds. "We must be well-organized because there can be as many as 200,000 visitors in the different parks on any given day. We are eighty-five miles east of Tampa and 185 miles from Miami. *Disney World* has 55,000 workers on its payroll. The parks cover 30,000 acres, 8,200 of which are protected."

Dinner is eaten on the edge of the Seven Seas Lagoon from where two other hotels are visible. The schedule is considered. Julie and Juanita are in a hurry to see Epcot Center. Dominique and Maria seek a more systematic solution. "Tomorrow, Magic Kingdom, the next day, Hollywood Studios, and finally Epcot Center. There is no way that we will be able to see everything."

* * *

Mothers and daughters arrive early at the Magic Kingdom the following morning while it is still cool and before the park has become crowded. They are immediately impressed by the entrance. The train of the Walt Disney Railway passes overhead and runs along the periphery of the park. "We can take a ride at the end of the day before going back to the hotel."

Main Street USA beckons and leads to Cinderella's Castle. One is reminded once again of the Old West. City Hall provides answers to everyone's questions. A horse-drawn carriage travels slowly one way while an old convertible carries passengers in the opposite direction. The drivers are in costumes from an earlier time. The jitney horn announces its arrival.

The teenagers and their mothers stroll up *Main Street* and enter a small movie theater featuring silent movies starring Charlie Chaplin. A standing audience of some thirty spectators finds his antics hilarious. It is a fine way to start the day.

Window-shopping before a hat boutique, Julie asks her mother if she would dare wear the one with the yellow flowers? "A bit audacious, I must say. But I am not the Queen of England. I prefer the less flashy one with the blue feather. It reminds me of *Mardi Gras* in New Orleans."

They hop on the jitney that brings them to the castle. It is 10:30 and a loudspeaker announces a parade for 2 p.m. Maria and Juanita are excited. "We will make a point of seeing it. In the meantime, we can go in different directions. But let us agree on where to meet in one hour."

Julie and Juanita consult the map before choosing: Adventureland, Frontierland, Liberty Square, Fantasyland and Tomorrowland. Frontierland is their first destination. The Thunder Mountain ride takes them over the mountains and across the prairie into a world of cowboys and assorted bandits. There are the deafening howls of wild animals and the cracking sounds of pistols and rifles. Juanita nudges her friend. "I thought for a moment that we were in the midst of it all."

The mothers choose Adventureland and visit the less rambunctious Swiss Family Treehouse and the Magic Carpets of Aladdin.

The Pecos Bill Café, a fast-food restaurant located between Adventureland and Frontierland, reunites the mothers and daughters for lunch. Subs and hamburgers are chosen "We will save a more gourmet meal for this evening." Dominique congratulates Julie for the ten-gallon hat that she is wearing and that she purchased for Philippe. "You remind me of John Wayne, your father's movie hero."

There is less than an hour before the parade. The crowd is already gathering on Main Street. Many children are sitting on the curb to have a better view, and in the shade as much as possible. At 2:00 p.m. sharp, music blares throughout the park. All the Walt Disney characters are present, including Goofy and Pluto, Pinocchio and Dumbo. Snow White and the Seven Dwarfs walk beside the floats, shake hands with the children and dance in step with the music. Mickey Mouse, alone on the main float, is clearly the star of the show. The crowd sings repeatedly the letters of his name. "M-I-C-K-E-Y M-O-U-S-E". He in turn responds with a wave and a bow.

A half hour later, the crowd dissipates and maintenance people appear out of nowhere to clean the premises. Armed with enormous vacuum cleaners, their chore is accomplished within fifteen minutes and not a scrap of paper or a piece of popcorn is to be found.

Maria proposes a ride on the Cinderella's Carousel. "We are never too old to ride on a merry-go-round."

* * *

The four vacationers decide to separate once again. This time, mothers and daughters will share the experience. Maria and Juanita select Tomorrowland. Dominique and Julie choose Liberty Square and head toward The Hall of Presidents where they first watch a film that retraces the history of the country through its presidents from Washington to George W. Bush. Highlighted are the Continental Army commanded by the first president, the Lincoln-Douglas debates, the industrialization of the country, the construction of the major cities and the two World Wars. Following the movie, each president is acknowledged in chronological order and life-sized mannequins that resemble each president respond with a gesture when their names are mentioned. Dominique is reminded of the *Musée Grévin* in Paris while Julie recalls the *JFK Library* in Boston.

From there, it is onto the Diamond Horseshoe Jamboree, reconstituted as a music hall that is depicted in any number of western movies. A balcony encircles the theater on three sides. Singers, dancers and magicians succeed each other onstage. Goofy descends from the balcony to engage with the children on the dance floor. They all clap their hands and stamp their feet in rhythm with a band playing lively Disney music.

The two couples meet once again in front of It's a Small World for coffee and soft drinks. After standing in line for twenty minutes, they embark in the boat that slowly takes them through the pavilion that houses hundreds of dolls representing different countries of the globe. A windmill identifies Holland; a pagoda, Japan; palm trees, the Islands of the Pacific; and naturally the Eiffel Tower, France. They learn afterward that this is the most popular pavilion in the Magic Kingdom.

A train ride around the park on the Walt Disney Railroad concludes the day. To be able to sit after hours of near continuous standing is a relief. Resting in a passenger car, they try to identify the many places that they have visited during the day.

A young lady dressed as Cinderella shakes hands with the visitors as they leave the park. Juanita asks if she may borrow her special slipper. Her mother takes a photo of her standing next to the smiling princess. "You will find your prince charming provided that the slipper fits you." A quartet dressed in costumes of the Roaring 20s plays jazz numbers that enliven the tired crowd. Julie buys a pair of Donald Duck earrings "I will wear them on the first day of the new school year."

* * *

Dominique estimates that the Hollywood Studios Park covers a surface area at least as large as the grounds outside the Louvre.

The Western theme is again obvious, suggesting movies out of Hollywood with which they have grown familiar. Some of the buildings to be sure are only facades, but further along is a saloon that is completely reconstituted and that might have been found in nineteenth century Dodge City. There, one may eat sandwiches and patisseries. Youngsters delight in heading to the bar where a variety of non-alcoholic beverages is available.

The Back Lot Tours Studio illustrates activities that take place behind the scenes. A make-up artist invites Juanita to sit for a complete makeover. Julie decides to engage with a staff person who offers to dress her in any number of outfits. "How would you like to be an Indian squaw girl or one of our old movie stars? Here are costumes that were worn by Vivien Leigh, Kathryn Hepburn and Grace Kelly. The boys prefer those of Gary Cooper and James Stewart."

"I should select the Grace Kelly one, our Grace from Monaco. I am from Nice. We were neighbors before her accident."

"Your Grace from Monaco and our Grace from Philadelphia. She played opposite Gary Cooper in *High Noon*, one of our classics from 1952. I can still hear the theme song. '*Do not forsake me, oh my darling, on this our wedding day.*' Here, let me comb your hair and you can put on this hat. She was beautiful in *High Noon* as she was in real life. She also starred opposite Cary Grant in *To Catch a Thief*."

"I can still picture her riding along the French Riviera, our *Côte d'Azur*," answers Julie.

At the Great Movie Ride, stuntmen perform some of their daring acrobatics that make action films so thrilling. The mothers and daughters are amazed upon seeing one person get out of a car wreck with not so much as a scratch. Another jumps from a high rise onto a street below, only to be caught by a net that of course one does not see. Maria and Dominique pick out a likeness of Indiana Jones who requests the help of an eight or nine year old boy from the audience to assist him in saving a teenage girl from four gangsters. As one might expect, they succeed in dramatic fashion and to the delight of the crowd with the help of Indiana's whip and the boy's blank shooting pistol. Dominique remembers that amusing scenes from *Raiders of the Lost Ark* were shot in the souks of Tunisia. "Indiana Jones never fails to escape from the bad guys, but he is completely intimidated by snakes."

* * *

The mothers decide to rest for the afternoon. Juanita and Julie take advantage to return to the Magic Kingdom.

While Juanita visits Fantasyland, Julie makes her way to the Haunted Mansion where she is half-terrorized by phantoms, skeletons and caskets. Spooky sounds and plaintive cries nearly 'freak her out'.

"You can't imagine, Maman, how frightened I was, and you were not there to protect me!"

* * *

Epcot Center is divided into two parts that are very different one from the other, the first one exhibiting the technological advances of this modern age, the second devoted to eleven country pavilions around the World Showcase Lagoon.

For this third day, we focus on the pavilions, stopping first at *Italy* where Maria purchases scarves for Juanita and Julie. In *Morocco*, a couscous is ordered. Dominique finds it a bit bland compared to those that she ate during her days in Tunisia. "It is true; it was not a real couscous. There were no meatballs in it."

Maria asks why she is laughing.

"I recall an evening at a restaurant in Paris. We had ordered a presidential couscous for the family, one with the usual vegetables like carrots, squash, string beans, turnip and chick peas. Ordinarily, this special couscous would also have included meatballs of one kind or another, but this one did not have any. Our son, Philippe, nine or ten years old at the time, kept repeating out loud. 'No meatballs! No meatballs! But this isn't a presidential couscous!' I tried to have him keep quiet, but he went on and on. The people at neighboring tables found it very amusing, but my husband and I were embarrassed. I must admit, however, that Philippe was absolutely right. It was not the presidential couscous that Mariem would prepare for us when we lived in Tunisia. Hers was a real presidential couscous that included an abundance of meatballs that we all loved."

A visit to *France* occurs in the afternoon and allows Julie and her mother to recapture the sights and sounds from back home. Young French girls are hostesses at this pavilion. Simone is here for a year and will return to resume her studies in Lyon for the next school year. Hélène is a black French citizen whose mother, married to a Frenchman, comes from the Ivory Coast. She hopes to remain in this country for several years and to eventually obtain a scholarship to further her studies here. The *Impressions de France* is a movie that they see before departing. It shows all the familiar scenes that invite Dominique and Julie to return.

England and *Canada* are the two countries that complete the tour. Properly attired with one of her magnificent hats, the queen is seen in a video to be leaving by coach from Buckingham Palace. Next door, the Royal Canadian Mounted Police are spectacular in another video. *Tourtières*, pies made of ground pork and potatoes in the tradition of the Canadian *habitants*, are enjoyed for the evening meal before the fireworks display that rises from the middle of the lagoon. The show illuminates the evening sky and ends with bursts of lights and sounds that leave the spectators gasping from sensory overload.

A bit overwhelmed by the experience, the women cross the lagoon by boat with perhaps two hundred other passengers to the debarkation point near the exit from the park. Back at the Contemporary Hotel, they turn in for the night after a wonderful day, but tired from all that they have seen and done.

* * *

Goofy seems to be everywhere and they meet him once again over breakfast. As ebullient as ever, he shakes hands with everyone and invites guests to have pictures taken with him. Recognizing the French accent, he encourages Julie and Dominique to visit Euro Disney. "You will be able to compare the two parks. I understand that wine is even served at the one in your country."

Juanita is wearing her scarf; Julie, her Donald Duck earrings. On the way to the airport, Dominique warns her daughter. "Now that the American school year is over, you will need to spend some time this summer studying for your baccalaureate requirements."

Julie's scowl is unmistakable. "It is kind of you to remind me."

Chapter 16.
July 2001 - Montana

The weeds frayed and edged back toward their roots. The air was thin and the sky grew pale; and every day the dust fell on the parched earth.

John Steinbeck
The Grapes of Wrath

Pierre contacted Dr. Mitchell one last time before the departure of his son. “Philippe, everything is in order.”

During the Christmas season, Philippe had jumped at the proposal. Now, on the eve of his departure, he is not as enthused. Dominique and Julie encourage him. “Relax, Philippe. You will have such a good time that you will not want to return. You already have been camping in Wyoming.”

“Yes, but I was with Papa.”

* * *

Philippe will fly tomorrow morning at 8:30 to Chicago. There, he will be met by the cousin of Dr. Mitchell’s uncle who will be waiting for him and who will show him briefly the shoreline along Lake Michigan. After that, he will board Amtrak, the former Great Northern Pacific Railway, that will bring him to Havre, a small town in Montana. This leg of the trip will take two days and will bring Philippe through the Twin Cities of Minneapolis and St. Paul and then through a number of small towns: Culbertson, Poplar, Glasgow and Saco. After he gets off at Havre, the train will traverse the rest of Montana, will cross the Rocky Mountains and will make its way to Washington State.

"And what should I do if there is nobody to meet me in Havre?"

"The Hoaglunds will be at the train station. You would not have made a trip such as this a year ago, but all our friends tell us that this kind of travel is very doable here. We have taken every precaution. You could have flown the entire way, but this train ride, we are told, should be a real experience."

* * *

His mother embraces him at the airport. "Take good care of yourself and keep an eye on your luggage."

Julie is more solicitous toward her brother than usual. "I am sure that you will have a good time and that you will be an excellent cowboy."

Pierre shakes his hand and gives him a big hug. "You will come back with many stories. Bring honor to the family!"

Philippe is touched. "I will call you from Chicago and from Havre after I have reached the Hoaglunds." Misty-eyed and walking quickly toward Gate B-11, he does not dare to turn around.

The flight from Washington, the arrival to and the departure from Chicago, the train stops along the way in cities large and small, and the crossing of the Great Plains of the country are without incident. He was pleased to meet Mr. Hoaglund's cousin and to have eaten along the shores of Lake Michigan. He saw the skyscrapers along the lake and he had a rapid tour around the Loop. He heard briefly about some of Chicago's gangsters, Al Capone and Eliot Ness, the Incorruptible. He found on occasion that time dragged as the fifteen hundred-mile trip wore on. He read the sports magazines that he had carefully packed beforehand and he followed his positions on a map. He took his meals in the lunch car. He became friendly with one of the conductors who provided him with many tales of the Wild West that he sensed were more or less true. He determined finally that he had an ability to sleep anywhere.

* * *

Philippe disembarks with two other passengers at the Havre stop. Being accustomed to the much larger French train stations, he is immediately surprised. This is but a small wooden building. The schedule is posted and is not complicated. The train arrives from Chicago at 4:45 p.m. every day. It remains in Havre for no more than three minutes. In the other direction, the arrival time is 9:25 a.m. and the departure at 9:28. Philippe is astonished for the ticket counter closes after the train has pulled away from the station and he is left to wonder what the employee does for the rest of the time.

Philippe makes his way to the dirt parking lot. He sees but one vehicle, an old Chevrolet pickup truck. The occupants, an older couple, introduce themselves: "Charles Hoaglund and my wife, Mildred. Scott is scheduled to arrive tomorrow. Are you hungry?"

"I could very well eat something, thank you."

The luggage, a suitcase and a backpack, are tossed in the back of the truck. With its dents and rust, the vehicle is as old-looking as its owners. Mr. Hoaglund climbs behind the wheel, lights his pipe and explains as they leave the station, "We find ourselves here in the eastern part of Montana. We are thirty miles from the ranch which is close to the Canadian border. This is the prairie; it is grazing country. To the west, there are the Rocky Mountains and the third of the state on the other side is more suited to farming. So, to the west there are farms and, here in the east, there are ranches. All depends on the amount of rain. When it rains, all is well. When it doesn't, that is another story."

After several miles, the pickup leaves Route 233 and follows a dirt road. The prairie extends as far as the horizon in all directions. It is the 'Big Sky' about which Philippe had heard. There is a feeling of immensity and space, a bit like in Maine but more so. He is brought back to a place in France in the area of the Var between Saint-Maximin and Rians; a sense of emptiness without a human trace apart from the road itself. With the turns that the old man takes and with no visible landmarks, Philippe is quickly disoriented. Mr. Hoaglund names a few of the ranches whose fences abut the road. There is hardly a building in sight apart from an occasional silo.

Mildred, seated in the middle, tells her story and that of her husband. "We are of Norwegian ancestry. Our grandparents came to the United States toward the end of the nineteenth century during the great wave of Scandinavian immigration. They settled in Wisconsin where they found life to be harsh. At that time, the railroad tycoons promised a better life further west. These companies, wanting to construct their lines as far as the Pacific, needed a population that would use this means of transportation for the products that they would send back east. Our parents settled in Montana to take advantage of the Homestead Act of 1862 which granted land free of charge to those who agreed to put it to good use. A family was entitled to receive 160 acres if its members were either American citizens or if they were to become citizens within five years. Also, if the government deemed the land to be well-developed after five years, a formality in most instances, the settlers would become definitive owners of the property for a nominal fee of sixteen dollars."

"How did you meet?"

"Charles was born in 1928, I in 1930. My parents arrived here in 1915, five years after those of my husband. We met at a church gathering that regularly brought together people of the region who were of Norwegian extraction. We were soon married and then the children were born."

Mr. Hoagland completes the narrative. "The railroads made their profits quickly enough, but the better life for all farmers was not as certain. Montana experienced a terrible drought during the Great Depression between 1932 and 1938. The parching of the land contributed to the formation of clouds of dust that gave rise to the expression 'Dust Bowl'. These awful conditions spurred a new migration that was immortalized by John Steinbeck's novel and John Ford's movie, *The Grapes of Wrath*. Many left for Spokane and Seattle; others like our parents decided to stay and to buy the abandoned land for next to nothing. Our parents worked tirelessly to transform their farms into ranches and, without getting rich, they were able to live decently and to see the fruits of their labor passed on to their children."

Philippe asks the significance of the Havre name "for we have the port of Havre on the Normandy coast in our country."

"We find in Montana several names of cities that remind us of our European origins: Glasgow, Malta, Dunkirk, Essex, Amsterdam, Waterloo, Zurich. Our ancestors remembered their past as they settled in this country. There might have been some French among them."

After a half hour, Mrs. Hoaglund points to a white building in the distance. “There is our home. We will be there in a few minutes. Dinner is ready.”

Approaching the Crooked Cactus Ranch, Philippe sees, in addition to the house, a barn, a stable, a tractor, a few old cars, another pick-up truck, a garden and an assortment of tools. The property is surrounded by a barbed wire fence.

“What is this building?”

“It is the bunkhouse, the building where the cowboys who work for us stay. You will meet them tomorrow morning.”

Dinner finished, Mildred shows Philippe to the room on the second floor that he will share with Scott. “It is small, but it will serve your purposes. After you have unpacked, come back downstairs and we will talk before you turn in.”

The room is unpretentious; no television. From the window, there is nothing to see but the prairie. Emptying his suitcase, Philippe questions the wisdom of coming out here to spend the next three weeks in such a desolate place. Looking around, he determines that there is a bathroom and another bedroom at this level. He noticed the kitchen, a parlor, another bedroom and a small office downstairs.

Philippe rejoins Mr. and Mrs. Hoaglund. “Here are some clothes for you to wear. These levis seem to be about your size. This long-sleeved shirt will protect your arms and, naturally, this stetson is obligatory. Try on these boots. With this belt, you will look like a real cowboy!

“Wake-up time tomorrow, 5:00 a.m.”

“A real cowboy,” thinks Philippe. “But no six-shooter? And tomorrow, a horse?”

* * *

Philippe is awakened by Mrs. Hoaglund. She has been up since 4:15 and has prepared a solid breakfast: eggs, sausages, home fries, bread. Philippe finds the coffee a bit weak.

Mildred presents the young Frenchman to the six cowboys with whom he will share breakfast. "Eat well, young man. It will be a long day. You will spend your time with Lenny. He will take care of you."

The tasks of the day are parceled out during a second cup of coffee. Philippe, in his cowboy outfit, boots and stetson, follows Lenny out to the corral where he is introduced to Gabby, a gentle horse that has been selected for him.

"Have you been on a horse before?"

"Huh?"

"Okay. We will start at the beginning. First, we must saddle the horse."

Lenny helps his student to mount. "We have the entire morning for you to get acquainted with him."

Philippe handles himself quite well. After a few times around the corral, first in a walk and then in a trot, and after a few falls without injury, he is able to hold himself upright in the saddle.

"Speak to him. He will come to recognize your voice and he will obey your commands. This afternoon, we will go out toward the well at the eastern end of the ranch to examine a few sections of fence."

"If only Maman could see me," thinks the understandably timid Philippe. "She would be frightened out of her mind. But still not as much as I am. Okay, Gabby, be good to me; be gentle; don't get too frisky."

Around noontime, the two companions stop for a sandwich. Lenny explains that the Crooked Cactus extends over an area of ten sections, each of which measures 6,400 acres,

64,000 in total. Philippe makes a mental calculation of 2,500 hectares for each division, or 25,000 in all.

"I am impressed by the dimensions of this ranch. It extends as far as the eye can see."

"Yes, that is true, but some ranches are much larger. The Crooked Cactus has 64,000 acres with 550 to 600 cows that are raised for their meat. About twenty horses are also on the property. In Texas, the King Ranch covers 400,000 hectares, or one million acres.

"4,000 $km.^2$; 100 km. x 40 km.!"

"It is said that the cowboys supervise their herds by helicopter."

"They are heliboys?"

"This ranch belongs to Mima and Pepe, the names that we have given to Mr. and Mrs. Hoaglund, but it is Jim, their grandson, with whom you ate this morning, who is in charge of the ranch. He is careful to always consult his grandfather as a matter of courtesy. If any problems arise, and there are always some that do, they call Jim's father whose name is Jack. Jack, the oldest son of Mima and Pepe, works for the Bureau of Land Management, a federal administration that oversees public land that can be loaned out to certain ranchmen. You will meet him later for he visits his son and his parents at least once a week."

"What kinds of cows do you raise?"

"Especially two types: Black Anguses and Herefords. Most will soon be sold for we will be organizing the roundup in two weeks."

While assessing the repairs that the fences will require, Lenny tells the story of his life as a cowboy. He loves his work, hard at times and with modest pay, but offset by an appreciation of the great outdoors. "It is true; I have few opportunities to spend my money on the ranch and so I am satisfied. I'm not sure what I will do for my retirement, but that is a long time from now. I respect the hard work that my employers have put forth to get to this point. I also enjoy the camaraderie of those who work here with me. I cannot see myself as a city person, away from the fresh air. What could I do there? I have been a ranchman for most of my life."

The end of the afternoon approaching and the inspection of the fences completed, they make their way back to the house. Philippe finds himself given another task: to clean the stable of the milking cows, a dozen Holsteins that furnish Mildred with the milk itself and with that which she will need to make her butter and cheese.

As mentioned earlier, the day has been long and tiring for this unaccustomed teen. He and Lenny, actually more Lenny than he, did a broad survey of the fences. They will return later in the week with the pick-up to replace damaged posts here and there and to repair the broken wires.

Dinner is eaten together. Philippe renews his acquaintance with Scott who arrived early in the afternoon. Lenny gives him a favorable summary of his helper's day and declares that Philippe can accompany him whenever else he might be designated to be his mentor.

The two adolescents are happy to see each other again. "I did not waste my time today. I had an excellent teacher. Lenny showed me many things and I really like my horse, Gabby. I never thought beforehand that I would be able to mount him on this first day."

Pepe assigns Tex to work with Philippe and Scott tomorrow. "You will find that each cowboy has his own specialty."

The Crooked Cactus is fortunate to have capable and devoted help. Along with Jim, Lenny and Tex, there are Johnny, Randy and Will who complete the well-organized team.

Mima is responsible for the cooking. She naturally serves a good deal of beef and potatoes. She bakes her own bread. She tends to a garden next to the barn for her vegetables. The chickens furnish her with all the eggs that she needs. She realizes that the first principle on any ranch is to provide good food with ample servings for the help. The work may be difficult, but it will always be done well provided that the cooking is good.

Philippe has eaten well. He feels tired at the end of the meal. He will turn in early after a busy day. After ten minutes of conversation with Scott, he falls on his bed and is soon asleep.

* * *

The economy of the ranch is dependent upon the round-ups. The herd is gathered twice a year and brought to Chinook to be sold. Scott and 'Phil' will participate in July's activity during their third week. The days are particularly long and arduous during these round-ups.

Philippe has had no days off. He is comfortable in the saddle by now. His work is appreciated by the Hoaglunds and their cowboys.

Before the departure day, the buyer, Gary Burns, came to the ranch to examine the animals and to agree, after a long exchange with Jim and Pepe, on the definitive price. Jack did not participate in these negotiations, but he advised his father beforehand. "Don't forget that Gary will earn a tidy profit at the slaughterhouse." Philippe has observed these transactions from a distance without understanding all the details. He is surprised, however, to find that no contract is signed. A handshake suffices to conclude the agreement. "That is the custom here and we never have any problems with Gary. Having said that, we can also affirm that he is a tough negotiator!"

The afternoon is spent weighing the animals. Pepe is honest and has not had the cattle drink beforehand. The work completed and the price established, Mima serves a special meal for everyone. Payment will take place upon delivery of the animals in Chinook. With the agreement in place, the conversation changes abruptly. There is no more talk about cows!

* * *

The Crooked Cactus keeps a few bulls to perpetuate the herd. On occasion, one or more of good reputation is rented to maintain the quality of the stock. The calves are separated from their mothers before the round-up to undergo an unpleasant set of treatments: branding of a cactus on their flank, then castration and vaccination. The procedures take but three minutes per animal. Standing dizzily, the calves bellow plaintively while aimlessly seeking their mothers. Their futile cries are known frequently to soften the most hardened cowboys. While a bit reticent, Scott and Philippe participate in these activities by immobilizing the legs of the poor animals.

One hundred or so of these calves will be sold along with the cattle when they have reached six to twelve months of age. The rest will be retained and the cycle will begin anew.

After dinner on the eve of the round-up, Scott and 'Phil' spend some time at the bunkhouse. There, they play cards and watch a few television programs. They return to the main house early, given the anticipated 4:00 a.m. awakening. While crossing the field, they are obliged to hold onto their stetsons and to shield their eyes as the wind has picked up. "This might have been the constant conditions during the years of the Dust Bowl."

* * *

The convoy to Chinook needs to be very well-orchestrated. Four more cowboys have been hired for the task. Jim makes a few suggestions that will allow the city boys to participate without finding themselves in harm's way. Philippe remains apprehensive. He wonders if he has the equestrian ability for such an activity. Scott reassures him. "I have watched you become more comfortable with Gabby every day. You will do fine. You can't let us down now."

"You're right; I don't want to let myself down at this point either. Okay, for the glory of Saumur[16] and the French Cavalry. I'll give it my best shot!"

As Lenny had predicted the very first day, Gabby does recognize Philippe's voice and he responds to his commands. The young helpers were advised to keep their distance from the cattle for working in the midst of these undisciplined animals is not a task for amateurs. Quite the contrary, one must be aware of the potential danger. In fact, an accident wherein a cowboy might be trampled has been known to prove fatal. Scott and Philippe will hang behind the herd and will assist Johnny, one of the most experienced cowboys, to retrieve those occasional cows that might stray from the herd.

Everyone gathers at the corral before sunrise at 4:30. It is one of the two most important days of the year. Jim has left nothing to chance; he has organized every aspect of the journey. Each person is keenly aware of his responsibilities. "We need to deliver this livestock to Gary Burns by early afternoon. We have at least a seven-hour journey ahead of us. We should not waste any time."

Jim yells out the command upon noticing the first rays of light. "Let's go. It is almost five o'clock. Open the gate; onto Chinook!"

---

[16] The French Military School.

Crazed by the yells of the cowboys, the bellowing cattle press against each other as they exit the corral. The cowboys orient the first of the herd to emerge and surround the near-stampeding animals. Tex and Will direct the head of the pack with their curses and prodding. Those that wander off in opposite directions are retrieved by Lenny and his assistants.

Sunrise makes the task more manageable. The wind from the previous evening has subsided. Philippe is momentarily able to admire the Big Sky. In spite of the noise and ruckus, he senses a certain peace and tranquility. He appreciates the difficulty and danger of the work. Will tumbles from his horse, unable to avoid a cow that bumped him from behind. Bleeding from his arm is noted. Fortunately, his injury is minor. Tex quickly bandages him and the convoy continues. A ten-minute break is scheduled close to every two hours at foreseen watering spots. The cowboys also indulge, sometimes drinking more than water.

Under these circumstances, Philippe grasps what Lenny had explained while inspecting the fences that first day. "The horses must obey the slightest commands. You will appreciate this the first day of the round-up. But beforehand, we need to 'break' them so that they will be serviceable under pressure."

Having made it to Chinook, they are greeted by Mima and Pepe who not surprisingly traveled there by pick-up. Gary Burns is also there to welcome them in the field that will serve as a holding area. He counts each head before the next step.

* * *

A train will bring the cattle to Nebraska, near Omaha, where they will be fattened on a corn diet for four to six weeks. Burns will then sell them to the slaughterhouses, the final destination of the 457 cows carrying the Crooked Cactus branding. As noted, he will be paid a handsome sum of money for his efforts.

Philippe learns that a tribe of *Nez Percés*[17] had occupied the Chinook region before the arrival of the white man. The Indians had resisted, but they had been forcibly regrouped by the government in 1877 and displaced to Idaho and Oklahoma. Some among them managed to find refuge in Canada.

In the presence of Pepe and Jim, Gary Burns writes a check for the previously agreed upon price. He hands it to Pepe in an almost solemn moment. The ranch will be able to function until the next round-up. Once the cowboys have been paid, the money will be deposited in the bank. The cowboys will have no chores for three days and they will have occasion to go into town where they will meet up with cowboys from other ranches.

Scott and Philippe will also go into town, but not with the men, for some of the distractions are not for people of their age. Instead, they will accompany Mima and Pepe to restock the provisions required by the ranch. They will also receive fifty dollars apiece for their own expenses in anticipation of the modest pay that they will receive on the day of their departure.

"Tomorrow, we will take advantage of our trip into town to meet up with our son, Jack. You can wear your everyday clothes. Philippe, you can drive the pickup as far as the first paved road."

* * *

Philippe and Scott are awakened at 6:00 a.m. The extra hour of sleep is welcomed. Departure is set for 7:30. Pepe

---

[17] *Nez Percés = Pierced Noses.*

encourages the young *chauffeur*. “Don’t worry; this old truck is indestructible.” Philippe is in control for twenty minutes before handing over the wheel. Pepe has taken the check out of his pocket. “Our first stop will be at the bank and we will then go to the post office. After that stop, we will drop Mima off to do her food shopping. You have your list, I hope.”

“I have my list.”

“While you are stocking up, I will bring these young men to the hardware store. We need to have our saws sharpened and a few tools should be replaced. We will meet you at the supermarket.”

Mima will buy only a few items, but she will purchase in bulk to satisfy the appetites of all those for whom she is required to cook.

The group visits the blacksmith to buy a fair number of horseshoes. Tex and Lenny will attend to the needs of the horses and some will certainly need to be shod.

The errands quickly run, the pick-up is directed toward the Dry Gulch Café where Jack is waiting. The couple’s oldest son inquires about the activities of this past week.

Having acquired a Master’s Degree in Agriculture, Jack became a government employee. He had previously worked on the Crooked Cactus Ranch for eight years to secure the transition between his aging father and his own son. At the Bureau of Land Management for the past seven years, he has represented the government, but he has maintained good relations with the ranchers, even though he is required to collect taxes from them. He knows their problems. He helps to regulate the flow of water for example after heavy rains and he takes whatever measures are necessary to prevent the erosion issues that were so common in earlier times. He studies the prices that cattle should bring and, while he does not have the power to set them, he can exercise a certain influence to protect those like his father who need a favorable market to live decently and fairly.

During lunch at the Dry Gulch Café, Philippe listens intently to the conversation between Pepe and his son. He can't help but detect a certain suspicion that they both have of the federal government in Washington that sends out any number of directives for the management of federal lands, "a bunch of bureaucrats who know nothing about agriculture." Philippe's take-home message is that it is not only in France that bureaucrats are chastised.

* * *

The ranch activities are somewhat more leisurely now that the round-up is over. Care is given to the horses for they too have worked hard. Attention is paid to replacing their shoes as needed. The part of the herd that has not been sold still requires daily maintenance. Mima spends more time in her garden. Pepe visits the neighboring ranches. Repairs on the main house and bunkhouse are completed. Scott and Philippe have occasion to participate in the birth of a few calves.

* * *

At last, the Saturday before their departure, 'Phil' and Scott attend the most anticipated celebration of the region, a rodeo hosted by the town of Saco. More than one thousand spectators are gathered in the stands surrounding an oval dirt arena. Workers from several ranches are assembled to compete against each other for token prize money and especially for bragging rights.

Will is the lasso representative for the Crooked Cactus Ranch. His task is to throw the rope around the calf's neck, to dismount from his horse, throw the calf to the ground and tie his legs in as little time as possible. Unfortunately, his time is second to that of J.D. Crenshaw from the Silver Horseshoe Ranch. Tex, on the other hand, wins the bucking-bronco competition, remaining in saddle 1.8 seconds longer than his closest rival.

A square dance that evening brings the festivities to a close. Beer flows abundantly for the adults, Coca-Cola for the young people. Philippe and Scott are introduced to girls of their age. Philippe jots down Donna's address on a scrap of paper before the last dance. It will be his secret, although he may raise the subject with his sister at a later date.

* * *

The departure time is at hand. Mima has prepared a special breakfast on this Sunday morning. She put a pie in the oven to serve after the eggs, ham, sausages, pan fries, biscuits and toast. The cowhands have gathered a last time to wish the young folks off on their journey.

Pepe congratulates the two friends for their good work. "I hope that you are pleased with the time that you have spent with us. You are always welcome to return."

Philippe is grateful. "I thank you for having received me so graciously and to have given me this experience. I will never forget these three weeks that I have spent among you. Your days are long and you do your work with good cheer." He goes to the corral a last time and caresses Gabby. "So long, good buddy. You were great and I wasn't too bad either, don't you agree?"

The teens throw their luggage in the back of the pick-up. A final stetson salute is offered by the cowboys lined up with Mima in front of the barn. The pickup pushes forward. Philippe recalls Julie's words from three weeks earlier. "I'm sure that you will be a great cowboy."

"Hey, I think I did pretty well after all. Phil in the Wild West! But I did not see any *Nez Percés*."

Chapter 17.
August 2001 – Quebec, P.Q. Canada

I remember
Je me souviens

After an overnight Washington-Quebec train ride and an on-time arrival, the Benoits are settled in the Château Frontenac Hotel which overlooks the St. Lawrence River.

To begin their stay, they decide on a horse-and-buggy tour of the Old City. Pierre warns everyone not to make fun of the Canadian accent, "our cousins being a bit touchy on the subject." Dominique interjects, "In Tunis, we had invited an American acquaintance and his French-Canadian companion to dinner. In the course of the meal, Fred asked if I found that Claire had an accent. I did not have a chance to respond as she vehemently replied, 'It is they who have an accent.' That is true; the accent always belongs to the other person."

Leaving the *Château* this Friday morning, they cross the street to the *Place d'Armes* where several *calèches* are waiting. The coachman and his horse are hired for one hour.

"Ah! French from France. Welcome to our country. Are you staying long? Three days? That is hardly enough. You will need to return. My name is Henri and my horse answers to Gustave."

The driver's *conference* is a nonstop narrative. "Quebec is a French-speaking province in a larger English setting. Young man, would you like to sit next to me? You can help me with Gustave.

"First, a few historical comments. Jacques Cartier discovered the region in 1534. The community of New-France as it was called was subsequently settled. The Upper City rises sixty meters above the river and the Lower City. Samuel de Champlain saw the strategic value of this site and he settled here in 1608. From your hotel, you can appreciate how this promontory, *Cap Diamant*, offers an excellent vantage point from where our ancestors could defend themselves. In fact, they were convinced that this location would be impenetrable, thanks to the ramparts that they had built and that we have maintained.

"But that, alas, was not the case. I will show you in a few minutes the ravine over which the English, under the command of General Wolfe, ascended onto the plateau.

"Okay! We will continue our story while trotting along. Come on, Gustave! You need to earn your next meal. Talk to him, young man. What is your name? Philippe? Yes, Philippe; tap him gently with this whip."

Seated comfortably in the carriage, Pierre, Dominique and Julie hardly have a chance to comment as Henri continues. "You can see the *Château* in front of you. It is our landmark, the equivalent to your Eiffel Tower. You are staying in the most famous hotel in the city. To your left is the statue of Samuel de Champlain. Our buggies are parked here on the *Place d'Armes*. We are now passing the funicular."

"Like at Montmartre in Paris."

"I have never visited France, the Old Country. My relatives would have come from Normandy. One of my cousins died in Dieppe in 1942.

"You can see here that we are overlooking the St. Lawrence River. On the other side as we gaze south is Lévis. Toward the east is the Island of Orléans."

Gustave's clip-clop does not diminish the lecture. Philippe has responded to Henri's invitation and recalls his dealings with Gabby. "Don't plunge us into the St. Lawrence," implores Dominique.

Henri continues. "There is the road that leads to the Lower City. On the corner is the *Musée du Fort* where you can hear a narrative of the sieges of Quebec between 1608 and 1775. I recommend a visit there if the subject is of interest to you."

The Old City is surrounded, European-style, by a wall measuring nearly three miles. It was first constructed in the eighteenth century by the French, was destroyed and subsequently reconstructed by the English. It was originally built to protect the city against American attacks. The streets are narrow. Henri points out the *Séminaire de Québec*, founded in 1663 by François de Laval, the first bishop of New-France and, beyond, the *Basilique Notre-Dame-de-Québec* and the *Couvent des Ursulines*.

"We saw another *Couvent des Ursulines* in the French Quarter of New Orleans when we were there for *Mardi Gras*."

"Here, as likely in New Orleans, it was in its time a school for young girls."

Henri resumes his lecture in history. "In the seventeenth century, this area flourished as a trading post and became a principal economic center. The New-France colony achieved a certain prosperity. The English attacked for the first time in 1629 and were driven back. Other attacks on the city were successfully resisted until September 18, 1759. The English overcame the ramparts that we are now straddling. This is the *Champs-de-Bataille*, known also as the Plains of Abraham, where the English won the final battle for Quebec. The two commanders, Wolfe and Montcalm, died, Wolfe during the battle itself and Montcalm of his wounds the following day. That is why we are no longer French."

"It is said", interrupts Julie, "that the results might have been quite different had the French awaited the arrival of reinforcements under Colonel Bougainville, held up behind the English at *Cap Rouge*."

"Perhaps. We always consider the 'what ifs'. It is true. The colonial militia had positioned itself at Beauport that we can see from here to the northwest. The soldiers were tired from having marched that considerable distance. The English were also more numerous. If we had awaited the reinforcements, might we have won? We will never know.

"There were other battles to follow, but this one really sealed the fate of New-France. The Treaty of Paris in 1763 ceded all of the territory to the English, except for the islands of Saint-Pierre and Miquelon, which remained French. That territory included most of the Mississippi Valley and what is now Louisiana. The people were assimilated into the English minority that also lived here. Eleven years later in 1774, the Act of Quebec granted the French a return of their language, their religion and civil rights that they had lost in 1763.

"It is estimated that there were seventy thousand French-Canadians here at the time of the Treaty of Paris. They lived in rural areas for the most part. The English were far less numerous. They were especially merchants who lived in the major cities such as this one and Montreal.

"Look at that precipice that goes down to the river. That is the exact path that the English troops probably followed to reach this more elevated level."

Philippe notices the children playing soccer in the park. "The teams are undoubtedly completely oblivious to what took place here so long ago."

Julie inquires. "And what do we see over there?"

"That is the Citadelle, the center of the English defenses of the nineteenth century. Today it is one of the two official residences of the governor of the Province of Quebec and it still doubles as military barracks. It is ten o'clock. Let us pause here for the changing of the guard. You will certainly be impressed by their red coats and fur hats."

"Like in London."

"Afterward, I will show you the place where General de Gaulle shouted '*Vive le Québec libre*'[18]. We were happy when he said that, but, unfortunately, our status has not changed.

"Here is the Cross of Sacrifice, dedicated in 1924 to the Canadians who died during World War 1 and rededicated in 1947 to those who died in both World Wars.

"Okay. We will return to your hotel and will pass by City Hall. '*Vive le Québec libre*' was spoken from that balcony. Here we are back at the *Place d'Armes*. Three days is not enough. You could stay for two weeks. Don't forget to visit the *Musée du Fort*. Thank you and perhaps we will meet again. Have a good stay."

* * *

[18] *'Long live Free Quebec.'*

"Nobody asking my opinion," offers Pierre, "let me propose the following: a quick lunch and a visit of the Lower City, then a cruise along the St. Lawrence to please your mother. It is nice weather and no likelihood of a shipwreck. And, for this evening, supper consisting of a traditional meal. Whoever likes these ideas may follow me."

From the *Place d'Armes*, they descend to the Lower City to the *Petit Champlain* neighborhood by the *Casse-cou*[19] steps that connect the Upper to the Lower City, the incline of which justifies its name. They end up at the *Place Royale.*

"It is here that the French presence in North America began. After Champlain's arrival in 1608, merchants established themselves and many became rich. Unfortunately, it was also the site of conflicts between the French and the English on a number of occasions in the seventeenth and eighteenth centuries."

"Thank you, Julie, for having studied the history of this area. You may continue."

"This church, *Notre-Dame-des-Victoires*, was built entirely of stone in 1688 and it is the oldest of this style on the entire continent."

Sensing little enthusiasm from Philippe, the family will spend very little time inside this impressive structure.

From the paved street in front of the church, several shops have replaced what had at one time been a number of warehouses. The *Petit Champlain* area is fifty yards beyond and caters to the tourists. It is from there that passengers disembark from the funicular. The family enters a glass factory at the end of the walkway where a glassblower is demonstrating his skills before an impressed audience that applauds upon completion of an intricate vase.

"As in Murano," comments Dominique.

---

[19] *Casse-cou = Breakneck.*

"Like your daughter, you too are very French with your comparisons."

"I suppose, Pierre, that you are right. With that said, let us find a place to eat."

* * *

"Well, children, you can be on your own. We will meet in front of the funicular in one hour. Your mother and I will shop for a souvenir of Quebec. In the meantime, don't spend all your money."

Having watched the glassblower one more time and having spent a half hour in an art gallery, Pierre and Dominique visit a boutique where they purchase a painting of the *Château Frontenac* viewed from the Port. "If you could hold it for us, we will fetch it upon our return from our afternoon activities."

Continuing their stroll, they come upon a harpist surrounded by a dozen listeners. Between traditional Canadian songs, the musician engages those who are interested in purchasing his CDs. *David O.* is from Chile and has lived in Quebec for several years. They listen to him for ten minutes, make a request for '*La vie en rose*', hum a few bars, buy a disc and move along.

Rejoining the children, the group wanders toward the Old Port. The 4 p.m. cruise aboard the *MV Louis Joliet* is about to depart for a delightful ninety-minute journey up the St. Lawrence as far as the Montmorency Falls. The flyer indicates that the *Joliet* is the largest excursion vessel in Canada. It follows the channel that separates the Île d'Orléans from the northern bank of the St. Lawrence. "Joliet is a name that is linked to that of Marquette. They explored the valley of the

Mississippi as far as the confluence of the Mississippi and Arkansas Rivers."

Forty minutes later, the captain points out the Montmorency Falls. "The river of the same name falls into the St. Lawrence from a height of eighty-three meters, thirty more than the Niagara Falls, a fact of which most people are unaware. There is a magnificent view from the summit. Take it in if you have a chance."

On the return leg of the excursion, the family is surprised by the imposing view of the *Château Frontenac*. Dominique comments that the painting that they purchased recaptures this scene nicely.

* * *

The concierge recommended the nearby restaurant *Aux Anciens Canadiens*. "If you would like to eat *à la québecoise*, you will do well to dine there. That establishment is located in the oldest home of the city, dating back to 1675. It is only a two-minute walk from here."

The hostess greets the family and shows it to a corner table. Consistent with the period of its construction, the ceiling is low and the overhead beams are exposed. The room is dimly lit. The atmosphere is conducive to total relaxation. The waitress is dressed as a peasant girl of an earlier time: starched white blouse, long dark blue skirt, light blue ruffled bonnet. "Greetings; my name is Hélène. Oh, you are French from France. Welcome to our country. Let me go over the menu with you. I might point out some of our traditional dishes."

"Please suggest a few to us."

"Pea soup, ragout with meat balls and beans cooked in bacon fat."

"Can you recommend a Canadian wine?" predictably inquires Pierre.

"Definitely."

"Really. What a surprise. Please choose one for us."

Hélène leaves to fill the orders.

"Papa, she is no older than I am. But her accent."

"Hush, Julie. As I mentioned earlier, it could be a sensitive issue."

Hélène is delighted to speak with French *cousins* and she is most solicitous toward her guests. In the course of the meal, Dominique engages her in conversation. "Noticing your outfit, I am reminded of *Maria Chapdelaine*. I read the book and saw the movie that was based on it. That was a long time ago. It was written by a Canadian and it described the life of your ancestors."

"Madame, we still read it in school. I am very familiar with the story. Maria had planned to marry François, but he died prematurely. Maria considered her options. 'Life is difficult here. What is the point of staying?' It is very true. Our grandparents still say that. Life was not easy in the eighteenth, nineteenth and early twentieth centuries. The winters were long and harsh. Many of our uncles and cousins, occasionally even our brothers and sisters, left for the United States. Maria would say to herself. 'It must be nice there, those big American cities! But there, it is different, people of different backgrounds, speaking a different language, singing different songs. Our ancestors are buried here, in communities that are familiar to us: *Lac à l'Eau-Claire, Saint-André-de-l'Epouvante, Saint-Cœur-de-Marie, Trois Pistoles, Pointes-aux-Outardes*.' Maria stayed, as we have stayed. But I have a great-aunt who settled near Boston, in Salem."

"The Witch City?"

“Yes, but my great-aunt is not a witch. She is a good Christian lady. She visits us once a year. Her children still speak French, but her grandchildren do not. We have been here for nearly four hundred years. On our automobile number plates is written *Je me souviens*, ‘I remember’. We have maintained our heritage, one of which we remain proud. After all, that is our history.”

Maple sugar pie is ordered for dessert. At the end of the meal, Philippe asks that Hélène sign the flyer of the restaurant that has her picture on the cover.

“As you can see, I am dressed very much as Maria might have been so many years ago.”

The evening ends back at the hotel at the *Bar de la Terrasse* from where one has a view of the illuminated countryside. Tourists are gathered outside at the railing. Their glances are directed downward toward the Lower City and the Old Port. “It is the time of lovers,” says Pierre, as he raises his glass toward his wife.

* * *

The lady who sold them the painting had sung the praises of the *Comté de Charlevoix*. “It would be a pleasant day trip.”

Pierre had told her that he would like to know if any Benoits had come to settle in the New World. “The genealogy of my family interests me. I checked the Quebec phone book but found very few Benoits.”

The saleslady explained that the name was not common, but was found occasionally. “*Les Eboulements*, a village in Charlevoix County, celebrated its 350th anniversary recently. A cousin of mine is the municipal secretary and has written a history of the community. She might be able to help you. Her husband owns the general store that is located across from the church."

"We are familiar with general stores from our time in Maine."

"The trip will take you less than two hours."

* * *

After a ten-minute drive, the family arrives at the Montmorency Falls that were seen the previous afternoon. Even though they are not as wide as the Niagara Falls, they warrant a brief stop. A tram ride carries them to the observation point. A magnificent view of the St. Lawrence, the Île d'Orléans and, beyond, of Lévis is seen from the summit.

Further along, Philippe is the first to notice the Basilica of *Sainte-Anne-de-Beaupré.* The architecture is a mixture of Gothic and Romanesque. Pilgrims flock to this shrine each year, particularly on the feast of *Sainte-Anne* on July 26th. Pierre mentions that this church reminds him of *Sainte-Anne-d'Auray* in France. "One of my grandfather's Jewish friends vowed to make a pilgrimage to that shrine if he survived the Buchenwald concentration camp. He did manage to survive and he kept his word. He dutifully and gratefully made his way to that holy place."

Many shops that sell religious articles surround the Basilica. One senses that the economy of the village is dependent upon the pilgrimage traffic. Philippe is content to remain outside. "I already saw *Notre-Dame-des-Victoires*. Take your time. I'll feed the pigeons while waiting for you."

Entering the nave, they are immediately aware of all the canes and crutches that adorn the walls and columns, left behind by pilgrims who were healed of their ailments. A Mass in progress sees many of the sick in wheelchairs approaching the communion rail as the organ plays *Veni Sancti Spiritu*. "I am reminded of Lourdes, both inside and outside," says Dominique. She lights a candle at the foot of the statue of *Sainte-Anne* before leaving.

* * *

Julie notices a bakery by the side of the road just beyond the village limits. The sign indicates that the bread is always fresh out of the oven. "Hélène indicated last night that we ought to eat a slice or two with butter or maple syrup."

They are greeted by an old lady dressed in black who shakes the flour from her hands. "This loaf is as fresh as it gets. It is a peasant bread. There is none like it and none any better." Not to be outdone by anyone, Philippe has a third slice and is seen to be generous with the maple syrup.

Leaving the community, they are struck by its cleanliness. It is as though all of the streets and walkways had just been swept.

Pierre continues along Route 138. From *Baie-Saint-Paul* one half hour later, a secondary shore road leads to *Saint-Joseph-de-la-Rive* where Julie takes a number of photos and from where a ferry brings them to a small island, the *Île-aux-Coudes*, where Jacques Cartier first landed in the sixteenth century. A narrow road follows its perimeter. The few families that inhabit the island seem proud of their history and of their island and seem oblivious to life on the mainland.

Returning to *Saint-Joseph-de-la-Rive*, Pierre regains the road to *Les Eboulements* which, like most other villages, is dominated by the church. Before entering the general store, they stroll across the road through the small cemetery. The names repeat themselves on the small tombstones: Audet, Tremblay, Bouchard.

Pierre explains to the storekeeper the reason for their visit. "You have come to the right place. My wife is the archivist of the community."

While the children wander the premises, the parents engage Mrs. Picard on a variety of topics. "You met my cousin in Quebec City. My position gives me access to all the town and parish records and I should be able to retrieve any information that you are seeking: births, deaths, marriages in particular. Included in my research are the names of everyone who might have worked in the public sector such as teachers and village officials. The names of those who moved away, especially to the United States, are also identified."

They spend over one hour examining the many recent and ancient documents. "I see indeed that a certain Geneviève Benoit taught here at the primary level in 1918. I can even tell you that she earned twenty-six dollars for her entire year of teaching. Her salary was quite modest but, of course, life was not expensive in those days."

Pierre is appreciative. "Very interesting. While we are here, may I ask you a question on a totally separate issue?"

"Certainly."

"I have often wondered why the French from Quebec did not enlist the help of the rebel thirteen colonies to the South at the time of the American Revolution."

"You need to understand that, after their victory in 1759 and the subsequent Treaty of Paris in 1763, the English had imposed their laws and their administrative structure over us. With the Act of Quebec in 1774, however, we had regained many of our former rights. Remember too that the American Generals Arnold and Montgomery did come as far as Quebec at the end of 1775, but they were repelled by English troops under the command of General Carlton."

"There must also have been a strong church influence."

"Indeed there was. You see, the Act of Quebec returned religious liberty to the French-Canadian Catholics. The Church naturally feared the influence of the Protestant New England population. The Church would maintain this important role in people's lives until 1960, a role that may have diminished since about that time. In spite of the submission of the French-Canadians to the English Crown, the relations between the two communities have remained strained. The differences of language and religion serve to explain de Gaulle's *Vive le Québec libre!"*

"That is very interesting. Getting back to the Benoit name, you mentioned a certain teacher, Geneviève. I will look for that name in the region of Poitiers when I return to France. That is the area from where my family originates. Thank you for your help."

The journey continues to *Sainte-Irénée* and *Pointe-au-Pic*, the latter being the location of the well known *Manoir Richelieu* and its casino. The family enters. "We are just looking," says Dominique. "I can see, Pierre, that you are itching to play that slot machine. Be patient. You will get your chance in Las Vegas."

"I thought of hitting the jackpot, but you are right. I will wait."

The return to Quebec is highlighted by the vivid sky colors enhanced by the setting sun.

* * *

Dominique senses that Philippe has had his fill of churches and museums. "We need to find some activity that will allow him to expend some of his pent-up energy. While Julie and I are visiting the *Musée du Fort* that Henri had suggested tomorrow morning, you might want to bring him to the Plains of Abraham where he could play soccer with boys of his age."

"Good idea."

* * *

Julie inquires. "Well, Philippe, how was your match?"

"I was well-received. As they mentioned: 'French from France? How interesting.' They have their own dialect that includes a multitude of local expressions into which any number of English words find their way. But they were very friendly and they made me feel at home." That said, 'Phil' gives his sister a detailed account of his every soccer move that impressed his adopted teammates.

Julie in turn gives her father a detailed account of what she learned at the *Musée*. While Philippe was playing, Pierre walked over to the Wolfe-Montcalm Monument to complete his own lesson in history.

* * *

There is one significant part of the city that has not been visited. "Let us go up *Rue Saint-Louis* after leaving the *Château Frontenac*."

It is a steady incline as the family walks beyond the wall that encircles the Old City. This main road becomes the *Grande Allée* along which a number of upscale restaurants are located. The facade of the Parliament Building with its statues of important Canadians of the past is appreciated for its French-Renaissance style. "The *Hôtel Loews le Concorde* harbors a surprise from its summit," in the words of the ever present *Château's* concierge.

The rotating restaurant, *l'Astral*, on the forty-second floor, makes one revolution every hour and offers an impressive view of the city, the river and the back of the *Château*. Philippe points down to the Plains of Abraham where he played earlier in the day.

After another traditional meal, they stroll leisurely back to their hotel. The restaurant patios are sparsely occupied at this late hour. There is time for one last visit to the *Place Dufférin* in front of the hotel. A light breeze has brought a coolness to the evening. A full moon is reflected off the St. Lawrence. The Old Port is asleep. The Lower City is tranquil. Another day is coming to an end.

An old accordionist is playing Quebec music of an earlier time by the *Monument Champlain* for what is now a sparse audience. Philippe retrieves a coin from his pocket and offers it to the appreciative musician.

Dominique pauses for a moment before the *Place d'Armes*. Henri and Gustave have retired for the night. The *calèches* are no longer to be seen.

Entering the hotel, Pierre offers a few suggestions for the next day. "We will visit the Lower City after breakfast before making our way to the train station and we too will say, like others before us, *Je me souviens*, *I remember*!"

Chapter 18.
September 11, 2001 – Washington, D.C.

L'Amérique frappée,
le monde saisi d'effroi ,
Le Monde, *12 septembre 2001.*

Terrorangriff auf das
Herz Amerikas ,
Die Welt, *12 septembre 2001.*

Hecatombe terrorista
contra Estados Unidos ,
El Mundo, *11 septembre 2001.*

Nous sommes tous Américains.
We are all Americans.
Le Monde

The Capitol is shining brightly this Tuesday morning. The children are in school. Pierre left the house early for an appointment with Ken McCabe from the *Post*. Dominique is not scheduled to teach. She will run her errands later in the morning. She answers the telephone. "Maman? Why are you calling from France so early? Have I seen what is taking place on television? No, I have not. An attack on New York? Okay, I will watch immediately."

She hangs up and, a few seconds later, she sees another airplane strike the second tower and an incredible burst of flames.

While usually not particularly interested in watching TV, she cannot take herself away from her set. She repeatedly sees replays of the two aircraft launching themselves into the Twin Towers.

President Bush has addressed the country from Florida at 9:30 a.m. "All means will be taken to assure the security of the country."

The phone rings a second time. Pierre sounds uncharacteristically agitated. "I have returned to the NIH and we are all gathered around a TV set in a conference room. Are you aware of what is going on in New York? It seems also that a plane has struck the Pentagon. The White House has been evacuated as will be all federal buildings shortly. It appears that all the bridges and tunnels in New York and all the airports of the country have been closed. Were you able to hear the Pentagon explosion?"

"No, we are too far away. And what about the children?"

"I am leaving now to retrieve them. Be patient."

After ten o'clock, the Twin Towers crumble in a cloud of dust. Dominique is horrified as she witnesses occupants of the towers, engulfed in flames, throwing themselves into empty space.

Mayor Giuliani appears, a handkerchief over his face, to console the injured and to exhort the able to distance themselves from the scene as quickly as possible. Sirens are blaring. Policemen and firefighters are everywhere.

Pierre, Philippe and Julie arrive home at 2:00 p.m. "It took me more than three hours to gather the children and to find our way back here. The city is a disaster. There are roadblocks at just about every other intersection. The smoke from the Pentagon is visible from every part of the city."

Philippe and Julie indicate that all the students were assembled in the gymnasium. “There was no way that we could continue our studies in our classrooms.”

“What should we do now?” asks Dominique.

“We should stay indoors and wait. I have called our parents. They are obviously concerned. I tried to reassure them. Let us stay calm and follow the events on television.”

“Stay calm? Easy for you to say!”

* * *

They tune in to CNN. Flights from abroad have been diverted to Canada. When asked at a press conference how many victims have been identified, Giuliani responds: “I have no idea at this point, but the number has to be substantial. I am told that there could have been as many as five thousand people in the two towers.”

At 4:00 p.m., CNN announces that, according to the FBI, the Al-Qaeda organization under the direction of Bin Laden is responsible for these reprehensible acts. Two hours later, Giuliani reappears to indicate that the city transportation system is up and running again but that it would be prudent for New Yorkers to remain at home tomorrow. The estimate during the early evening hours is that more than seventy policemen and at least two hundred firefighters have died. The fear is that the number of victims will exceed the earlier estimates. Many survivors are trapped beneath tons of steel and concrete and furious efforts are in progress in an attempt to save them.

Having returned to Washington after a detour to Nebraska for security reasons, the president addresses the nation once again. “These acts of terrorism may have damaged buildings, but they will not break the American spirit.”

It is revealed that an open cell phone on flight # 93 confirmed a struggle between passengers and the terrorists. The intent was to direct the plane to Washington to strike the White House, the Capitol or Camp David.

* * *

Multiple television channels highlight the heroism of the policemen and the firefighters who climbed into the towers as the occupants descended. Among these occupants were many who also showed remarkable courage, coming to the rescue of their neighbors. In one instance, a man carried a disabled lady down forty flights of stairs in his arms to rescue her.

Irony also came into the lives of others. A blind man was guided to the street by his dog. The story is told of a secretary who, arriving late for work, looked up to the upper stories and witnessed the plane crashing into the location of her office. It is said as well that an Australian Olympic swimmer who had won several gold medals had his life saved when he returned to his hotel to retrieve the camera that he had forgotten.

Drivers on Route 395 saw the plane that was about to launch itself into the Pentagon fly barely thirty to forty feet above them. Moments later, they witnessed a gigantic explosion and an enormous plume of flames. The aircraft had struck several telephone poles and electrical wires in its descent, one pole landing on the roof of a taxi. The terrorized cabbie escaped with only minor injuries. An officer at the Pentagon itself had returned to his car to fetch the glasses that he had left behind. Making his way back to his office, he was surprised to witness this same plane embedded in the western facade of the building. He spent the rest of the day looking for and transporting victims, some alive and some dead, toward makeshift clinics and ambulances.

The Benoits share the anxieties of the rest of the country… and are frightened. “What a day. What a disaster!”

Dominique obviously did not run her errands. Julie and Philippe will not go to school tomorrow. Pierre has consulted Harvey Kantrowicz. “We will need to call in the morning to see if the NIH will be functioning.”

* * *

At bedtime, Julie, in tears, asks if they were wise to come to this country. Dominique consoles her, but inwardly shares her feelings. Philippe thinks that the world has gone mad.

In spite of his own discomfort, Pierre draws the conclusions of the day. “We may never know the reasons for all that has taken place since this morning, but what is clear is that we have witnessed a series of events today the consequences of which will be felt for a long time throughout this country and throughout the world.”

Chapter 19.
October 2001 – Napa Valley, Sonoma County, California

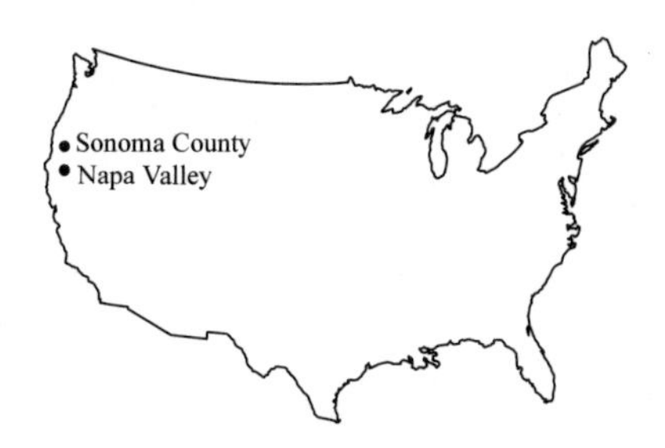

American wines?
Let us taste them!

"Good morning, gentlemen. I hope you are well-rested after yesterday's long trip. I should have let you sleep for another hour, but I would like to show you my property before breakfast."

It is seven o'clock. Pierre and Harvey Kantrowicz arrived yesterday evening in Napa Valley after a two-hour drive in a rented car from San Francisco. They are happy to get out of Washington after the turmoil of the past month. Self-proclaimed wine experts, they frequently discuss the merits of one or another vintage. They each have their preferences and they are rarely of the same opinion. They do appreciate, however, many of the French wines. Both find a number of American varieties to be very acceptable as well. Pierre felt recently that it would be worthwhile to visit a winery so, as he put it, "to, at least once, see how the Americans 'manufacture' their product."

Abby Murphy overheard their conversations at the laboratory on a number of occasions. It turns out that she has a brother-in-law, Walter Magnuson, who has a property in Napa Valley, north of San Francisco. "Would you like me to have him invite you to his vineyard at the time of the harvest?" An agreement was quickly reached and arrangements were put in place.

Walter offers some background information. "I was a bank employee for thirty-five years and I retired three years ago. Our children are grown and are scattered around the country. My wife, Helen, and I left Missouri and we bought these forty-seven acres of land, about twenty hectares. One-third of it is devoted to vines that are still young. We harvested our first crop last year. In addition, we have a few sheep, some ducks, a cow and, would you believe it, a llama."

"Much like you," says Pierre, "we have a number of ecologists in France, most notably a person whose name is Jose Bové."

"You can see that we have installed these solar panels near the house. The irony is that the sun shines brightly nearly all year long in California and yet the state lacks energy. We are self-sufficient for all of our needs and we sell a tidy surplus to the regional grid.

"And now, let us take a quick tour of the grounds."

Descending a slope between two rows of vines, Walter proudly shows them his ripened grapes. "This is a small vineyard and I do not make my own wine. I am part of a co-operative with four other small vintners. We function under the French name, *Clos du Bois*. We will have a chance to visit other vineyards during your stay: Mumm Cuvée Napa, which produces a sparkling wine, and the William Hill Winery.

"Mumm? Is it the same as the French *Mumm*?"
"I believe the two companies have made an agreement."

* * *

Walter and his wife find themselves in Napa Valley, which, along with Sonoma County, forms the heart of the California wine country, a region that is favored by its Mediterranean-like climate. Franciscan monks who came from Mexico in the seventeenth century actually planted the first vines around their missions for they needed wine for their Masses.

In 1861, Colonel Agoston Haraszthy, of Hungarian descent, brought 200,000 vines from a number of European countries to this state and planted them in a number of areas. He also improved upon the wines of the Franciscans and, for this, he is known as the Father of California Wines.

Over lunch, Walter offers a number of his red and white wines to his guests. "You will find no bottles with foreign labels this week. Here, you will drink only American wines and, more particularly, California wines. I must specify because there are also vineyards in other parts of the country."

"I have tasted a few wines from New York State that weren't that great," says Harvey.

Pierre adds: "I recently sampled a couple of Quebec wines that actually were quite good. One from the Eastern Townships in particular, a *Cep d'Argent*, pleased me a great deal. Back home, I have experienced a number of red and white Gallo wines that were more than acceptable and a few others that were not as good in my opinion."

Walter is sensitive to his own operation. "Those are very big companies that sell in large quantities and at a low price.

Our wines are more expensive, but we strive for a higher quality in our product."

"Also back home, we have uprooted many older vines by machine and have replanted newer varieties in the South, in the Languedoc region, near the Mediterranean."

Pierre inquires, "Do you have any climactic problems here?"

"Not really. We have vaporizers or sprays that form a fog to protect the grapes against freezing in February and March. Up to this point, we have been fortunate.

"In California, we gather our crops from south to north in August, September and October. By November, it is all finished.

"The larger wine producers have been around for a long time and the owners have a fine sense for the quality of their grapes. They know what goes into maintaining good vineyards, ones that often are passed down from father to son.

"This afternoon, I am scheduled to meet the Mexican workers who come each year to harvest our grapes. The members of our cooperative divide the labor costs that would be beyond what we could afford individually."

* * *

They are awakened at 6 a.m. Harvey and Pierre will participate in the morning's activities with the Mexican workers. Pierre will assist his namesake, Pedro, who has a fair command of English.

The Mexicans began their season in the southern part of the state where the warmer temperatures prevail. They worked their way northward in September toward Napa Valley and Sonoma County. They reached this cooperative this month. They are well-received and well-paid here. Walter assures his guests that all the workers have their green cards, so everyone can be at ease.

Pedro shows Pierre how to proceed. “Cut the stems slowly and place the clusters of grapes in your basket.” Pierre thinks that, in France, less care is given to the grapes except for those of the *Château Eyquem Winery*.

Pedro works much more quickly and moves to the next row. Pierre applies himself to the task. His load gradually gets heavier. He cautiously maneuvers to the bottom of the incline and deposits his yield into the bin that will be pulled by a tractor. Pedro mentions that the grape appears perfect and will make a fine white wine. “The harvest will be very good and Walter will be pleased.”

Harvey joins Pierre for a break after they have worked for two hours. He has not hesitated to taste the grapes and adds, “but this is some kind of hard work.”

“Our activities at the laboratory in Washington are much less strenuous,” replies his colleague.

Manuel is the boss of the group. He is pleased with the work of the morning and he congratulates Walter on the maintenance of the vineyard. “You have put forth a good effort and this year’s yield will be better than last year’s.”

“Next year, I hope to plant by the solar panels and add twenty-five more acres.”

“Be careful. Some of those areas are more exposed and could experience some freezing. Fifteen additional acres might be more realistic.”

Harvey and Pierre rest after lunch. A bit of back stiffness aside, they accompany Walter and Manuel late in the afternoon to the *Clos du Bois* where their grapes and those from other cooperatives will be turned into wine.

They are greeted by Luigi, the head of the operation. He and Manuel know each other. “Welcome once again. I hope you are bringing me a good sample of grapes.”

“It is a perfect sample. Our friends here from Washington helped in the picking. Please show them what you will do with this load.”

Luigi’s heavily-accented reply draws smiles from his audience. “Ah! I would not be able to tell you the entire story in fifteen minutes. Dare I say, however, that, from the grape to the bottle, Cana notwithstanding, a real miracle will occur.”

The first order of business is to separate the grapes from the stems, to weigh the grapes and to wash them. They then wander through the winery and pause before the press. “We first will retard the oxygenation of the *must*. At one time, sulfurized candles were burnt in the vats. Now we use the chemical, sulfur dioxide. It is a more scientific process and we can be much more precise in our measurements.”

Pierre recalls having visited wineries in the Beaune area at home a long time ago. “The handling of the grapes to make a red or a white wine was quite different.”

“That is certainly the case here as well and I will explain the difference. For red wines, we press less forcefully and we leave the juice in contact with the skins for a longer period. We obtain concentrations of 12 to 14 %.”

“In France, the Côte-du-Rhône attains 13.5 % and the Bordeaux-types reach only 12.5 %.”

Aligned along the walls of an enormous fermentation room are a dozen stainless steel vats with capacities of 100,000 gallons apiece. Harvey is impressed by the orderliness and the neatness of the premises. “This place is not unlike our laboratory.”

“It takes ten to fifteen days for the fermentation of the reds and frequently much longer for the whites. After a period that can vary anywhere from one to four weeks, the first portion is extracted. What remains in the bottom of the vat is returned to the press for what yields, as you would call it, Dr. Benoit, the *vin de presse*. This *vin de presse* often makes the best wine and the vintner generally mixes it with the first portion to arrive at his definitive product."

Luigi directs his guests beyond the vats to the area where fifty gallon barrels are stacked from floor to ceiling onto solid wooden staging. "We use oak barrels like the French. They are more expensive, but they yield a higher-quality wine. They last five or six years and are then replaced by new ones."

Looking all around like a child in a toy factory, Harvey comments: "This is hard work."

"It is as much art as it is work."

Bottling of the finished product takes place in the next room. "We fill millions of bottles and we ship them throughout the country and even to France. Like our neighbors, we produce several varieties: Chardonnays, Sauvignons Blancs, Merlots and Pinot Noirs."

"Those varieties also exist in France but our labels may be different from yours. The Château from which a Bordeaux originates, for example, is generally indicated on our labels. Certain local wines might mention the type of vine, especially if they are exported to England. For that matter, some of these lesser inexpensive wines that are locally produced with great care are often very good."

Luigi concludes this first session. "After the bottles leave here, the wine continues to develop. Kept in a cool environment, it will take two or three years for the wine to reach its complete maturity. That is a quick overview of what will happen to the grapes that you brought us today. We will make a good white wine from them, a Chablis."

Back at home, Walter announces that evening, "Tomorrow, gentlemen, we will go to the Mumm Cuvée Napa Winery."

* * *

Walter, Harvey and Pierre are greeted by Joan Danforth who is the Public Relations Director of this winery. She informs them that it is a Frenchman, Guy Deveaux, who purchased this vineyard and launched this particular brand that has become as popular as the Dom Pérignon variety.

"We cut the stems carefully and place the grapes in these yellow containers that are particular to our establishment. The workers carry them by holding onto these handles so as not to bruise the grapes. We harvest four different varieties that include principally Chardonnays and Pinot Noirs. The other varieties, Pinot Meuniers and Pinot Gris, are complementary to these first two.

"After five months in the vats, we select the wines that will undergo a second fermentation which is what characterizes the champagne method. We put these wines in bottles with a provisional cork after having added a mixture of wine, sugar and yeast, what the French call the *liqueur de tirage*. We then rotate the bottles automatically. In France, Dr. Benoit, workers known as *manipulateurs* perform this task by hand, manipulate if you wish, by rotating each bottle one-quarter turn every day."

"Which explains perhaps the high price of our champagnes."

"This maneuver goes on for six to eight weeks. We then add a mixture of wine and sugar cane and finally insert the definitive cork."

"How did you obtain the authorization to use the name Mumm?" asks Pierre. "I thought it was a trademarked name."

"The Mumm Cuvée Napa name was established in cooperation with a negotiator from the Champagne region, G.H. Mumm. Out of respect for him and by a tacit agreement, we do not give the name of champagne to our product. We do, however, use grapes of comparable quality as the French ones and we cultivate them in a similar soil and virtually identical climate. We are satisfied to use the term *champagne-like*."

Mrs. Danforth explains how sales of the Mumm Cuvée Napa brand are somewhat limited by the tradition in the United States to serve a sparkling wine primarily on the occasions of weddings and anniversaries.

"That is the case in France as well."

"But we would like our clientele to drink our product more often. At other receptions, white wines seem to dominate. We need to educate the masses and encourage people to serve sparkling wines more liberally."

She continues: "So, look at this sample. Notice the bubbles and the foam on the surface; smell the fragrance; observe the pale yellow hue of this *Brut* and the salmon color of the *Demi-sec* and the *Sec*. Drink it and savor it. Dr. Benoit, what do you think of our Mumm?"

"Madame, allow a Frenchman to give you a partisan answer. Your wines are excellent; our champagnes are incomparable."

Pierre raises his glass in Mrs. Danforth's direction and, with a smile, he gently bows to receive forgiveness for his nationalistic comment.

Not offended, she smiles in return and offers a bottle to each of her three visitors. Pierre purchases two more bottles "for our next anniversary."

* * *

Manuel and his crew completed their work in three days and they will next move to the fourth vineyard in the cooperative. Walter, Pierre and Harvey returned to the *Clos du Bois* two more times. Luigi gave them additional 'lessons' at the time of these encounters. They also visited the gigantic Robert Mondavi operation. The last day, they traveled to other vineyards in Sonoma County.

Walter summarizes: "There are ninety vineyards in Napa Valley and about thirty in Sonoma County which is closer to the Pacific. The climate there is milder and more humid, features that impart different flavors to their wines."

Our friends make their way to two additional wineries where they do not fail to taste the products. Ending at the William Hill winery, they sample a Chardonnay that they find particularly delightful. "This label is our signature-product, our standard-bearer," says Tina Adams, the winemaker of the establishment.

The next hour is spent comparing the qualities and subtleties of these Sonoma County wines. "This one is sweeter, that one is dryer, the next is lighter…"

Harvey solemnly renders his opinion. "I must admit that I like them all."

At the end of the session, Pierre invites Walter and Tina. "Now, you must come to France to taste our wines. We have well-organized tours and cruises along the Saône and the Rhône Rivers that would give you a wonderful experience of some of our principal wines from the Bourgogne to the Châteauneuf-du-Pape regions."

Shaking hands, promises are made to enjoy future encounters.

* * *

During the return to the capital, the two friends talk incessantly of their recent experience. Walter and Helen will visit Abby Murphy after they have tended to the vineyard following the harvest. Pierre proposes an evening wine-tasting party of their own to coincide with that trip. "We will not be limited to California wines or, for that matter, even to French wines. This could be an international event that would include, among others, Brazilian, Australian and South African labels."

Harvey is in complete agreement. "Our laboratory conversations are about to be elevated to a completely different level!"

Chapter 20. November 2001 – Wheeling, West Virginia and Appalachia

I have pleaded your cause everywhere, requiring better conditions in the mines. Those are rights to which you are entitled.

John L. Lewis,
President of the *UMWA*[20]

It is a tradition at the Woodrow Wilson High School to participate in social action programs. Accordingly, Mrs. Hébert is accompanying Julie and four classmates to West Medford in West Virginia. The purpose is to help symbolically in the reconstruction of a small community that has been recently ravaged by severe flooding following a long period of torrential rains over the Appalachian Mountains.

The students will work with Habitat for Humanity, which specializes in the building of new homes of good quality and at affordable prices for people of limited means. Habitat for Humanity was founded in 1976 by a philanthropic couple, Millard and Linda Fuller. This organization has since built more than 100,000 homes in eighty countries, thanks to the work of volunteers and the donations of many benefactors.

[20] *UMWA = United Mine Workers of America.*

Former President Jimmy Carter is perhaps the best-known among these volunteers. He has devoted one week of his time each year to assist in this effort. A trade specialty for the participants, while desirable, is not required. Each person contributes according to his or her abilities.

In order to miss 2½ days of classes, the students did extra homework and additional assignments before their departure. The brief Thanksgiving break beginning Wednesday noon until the following Monday will allow these five young people to spend an entire week with the family to which they have been assigned.

* * *

The drive on Saturday brings the group to Wheeling, West Virginia, which for a long time owed its prosperity to the National Road #40, the first major thoroughfare to be financed with federal funds. It was built to link the East Coast to the Great Plains and it allowed this industrial city of 35,000 to flourish. The city and its prosperity have long since been bypassed by Interstate 70 that carries 30,000 eighteen-wheelers each day. The noise from these downshifting vehicles, particularly those traveling east to west, is still easily heard within the community at all hours of the day and night. Wheeling is located in the northern part of the state, in the panhandle, on the banks of the Ohio River. The trip has taken five hours through this mountainous region where one quickly gains the impression of a significant amount of poverty.

The Civic Center in the heart of Wheeling is the first place to be visited. It is the most impressive building in this otherwise ordinary city. The hockey Nailers play their home games here, their name recalling the time when Wheeling was a leader in the nail industry. Those factories have all shut down. A plaque in the atrium indicates the exact place where a French explorer, Céloron de Bainville, arrived with a Jesuit priest in 1749 to take possession of the territory in the name of Louis XV.

After crossing the Ohio River, the group heads northward along its western shore. This waterway originates near Pittsburgh and is formed by the confluence of the Allegheny and Monongahela Rivers. It travels from there over nine hundred miles southwestward before joining the Mississippi River. The Ohio allowed explorers and hunters of an earlier time to penetrate into the interior of the country and to establish themselves on the other side of the Appalachian Mountains.

"Madame Hébert, there is an episode in the *Conquest of the West* starring James Stewart that is filmed on the banks of this river."

"That is right, Julie. The Ohio became a principal transportation route before the arrival of the railroads and the highways. Even now, it plays a major role in the transport of any number of goods. If you look on the opposite side, you will see the very well-known Weirton Steel Mill. This mill is unique in that it is owned by the workers themselves and, for now at least, it functions very well. By contrast, many mills have closed in recent years because of less expensive steel that is imported from Japan and other countries."

"The smoke appears dirty."

"This is nothing compared to what it had been. A chemical process now makes this smoke much less of a pollutant than that of a bygone era. I am well aware of this situation, having studied in the area at the University of Pittsburgh. Before the enactment of pollution-reduction laws, Wheeling and Pittsburgh found themselves in a continuous twilight zone, the smoke from the mines and the mills obstructing the light of day. We can breathe better now, but the costs of iron and steel unfortunately have risen considerably. The barges that you can see still transport iron ore and coal, both of which are needed in large amounts to produce steel. Being employed in these mills and mines is hard work and, while safety measures have particularly been taken in the mines, the conditions there can still be dangerous. Catastrophes are known to occur even to this day."

* * *

At 9 p.m. on Saturday evenings, the radio station WWVA[21] transmits its *Country Jamboree* program across the United States. Known for its country music, the station has established a longstanding reputation and has developed a substantial following. Cowbells can be heard in the background. People, old and young, are dressed casually and are dancing to their favorite musical requests.

The disc jockey approaches Julie, microphone in hand. "Your name, please?"

"Julie Benoit."

"Do I detect an accent?"

"Yes, I am French, a student at the Woodrow Wilson High School in Washington, D.C."

"Won't you greet our national audience?"

"Hello USA!"

"Do you have a song request?"

Julie turns to Randy. "He is our specialist in this kind of music."

Randy does not hesitate. "Could you play 'Country Roads' by John Denver?"

---

[21] *WWVA = Wheeling West VirginiA.*

"Perfect! Listen carefully to the lyrics as Denver sings of our beautiful West Virginia."

* * *

Before reaching West Medford the following afternoon, Mrs. Hébert explains that the mountains in this region have seen their vegetation disappear as a result of the strip mining that had been common practice until recently. "The result is that there is nothing to prevent water from flooding lower-level communities. With the abundant rains that the area has seen in recent months, you will discover the tragic results that have ensued. Erosion is better controlled now that laws have been passed. Mining companies are required to prevent the deforestation for which they were responsible."

The road winds down the mountainside toward an ordinary-looking community: post office, bank, movie theater, church, school, a few stores. Julie will stay with the Donaldsons and will help in the construction of their new house. Victims of severe floods that struck the town on a number of occasions, the family is now lodged in a trailer home that has been provided by the United Mine Workers of America. The parents and their five children are barely accommodated in these tight quarters.

The father, Keith, is a coal miner, as had been his father and grandfather before him. Like his wife, Heidi, he was born in this community whose economy is entirely dependent upon the mines. Also, like the majority of its inhabitants, he has grown up, he has married, he has worked and he will die here, this place where he will have spent his entire life. As everyone else, he is hopeful of a better future for his children, thanks to the educational opportunities that are now available.

Heidi continues the narrative. "My father-in-law died young of the Black Lung Disease which was common among the miners of his day. We see less of this illness now, thanks to John L. Lewis who headed the United Mine Workers of America from 1920 to 1960. Everyone recognized him for his bushy eyebrows. It is this union that he headed that built eight hospitals and several clinics throughout Appalachia and it is he who succeeded in winning a better standard of living for the families of miners. In fact, President Lyndon Johnson awarded him the Presidential Medal of Honor in 1964 for his efforts on behalf of people like us."

Julie will share a small bedroom with the two girls, Charlotte, age twelve, and Francine, age six. Charlotte informs her new friend, "As you can see, life is not easy under these conditions. We combined our efforts to bring our school, which has been closed for two weeks because of the floods, back to being fairly clean. We will make up a few of those missed days by staying in class longer at the end of the school year."

The three boys --Gary, seventeen, Willie, fifteen, and Quint, nine-- also share a small room. The kitchen and dining area are so small that meals are eaten in shifts.

"You can have my bed," says Francine. "I can sleep on the floor."

The Donaldsons accepted the generous offer of Habitat for Humanity, which has worked in Appalachia, one of the poorest areas in the country, over the past several months.

* * *

Julie and Randy will be part of the team that, over the next three days, will begin to make the new Donaldson home a reality. They are introduced this Monday morning to the three other members with whom they will work. Vinnie is from Virginia and is a plumber. He has participated in twenty such projects. Brian, from Columbus, Ohio, is an electrician. This is the first time that he has volunteered his services to this organization. Joseph Scully is retired from having worked in the construction industry. He had been the CEO of a major building firm in Atlanta, Georgia, before being recruited by Jimmy Carter four years ago to work with him on a project in the rural part of his home state. He is in charge of this crew. Compared to the high-rise challenges of his working days, this is a relatively simple undertaking. Of note, he had directed a project in Costa Rica last year.

Julie, dressed in sweatshirt and jeans and donning an obligatory hard hat, carries studs and boards. Brian is impressed. "Let me help you saw them to size."

"But what is it with these inches and feet? Have you never heard of the metric system?"

"I realize that Europeans like you prefer centimeters and meters. Be patient. You need only adjust for these next few days."

Julie gains increasing dexterity with hammer and nail as the day progresses. Randy and she are introduced to some of the power tools that they learn to operate under supervision that afternoon.

After classes, the Donaldson children arrive to participate in this effort. Gary makes a point of helping Julie. "I think I would prefer to work as a carpenter than to spend the rest of my life in the mines. Let me show you how we will use this plywood."

"You might be stronger than I am, but watch me bang this section into place."

"You are really catching onto the trade. You may be a card-carrying union member by the end of the week."

Mrs. Donaldson appears on the scene before quitting time. "We will be celebrating Thanksgiving at our place on Thursday. You are all invited to our trailer for a special meal at 1 p.m."

* * *

The Thanksgiving holiday is celebrated in the United States on the fourth Thursday of November. This day initiates the shopping spree that will extend through Christmas. New Year's Day one week later will conclude the holiday season. While not officially a holiday, many will not work the Friday after Thanksgiving in order to benefit from the large number of department store sales that are publicized for that day. Known as Black Friday, the profits generated from that shopping day and those of the succeeding four weeks will determine the success or failure of much of the retail industry. This will also be the case throughout Appalachia, but expectations are more subdued here compared to the rest of the country, given the economic realities of the area.

Thanksgiving Day recalls the gathering that took place in 1621 in Plymouth, Massachusetts. The survivors of the *Mayflower*, about fifty in number who had arrived the previous year, celebrated a good harvest that allowed them to settle into their new country. They gathered with approximately ninety natives from the Wampanoag[22] tribe under the leadership of Chief Massasoit[23] for a special meal of gratitude.

But before recalling that meal, there is the traditional football game between the neighboring high schools. While most games occur on Friday evenings or Saturday afternoons, this one begins at 10 a.m. For these schools, it is the most important and the last game of the season.

---

[22] *Wampanoag = People of the East* or *People of the First Light*. It must be said that relations between the two groups that had been cordial at the outset became much more hostile in succeeding years.
[23] *Massasoit = The Grand Chief.*

Gary left the trailer early this morning to join his teammates. West Medford High is favored in this forty-fourth meeting against Templeton High from the adjoining community. Not even the recent floods could prevent this game from taking place. Gary is a linebacker for his team that comes into this game with a 7 and 3 record. He had mentioned to Julie the previous evening, "My brothers will explain the game to you and you can count the number of tackles that I will make."

"What is a tackle?"

"It is a play in which I throw to the ground the person on the other team who is carrying the ball."

Julie sees similarities between football and the rugby game with which she is more familiar, but finds the American sport to be more brutal. The fans are ecstatic when a touchdown is scored, similar to the 'try' in rugby. The school band performances at halftime impress her. "The uniforms and music remind me of the parade that I attended in Phoenix on Memorial Day."

"So what do you think of our football, Julie?" asks Willie.

"I find it more violent than our rugby. I prefer our game."

Keith and his mining friends on their part awakened early to go hunting this morning. It is the beginning of the season and will be the main male social activity of this group for the next several weeks.

After a 24-14 West Medford victory and nine tackles, more or less, that Julie was able to count, the seven family members and five *Habitat* workers are tightly squeezed into the trailer to do honor to the twenty-two lb. turkey. It will be served with mashed potatoes, stuffing, peas, squash, carrots, olives and cranberry sauce. Apple cider, soft drinks and wine will be offered for beverages. Dessert will consist of apple pie to help fulfill the adage of which Julie has become familiar, *Mother, Country and Apple Pie.*

All the rooms of the mobile home are utilized to accommodate the crowd and plates are passed from person to person until everyone has been served. Keith, having returned from his hunting adventures, says grace, thanking those who have come to help them. Heidi adds, "We thank you, Lord, for our good health and we think back to the Pilgrims themselves who were grateful in spite of their hardships."

The meal is eaten slowly amidst much merriment, undiminished by the cramped quarters.

* * *

The next day is the last work day for the student volunteers. The new Donaldson home is beginning to take shape. The framing is well advanced as door and window locations are easily identified. Julie and the others can walk on the floor of the downstairs. The finished product will be comfortable without being pretentious.

The students will be replaced by other volunteers. As Julie, Randy and their three classmates who worked across town prepare to leave West Medford, they are thanked profusely by their hosts. Julie embraces Heidi and her daughters. Gary asks Julie for a photo as she boards the van that will bring her back to Washington.

"I will mail you a picture as soon as I arrive home."

Mrs. Hébert draws the conclusions of the experience on the way back to the Capital. "There was little time to do all that we wanted to accomplish. Your efforts, however, are appreciated. You worked well and everyone is grateful. You have a sense now, I believe, that poverty does exist in this country that might otherwise be thought of as only being rich and powerful. There are the working-poor among us and West Virginia is particularly afflicted by the poverty that you have witnessed. The mines still offer reasonably well-paid work in West Medford but, as you have seen, even here there are problems.

"Once again, thank you for your service."

Chapter 21.
December 2001 – Washington, D.C.

One learns in the midst of plagues that there is more to admire in man than there is to despise.

Camus, *The Plague*

During the second semester of the past school year, Dr. Clark had made Dominique aware of an opening at Georgetown University. The position would entail teaching a French Literature course for two hours once weekly. Not having taught at this level before, she was initially reluctant, but, after talking it over at home and following an interview with the Chairperson of the Department, she hesitatingly accepted.

Thus it is that Dominique has found herself before this class of students every Wednesday afternoon since September. The school is within walking distance of home. She has found the academic level of her students to be generally good, most of them working toward an M.A. in French with the intent of pursuing teaching careers.

The conversation at home indicated keen interest from the very outset. "So, tell us about your students."

"It is an interesting assortment, a different melting pot. Some are sons and daughters of diplomats. Others belong to families of government employees. The foreign countries represented are diverse and include Egypt, Lebanon, Morocco, Israel, Senegal, Canada, Haiti and Venezuela. There is even a student from France, Louis Lachaume, whose father is employed at the French Embassy and whose mother is a journalist. He obtained a Law Degree in Paris and is adding to his CV. The rest are American. It is a manageable group of sixteen students, nine women and seven men."

Pierre and Julie showed particular interest. Pierre wondered initially about her plans. "I am being given a good deal of flexibility with regard to the content of this course. I need to give this detail a bit more thought. We will read the likes of Balzac and Lamartine. I am open to any of your suggestions. Some of the students appear to be vaguely familiar with Camus and we will tackle some of his works later in the term."

It is this author that they are about to discuss as they approach the end of this first semester.

* * *

"As we gather today, we find ourselves at a different point in this course. We have covered some of the well-known classical authors: Corneille, Racine, Molière. We have read some of the *Fables* of Lafontaine. You have most recently written papers on *Madame Bovary*.

"We come now to discuss the works of arguably the most popular French author, Albert Camus. I believe that he is the most read and highly regarded French writer at the college and graduate levels and perhaps the best known among adults in general. We will deal with an entire different set of talking points than we have up until now, more serious perhaps and, in some respects, topics that you will find more sobering if not outright depressing. That's okay. I think we are prepared to handle Camus. You are a mature group of people. At the same time, you will be exposed to some of our French history and the issues with which my people dealt during World War II.

"With these introductory comments in place, let us begin. I have asked you to read *The Stranger* and *The Plague*, two of Camus' major works. You realize of course that Camus was a prolific author, playwright and reporter. We will concentrate on *The Plague* in these next two classes.

"Let us start with a summary of the story. I need a volunteer!"

Leïla, from Egypt, dressed in a long traditional skirt and with her hair covered, nods. "The story unfolds in Oran, a dusty city of 200,000 people along the Mediterranean coast of Algeria. Camus tells the story of a terrible plague that strikes the city and throws it into utter chaos and turmoil. Transmitted by fleas, the illness manifests itself first by the death of rats and then by the demise of the citizens of the city in large numbers. Oran is quarantined. People are not allowed to come into or to leave the city, a situation which is at the root of any number of problems."

"Thank you. That is a good start. I can recall having lived in that part of the world. The hot summer sun in a cloudless sky often made us retreat into the coolness of our dwellings. Imagine the desert winds, the siroccos, that arise unexpectedly from the Sahara and blow a suffocating heat as that of a furnace into the city. Sand is transported everywhere and finds its way into the smallest crevices of one's home. Such an epidemic as the plague extending through the summer months would be nearly impossible to bear.

"Well, who would like to present the main characters?... Rebecca?

"Dr. Bernard Rieux, approximately thirty-five years old, is a devoted physician. He cares for the sick and does everything within his power to fight this epidemic. He is largely responsible for the quarantining of Oran.

"Jean Tarrou chronicles the epidemic by describing in his notebook the day-to-day existence of the people in the midst of this catastrophe. He is found everywhere in the story. He befriends Dr. Rieux and becomes his confidant. It is said of Tarrou that *one can always count on him.*

"Raymond Rambert is a young journalist, recently married, and whose spouse remains in France. He left Paris and arrived in Oran recently to study the living conditions of native Algerians. The plague upsets him from many personal and professional standpoints. He is adamant on leaving Oran to rejoin his wife, but all legitimate and clandestine means of escape are futile. In the final analysis, and persuaded by the physician's example, he remains and works at Dr. Rieux's side.

"Joseph Grand is a government bureaucrat who becomes the doctor's secretary during these difficult times. He is responsible for keeping the statistics on the number of deaths throughout the epidemic.

"Father Paneloux is a Jesuit priest, respected and liked equally by believers and nonbelievers. He is influential in the community and is brought together with the physician over life-and-death situations.

"Cottard is a slippery character who benefits from the plague, profiting in a number of ways from the misery of others. Through a number of shady connections, he tries to help Rambert leave Oran to rejoin his wife in Paris, but is unsuccessful."

Dominique smiles approvingly. "Many thanks, Rebecca. There are other lesser characters about whom we might talk, but this is sufficient for us to begin our discussion.

"Who would like to comment on the mood that the author is trying to create in this story?… Charles?"

"Camus gives us a pessimistic view of Oran, *an ugly and dusty city*, a city *with no pigeons, no trees and no gardens*, a city *with no soul*. It is a city where real love does not exist. Everyone is just there to make money and survive."

Dominique agrees. "It is part of the classical theme of the absurd for which Camus is so well-known. *The Stranger* also complies with this theme of the absurd. We sense an existence without passion, an emptiness in one's everyday life. The ultimate absurdity of course is symbolized by death, particularly unjust death or death without reason. But I am getting ahead of myself.

"Who would like to comment on the results of Oran's quarantine?… Mr. Donovan?"

"There is, first of all, the element of fear, fear of being afflicted by the disease and fear of being isolated. Imagine hundreds of citizens dying a tortured death every week over a period of nine months. The disease strikes in two forms: the bubonic version and the pneumonic one. The bubonic type is characterized by painful *buboes* or swollen inflamed lymph glands in the groins, arms, and neck. The pneumonic type is more violent and involves more respiratory symptoms consisting of a bloody cough *…as if a wind spread a fire in a person's chest*, and accompanied by a high temperature, delirium, profuse sweating and extreme thirst. Both types kill, the latter kind more quickly than the former.

"The medical infrastructure is overwhelmed and all the basic necessities of life are eventually lacking. Victims are transported from hospitals to cemeteries in the dead of night and are buried more or less unceremoniously in common graves. In all of this, there is too often the separation among lovers and among family members. The isolation created by the plague is tantamount to an exile, both from outside of the city as well as from within."

Tanya Rodriguez raises her hand. "There seems to me to be an element of solitude that contributes to the author's pessimism. A sick person about to die feels very much alone. Even those who are not sick are lonely… *alone under the heavens. In solitude, nobody could hope for the neighbor's help. Each person remained alone*."

Yasmina adds, "I would even go beyond pessimism to indicate a certain fatalism. There is nothing but uncertainty during this scourge."

"That is true," interjects Dominique, "but it is the physician who identifies his own personal certainty. Listening from an open window, he hears the noise of an electric saw arising from a neighboring shop. '*There is certainty in everyday work. The essential thing is to carry out one's calling and to do it well. All the rest hangs from tenuous threads and insignificant commotion.*' This is his personal certainty and the guiding principle that allows him to minister to his patients against all odds in the midst of all the confusion and chaos."

Linda Malone is recognized. "We have spoken of fear, solitude and exile resulting from the plague, but what is the point of the plague?"

"Excellent question. First of all, Camus needed an extraordinary event to be able to promote his philosophy. This plague was the vehicle that allowed him to isolate a population, to cut it off from the world, to establish in a dramatic way the setting that would allow him to speak to his reading audience.

"Having said that, the plague is really a symbol, and specifically a symbol of Nazism, also known as the *Brown Plague*. You realize of course that the infection that ravaged Europe in the fourteenth century and killed one-third of its population was called the *Black Plague* or the *Black Death*. While Nazism is never mentioned by name, many feel that the story reflects this issue. You must remember the historical context in which the story was written.

"Given the plight of the citizens of Oran, can anyone think of another term to describe their situation?… Yasmina?"

"They were prisoners in their own city, in their own homes."

"Exactly. Camus started writing *The Plague* after Germany had overrun France in 1940. The new French government under Maréchal Pétain explains many of the events that were taking place. The Vichy government that Pétain headed had established itself in much of the country as well as in Algeria. The author felt that this Vichy group had lost its moral compass and was alien to the noble qualities that had been responsible for the grandeur of France. Dr. Rieux proclaims: *A catastrophe has struck our country because we have forgotten our traditional values*. The plague is a condemnation of Nazism and Vichyism. Pétain of course was subsequently repudiated for having collaborated with the enemy and was stripped of his title of Maréchal.

"Against this backdrop, there were more than two million Frenchmen who were prisoners of war in Germany. *Prisoners* is a stronger term than *exiles* and that term reflects the reality of which Camus was writing. The daily and weekly deaths recorded by the bureaucrat, Joseph Grand, are an indication of what was going on in the world in which the author lived.

"I might add parenthetically that Camus condemned the anti-Semitism that was integral to the Hitler regime. Growing up and working in Algeria as he did, he associated with the substantial Jewish community that lived there and he had many Israeli friends. He also wrote extensively for *Free French* newspapers in support of the Resistance movement that repudiated everything for which Nazism stood.

"But I should not be doing all the talking. Are there other topics that can be covered?… Claudine?"

"This all makes sense, but life did go on. The Oranians continued to *circulate in the streets, to sit at café terraces*. They went to the movies, seeing the same films over and over. With an abundance of foot traffic, there was a *mistaken holiday atmosphere*. Men continued to drink."

Dominique agrees and adds, "Recall that the German occupation of France extended over a long four-year period and, yes, life did go on, but with many humiliations, hardships and deprivations. Food shortages were particularly common. In the midst of the realities of the day, a certain adaptation occurred, a tribute, I suppose, to the human spirit. The underground Resistance movement was also able to operate under this cover."

Roberto Sosa intervenes. "There seems to be much in this story that reflects what was going on in the author's personal life. I have read, for example, that Camus was born in Algiers and was well-acquainted with life in Algeria. He knew Algiers and Oran well. I wonder if there are allusions here to the colonial dimension of life in this country."

The teacher reflects before answering. "That is a complicated topic. The story itself speaks very little of the Arab population, but we know that Camus sympathized with their plight under French colonial rule. He wrote often in the newspaper *Alger Républicain* on behalf of their cause.

"The Algerian War remains a sensitive topic among the French to this day and the debate persists between the civilizing role of France and its, shall I say, paternalistic tendencies toward this country; a vast debate in the words of General de Gaulle who, it might be said, finally brought an end to that seemingly unending conflict. Our Algerian War has often been compared to your Vietnam engagement.

"It is known that Camus hated Oran and loved Algiers, *his* city as he would put it. He delighted in the simple pleasures of Algiers where he had been born and where he grew up: the sun, the sea, the cafés, soccer, reading and jazz. He was also a very charming and engaging person. We have already spoken of Oran and what Camus thought of it."

Louis Lachaume gets back to the separation issue engendered by the plague. "Camus experienced his own version of being pulled apart from his wife when he left Algeria to return to France for treatment of the tuberculosis that afflicted him. In those days before the appearance of sulfa drugs and penicillin, tuberculosis was treated primarily with a high-caloric diet and by breathing fresh mountain air. His wife, Francine, who had accompanied him to a mountain sanatorium, made her way back to teach in Algeria in 1942 during her husband's treatment and they were separated from each other for nearly two years. Camus' thoughts on love and separation imposed by the plague are undoubtedly a reflection of his own experience. He had the same emotions that Rambert might have had after Oran had been quarantined."

* * *

Seeking to bring some of the principal characters into the discussion, the teacher invites someone to elaborate on the plight of Raymond Rambert. "After all, he had been recently married and now he is confined to this place that he does not particularly like. He would much prefer to be back in Paris with his wife."

Jean-Baptiste, the Haitian, catches Dominique's eye. "Rambert approaches Dr. Rieux. Could he help him to leave? The physician answers. 'Now, unfortunately, you will remain here like everyone else.'

'But I am not from here. I am a stranger in this city. You think of nobody. You speak of public service and yet the public good consists of each person's happiness.'

'There are some things that my position prohibits. I cannot help you.'"

Jean-Baptiste continues. "It is the eternal conflict between private happiness and the common good. Rieux himself had been separated from his wife who had sought treatment abroad before Oran's quarantine. He even refused to pull strings for himself.

"To Rambert's credit, after this encounter and following his unsuccessful attempts to leave using other means, he joins the physician to labor against that from which he was seeking to escape."

"Thank you, Jean-Baptiste. You addressed well the topic of individual versus collective good.

"Mr. Donovan, what is on your mind?"

"Madame, apart from Tarrou, none of the characters speaks of his father. Is that not a bit curious?"

"That is true. You may or may not be aware that Camus never knew his father. He was raised by his mother and his grandmother. His father died in France during World War I when he, Camus, was just a one-year old."

"That helps to explain," replies Brendan, "so much of the heaviness of this narrative."

With time winding down, Dominique seeks to cut off the discussion. “Our classes always seem to go by too quickly. You have a good grasp of the circumstances surrounding this story. It is important, as you can see, to know the historical context in which it was written.

“We will let it go at that for now. At our next meeting, we will get more involved with some of the other characters themselves. In the meantime, pay attention to Father Paneloux. We will begin with him.”

Chapter 22.
December 2001 – San Antonio, Texas

Remember the Alamo

Dominique and Pierre have been invited to dinner at the Winships before leaving on vacation for the holidays. Jerome and Loretta, the parents of Larry and Louis, live in Ballston, a suburb of the Capital. Jerome has held a fairly important position in the Department of Fisheries after his long career as a lobsterman in Maine. His son in turn inherited his business.

Louis and his wife have come from Rockland for a visit. The conversation naturally gravitates toward last year's lobster yield. "Have you increased the number of traps since we last saw each other?"

"Yes, Dominique. I now have 350 traps. I could take Philippe back to Maine with me to give me a hand."

"He could spend three weeks in Presque Isle to pick potatoes and three weeks in Rockland to catch your lobsters, but I doubt that he will want to stay beyond our departure date for France."

“Are you aware,” says Jerome, “ that there was a time in the nineteenth century when Maine prisoners were fed these delicious lobsters on a daily basis? This delicacy was considered very ordinary at the time and the unhappy prisoners revolted in protest. That outcome was actually better for us lobstermen. We could sell them for a higher price to the local restaurants.”

As has been the habit since September 11th, the conversation gravitates to the events of that day. Jerome thinks increasingly about his retirement. “It is not easy working under these security conditions. I think frequently of Rockland where Loretta and I hope to return. I’ll take Philippe’s place but, at my age, for only a few hours a week.”

Pierre recalls the feast on Vinalhaven Island. “Hail to the lobster and to the American clambake.”

* * *

The Benoits and Mitchells have stayed in contact and decided some time ago to celebrate the holidays together as they did last year. San Antonio, Texas was the favored destination. Julie asked why people referred to Texas as the *Lone Star State*. “Why only a single star?”

“Because, for a long time, Texans preferred to remain independent of Mexico and the United States,” says Pierre. “The eventual outcome was obviously different. We may discover why in the course of our trip.”

* * *

While Philippe and his father are exercising at the hotel gym, Dominique and Julie, in summer dresses, are out for a stroll. It is quite warm, San Antonio being roughly at the latitude of New Orleans. “We are further south than Tunis,” says Dominique.

Advertisements in English and Spanish indicate that a basketball game is scheduled for this evening: San Antonio Spurs vs Washington Wizards. “Our fellow Frenchman, Tony Parker, will play tonight. What would the men think if we were to attend and support our compatriot? It would be a complete surprise, especially for your brother who has become interested in our team from the Capital.”

* * *

The Alamodome is a gigantic sports complex that can seat in excess of 60,000 spectators. It is the regular scene for basketball games, but also for many other sports and entertainment spectacles. The Spurs were the National Basketball Association champions in 1999. “According to our French press, Tony Parker is the star of the team. Don’t you remember, Julie, the many headlines that the newspaper *L’Equipe* ran with Parker’s name on the front page?”

Philippe is thrilled. The substantial crowd assembles at the entrance. “Here are your tickets,” says Dominique, “in the event that we were to become separated.”

Pierre looks around the arena before being seated. “Look, Philippe, at all the people in the two levels above us. There must be 40,000 fans here. They clearly like their Spurs, but I will cheer for the Wizards. We must. We are from Washington now and the Wizards are our team.”

“But Tony Parker is French.”

At precisely 7:00 p.m., the Texas Belles make their appearance, twelve young ladies wearing red, white and blue outfits and donning stetson hats. They will entertain the crowd before the contest with a spirited dance routine that will be accompanied by deafening rock music. Their movements are perfectly synchronized. The fans are completely engaged, clapping their hands, cheering and singing, or eating and drinking.

Suddenly, a fireworks display engulfs the hall with an amazing sight-and-sound extravaganza that reaches the highest point of the roof which is quickly obscured by smoke. The sprinkler system is abruptly set off over half of the arena, drenching the spectators and the Texas Belles.[24]

The basketball court is flooded. Screeching is heard from the affected sections as the entire Alamodome is in total darkness for an interminable thirty seconds. After several minutes, the administration apologizes and announces that whoever chooses to leave the premises will be reimbursed for the inconvenience. "We are distressed over this turn of events."

"What should we do?" asks Dominique.

Wiping his face with his shirtsleeve, Philippe does not hesitate. "It's not the end of the world. We will dry rapidly. This is Texas and all sorts of unusual things happen here."

The crowd cheers and bursts into laughter upon seeing a dozen janitors appearing on the playing surface with five or six brooms, a few buckets and eight or ten mops. "Here we are in this high-tech society, we have been to the moon and the most that the owners of this place have to offer are the most rudimentary instruments. If at least they could come up with a few large fans." So pontificates Philippe's neighbor.

"But at least we know that the sprinkler system works. Look at those enormous pipes. Is it any wonder that we are as soaked as we are?"

Most of the fans maintain their sense of humor and very few leave. The game is delayed an hour to allow the floor to dry.

---

[24] Incident experienced by the American author and his family.

Thanks to a vintage performance by Tony Parker and the loud support of his fans, our friends are treated to an exciting game in which the Spurs prevail. "Hooray for Tony Parker. But what an adventure," says Pierre. "Dominique, this will be some kind of story that you will be able to relate to the grandchildren when that day comes."

* * *

Pierre is the first to arise the next morning. "We will start by visiting the Alamo. Our clothes are dry. Hopefully, we will not get caught in a thunderstorm."

Julie bought a local newspaper. "The front page talks of yesterday evening's 'Texan shower'. They are serious when they say that everything in Texas is big. Look at the photo, Papa."

"I doubt that there will be fireworks where we are going today and so we can be at ease. It is time for us to learn a bit of history and to see if the film with John Wayne and Richard Widmark is faithful to what took place in this town. Let us rejoin the Mitchells."

The Alamo was originally a Spanish mission. The Franciscan priests intended to christianize the Indian people. They in turn resisted this conversion. An epidemic of smallpox decimated the native population in the eighteenth century and resulted in a lesser influence of the mission which in subsequent years was transformed into a convent, one of four built on the banks of the San Antonio River. It included a chapel and a square courtyard with small cells occupying three of its sides. "It is not a very impressive building," says Julie.

"And yet," answers Viola, the guide, "it became a fort in 1801, and it played a decisive role in the history of Texas and that of the entire Southwest of the United States in 1836 by blocking Mexico's expansion to the north."

Viola refers to a map of the nineteenth century. "Mexico had gained its independence from Spain and had acquired the vast territory corresponding to Texas, New Mexico and California of our day. On the other hand, the United States since its independence did not hide its intentions to expand into these territories as far as the Pacific Ocean. The Louisiana Purchase from France in 1803 had doubled the size of the country, but it then felt frustrated in its further expansion.

"At that time, Mexico found itself in total disarray. It could only be described as being in a virtual state of anarchy, particularly in the North, where the law of the jungle prevailed."

She continues. "For the Americans, Texas represented a frontier to be explored and one that held the promise of a better life. There was gold and silver, a favorable climate and lots of open space. Of great significance as well, there was land in unlimited amounts and it was cheap. An acre cost less than three cents whereas the price rose to thirty cents elsewhere."

The enraptured group approaches a more regional map near the door leading to the courtyard. "When and where does General Santa Anna come into the picture?" asks Philippe.

"In 1836, the Mexican army under the command of Antonio Lopez de Santa Anna marched toward San Antonio to put an end to an old conflict. The general, known for his brutality, provoked a sense of terror wherever he ventured.

"Texas found itself under the direction of an American governor. The army, composed of volunteers from every state in the nation, was undeniably weak. The soldiers were poorly trained, poorly armed, and rarely paid. Discipline was completely absent and it is said that each man needed to be completely self-reliant, to be his own cook and bottle washer. Within this ragtag assembly, however, were a few capable officers.

"Fate had brought this disparate group together and each person was there for his own reasons. Surprised by the arrival of Santa Anna toward the end of winter, they were united in combat and they inwardly knew the outcome that awaited them. Two officers, Jim Bowie and William Travis, shared their sense of doom. At the same time, they also knew that Santa Anna had to be stopped in this place. Otherwise, all of Texas would be lost. The freedom sought by these frontiersmen could only be preserved if a successful defense were to be mounted here and now… here at the Alamo."

The guide extols the heroism of the defenders and of their leaders. "Along with Davy Crockett, there were fewer than two hundred men who were present to face the five thousand fighters under Santa Anna. The Alamo commanders themselves were no saints. Jim Bowie had enriched himself through the slave trade and had been obliged to flee Louisiana after having killed two men with his famous Bowie knife. Travis, an attorney, had made his way to Texas following his murder in a fit of anger of a South Carolinian whom he suspected of having a relationship with his wife. Under these two individuals, 183 men and a few women and children were gathered here to resist the enemy. Santa Anna's goal by contrast was simple: to crush the *Norteamericanos* and to show no mercy, to take no prisoners."

Julie, Philippe, Scott and his sister Katherine reflect while moving around the chapel. Scott looks around the courtyard from one of the windows. "Imagine the cannons and guns that Santa Anna was able to aim at this fort during a thirteen-day siege."

Viola agrees. "By even the second day of the confrontation, Jim Bowie, already weakened by a case of tuberculosis, had been seriously injured while maneuvering a cannon within the fort. Being in bad straits, he relinquished his part of the command to William Travis.

"Each defender would ask himself repeatedly why he was here. Travis held the answer. San Antonio must be defended until the death. Otherwise, all of Texas would be subjected to the whims of Santa Anna. But reinforcements would be needed.

"On several occasions during the succeeding days, Travis sent messengers to other missions. After nine days of sporadic fighting, thirty-two volunteers arrived from Gonzales, located east of San Antonio. They too knew that they would suffer the same fate as those who were encamped within the fort. James Fannin from the Goliad mission also tried to come to the aide of his comrades but, for a variety of reasons, he was unable to reach the Alamo.

"Lacking ammunition, the defense could fire at Santa Anna only sporadically. Realizing their diminishing chance of survival and sensing his men's faltering morale, Travis assembled them on March 3rd and gave each soldier a choice. He realized that he had been mistaken in assuring them that they would receive all the necessary support and reinforcements. Those who preferred, therefore, might slip away during the night. Taking his sword, he drew a line in the sand. Those who would jump over it would engage themselves in the defense of the fort to their death if necessary. For a seemingly interminable time, nobody responded. The immobile soldiers lowered their heads in silence, looking neither to the left nor to the right. Finally, one volunteer crossed the line… and then another… and another. Slowly, more volunteers made their way to the other side and eventually all but one chose to remain, ready to die for the Texas cause. From this moment on, the defense was much more engaged.

"The Mexicans launched their last assault on the morning of March 9, 1836. The fort fell after three hours of relentless fighting. All the defenders perished and almost fifteen hundred of the attackers were killed.

"The news of the massacre spread like wildfire and immediately generated a sense of horror throughout the country. The resistance of the men under Travis was not to be in vain as the cry of *Remember the Alamo* reverberated everywhere and, six weeks later, Sam Houston decimated the Santa Anna forces at San Jacinto in a battle that lasted a mere twenty minutes."

Philippe has engrossed himself in the guide's story and poses a question. "Ultimately, what did Santa Anna hope to gain in all of this?"

"As a committed Mexican, Santa Anna in a way was fighting against both Spain and Texas. His hope was to expand his own country and his own personal power. The Texans for their part wanted initially to remain independent, as indeed they were after Sam Houston's victory. Eventually, though, annexation of the territory took place and Texas was added to the Union in 1845, becoming the twenty-eighth state of the United States."

"Thank you. This entire region would certainly be much different if Sam Houston had not defeated Santa Anna."

"We can always invoke the *what ifs*… The *Manifest Destiny* was certainly facilitated after this heroic, albeit tragic event."

There is a life-sized picture of Davy Crockett in his coonskin hat that attracts Scott's attention. "Crockett also died in the conflict. He was a giant among men, a storyteller, claiming *to have killed himself a b'ar when he was only three*."

"We know," says Viola, "that he was a great braggart, but he was also a man with a big heart who never forgot the less fortunate when he represented Tennessee in Congress. He also had a reputation for being a sharpshooter, able to snuff out the flame of a candle with a rifle shot from a hundred yards away… when he was sober, for he was also a heavy drinker. He was among those who jumped over the line in the *Alamo* courtyard to defend the Texas cause to the end. One of the great figures of the frontier, he is revered in the annals of American folklore."

The children, who have separated themselves from the adults, leave the chapel and wander into the courtyard. It is actually not as large as first anticipated. The rooms on three sides give witness to the austere lives of the nuns. A cannon remains at each corner. Julie approaches one of them. "Imagine the chaos of that March 9th morning of 1836: cannons, rifles, bayonets, knives. It must have been a horrible scene."

* * *

San Antonio is the ninth most populous city in the United States with 1.7 million inhabitants. It is built on the banks of the river which the Indians called *Yanaguana* or 'Refreshing Waters'. Spanish missionaries baptized it San Antonio after the saint of the day. In 1718, Father Antonio Olivares established a mission at today's site. The river is bordered by the Riverwalk, *El Paseo del Rio* in Spanish, a favorite strolling place for the people of the city, the majority of whom are of Mexican descent.

"There are but two days before Christmas for us to do our shopping. Let us go to the *Paseo*." Dominique thinks of the stalls along the Seine in Paris, but this site is much larger with all its stores, boutiques, cafés and restaurants. The signs here too are in English and Spanish. The passersby also speak both languages.

The Riverwalk is at a lower level than the streets of the city. Walking down the steps, Pierre suggests a ride on the river aboard the *Yanaguana Cruise*. "After our return, we can separate to do our shopping. Should we not find what interests us here, we can go to Market Square, *el Mercado*, the largest Mexican market outside of Mexico City."

Christmas carols in Spanish are heard from the boat. A group of young women dancers in traditional costumes, brightly colored gowns and white blouses, is elegantly performing on a stage along the banks of the river. Musicians wearing enormous sombreros and playing trumpets and guitars are equally festive.

In the midst of this carnival atmosphere, Dominique inquires, "Is this a religious or a commercial holiday?"

"A bit of both, I would guess."

"But, seriously, Pierre!"

"Not unlike in France."

The children shake their heads upon hearing this philosophical discussion.

The father brings the conversation back to the task at hand. "Let us regroup at five o'clock. We will feast on Tex-Mex food for supper. You have your money, but don't spend it on anything foolish and keep the gifts simple."

Julie and Philippe go their separate ways. Dominique suggests a cup of coffee. "We can do some people-watching before doing our own shopping."

Two hours later, the family reunites. Pierre, as usual, has studied the choice of restaurants and their menus. "*Pico de Gallo* serves everything that we might want: guacamoles, tamales, enchiladas, tacos, tortillas and frijoles to name just a few items."

* * *

Christmas Eve is spent with the Mitchells. "No appendicitis, Philippe," says Frank, "unless you have a second one hidden on the other side."

"It could be Katherine's turn this year."

"I am afraid of hospitals. Why not Julie?"

"Thank you for considering me, but I will pass!"

"Well, what about this Mass, Dominique?"

"It was said in Spanish, Estelle, and it was quite different from those that we have attended back home. We found a chapel, Santa Maria Guadalupe. The Mass concluded with a beautiful *Feliz Navidad* sung by a children's choir. We sensed the continued presence of the Franciscan Fathers."

Philippe understood some of the words of the homily, "thanks to my classmates, Miguel and Roberto, and to my Spanish teacher. I was half-asleep at that point and so I can't summarize it all that well for you."

The exchange of gifts takes place with great fanfare. Estelle smilingly offers Dominique a French recipe book by Julia Child. "She was a longtime television star and a tall lady at that. She studied in France and always concluded her program with a cheerful *Bon appétit*."

"Thank you. Let me read you her dedication: *To the beautiful France... and to those who created one of the most wonderful arts in the world.*"

During the rapidly prepared meal, plans are made. "Next year," offers Pierre, "you should come to Nice and we can consider skiing in Grenoble."

Frank looks at Scott. "You will need a job to pay your way."

"If I don't find gold in the Superstition Mountains, I will hire myself out at McDonalds!"

* * *

It is Julie who offers her bit of wisdom before returning to Washington. "The Alamo notwithstanding, I am still impressed by the Latino element in the area. We have seen so many people who have migrated here from Mexico. Maybe Santa Anna was not totally defeated at San Jacinto after all."

"Bravo for presenting us with this geopolitical assessment," says Philippe, while winking at his parents.

Chapter 23.
January 2002 – Washington, D.C.

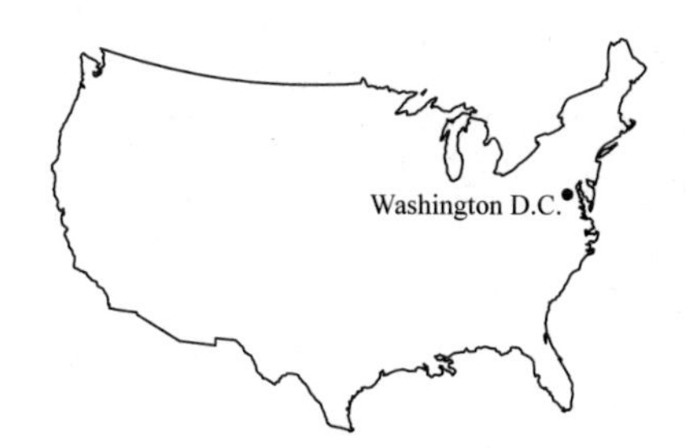

If there is something for which a person can always hope and can occasionally obtain, it is human tenderness.

Camus, *The Plague*

"As mentioned before we left each other last time, we will begin today by discussing Father Paneloux. You may remember Rebecca saying that this Jesuit priest was liked and respected by both believers and nonbelievers. With that in mind, who would like to comment on the two preachings that he gives in the course of the plague?

"Recall, if you will, the setting of the first preaching. Father Paneloux delivers this first sermon during the early phase of the plague. People are frightened. It is cold and damp, a dismal day. The church is full and the crowd spills beyond the main door onto the front steps.

"Your throughts? Charlotte."

"His first sermon justifies the concept of divine punishment falling upon these people. *My brothers, you have all fallen into this affliction! The wrath of God brings the proud and the blind to their knees.* Father Paneloux chastises those in the pews for their *lack of love*."

"Yes?"

"But, thanks to this disaster, those who are repentant may ultimately benefit from this divine punishment."

"Claudine?"

"I find this sermon terrifying, closer to an apocalyptic message than to a gospel one. It is a diatribe that overlooks the punishment of innocents. It ignores the fact that the plague strikes haphazardly. How can Father Paneloux speak of the road to salvation as a *red hot spear that gives one a glimpse of eternity*? He seems to be proposing that deliverance may only occur through suffering and that the inhabitants of Oran have brought the plague upon themselves."

"He does sound severe, doesn't he?"

"I believe that, back home in present day Quebec, the Church is much more open, more generous than in the past, speaking more of love than of sin, judging and condemning less the *miserable men* of whom Father Paneloux speaks. May I add *miserable women* as well? In our day, we speak less of the fear of hell and insist more on divine love and forgiveness."

"Thank you, Claudine... Rebecca?"

"I am not Christian. It seems to me that Father Paneloux speaks of a God who judges and punishes. *My brothers, you are in the midst of this calamity; my brothers, you have deserved it. Weary from your sins, God has restricted his gaze. The wicked have reason to tremble*. The just seemingly have nothing to fear."

"Louis?"

"Father Paneloux does end his sermon with a flicker of hope. *Our fellow citizens may raise their voices to the heavens where they will speak the Christian concept of love. God will do the rest.*"

"You both make valid points, Rebecca and Louis. Actually, you do as well, Claudine. Thinking back to our last class, the sermon can also be interpreted in terms of Camus' thinking about the German occupation of France during the war. He may be saying in effect that the French deserved their unhappy fate because they had lost their moral compass. They had replaced their traditional republican motto of *Liberty, Equality, Fraternity* with the Vichy one of *Work, Family, Country* which, while perhaps honorable enough, was a deviation from the one that truly reflected the glory days that France experienced at an earlier time."

Dominique continues, "Many commentators believe that Father Paneloux's first sermon heads in this direction. It raises of course the issues of faith in the existence of God and the problem of suffering in the world. Dr. Rieux, who is perhaps Camus' main spokesperson in a conversation with the Father, refuses to believe in a creating God who allows the existence of evil and suffering. Hovering together over a dying child, the doctor says *that one at least was innocent* to justify his disagreement and to rebuke the priest's pronouncement of guilt to the suffering of the citizens of Oran."

"Who would like to pursue this theme?… Tanya Rodriguez?"

"Later in dealing with the same issues, the doctor says to Tarrou: '*I believe that I am on the path of truth in fighting against creation as I find it.*"

"Your conclusion, Tanya?"

"Rieux's beliefs are not militant, but they reflect the hopelessness in the midst of the realities of evil and suffering. As mentioned in our last class, it is the absurd symbolized by death."

* * *

"Myrianna?"

"The tortured death of the child to which Father Paneloux is witness completely unravels him and leads him to deliver another sermon that is quite different from the first. One senses in this second preaching that his theology has evolved."

"Could you elaborate?"

"He is less stern. He speaks more softly. He does not say '*you*' but rather '*we*'. He goes from a collective punishment that strikes the innocent and the guilty alike to a more individual one. Having said that, he retains the element of suffering as an invitation to repentance. There appears to be redemptive value to suffering in Father Paneloux's thinking."

Yasmina raises her hand. "Dr. Rieux disagrees. *No Father, I will always refuse until the day I die to accept the creation that you propose wherein children are so tortured.* The doctor and Father Paneloux are far apart in their thinking and they seem not to agree on much."

Claudine is a bit more forgiving of the priest after his second preaching. "Father Paneloux does not deny this problem of suffering, dramatic as it might be. *There is nothing more important to explain than the suffering of a child.* He goes on to say. *Who in fact would dare say that the joy of eternity can offset a single instant of human suffering?*"

Brendan Donovan interjects. "Is this not, Claudine, Camus who is speaking here for himself?"

"I suppose so."

Dominique adds her own comments. "Father Paneloux continues, *We should remain faithful to this tearing apart when one is faced with the death of a child.* There is, he claims, within the concept of evil, that evil which is *necessary* and that which is *useless* for *if it is just that the dissolute should be punished, one cannot fathom why a child should be.* As it turns out, the child, Jean Tarrou and Father

Paneloux, all good people, eventually succumb to the plague. Cottard, the *slippery* character of whom Rebecca spoke last time, survives. Life is not fair."

"Exactly," responds Rachel. "It is not for us or even for the priest to judge. Only God."

Dominique senses that the conversation is heating up. "Julio?"

"Father Paneloux then poses an eternal dilemma. *One needs to believe everything or reject everything, believe in spite of suffering because God wills it, to abandon oneself to the divine will, but without inflicting suffering on others*. On the other hand, in the words of Father Paneloux, *neither to seek out suffering to fulfill some kind of proud satisfaction. To the contrary, one should combat the plague, that symbol of suffering, with all one's might.* This, I believe, represents some of the evolution in the priest's thinking."

"If I read you correctly, Julio, suffering then forces man to take a position: to believe and accept or to deny and refuse the will of God."

"Yes, to believe or not, a fundamental decision, is it not?"

"Good points, Julio."

Brendan engages in the discussion. "I see a parallel between the missions of Dr. Rieux and Father Paneloux. *We fight against death with all our being.*"

The teacher senses that the entire class wishes to contribute… "Leïla?"

"I would like to comment on this second sermon as well. Submission to the will of God is one of the fundamental principles of Islam. As a Muslim person, I can understand the direction in which Father Paneloux is heading."

Dominique appreciates these remarks but offers the doctor's opposing view. "Rieux cannot accept a morality of submission, even a divine submission. *I have spent too much time in hospitals to accept the idea of collective or individual punishment....* Yasmina?"

"I agree with Leïla. Islam means submission, but I believe that it should be an active submission. Illnesses and suffering exist and we should accept them as realities in our lives. Those are part of the human condition, but we still need to treat the sick and combat against suffering. We need to oppose this plague and, by extension, all plagues. Camus seems to express a pessimism and fatalism that ends in resignation. Is this not his submission?"

"I understand what you and Leïla are saying. I just don't think that Dr. Rieux, that is to say Camus, totally agrees. The doctor's comments would seem to refute this position. *When one sees the misery and suffering that it brings, one would need to be crazy, blind, or lazy to resign oneself to the plague*. It is also mentioned that *even your victories will always be provisional*. Camus is less sanguine in this regard."

* * *

Dominique takes a deep breath. "Okay, having in mind all that we have discussed, let us try to clarify Camus' philosophy... Julio?"

"His is a pessimism founded on the absurdity of death. We have already said that. But he also has some serious considerations on love, freedom and justice."

"For example?"

"Love is seen as being merely physical."

Linda Malone gives a more noble view as individuals who are linked '*...in their intelligence, their hearts, and their flesh*.'"

The teacher smiles. "Claudine?"

"And *the great desire of a restless heart to forever possess the person that one loves*. I find Linda's analysis of love and the one that I have just quoted to be more to my liking."

Dominique agrees with Julio, Linda and Claudine. "I believe that Camus experienced each of these extremes."

Brendan Donovan shifts gears and introduces the subject of Camus' pacifism. "He opposed violence in all of its forms."

"But Brendan," asks Rebecca Weinstein, "how could Nazism have been defeated without the killing that the war effort required?"

"I don't have the answer to that question. I just think that Camus, as a committed pacifist, appealed to non-violence."

"Having said that," adds the teacher, "he was very active within the Resistance movement. He knew many who saved Jews from being deported. He also wrote on their behalf in the newspaper *Combat*.

"In any event, I hope that you will not be put in the position of having to make those decisions."

Dominique seeks a redeeming theme to this serious discussion. "Is there a moral issue in all of this? Recognizing the submission comments of Leïla and Yasmina, who might add anything that might be considered positive?… Linda?"

"Through Dr. Rieux, Camus offers his personal morality. Against the scandal of death and of life's absurdities, one must resist, plod on, even without hope, consciously and lucidly against all plagues, against illness and death to be sure, but also against all forms of foolishness including wars, revolutions and angry dictatorships. This entails carrying out one's day-to-day calling in spite of setbacks, doing one's work honestly and honorably."

Dominique agrees. "If there is an underlying theme to this work, I submit this last phrase that Camus has given us for your consideration; that is, to respond to our daily calling honestly and honorably."

* * *

Dominique seeks to bring the discussion to a close. “We finally come to Oran’s deliverance from the plague. The cats return to the streets and we find the rats in good health once again in the cellars and in the alleyways. The quarantine is lifted and the city gates are opened *at dawn on a pleasant February morning.* The people resume their suspended lives and celebrate with *joyful singing.* The women come down from the roof terraces to run their errands and *the films change in the cinemas*! Think of the eventual liberation of Paris at the end of the war. After so much hardship, what joy!”

“But Madame,” adds Myrianna, “the plague, that is to say the war, in the words of Tarrou upon facing his own death, was the *ultimate defeat* that even peace cannot rectify any-more than *there can be an armistice for the mother who is separated from her child or the man who buries a friend.*”

“You make a good point, Myrianna. Still, one needed to savor the moment when *the sufferings had ended and the time of forgetfulness had not yet begun.*”

Louis adds: “It is true that they rejoiced, but the plague had left its scars. It had changed the people of Oran.”

“For example?”

“Father Paneloux’s second sermon, as has been men-tioned, shows how his theology has changed. Rambert in finally seeing his wife again would ask himself *if the plague can come and go without men’s hearts being changed.* People would resume their lives, but their views of the world and of themselves would be different. The French had suffered much during the occupation. They had changed as a result of the war and Camus acknowledges this.”

“And yet,” adds the teacher, “he also realized that they soon returned to their faults, their failings and their petty squabbles.

"So, Mr. Sosa, what do you think the people gained in all of this?"

"Camus states that all that man can hope to gain from plagues is knowledge and remembrance."

"Maybe that is what Tarrou means when he calls it *winning the game*."

Sosa pauses and then continues. "Tarrou adds: *the events of life and the image of death, that is knowledge*. It is not a very optimistic worldview, is it? Tarrou had never had any semblance of hope."

Dominique agrees with this assessment of Tarrou. "How hard it must be to live only with what one knows and with what one can remember but deprived of that for which one can hope. There can be no peace without hope and there certainly can be no joy."

Jean-Baptiste dislikes this pessimism. "The doctor tells us that *joy is a burn that cannot be savored.* I find this depressing."

Dominique stares briefly out the window. "But you must finish his sentence. *If there is something for which a person can always hope and can occasionally obtain, it is human tenderness*.

"It is on this last thought that we can perhaps end and it is this human tenderness that I wish for you because, without it, there is no future and, with no future, there is no hope. It is possibly human tenderness that offers us a single ray of happiness in the midst of a world that the author recognizes as miserable, *a world that is upside down*, that is topsy-turvy."

The students are hanging on their teacher's every word. "For the believer, there is faith, the first cousin of which in some circles is said to be doubt. Camus describes for us the human condition according to the historical context in which he lived and according to his own personal experiences. Literary critics are in agreement in saying, as we have seen, that the author expresses his ideas, both philosophical and political, through the characters of his novel. You might also notice that these characters all express the need to resist, even if the word is not used. Dr. Rieux does his duty in spite of so much adversity. Father Paneloux, after his second sermon, stays the course. Rambert finally remains to work at the doctor's side. Camus seems to leave the door open ever so slightly for some good in the world.

"Some of you will go on to teach other students. Much more can be said about this author who, as I mentioned previously, was prolific in his writing and whom you may choose to cover if you offer a course such as this one. You will perhaps want to read some of his plays as well.

"I commend you for having reflected well on the subject matter of these last two classes."

* * *

Camus received the Nobel Prize in literature in 1957 *for the collection of his work that brings to light with serious insights the problems that weigh upon man's conscience and that are posed in our times*.

The teacher concludes. "Interpersonal and societal relationships need to be fostered and developed and one must remain vigilant to the lessons of history for, if they are not heeded, the plague bacillus, lying dormant in unsuspecting places, may resurface to afflict us anew.

"Albert Camus died in an automobile accident in 1960."

Chapter 24.
January 2002 – Chicago, Illinois

I have a dream…

Shortly after her return from San Antonio, Julie accepted an invitation from Dawn Walker to visit an aunt in Chicago over the Martin Luther King holiday weekend. "You will get to meet another African-American family."

During the past 11/2 years, Dawn has become one of Julie's best friends. Julie is not completely unaware of black people for she associates with several of them every day in Washington, and particularly in school, but without having serious contacts, those with Dawn being the sole exception. The expenses will be modest, for the two adolescents will avail themselves of their airfare using the frequent-flier miles of their parents.

They embark at Reagan Airport for the two-hour flight to Chicago. It is Dawn's first trip without her family. Her father, Harold, is emotional in seeing his daughter off. "Don't miss your aunt and your cousin at the other end."

"But I am eighteen years old. I am no longer a little girl."

* * *

Georgina Walker and her daughter, Sophie, are awaiting Dawn and Julie at O'Hare Airport. They live on the North Side of the city, not far from Loyola University, a well-recognized Jesuit school. During the trip home from the airport, they get acquainted. Georgina works for World Relief, a non-profit organization specializing in the welcoming of refugees. "After receiving many Bosnians, we are now greeting those fleeing Sudan and the Ivory Coast."

During the meal, the three young ladies talk about their studies. Julie explains the French system and how it differs from the American one. Sophie, aged nineteen, is studying journalism at the University of Chicago. She will be responsible for entertaining the two visitors. "I have thought a great deal about this weekend over the past few days. Sleep well for we will get an early start tomorrow. It will be a full day."

* * *

They leave the house at nine o'clock this Saturday morning. It is four degrees and a cold breeze from the lake justifies the nickname of the 'Windy City'. The three friends are bundled up in heavy jackets and face masks for the ten-minute walk to the El that feels more like a half hour. The streets are bordered on both sides by identical three-storey brick row houses surrounded by small yards. It is a middle-class neighborhood.

Julie discreetly observes the commotion on the El. The passengers, mostly black, seem frozen. Many are wearing red and blue Bulls parkas that celebrate the glory days of Michael Jordan who dominated the National Basketball Association for so long. Sophie makes Julie aware of the six titles captured by his team from 1993 to 1998. "Unfortunately, we have fallen to a level of mediocrity since his retirement."

The ride takes them along Lake Michigan and their destination is the Magnificent Mile, the Champs-Elysées of Chicago. There they will find all the high-end stores: Marshall Fields, Nieman Marcus, Crate and Barrel, F.A.O. Schwartz, Borders, and many others! Julie compares them to the Galeries Lafayette, Le Printemps, and La Samaritaine back home.

"Here we are in the shopping center of the world," says Sophie.

Julie thinks of Paris but refrains from commenting, "That may be a bit presumptuous even though these stores are impressive," muses she.

"We are going dancing tonight and we need to dress you up for the occasion. My cousin brought everything that she will need, but you will not be accepted with what you are wearing. We are about the same size and I will loan you some of my clothes, but we need to buy you a blouse."

"Sophie, where are you bringing me tonight?"

"Don't worry, Julie. There are several discos for young people who have not reached drinking age and where alcoholic beverages are not served. We will go to the *Mirage Club*, one that is known for its hip-hop music. You will need to be brave for we are going to make a real Chicagoan out of you."

"I am hardly reassured. I have to ask myself what you are thinking."

They hustle along from store to store, pausing at intervals to sort through items of interest. They finally find themselves on the third floor of *Nieman Marcus*. While Julie is distracted in the perfume section, Dawn and Sophie consult the make-up person.

"Julie, Stephanie will prepare you for tonight. You are a bit too pale."

The stylist, wearing a long white coat, gently grasps Julie by the chin. She turns her face from side to side and runs a comb through her hair. "I will make a real beauty out of you. You have very nice features and you will be a real princess when I am finished with you. I will give you a Cindy Crawford look."

"No, no!" says Sophie. "My mother will be doing up her hair for tonight's event. Give her a Halle Berry look instead."

Stephanie takes her mission seriously. A substantial audience gathers during the half hour session. The assembled women show interest and amusement at the transfiguration that is taking place and they applaud when the task is completed. Stephanie applies the final strokes and steps back. "You are a black goddess… in white skin!"

Julie gazes in the mirror. She is a bit surprised but not at all displeased. She thanks Stephanie, offers her a generous tip, receives a number of perfume samples, and walks away with her companions.

* * *

Sophie takes Julie by the arm. "We will now take the El to the Sears Tower where we will eat a sandwich before making our way to the summit. With 103 storeys and rising 1,350 feet, this skyscraper is the second-tallest building in the world."

The three companions have a view of the entire city from the Skydeck and can see forty miles beyond. Dawn and Julie look through the binoculars. They follow the Chicago River that flows at the foot of the Tower toward Lake Michigan[25]

---

[25] The Great Lakes – Superior, Huron, Michigan, Ontario, and Erie – formerly explored by Cartier and Champlain, combine to form the largest source of fresh water in the world and extend across nine hundred miles from east to west and seven hundred miles from north to south.

alongside of which they are able to distinguish Lincoln Park and the Oak Street Beach. Sophie indicates other points of interest including several details of the Loop.

* * *

"How beautiful you look," marvels Aunt Georgina. "You will be the queen of the ball this evening."

"Not until you have done up her hair," interjects her daughter.

"I agree. Sit down on this chair by the table, Julie. You have very nice hair, but it is fine. Hold on while I pull it and braid it. Your head will feel tight."

After a productive session, Aunt Georgina is satisfied. "You are ready now to choose the outfit that you will be wearing."

Sophie offers her black slacks, the shiny emerald green blouse that they purchased earlier, a handbag, and flashy costume jewelry. "These earrings match your blouse. No need to frown. You are not going to church but to a ballroom. You need to make a statement with your outfit."

While keeping her thoughts to herself, Julie feels that this assortment of clothes is much more assertive than what she would ordinarily wear. She quickly mentions, "Hey, there is no way that I will meet any of my friends or, for that matter, grand-mère or Sister Angela. So, let's go for it. These slacks, however, are so tight that I will never be able to sit."

"You are not going there to sit but to dance!"

Sophie completes Julie's wardrobe with high heels. "What do you think of her, Dawn?"

"Julie, you will be irresistible."

* * *

The *Mirage* is a discothèque on North Green Street that is known for its hip-hop music, a style that originated in the parks of New York City in the early 80s. This music subsequently became popular throughout the country. Often containing violent or erotic themes, the lyrics expressed the anger and frustration of the youth living in inner cities. The *MTV* television channel was the vehicle that popularized this style. The themes were propagated in spite of the indignation and opposition of many authorities and parents from the middle and upper classes of society.

Sophie warns her protégés: "Ignore the lyrics. We are going to the disco to dance and to have fun with my friends."

The blinking neon lights illuminate the facade of the dance hall. Sophie and her companions descend five or six steps and arrive at the basement level. The ear-splitting music sets the tone for the evening.

Upon entering, Julie feels self-conscious. There are but a handful of whites in the audience. Sophie's friends, forewarned, greet her warmly and she is quickly set at ease. The hall is dimly lighted. Small round tables are set along the perimeter of the room. From the walls hang pictures of stars, both black and white, both former and current. Curious, Julie notices photos of Nat King Cole, Chubby Checker and, of course, Elvis Presley. Sophie points out one of P. Diddy, a contemporary artist among her favorites. At least three hundred dancers are assembled in front of the stage, singing and clapping, swaying in place with the music. Julie joins the crowd, hesitant at first, but swaying in harmony with those around her soon enough. The black group onstage is warming up the gathering with renditions of Eminem, Ice Cube and Snoop Dogg.

Dawn congratulates Julie. "You handle yourself quite well."

"Dawn, my dear, not too many compliments. She will never have our sense of rhythm. It is like in basketball. The whites can never jump as high as we can!"

Overhearing the conversation, one of Sophie's friends, Antwain, invites Julie to dance. "Come and rap with me!"

Antwain is sensitive to Julie's initial discomfort and he shows her a few simple steps. The music goes on at length and Julie masters her first 'lesson'. She quickly becomes aware that there is no set pattern to the dancing routine and she is encouraged to 'hang loose'. She absorbs the message and soon loses whatever inhibitions she might have had upon arriving as the group plays a few P. Diddy renditions to Sophie's delight: 'Child of the Ghetto', 'Blast Off', 'Shiny Suit Man'.

Dawn, Julie and Sophie are joined by a dozen other young people during a break. Over soft drinks, the conversation is directed toward the musicians who have descended from the stage to engage with the crowd; Julie is introduced and is complimented on her striking appearance.

The evening goes by quickly, with singing, laughter and more dancing. Dawn reminds Sophie, "I hate to say this but we must leave by midnight. Aunt Georgina set the return hour and she was adamant on a curfew."

Julie is sorry. "It is a shame that the time has gone by so quickly."

"Well," says Antwain, "let us have a last dance before you leave."

He congratulates Julie after their evening together. "You have made tremendous progress in such a short period of time."

“Thank you for all your help. I could not have made it without you.”

* * *

Aunt Georgina raps on the door. “Ah, you are tired this morning. It is ten o’clock. Breakfast is ready and we will be leaving in one hour.”

The Walkers are a pious family that never misses the Sunday service at the Southern Baptist Church on Lake Shore Drive. Sophie, Dawn and Julie are completely immobile. Aunt Georgina addresses Julie: “I was not asleep when you came in this morning. You sure had a ton of stories.”

Julie finds herself once again in the midst of a black congregation. Listening to the gospel music, she discovers that the rhythm is not so different from that of the previous evening. The singers, mostly women in blue gowns and a few men in black suits and bow ties, sway to renditions of ‘Bless the Lord’, ‘Amazing Grace’ and ‘It Is Well with My Soul’. The faithful join in. Julie is impressed by the enthusiasm of the congregation and cannot help comparing it to the stiffness of the church assemblies in Nice.

After the singing, the pastor delivers his sermon memorializing the life of Martin Luther King. “Tomorrow we will celebrate a very special holiday wherein we will remember a person who did much for our people.”

He evokes the boycott of the bus system of Montgomery after the arrest of Rosa Parks. He recalls the peaceful marches and the brutal police responses. Julie revisits in her mind the television images that she had previously seen of dogs threatening the demonstrators. The minister highlights the 250,000 people in front of the Lincoln Memorial in the Capital and the millions who watched on television as Martin Luther King delivered his *I have a dream* oration.

The pastor raises his voice. “The struggle is not over. We can proclaim our victories, but we must continue the work that remains unfinished. We can celebrate tomorrow with pride and joy the life of the person who is responsible for so much of our progress. Beyond tomorrow, however, we must continue to strive for the equality that still eludes us.”

“Amen, Hallelujah!” comes the answer. The community strikes up ‘It Is Well with My Soul’ a second time.

Aunt Georgina tells the story of Horatio Spafford, the composer of this last hymn, during the ride home. “He was a white lawyer whose son died young in 1871. Horatio was later ruined when he lost all of his property in the Great Chicago Fire. He subsequently decided to take a trip to Europe with his family, but he was detained in Chicago for business reasons at the last minute. His wife and four daughters sailed without him on the *Ville du Havre* which was struck by another ship and sank quickly in the middle of the Atlantic Ocean. The mother somehow survived and sent her husband a cable a few days later from France: ‘*Saved Alone.*’ In spite of all these tragedies, Horatio kept the faith and composed this hymn as he crossed the Atlantic to rejoin his wife: ‘It Is Well with My Soul’.”

* * *

The conversation naturally turns to Martin Luther King during the meal. The aunt tells her story and that of her family. “I was young in 1968 when King was assassinated, but I remember my father’s experiences as a young man in Mississippi. He participated in the march from Selma, Mississippi to Montgomery, Alabama with King and he was subjected on any number of occasions to the contempt of whites and to the physical abuse of the police. He subscribed to King's peaceful resistance. He compared this model to that of Lincoln who a century earlier had freed the slaves. Other blacks, however, chose a more violent approach."

"In France, my father spoke of Angela Davis and the Black Panthers."

"Their violence is understandable. A few days after the *I have a dream* speech, a bomb killed four young black girls in a church in Birmingham, Alabama.

"My parents were poor. My mother worked as a maid for a white family. My father worked two jobs: as a porter during the day and as a gas station attendant at night. The working poor are not an invention of our time. But they were driven people who toiled tirelessly in order that their four children might get an education. Their tenacity was facilitated by the civil rights legislation passed by President Lyndon Johnson."

"How did you manage to find your way to Chicago?"

"I came here with Sophie when she was three years old. As a single mother, I was determined to turn my life around and to find work. Opportunities were better here in the North. Still, it was not easy. At first, Sophie was enrolled in a Head Start program while I worked in a fast-food restaurant. At night, she came with me to my second job in a family where I worked as a nanny. At the time, we lived on the South Side of Chicago where there was a high level of violence. Fights and murders were common. Our apartment in a project was a disaster. It was dirty and was infested with rats. The hallways smelled of urine. We went outside at our peril and only when necessary. Drugs were sold openly in neighboring vacant lots. It was disgusting… and dangerous."

"How did you ever make your way into this more middle-class neighborhood?"

"I benefited from a number of public assistance programs: a subsidized apartment, food stamps, and reduced fares on the El. I took some courses and eventually earned a degree after five years. This allowed me to find a better paid job. I will never be rich, but I am happy to have left the ghetto where we had lived for so long."

Sophie continues the narrative. "It was terrifying to live in that kind of environment. I was always frightened to come home from school, but I learned to avoid the traps. I became streetwise and independent of necessity at a very young age."

The aunt agrees. "Sophie refined her survival skills well. In the end, we were helped a great deal by the safety net. Sophie did well in high school and received a modest scholarship which has allowed her to pursue her studies at the college level. Yes, we are now part of the middle class, but, as the pastor mentioned this morning, the struggle is not over. There are still, as statistics indicate, significant economic differences between blacks and whites."

"We have the same problems in France with immigrants from North and Sub-Saharan Africa."

"But you have not come here to listen to our story. We experienced poverty and witnessed violence on the South Side, but we are not alone. Alas, violence seems to be a reality in most of our large cities. I might add though that there are some very desirable neighborhoods on the South Side. I should not paint that part of the city as being completely deprived."

* * *

The afternoon is devoted to a football game between the Chicago Bears and the New York Giants. "The Super Bowl will be played in New Orleans next month. It will almost be another national holiday. The Super Bowl is the most popular sporting event of the year and the game that is the most watched on television. Our team is not favored to make it that far," says Aunt Georgina.

"Do you know much about our American-style football, Julie?" asks Sophie.

"I attended a high school game in West Virginia on Thanksgiving Day and a friend tried to explain the rules to me. I don't understand all of them, but I am aware that the ball carrier must be thrown to the ground. My brother and I prefer our football, the sport that you call soccer."

"Look, Julie," exclaims Dawn. "More than half of the players are black. Whether it be in football, baseball or basketball, we are disproportionately represented. In basketball, more than 80 % of the players are black."

Sophie adds: "As I mentioned yesterday, we just jump higher than you do."

* * *

The two visitors from the Capital would very much like to stay longer this Monday morning. They attended a concert the previous evening at the nearby University of Loyola and they quickly wandered across the snow-covered campus. Aunt Georgina and Sophie will drive them to the airport. They will have lunch at the Bistro 110 along the way.

At breakfast, Julie asks how she should manage her hairdo.

"But you should hold onto it. Sit down and don't move. It will only take me five minutes. I will tighten your hair once again. Were you aware how you were admired at the concert last night?"

Sophie chimes in: "Do you want me to call Stephanie so that she can make you up once more?"

"I don't think so. My parents won't recognize me. The hairdo will suffice for our return."

* * *

Julie thanks Aunt Georgina and Cousin Sophie and hands her ticket to the airline stewardess. "I could easily stay for another week. Sophie, you have been magnificent. I would love to return to dance at another club. Thank Antwain for me. I agree that he is a great dancer and he kept me from looking ridiculous."

Dawn embraces her aunt and cousin. "I will keep good memories of the city, but I wish that it were not so cold."

"You can visit us during the summer next time and you can swim in the lake at the Oak Street Beach."

Dawn and Julie review the adventures of the weekend during the return flight. "We will have many stories to tell our classmates tomorrow. I will comb your hair one last time on the school bus before our first class."

* * *

At the airport, Philippe runs to greet his sister. "What is this with your hair?"

"Aunt Georgina and Sophie insisted. What do you think of it?"

"I'm not sure. And, what about this perfume?"

"It's a long story. I'll tell you later."

Pierre and Dominique are equally surprised at their daughter's appearance, but they don't comment in front of the Walkers. Dominique kisses her daughter. "I have the impression that you had a good time."

"Julie was fantastic. My cousin had prepared many surprises for us and do you realize that your daughter received compliments for her dancing?"

Julie blushes. “Don’t reveal all our secrets.”

* * *

Pierre can’t help commenting during the ride home. “I wonder if you intend to send a photo back home to your grandparents. You know them. Their tastes tend to run along classical lines. It will give them a completely new outlook on their granddaughter.”

Chapter 25.
February 2002 – San Diego, California

San Diego: the most refined city in America.

Peter Wilson,
Mayor of San Diego, 1971-1983

Mother and daughter arrived in San Diego the evening before to visit one of Dominique's first cousins whom she has not seen in twenty years and with whom her contact has been limited to birth announcements and to the exchange of cards at holiday time. In her most recent note, Nicole invited the Benoit family for a visit. Unable to free himself, Pierre encouraged his wife to accept. "I have been to San Francisco," he told her, "and it is your turn to see the Pacific Ocean. The temperature is mild at this time of year, and you and Julie could avail yourselves of a long weekend during the winter school break."

* * *

Very close during their childhood and adolescence, their mothers being sisters, the cousins had separated after lycée, Dominique having enrolled at the Sorbonne and Nicole having chosen studies elsewhere in nursing. Following her graduation, Nicole had been recruited by an American hospital in Riyadh in Saudi Arabia. There, she met Barry, an engineer employed by Mobil Oil. They married and she then followed him to Algeria, Libya, Iran, and the United States where they lived in New Jersey, Oklahoma City and Houston, before moving to San Diego. She now works as an Emergency Room nurse three days a week at the UCSD Medical Center[26].

Over breakfast, Nicole and Dominique recall the events in their lives that have brought them to this point. "Barry has a very responsible position and, as long as automobiles are to run on gasoline… Mind you, I am basically an ecologist even though I appreciate the luxury that you see around you. I still am opposed to this complete reliance on foreign oil, but here we are and what can I say. If we find alternative forms of energy for our vehicles, many of us will be searching for other ways to make a living. When we met in Riyadh, Barry and his company assisted the Saudi government in the exploration of this precious commodity. Thereafter, we moved every two or three years to accommodate Mobil Oil. He has advanced within the company and he now holds an important managerial position. He has benefited from a nice series of promotions."

"Your time in Riyadh might compare to our stay in Tunis. Describe, if you would, this place about which I have heard much but have never had the opportunity to visit."

"I enjoyed my two years in Riyadh, the capital of the country, where we saw first-hand the results of all the petroleum profits. It is an ultra-modern city that sparkles in the middle of the desert. The hospital where I worked is magnificent and has all the up-to-date equipment. The generous

[26] *University of California at San Diego Medical Center.*

salaries attract physicians and nurses from many parts of the world and all the specialties are more than adequately represented.

"Many Mercedes cars circulate everywhere on well-paved roads. All the buildings are air-conditioned. We could find every imaginable product that was imported from Europe or the United States in the stores where we shopped. We enjoyed all of the comforts in our everyday living."

"Did the Saudis have access to this prosperity?"

"The country remains very traditional. The women do not drive all these Mercedes cars and they do not sit in the cafés. They are always accompanied by a man from within their family. The government controls the press and thereby controls public opinion. Everyone watches *El Jazeera* on television. That said, the oil wealth is obvious and the people do benefit to a point."

Dominique shares her own Tunisian experience. "We would often see veiled women in the medina of Tunis while they were running their errands."

"In Riyadh as well. But, at times, we also saw them remove their veils in the stores to try out samples of our French perfumes. To be sure, the fashion-conscious young girls wore long robes, the *jabithas*, but with skin-tight jeans underneath."

"It is the country where Mecca is located."

"The country of the hajj, the pilgrimage, as you know from your time in Tunis, to which all male Muslims aspire in their lifetime. Yes, religion is very much a part of daily life there. The imam's chant calls the faithful to prayer five times a day and the men go to the mosque on Friday afternoons. There is also the month of Ramadan. At sunset, the blast of a small cannon that was located in front of our house signaled the end of that day's fast."

"Where were your children born?"

"Laurent was born in Tripoli, Antoine in Newark and Christine in Oklahoma City."

"You certainly moved around. Your children must be very resilient and Barry must enjoy his work."

Nicole presents her cousin with a generous serving of pancakes. "I find that Barry's oil poisons this society of overconsumption. I must say that it bothers me a great deal. I realize that the same also holds true in Europe, but here the waste is even more obvious. The cars are so big and one-third of them are SUVs, small trucks really.

"Life was simpler in Oklahoma City. There were also fewer racial tensions there. In all candor, I enjoy it here in San Diego where we have lived comfortably for the past two years. We are constantly reminded that we are close to the border and immigration is an issue here as it is elsewhere in the country. Many workers have their green cards that allow them to work legally in the United States, but the majority do not. It is estimated that more than ten million residents have entered through clandestine means, hidden in the backs of trucks or crossing, often on foot, the deserts of Arizona or New Mexico. There are two thousand miles of frontier between the United States and Mexico. It is impossible to oversee every point of entry into the country."

"There are probably advantages and disadvantages to being so close to the border."

Nicole thinks a bit before answering. "Barry worries that these folks work for lower wages and take jobs away from Americans. They often have no insurance and several hospitals in California have closed because they were obliged to treat too many immigrant patients at little or no charge. I see this situation arise everyday in our Emergency Room, accepting as we do everyone who presents himself or herself at our door. Yesterday, for example, an immigrant child with meningitis was brought to us by her mother. We obviously admitted and treated her without asking who will pay. It turns out that the family is indigent and the hospital will be obliged to absorb the costs.

"We also need to educate these children from beyond our borders, many of whom do not speak English, in our schools."

"But you are a country of immigrants."

"Yes, but there needs to be more control over the situation."

"Similar to ours in France for that matter."

"Loma Point, our neighborhood, is very desirable. It is a residential community; maybe not Beverly Hills, but still quite nice. The children have adjusted well. The ocean has a moderating effect on the climate. During the day, it is mostly between 65 and 75 degrees and it is almost always sunny. We are comfortable in San Diego, even during the summer. One could be on the *Côte d'Azur*, while thirty miles further inland, one feels the heat of the desert, hot as a furnace."

"What will Laurent do next year?"

"He has chosen to stay within the higher education system in the state. Our public universities are dispersed throughout California. He is completing his last year of high school. We would have preferred that he enroll here in San Diego, but he is seeking his independence. He has been accepted at Berkeley in natural sciences."

The cousin concludes: "But enough about us. How have you adapted to American living?"

Dominique pours herself a second cup of coffee. "This is not the first time that we have lived abroad; we spent two years in Tunisia where our standard of living was good. I learned a bit of Arabic, even though the merchants and colleagues of both Pierre and me spoke French acceptably well and, at times, even quite fluently."

"We became acquainted with American Peace Corps volunteers. Life in the major cities was not all that different from what it had been back home. Women were dressed *à la européenne*, except for the more elderly and poorer ones who still went out veiled in public. In the smaller villages, a more traditional way of life and dress prevailed of course. The *barnouk* or veil was more usual there.

"In this country, Pierre has been well-integrated within the NIH community. He is working on the flu vaccine and continuing his research on other vaccines as well; most notably, those to combat the West Nile, Hepatitis C, and AIDS viruses. He travels a fair amount to present the results of his research and to study a variety of epidemics that might arise throughout the country."

"You mentioned that you have resumed your teaching career. How is that going?"

Dominique smiles at the question. "I am holding my own at the Duke Ellington School of the Arts and my colleagues have been very solicitous toward me. I have been touched by their reception. I am a bit concerned over certain tensions between racial groups, but there is no violence. Unfortunately, foreign language studies are not a priority among most of the students. They are more oriented toward math and sciences. The curriculum at this secondary level is not as broad as ours in France. We are occasionally accused of our encyclopedic education, what others might call our general culture."

She continues. "It is a multi-ethnic population of students. There are more distractions here than there are in France and the school day is shorter than ours. I often ask myself if many of my students are really that interested in their studies. There are exceptions of course."

Nicole agrees. "We need to shut off the television set at home and monitor what is taking place on the internet. Barry and I are quite satisfied with the schools that our children are attending. Antoine requires special assistance in some of his courses and the administration has been able to meet his needs."

"We also think a great deal about our children's education. This year, they are following the American curriculum, focusing particularly on their exposure to English. Julie has adapted more easily than has Philippe. There are also some French courses that they follow on weekends in order to not fall behind upon their return to France. They are helped in that regard by the internet."

"I still maintain that the secondary level of education is inferior to ours in France, but the difference is made up at the college level."

Dominique agrees. "I also teach a French literature course at Georgetown University where the students are generally very bright."

* * *

Nicole becomes aware of the time. "There is so much of our lives to share, but do you realize that we have in San Diego the most famous zoo in the country? The first question that you will be asked back in Washington is if you enjoyed visiting our zoo and botanical gardens. We will go to Balboa Park where, in addition to the zoo and gardens, we will find a number of museums and art galleries."

"Balboa?"

"He was the Spanish explorer who was the first to arrive along the Pacific coast in 1513."

The bus tour through the zoo is narrated by a young lady who introduces herself. "My name is Sonya. Our visit through the park will last forty minutes. Please keep your hands inside the bus and do not feed the animals. You may, however, take as many photos as you like.

"The zoo is home to 3,500 animals. The botanical garden boasts 6,500 species of plants."

At the end of the tour, Sonya points out a section that has been set apart. "Those are bears that have been loaned to us by the Beijing Zoo. The mother just gave birth to two pandas within the past few days. You may have seen them on television."

* * *

"We will meet Barry in the Old City for dinner. The architecture there is primarily Mexican, as is also the case in much of the rest of the city. We are only ten miles from the border and San Diego belonged to Mexico during the first half of the nineteenth century."

The cannon in the *Plaza de Los Arenas* is a vestige of the Mexican-American War of 1846-1848. Stores, boutiques, restaurants and museums line the periphery of the square. Antoine leads the group to the Seeley Museum that is devoted to the first transportation company of California. A former stable, one finds models of stagecoaches and their trappings that were used during those early days when Albert Seeley founded the first service between San Diego and Los Angeles. Antoine plays a cowboy role by hopping onto the driver's bench of the first vehicle, but is persuaded to get down by the employee dressed in an outfit from those earlier times. "I would encourage you to watch the video in the visitors' auditorium. It will give you the entire history of this city."

* * *

Before the arrival of the *Conquistadores*, the region had been inhabited by the Kumesaay Indians who had welcomed the first Spanish colonizers. But they quickly revolted after being decimated by the epidemics of smallpox and measles that were introduced by these new immigrants.

The serious colonization of San Diego began in 1769 when the first of twenty-one missions was established by the *Padres* in what is now the state of California.

Independent since 1821, Mexico built a garrison in San Diego, a small village at the time, where the bay served as a significant commercial site. The colonists brought their costumes, their fiestas, their processions and their bullfights along with them. The frontier of the Rio Grande was definitively established by the Guadalupe-Hidalgo Treaty in 1848 at the end of the Mexican-American War.

San Diego expanded rapidly after getting caught up in the Gold Rush and the government established itself in the New City that had been developed by Alonzo Horton in 1867. Destroyed by fire in 1872, the Old City was restored in a Hispano-Mexican style, becoming thereafter a historic park and tourist center.

The group joins Barry at the Casa Bandini restaurant in the Old City for a Mexican meal. Orders are placed for quesadillas and enchiladas, fortified with a jalapeño sauce. Dominique compares the hot taste to that of the Tunisian cooking that she has experienced, the jalapeño sauce similar to the harissa found in the souks of Tunis and the rest of the country.

After the meal, a quick tour of the *Bazaar del Mundo* allows Julie to purchase a few souvenirs following which Nicole suggests a ride over the Coronado Bridge to get another view of the city.

* * *

"Barry is free today and he will be our driver, in our SUV of course. There will be ample room for everyone. We will go first to Horton Plaza. We spoke of Alonzo Horton yesterday when we were in the Old City. It was he who started construction of the New City after 1870."

While the young people delight in shopping, the parents have lunch in the Gas Lamp District where Spanish is spoken as much as English.

"Barry," asks Dominique, "how did you ever find yourself in Saudi Arabia?"

"When I left for that country, I had never been outside of the United States, not even to Canada. I had spent the days of my youth on a farm in Nebraska."

"In the interior of the country."

"Yes. I studied geology in Texas. While this was not a foreign country, for me it was very different."

"For those of us from Nice, the northern part of France would be much the same experience as yours had been."

"Absolutely. Following my graduation, I went to work for Mobil Oil and, after two years in Galveston, Texas, I was sent to Saudi Arabia from where I wandered throughout the region: Yemen, Bahrain, Qatar, Oman. Through my associations with laborers, merchants and colleagues, I learned enough Arabic to make myself understood in the souks. Over time, I met Nicole."

Nicole slaps her hand on the table. "How fortunate for you."

Barry ignores the comment. "We traveled around as I was transferred from place to place."

"I told her that story."

"So here we are in San Diego, while perhaps awaiting Alaska where we think there are important oil reserves. However, many environmentalists, my wife included, are opposed to our drilling there."

Nicole stiffens and cannot keep from commenting: "That would be a real travesty and would violate my own ecological principles."

Dominique feels caught between these divergent views as Barry snaps back. "You can't have it both ways, my dear. To become energy-independent, we must find other sources and it is our opinion at Mobil that Alaska represents part of the solution. Don't worry, we have the technological wherewithal to drill safely."

"That is the government's argument and that of all the big oil companies."

"Well, otherwise we will forever be dependent upon the Middle East and the uncertainties that we find in that part of the world."

Dominique seeks to defuse the tension between husband and wife. "Is there not another dimension that you are both overlooking? I wonder if there is not an element of over-consumption in this country. Your automobiles are big and I find that most Americans are not serious when it comes to energy conservation."

Barry tilts his head back. "Your point is well-taken. At the same time, you must realize that I am not the one who makes the rules. Much of this becomes a political issue. You, the French, have decided to go the nuclear route, which poses the problem of nuclear disposal. To be sure, the ideal may be found in sun and wind, but we are a long way economically from relying exclusively on the two of them."

"I have heard of liquefied gas to propel your autos and France is even experimenting with compressed air. Cars will be smaller and will travel more slowly, but there will be no pollution. Let's hope that new technology will solve some of these problems."

The children's return defuses the controversy. "Maman, I made out very well in my shopping. Laurent showed me around and I found some pretty things."

* * *

Luxury yachts fill the docking spaces along Harbor Drive. Dominique is overwhelmed by several hundred of them. They make their way once again to the Coronado Bridge which spans two miles over the bay and which brings them to the town of Coronado. "This is not the Golden Gate Bridge," says Barry, "but I am always impressed whenever I come in this direction. Look over there at the *Embarcadero* where we just saw all those yachts. You can get a better sense of how many there are from this vantage point."

They come to the Coronado Hotel after crossing the bridge. Nicole indicates that movie stars and political figures can frequently be found here. "You can also see the airport from this location. Arrivals and departures occur practically every minute. The Naval Station of which you may have heard also serves an important role in the economy of the city."

"See those surfers under the bridge, Maman," points out Julie. "That is where Laurent and I went yesterday. I was not all that bad toward the end, Laurent, was I?"

"Julie, you were magnificent."

* * *

Barry made arrangements to use his supervisor's yacht for a short trip along the coast. In her invitation, Nicole had said, "If you come to San Diego, we will definitely need to go out on a cruise."

The Shermans are the owners of a luxurious 75-foot yacht, the *Westward Ho*, which can easily sleep six people. One part of the cabin has a kitchenette with all the imaginable conveniences and a spacious sitting area with two couches, a coffee table, and three deck chairs. Dominique surmises that she need not bring up the subject of ecology.

The vessel departs from the bay and takes a northern course, passing the beaches of Sunset Cliffs, Pescadero, South Mission and North Mission as far as La Jolla where the University of California at San Diego is located.[27] A delicious buffet is served before the turnaround at La Jolla: sliced ham, shrimp, lobster tails, potato salad, caviar, a variety of cheeses, a number of choice California wines and soft drinks.

Before heading back, Barry says that they will move away from the coast. "I will show you a surprise that you are bound to like."

Dominique turns pale.

"Put on your safety vests. The Coast Guard patrols the area and significant fines are levied if you are not properly equipped."

Dominique smiles timidly.

Twenty minutes after leaving the shoreline, Barry shuts down the motor. "Let's just be still now. We are going to wait. Hopefully, we will be lucky."

Dominique wonders what to expect.

"Chut."

The children have wandered into the cabin to whisper quietly. Everyone is motionless on deck for another fifteen minutes. The adults are transfixed by the gentle rocking of the boat and the silence contributes to total relaxation.

Suddenly, Barry points toward the starboard side. In a hushed voice, he attracts their attention. "Look there."

---

[27] There are fourteen Universities of California in different cities: at San Diego, at Berkeley, at Sacramento, at Los Angeles (*UCLA*), etc.

For at least thirty seconds, they are treated to the leaping and plunging of two whales who are seemingly unaware that their antics are being observed. Barry is pleased that the adventure has been successful. "At times, we can also see dolphins putting on a show around boats, but we will settle for this whale extravaganza today."

"We had such a dolphin experience while sailing from Tunis to Marseilles. They actually followed us for over one hour."

The return to the *Embarcadero* takes place in silence. The setting sun reddens the western sky. The last rays of light impart an impressionistic touch to the yachts that are docked there, as well as to the city itself.

* * *

Before leaving San Diego, Dominique invites her cousins to visit Washington and, later, France. "Nicole, you must come. Twenty years between visits is too long. Barry, we don't have much oil back home, but there are interesting places for you to visit."

"I would love to see Normandy. One of my uncles died on Omaha Beach. I also developed a few friendships among French colleagues in the course of my Middle East travels. It would be a pleasure to reconnect with one or two of them."

Julie shows off her local treasure: a Mexican gown with vivid colors. "With my castanets, I can do the fiesta. *Ole!*"

Chapter 26.
March 2002 – La Gaspésie, P.Q., Canada

Many a weary year had passed since the burning of Grand-Pré. When on the falling tide the freighted vessels departed. Far asunder, on separate coasts, the Acadians landed; Scattered were they, like flakes of snow.

Evangeline, by Longfellow

The Benoits have become good friends with Larry and Melanie Winship. Pierre and his colleague have worked together on a number of projects. They collaborated on a report for the Capitol after the Vancouver conference. They traveled together to Kansas City to study an epidemic of hepatitis. They are planning a trip to San Francisco next month for a final seminar. The wives have also become close.

The parents of Melanie, Gérard and Françoise Tremblay, came from Quebec to settle in Maine. They continued to speak French at home and Melanie has retained a fair amount of it, given her attendance at parochial schools taught by nuns. She pursued her studies at Colby College before moving to Paris where she followed courses at the Louvre. Following her return to the United States, she accepted a position at the National Gallery of Art in Washington where she now holds an important administrative position. In that capacity, she was able to find a substantial number of French books for the library collection at the Duke Ellington. Dominique also brought groups of students to the Gallery on two occasions: one time for a slide show in French on the cathedrals of France and another time for a lecture on the châteaux of the Loire.

Pierre outlines the itinerary. "The Winships have planned a short trip to *La Gaspésie.* Larry is familiar with the area. We will leave Wednesday evening after your class at Georgetown. They have planned everything. Melanie has a cousin who owns a B&B in Port-Daniel where we will stay for two nights. We will first fly to Campbelton in New Brunswick, near the Quebec border."

Dominique has tended to the children. "Philippe will enjoy his stay with Ross Appleton and Julie and Juanita have already figured out their few days together."

* * *

La Gaspésie is named for the Gaspé peninsula which advances into the Gulf of St. Lawrence, between the river itself and New Brunswick. In the Micmac Indian dialect, *Gespeg* means 'the end of the world'. While the mountainous interior of the peninsula is essentially deserted, the coast is well-populated during the summer. Life is much more tranquil during the rest of the year for the 150,000 permanent residents. A 600-mile road follows the coast around the peninsula through a number of fishing villages.

Following a restful night in Campbelton, the two couples leave the city by car, crossing the bridge into the Province of Quebec. They enter Pointe-à-la-Croix on the Quebec side and then take the road that leads to Gaspé, located at the far-end of the peninsula. Along the way, they pass through villages carrying picturesque names: Escuminac, Saint-Omer, Maria, Grande-Cascapédia, Saint-Godefroi and Bonaventure. Most are built around a Catholic church, different from the many towns of the United States where small churches of different Protestant denominations are more common. They notice at the same time that one of the churches is in the form of a wigwam in the center of the Gesgapegiag Indian Reserve where seven hundred Micmacs belonging to the large tribe of Algonquins worship. Melanie indicates that the Micmacs have resided here for thousands of years. "They arrived on the scene well before the Vikings, the Basques, the Italians and the French. They now live in permanent housing, having long since given up their tents."

One of their souvenir shops is found along the main road. Three ladies in native garb are weaving straw baskets. Their language is incomprehensible to the visitors. Dominique, fascinated, asks if she may watch them work at their craft.

"By all means. Please sit down and we will show you how to make one of these baskets."

The twenty-minute lesson proceeds with much laughter. Dominique's skills clearly lie in other areas, but she is offered a basket as a gift. She in turn buys four necklaces that will pack easily upon returning to France.

Pierre sifts through the moccasins and thinks of *The Last of the Mohicans* which he read in the days of his youth.

One of the ladies puts a feathered headdress on Larry Winship who throws himself into a spirited dance around the store, much to the delight of the assembled patrons.

* * *

The friends proceed along Route 132 between the coast and a railroad. Melanie gives a history of the region and that of her family during the leisurely ride.

"A Quebec young lady told us of some families that moved to the United States while others chose to stay here," recalls Pierre.

"That is essentially my story," says Melanie. "My ancestors initially came from Brittany in your country. Many Acadians also traced their roots to Poitou and Saintonge in France. The French who settled in the St. Lawrence Valley near Quebec and Montreal originated mostly from Normandy, Picardie and the North of France. Around 1632, others came to Acadia, what is today Nova Scotia, which, along with New Brunswick, Newfoundland and Prince Edward Island, form the Maritime Provinces of Canada. France and England had their disputes over this territory and the settlers found themselves in the middle of this conflict.

"At the beginning of the eighteenth century, France had designs over the Island of Saint John, today's Prince Edward Island, and the northern part of Nova Scotia, what corresponds today to New Brunswick and the northern part of Maine. France constructed a fort at Louisbourg costing fifteen million dollars, a hefty sum at the time, to protect its interests. Subsequently, through the Treaty of Utrecht, England was granted Nova Scotia. As a result, the Acadians were obliged to swear their allegiance to George II, a decision that posed serious problems, for this potentially would put them in opposition to their own French brethren.

"In 1755, Governor Lawrence required the total submission of the Acadian delegation to the English Crown. These strong-willed French immigrants refused to obey this high-handed directive and they were imprisoned without due process in a church in Grand-Pré. They were then deported. This was the beginning of the *Grand Dérangement* wherein eight thousand Acadians were dispersed along the Atlantic Coast from Boston to the Gulf of Mexico. A few vessels even transported some Acadians back to France, England, the East Indies and Corsica. Many family members were separated from one another and their lands were confiscated. The Acadians eventually sought to regroup and this explains why many are found on this peninsula, in northern Maine and in Louisiana."

"We discovered in New Orleans," relates Dominique, "that the descendants of these exiles who made their way to Louisiana are called *Cajuns*, a bastardized version of *Acadians*."

"I have distant cousins who live there whom I have never met."

"But why this fateful decision?" inquires Pierre.

Larry picks up the conversation. "Historians are not in complete agreement on the details, but it can be said that the American colonies had been neglected by Louis XV. England at that time was seeking to extend its sphere of influence in this area, particularly since the ascension of William Pitt. The English feared that the Acadians would join with the French-Canadians from the St. Lawrence Valley and oppose them. This cruel expulsion was their solution to the dilemma."

Pierre adds, "We met a Mr. Villette when we visited Maine a short time after our arrival here. He has an Acadian background and he is part of this regrouping in Presque Isle to which you refer."

* * *

They arrive in Port-Daniel, which overlooks the *Baie des Chaleurs*, a bit before sunset. They have covered half the distance to Gaspé. The Tremblay home is easily found. It is a large two-storey Victorian, *Bleu sur Mer*, with a *Deux Chevaux*[28] French automobile parked in front. Melanie points out the five suns on the outside sign, *Gîte pour Fins Routards*, *B&B for Refined Travelers*. "The five suns give this *B&B* a rating that is equivalent to a five-star hotel."

Armand, Melanie's cousin, and his wife greet them warmly. They are shown to their rooms before dinner. It has been a full day and everyone is weary. Having visited the golf course in Carlton, Pierre is reminded while falling asleep of a round that he played with Larry in Washington. His last thought of the day is that of a bunker shot that he successfully negotiated to save par in a match that won him a five-dollar bet and bragging rights until the next round.

During an early-morning breakfast, the Tremblays relate their B&B story to their guests. "I was a lawyer and Carole a reporter in Montreal and we led a frantic life. While vacationing in this area two years ago, we saw a 'For Sale' sign in front of this house and we made the big decision to buy the property. After the purchase, we found ourselves with a great amount of work to restore it to its present condition. I still tend to some legal affairs through the internet and I return to Montreal from time to time to handle matters there."

"You have a beautiful hearth and the furniture is in good taste."

"You may purchase whatever appeals to you. Many of these pieces are of antique value. Carole and I are always shopping for old furniture and we sell to tourists who stay with us and to passersby who have been given our address. This is a lodging-boutique. As soon as we sell an item, we seek immediately to replace it."

---

[28] Built along the lines of a Model T Ford.

"Even these paintings?"

"Yes. The painting over the foyer is a Haitian piece that was brought to us by our local pastor whom you will meet this evening. He will dine with us. The sale of this piece will assist in his missionary effort."

"And how did you settle upon the name *Bleu sur Mer*?"

"When we came upon the 'For Sale' sign, the exterior was this pale blue color and, of course, we overlook the water. The name seemed appropriate. We needed to gut the interior and do a good deal of remodeling to bring it to its present state. While we have only three rooms for our guests, we believe that they are tastefully decorated. We have chosen to be a high-end residence, deserving of the five suns that we have been granted by *Tourism Québec*. Of the 1,700 B&Bs listed in the Province, only eighteen have achieved this highest rating and we are the only one in all of *Gaspésie*. In all modesty…"

"You are most deserving."

Carole outlines their future plans. "We hope to purchase another lodging in Montreal and to call it *Bleu en Ville* and eventually one in southern France and to call that one *Bleu en Provence*. This last one will be the ultimate fulfillment of our dreams."

Dominique shares Carole's enthusiasm. "We will certainly stay with you when you reach your goal in Provence."

Armand continues, "You are here before the busy season. It is still cool but not nearly as cold as the northern side of the peninsula. The Chic-Choc Mountains protect us. The *Nordais* is a wind farm at *Cap Chat* that takes advantage of the wind that howls continuously on that side of the mountain. It satisfies a large portion of our energy needs and without pollution. It is by far the largest development of its kind in all of Canada."

"We went by the train station yesterday. You have railroad access from all appearances?"

"Rail Canada originates in Montreal, crosses this peninsula from north to south, and follows the shoreline, as you will see on your trip today, all the way to Gaspé."

* * *

They travel on Route 132 as far as Percé. Before arriving there, they come upon the Bonaventure Island and they are surprised by the enormous *Rocher de Percé.*

Consulting the guidebook, Melanie informs the group that the Rock measures five hundred and fifteen feet long and ninety-five feet high. It dates back four hundred million years and is a protected refuge for some two hundred species of birds, among which are gannets, cormorants, guillemots and kittiwakes.

Larry drives around the Forillon National Park. Too cold for a picnic, lunch is eaten at a local restaurant before reaching their destination.

* * *

Gaspé is located at the northeastern tip of the peninsula at the mouth of a bay that faces the Gulf of St. Lawrence. In 1534, Jacques Cartier had claimed the area by raising a cross in the presence of the Indians of the area. He did this ceremonially in the name of François I. Gaspé subsequently gained the title of 'Cradle of Canada'. A monument is found near the Gaspé Museum, six scenes on a vertical marble stone commemorating the event. Cartier had come to this place before making his way up the St. Lawrence River, stopping briefly at the Île-aux-Coudres before settling definitively at what is now the city of Quebec.

Time is well spent in the museum to better understand the country that was to become known as New France.

The first room tells the story of the explorer himself. Cartier showed a love of sailing as a youngster. He rose through the ranks from being a lowly shipboy to becoming a seaman over several years. On the recommendation of the Abbot of the Mont-Saint-Michel, he received the distinguished title of *Capitaine du Roi*, 'The King's Captain', and he was later commissioned to lead an exploratory voyage to the New World, taking possession of the lands that he would find along the way.

Pierre takes great interest in the navigation tools of the sixteenth century: quadrants and astrolabes to view celestial bodies before the appearance of the sextant. Other rudimentary instruments would also help to calculate latitudes on the open sea. Cartier was familiar with the usage of this equipment that had been developed by his precursors. "They made out quite well before having access to our modern technology."

Dominique finds a map that retraces Cartier's itinerary as he made his way to Gaspé. "He skirted to the northeast of Newfoundland, entered the Straight of Belle-Isle to cross the Gulf of St. Lawrence, naming as he went *Havre de la Baleine*, *Blanc Sablon* and the *Isles de Brest*. Another map indicates that he penetrated into the *Baie des Chaleurs* before actually landing at Gaspé, stopping for a time at Port-Daniel. Returning toward Gaspé, he planted his cross on July 24, 1534, an important date in the history of this country as well as ours."

* * *

On the ride back toward Percé, they stop at a flea market where they find inexpensive items of interest. Dominique discovers a scarf between irons and toasters. She also buys table settings that she will pack for relatives back home. Melanie chooses jewelry pieces for Christmas gifts for her daughters. Pierre and Larry browse outside amidst some of the farm machinery. Pierre sits on a tractor and offers to buy it for Dominique.

"Very funny, dear, but you will have trouble getting it home."

Back at the inn, Carole is at the door to receive them. "Have you had a good day?"

Dominique, while tired from the long ride, is enthusiastic. "We fell in love with all your picturesque villages. They are such a contrast to all the big cities that we have seen since we have been on this side of the Atlantic."

"This is exactly the tranquility that we were seeking when we purchased this lodging. It is a pleasure for us to share this lifestyle with you, however briefly."

* * *

While away for just a few days, the two couples sense a change in mood upon returning home. The atmosphere in the Capital appears more somber, even more ominous. There is a growing awareness that an invasion of Iraq could be looming on the horizon.

Sensitive to the politics of the city, Dominique is fretful. "Hopefully, this can all be resolved peacefully."

Chapter 27.
April 2002 – Toronto, Ontario, Canada

Primum non nocere.
First, do no harm.

Medical aphorism

Responding to the invitation of Dr. Grabowski whom he had met in Vancouver, Pierre will deliver a series of lectures at the University of Toronto, considered one of the best in all of Canada. Upon his arrival, he is met by Dr. Floyd Spence, Dean of the Medical School. "You will be teaching our second-year medical students. Are you familiar with our curriculum?"

"I have reviewed the material that you sent me. It is different from ours and I will adapt my talks accordingly."

"Our students have completed four years of college and we accept the best among them, both men and women, using strict academic and personal standards."

* * *

Over a three-week period, Pierre's lectures will constitute a short course in microbiology. He will also oversee practical applications of his material in the laboratory. Finally, he will collaborate with Dr. Grabowski in the study of a pulmonary infection that has ravaged the city these past few weeks.

Dr. Spence offers Pierre a long white coat. "Let me give you a brief tour of the dissection hall used by our first-year students in their Gross Anatomy course."

Thirty groups, each with four students, can be seen, scalpels in hand, hovering over cadavers that they are meticulously studying.

"Where do you find these individuals?" asks Pierre.

"They are mostly indigent people who have come to us from the streets of the city or who have died on our wards."

"That is also the case in our country."

Concentrating on their tasks, the students, in their blood-stained lab coats, are oblivious to the presence of the dean and of the visiting professor.

"In my day," says Dr. Spence, "we worked with bare hands. The students now wear rubber gloves because of the AIDS epidemic, even though we test these cadavers beforehand. The students consult the *Gray's Anatomy* textbook every step of the way. They are now studying the respiratory and digestive systems."

A skeleton is hanging from each of the four corners of the dissecting lab. Pierre recalls the mnemonic that helps identify the bones of the wrist and he and Dr. Spence chuckle as they recite it in unison.

The microbiology laboratory is the next to be visited. "You will spend much of your time here. Your NIH research is known to some of us and will be instructive to our students; I should perhaps say your students."

"As you might well imagine, we have excellent working conditions in Washington. I met your colleague, Dr. Flanagan, from this institution last month. I worked with him as we studied an epidemic in Indiana that resulted from inadequately cooked hamburgers. I would point out that we came across thirty-seven cases, two of which proved to be fatal. I will also discuss other outbreaks that should be of interest to the students."

* * *

The telephone rings. Dr. Spence's secretary answers. "Dr. Kantrowicz calling for you."

"Hello, Harvey. Are we dining together this evening?"

Dr. Kantrowicz has been here for a week, participating in the intern and resident teaching program of the University Hospital. "I will meet you in the lobby of the Intercontinental Hotel where I am staying. I am thinking of a restaurant on Queen's Wharf."

"So, Harvey, what have you done since you arrived here last week?"

Over a cup of coffee, Harvey summarizes his experience with these young physicians. This is the third year that he has shared his expertise within this program. "I spend most of my time in the hospital. I am the Chief of the Infectious Disease Department and am responsible for the team of four women and two men who make up the house staff within the training program."

"The profession is feminizing itself."

"About 50/50 at this point."

"They completed their four years?"

“Those four years of college and an additional four years of medical school. And that is not the end of it. After that, they will have at least three additional years of postgraduate training, a year of internship and no less than two years of residency. Surgical specialties can even be a few years longer. The physicians with whom I am dealing are fulfilling their postgraduate requirements.”

“I am familiar with *ER* on TV.”

“That program gives you a romanticized view of the process. The team also includes three nurses. A fourth-year medical student or two occasionally join us as well.”

“With what kinds of illnesses are you dealing?”

“The usual respiratory and gastrointestinal infections to be sure but, at the moment, we are also occupied with two patients suffering from more serious infections: one with AIDS and the other with a serious pulmonary disorder.

“If you would like, you could join us some morning on our ward rounds. I am generally in agreement with the diagnoses and treatments of the interns and residents. I rarely give an opposing plan of management, but the responsibility of care is ultimately mine and I do propose alternative treatments from time to time.

“Once a week, Fridays at noon, we have our Grand Rounds, a conference that brings together all the interns and residents, many of the staff physicians and many medical students. A patient with a particular problem of interest is presented and a discussion ensues over the management and treatment.

“That said, let us talk about other things. I will start by showing you the *Casa Loma*.”

The *Casa Loma* was built for Sir Henry Pellatt, an English industrial tycoon, who wanted a European-style palace. It was constructed in 1913 on the occasion of a visit by George

V and it carried the substantial price tag of three million dollars. Consisting of ninety-eight rooms, two towers and secret passages, it was and remains an impressive structure, but it never was the commercial success for which it had been intended.

From the Grand Hall, the two friends have a magnificent view of the city. "This room is rented for many receptions. It is the local government that now owns the building and grounds and the proceeds from all the functions that take place here help support several non-profit organizations."

* * *

After his first week, Pierre is more familiar with the campus. He has met several faculty members with whom he dines regularly in the cafeteria. He spends an hour or two each evening preparing for the classes of the following day. The university has made an apartment with all the necessary comforts available to him.

The students are attentive during this first lecture of the day. Each one is seen to be taking abundant notes. It is in the tradition of medical studies to record verbatim everything that the professor says for one never knows when one will be obliged to *spit back* this information in an exam at a later date.

"Let me propose to you this morning a few of our NIH studies. Generally speaking, sick patients arrive at your doorstep one by one. At our institution, by contrast, we have the capacity to study many cases that might appear together or separately in hospitals in any part of the country. It is truly the study of epidemiology."

Pierre begins with the Listeria organism, responsible for cases of meningitis in infants. "As you will come to recognize in pediatrics, these sick infants for the most part represent isolated cases. But several kinds of food have been implicated in outbreaks from this organism. In Canada, for instance, several cases occurred following the ingestion of cabbage; in Massachusetts, from non-pasteurized milk; in Los Angeles, from soft Mexican cheese, and in Switzerland, from a different soft cheese; in England, from paté; finally in France, from frozen pork tongue. Most recently, insufficiently cooked poultry has led to several deaths. Even milk pasteurization has occasionally not been sufficient to prevent this infection. Figures from before 1989 showed nearly two thousand cases of listeriosis worldwide, one-quarter of which were fatal. Strict measures designed to clean up slaughterhouses and regulate appropriate sectors of the food industry were very effective. After 1993, the figures were cut in half. While not a perfect result, this would nonetheless represent significant progress.

"Might I add, however, that we in France have been eating cheeses made from raw milk for two thousand years and we are still around."

The students break out in laughter and some applaud.

Following two questions, Pierre offers another example. "I present this other bacterium for your consideration, the *E. coli*. You might be aware of the outbreak provoked by hamburgers that were eaten at a fast-food restaurant in Washington State not too long ago. You will learn later about the consequences of the syndrome that was identified. It suffices to say for the moment that ground meat may be well-cooked on the surface but inadequately cooked in the center where the *E. coli* organism may not be killed, a situation that can have tragic consequences. The lesson to retain here is obviously to thoroughly cook ground meat."

The professor next indicates that honey ingested by an infant in the first months of life can give rise to cases of botulism, another infection of bacterial origin. These can also be fatal as can be cases of salmonellosis brought on by contaminated eggs.

"It is not my intent to frighten you by relating these stories. At the same time, you can appreciate the importance of microbiology. The preventive measures are often simple as in the case of the cooking of hamburgers. For that matter, we could also talk about toxoplasmosis which we see often enough in France.

"By applying simple hygienic measures, as you can see, we can, if not eradicate, at least significantly diminish the propagation of these epidemics. Physicians that you are about to become, you can understand the necessity of taking these easy steps and you might also remember to wash your hands well between each intervention."

* * *

"Did your lecture go well?" inquires Harvey.

"I think so. The students seemed engaged and they asked pertinent questions. It has been an intense hour and I am ready to see more of Toronto."

"Let us begin with the CN Tower. This is Toronto's symbol, its Eiffel Tower if you wish. It was built in 1976 as a telecommunications instrument."

The elevator takes its passengers up to a height of almost 1,800 feet. Harvey points out several interesting sites from the summit. "As you can see, it is a huge city of between three and four million people. It is the largest city in Canada, the only one along with Montreal to have a baseball team in the United States American and National Leagues."[29]

"You seem passionate about baseball."

---

[29] The Montreal Expos moved to Washington, D.C. in 2005 and became the Washington Nationals.

"Most Americans are. You can see the Skydome, home of the Blue Jays, from here. The roof is closed now, but it is open during the season, weather-permitting. During cold or inclement weather, the roof remains closed and the game is played in a climate-controlled environment. This is the first retractable roof to have been built and the stadium is magnificent, particularly when the roof is open."

"Harvey, you impress me!"

"But the favorite sport in this city is hockey. Toronto is proud of its Maple Leafs.

"Further on to Lake Ontario, you can see the Islands of Toronto. At one time, the shore of the lake had been heavily polluted from all the maritime activity that occurred here. Since 1980, a massive clean-up campaign paved the way for the development that you will experience this evening when we dine at Exhibition Place on Queen's Wharf."

Spadina Avenue at the base of the tower brings out the different waves of immigration for which the city is noted. "Are you looking for a Chinese restaurant, a kosher market, a Portugese *epicerie*, an Indian jeweler? You will find all of these on this street with their multicolored signs and their distinct languages and accents."

Pierre thinks of the globalization phenomenon and admires the acceptance of these diverse nationalities.

"It is one of the attractive features of Toronto," says Harvey, "and one of the reasons why I return each year."

* * *

Before beginning his hospital rounds, Harvey introduces Pierre to the interns and residents. "Dr. Benoit will accompany us this morning and, if he wishes, he may participate in our discussions."

It is a third-year woman resident who is responsible for her junior colleagues and who in turn answers to Harvey. The team comes together on the twelfth floor of the hospital, next to the nurse's station, and the rounds begin with a report of what has transpired overnight. The stories of two patients who were admitted are presented, one of whom is more seriously ill than the other. Both will be examined after the conditions of the current patients have been reviewed.

The team walks from room to room. Harvey mentions to Pierre that the patients remain in the hospital for no longer than necessary as costs are significant and insurance companies are always reluctant to cover any unnecessary procedures or extended stays.

Two patients with pneumonia are progressing satisfactorily. Another woman with a respiratory illness is not responding to ampicillin. A dressing on a shoulder injury needs to be changed.

"Have we recovered an organism from that wound?"

"A *Staph aureus*," responds Dr. Boulanger in French.

Pierre smiles and nods his approval.

One of the patients with AIDS is terminal and is not expected to survive the day. "Is it, as in France, the result of unprotected sexual activity or through drug usage?"

"Absolutely."

A twenty-eight-year-old lady who has received a kidney transplant is convalescing in a private room. "Let us continue the Gancyclovir."[30]

A patient across the hall with a cerebral abscess is responding well to a three-antibiotic regimen. "We can continue the same cocktail, but we should order a follow-up MRI."

---

[30] Antiviral medication prescribed after transplants.

The group next focuses on one of the patients who was admitted late last evening. Dr. Granger, the intern in his first postgraduate year of training, presents the history of the illness and the treatment initiated with the approval of Drs. Boulanger and Kantrowicz.

Pierre asks a few pointed questions on the antibiotic selection. After an animated exchange, Harvey intervenes. "Your diagnosis and treatment are on target, judging by the initial response. Ms. Wu, let us monitor this situation closely and give us another report this noontime."

The second overnight admission appears to be suffering from the respiratory infection that has been plaguing Toronto in recent weeks. The team uses the next forty minutes examining the sick person and discussing the early treatment measures to be taken.

* * *

Pierre spends the next three hours in the microbiology laboratory, looking through microscopes and answering questions.

"Do you think, Professor, that this parasite is an amoeba?" asks the first student.

"This malaria organism," inquires a second student, "would it be the *falciparum*, the *ovale*, or the *malariae* type?"

And still a third request. "Is this egg that of the ascaris worm?"

"No, this is not an amoeba… This is the *falciparum* type of malaria… Yes, this is an *ascarid* egg." He draws the egg of another parasite for a fourth student.

* * *

Harvey, Pierre and Dr. Grabowski preside over the Grand Rounds[31] Friday at noon. This particular session will be devoted to the presentation of the second patient admitted two nights ago[32]. Dr. Grabowski will deal with the highlights of the infection and Pierre will make selected comments. This illness has particularly affected Toronto and the entire city has been concerned. The personnel of this hospital has been appropriately alarmed, given that several physicians and nurses from around the world have been fatally infected.

Pierre, Harvey and Dr. Grabowski have met a bit beforehand in the Doctors' Lounge to compare notes.

Dr. Grabowski begins by retracing the course of the epidemic which, originating in China, has rapidly spread to Vietnam, Singapore, Ireland, the United States and Canada, arriving most recently in Toronto. "On February 28 of this year, the French Hospital of Hanoi requested that the World Health Organization study the case of a sick person who presented with symptoms of an unidentified respiratory infection. Dr. Carlo Urbani, a specialist in infectious diseases, responded to this Vietnamese request. But he himself and the five additional specialists who accompanied him became infected with the virus. During the subsequent weeks, Dr. Urbani courageously treated the patients of the hospital and searched for the cause of this illness. On his recommendation, the French Hospital was quarantined by the Vietnamese government to prevent a serious outbreak. The doctor never saw the results of his work as he died on March 29. Members of Doctors Without Borders and the CDC of Atlanta, Georgia

---

[31] Conference in the hospital amphitheater that brings together the personnel from multiple disciplines.

[32] Description of SARS (Severe Acute Respiratory Syndrome) which will occur in 2003.

continued his work that may well have prevented a world-wide catastrophe."

Dr. Grabowski projects a photo of Dr. Urbani. "Many believe that the microbe responsible for this infection could be named after him because of his early contributions."

The physician continues: "The illness developed into a pandemic in a very few weeks, traveling by plane through Asia, America and Europe. The first cases in Canada were discovered last month, nine here in Toronto and one in Vancouver. The virus was brought here from Hong Kong by a Toronto resident of Chinese origin."

Harvey picks up the narrative: "This lady had traveled to Hong Kong with her husband to visit their son. She contracted the illness which she in turn transmitted to her family and to other people with whom she came in contact upon her return. Soon thereafter, she died, as did the person from Vancouver who had stayed in Hong Kong in the same hotel and at the same time as she had.

"If Guangdong, a province in the southeastern part of China, served as the original site of the infection, it spread quickly to Hong Kong and beyond. In February and the early part of last month, 138 people were diagnosed and treated for this infection and five succumbed. Among these 138 patients were twenty physicians, thirty-four nurses, sixteen medical students and fifteen other medical workers."

Dr. Grabowski concludes this part of the presentation by indicating that all the hospitals in Toronto have been affected by this infection. "Apart from the human toll in the city, there has been an enormous economic downside as well. Hotel reservations have been cancelled and restaurants have become deserted. Our baseball team has had to lower its admission prices to the Skydome and the players from visiting teams have been required to stay in their hotels except for their bus rides to and from the stadium.

"There have been more than eight thousand cases worldwide in twenty-six countries on five continents with 774 fatalities, among whom was a French doctor who came from Hanoi where he worked in the Franco-Vietnamese Hospital."

Dr. Grabowski introduces Dr. Benoit who describes the microbiology of the infection. Pierre commends the Centers for Disease Control from Atlanta for quickly identifying the organism, "helped immensely by the laboratory of this hospital. This new virus has affected humans and presumably has been contracted from animals that have served as reservoirs."

Dr. Grabowski returns to the podium to describe the course of the illness. "Patients initially present with a flu-like illness that quickly evolves into a severe respiratory illness, frequently requiring assisted ventilation. The treatment modalities include very intensive and costly care."

Pierre points out that, at least in the United States and Canada, children have been rarely affected and there have been no fatal cases in the young age group. "I might also cite the example of the transmission of this infection on a Hong Kong-Beijing flight on which twenty-two passengers became ill among the 119 persons aboard, eight of the cases being seated within three rows of the index case."

Harvey projects a few slides and indicates the preventive measures that need to be taken in view of the communicability of this potentially lethal virus. "All of you in this room have felt the consequences of this infection. The patient that was hospitalized here the other night remains in our ICU. It is too soon to predict whether he will survive or not."

Pierre makes a few summarizing comments and the three presenters answer questions from a visibly concerned audience.

Pierre rejoins his students in the laboratory for a last practical session. He indicates in his concluding remarks that infectious diseases will be the most common illnesses that they will encounter in the fields of General Practice, Family Medicine and Pediatrics. "Be attentive to what you see under your microscopes and you will be successful."

* * *

A reception is held at the *Casa Loma* on the eve of the departure of the two visiting professors. Pierre and Harvey are the guests of honor at this event that is attended by many of the medical students, interns and residents. Dr Spence thanks Harvey and Pierre for their services. He approaches Pierre during the meal. "I look forward to meeting you in Washington and later in France."

"It will be my pleasure to be your host."

* * *

During the return flight, Pierre gives thought to the work that remains during his final days at the NIH. Karen Miller will have organized his calendar by the time he arrives at his office next Monday. He will travel for a last conference to San Francisco and Dr. Mark Chase has asked him to return briefly to Tulane University. Between these trips, much of his time will be devoted to his laboratory research and he will need to prepare a report of the past two years for the Pasteur Institute before his return to France.

Harvey implores Pierre to keep good statistics. "We will need to consult them in the coming months and you won't be here to bail us out."

"It might be a good excuse for me to return!"

Chapter 28.
May 2002 – Las Vegas, Nevada

Place your bets;
place your bets...
No more bets.

"Beverages, tea, coffee, cigars, cigarettes."

Pierre makes a half-turn and orders a gin and tonic from the waitress wearing a dark-green and purple miniskirt and a low-cut white blouse. He muses, "Is this some kind of Playboy Club?" He smiles at her and returns to his Blackjack game, "our Twenty-one." The croupier has dealt him an eight and a king and her upturned card is a five. “For my 10-dollar bet, this one is in the bag.”

Four men and three women are seated at the crescent-shaped table. They are very serious and completely focused. Two of the women are chain-smoking. Pierre thinks that he could be at an international conference as two players are Asian, three are African-American and the sixth could be Italian. The croupier is Hispanic. Each player has received two upturned cards. One of the croupier’s two cards is down-turned.

Pierre showing eighteen does not want any additional cards; he passes with a smooth hand signal. The dealer directs her attention to the other players and then turns over her second card, a four... nine with her upturned five. She draws a queen that adds up to nineteen. Pierre grimaces. “Not my luck this time unfortunately.”

One of the smoking ladies was dealt a blackjack hand, a king and an ace, enabling her to win 1½ times her bet of ten dollars. She leaves three five dollar chips on the table for the next hand. One of the Asian men split a pair of sixes, drew a five on one of them, doubled that hand and was dealt a jack. He drew a two on the other six, requested another card, an ace[33] for a draw, what the croupier called a *push*. He managed to double his original bet of twenty dollars on the first of the split-sixes and scooped up a total of forty dollars.

Some players can win considerable amounts of money. Pierre had decided to play no more than one hundred dollars that he had exchanged for twenty five dollars chips. He finds himself down to sixty dollars after several hands that have mostly favored the dealer.

The waitress returns with her tray of drinks and extends her free hand. “Your gin and tonic, sir.”

---

[33] An ace can count for either one or eleven in Blackjack.

"Thank you."

Pierre smiles again, gives her a $5 chip as a tip and catches an elbow in the ribs. "Pay attention to your cards and not to the playmate."

"My dear, might you be a bit jealous?"

"Be careful or I could create a scene."

"Not at all. You are my playmate and you are going to bring me good luck."

Sure enough, Pierre is dealt a blackjack, a pair of eights that he successfully splits and a four and seven combination that he doubles and wins. The croupier busts a few times and Pierre is soon holding more than two hundred dollars in chips. "See, darling, you are truly my good-luck charm."

At the end of the 'shoe' and before the next shuffle, Pierre 'colors' in his chips and leaves the table with one black, two green and three red ones that he will cash in for one hundred and sixty-five dollars at the redemption window. He and Dominique then decide to rejoin the children.

"That waitress really wasn't too bad!… Just kidding."

Pierre continues, "One of the smoking ladies lost at least three hundred dollars, but she was not a good player. She drew cards when she should not have and she passed a few times when she needed to improve her hand with another card. For my part, I won sixty-five dollars and I am pleased. I had a good time."

It is said that those who are able to count cards can regularly win at Blackjack. The story is told of teams of players who unite against the House to win particularly large sums of money. If the casinos become aware of these strategies, those players can be summarily excluded from playing anywhere on the Strip. Using such techniques, a group of MIT students won more than $100,000 in the course of a single weekend!"

* * *

The Benoit family has come here on the advice of Harvey Kantrowicz. “You absolutely must see Las Vegas before going home!” Dominique had found an ad in *Time Magazine*: three days at Caesar’s Palace, airfare included, for $369 per adult and half that amount for each child, “a deal to not pass up.”

The children have wandered around the hotel and have been impressed by the upscale lobby: simulated Roman columns and statues, one of which is a replica of the *Venus de Milo*. Julie and Philippe have found it amusing. For Dominique, it is a bit “over the top!”

They stroll along the Strip, the grand boulevard between the luxury hotels and casinos: the Sahara, Circus Circus, the Mirage, Harrah’s… more than twenty in all. Taxis, limousines with tinted windows and late model cars bustle about. An occasional delivery truck is also seen. On the opposite side, a reproduction of the Eiffel Tower near the *Hôtel de Paris* catches their eye. “Will we get a glimpse of stars from Hollywood? I would love to see Harrison Ford or Brad Pitt.”

“Of course, Julie,” answers Philippe. “That is the girl in you. But why not Julia Roberts or Nicole Kidman?”

It is a dry heat. Las Vegas, ‘the Prairie’ in Spanish, is an oasis in the middle of the desert. In 1829, a Mexican had lost himself before finding a water source around which a growing population settled and which later grew through the arrival of the railroad toward the end of the nineteenth century. The city itself was founded in 1905 and it rapidly became the Gaming Capital, close to the border with California where gambling was not allowed. It is estimated that thirty-three million tourists descend upon this site annually in search of that elusive fortune that everyone seeks.

Weddings that take place in the chapels of most of the hotels are another industry of Las Vegas. The formalities are perfunctory, quick and easy; no questions asked of the spouses and no waiting period. All that is needed is a priest, a minister, a rabbi or, more often than not, a justice of the peace who in many instances might even be the concierge of the hotel.

The ceremony itself can range from the most simple to the most elaborate, according to the means of those who are being married. The format might be traditional, a situation which arises from time to time. More frequently, a more casual atmosphere prevails. More than 100,000 couples marry each year, Valentine's Day in February being by far the most popular day. To see recently married couples in their wedding gowns and tuxedos at the gambling tables surprises nobody.

* * *

A visit to the Luxor Hotel, a kilometer from Caesar's Palace and a short bus ride away, has been planned for the afternoon. Built in the form of a pyramid, it easily stands apart from the rest of the hotels. The family enters between the paws of a gigantic sphinx. Inside, they immediately gaze at a tall obelisk, not unlike the one on the Place de la Concorde. The lower part of the walls is covered with hieroglyphics and photos: pharaohs, queens, pyramids and temples. Statues and columns are scattered about the spacious vestibule which surrounds the obligatory casino. The visitors are attracted by the noise of slots. "How can we possibly resist?" asks Pierre.

"You will have your chance later."

Looking upward, they are struck by the rooms that appear, level by level, to be hooked to the inner walls of the pyramid. The floor above the casino houses a museum that tells the story of ancient Egypt. The guide brings a group into a room that has been meticulously reconstituted as the tomb of

Tutankhamen. Panels explain how in 1922 Howard Carter, an English archeologist, discovered somewhat fortuitously the tomb of the young sovereign in the Valley of the Kings nearly thirty-three centuries after his death. These rooms have been designed with the assistance of Egyptian historians to guarantee the authenticity of the reproduction. In the simulated words of Howard Carter, they learn of the serendipitous way in which the tomb was discovered.

The parents are surprised at the interest that Philippe shows. Julie is amazed by the opulence of the rooms covered with gold.

"Don't forget that it was on the backs of the poor and the voiceless that these marvels were built, not unlike our cathedrals and the palace at Versailles!"

Philippe replies, "I never thought that I would receive an egyptology lesson in Las Vegas."

"Casino culture; that's America."

* * *

The *Bellagio* serves as the next setting that the family visits before attending the presentation of the *Cirque du Soleil O* performed by a troupe that is permanently attached to this hotel.

In this city that constantly dazzles, there is no escaping the luxury that is continuously on display: abundant marble, exquisite tapestries, authentic crystal chandeliers. There is a gallery that presents priceless works of art that have been loaned from prestigious places such as the Boston Museum of Fine Arts and the Metropolitan Museum of Art of New York. For a modest price, one can visit at one's leisure. "I hope they are well insured," comments the ever-practical Pierre.

Naturally, there is the quick walk through the casino on the first floor.

The *Cirque du Soleil* was created by a group of amateurs in the Baie Saint-Paul area of Quebec in 1984 on the occasion of the 450th anniversary of Jacques Cartier's arrival in Canada. The remarkable skills of this group were quickly popularized and the ensuing tours were a hit wherever they went. The synchronized swimming is particularly delightful and Philippe is amazed upon seeing the piano player on a stage in the middle of the water disappear before his eyes, apparently submerged with his instrument to the bottom of the pool.

Julie agrees, "They deserve their acclaim."

In front of the hotel is the sight and sound display of the 'Dance of the Fountains', geysers of water rhythmically and colorfully rising and falling to blaring music.

Philippe wonders how they manage to find so much water in the middle of the desert. "It comes from Lake Mead, retained by Hoover Dam on the Colorado River," answers a bystander. "It is the largest artificial lake in the world."

* * *

Pierre suggests a visit to New York-New York this Saturday morning. The NY-NY is located at the intersection of Tropicana Avenue and Las Vegas Boulevard along with the MGM, the Tropicana and the Excalibur. These four hotels combine for a total of almost fifteen thousand rooms.

A sixty-foot Statue of Liberty in the middle of a version of the East River greets the visitors at the foot of the NY-NY facade. Frank Sinatra's voice is heard in the background singing his rendition of 'New York, New York'. A semicircular barrier surrounding the East River water is draped with the shirts of firefighters and policemen from all the states in the country in memory of their comrades who perished in the attack of September 11th of last year.

The visitors are further enchanted by songs of 'The Voice'. The neighborhoods of Old New York are reproduced: Greenwich Village, the Bronx, Brooklyn. Large photos bring back those earlier times and Italian, Irish and Jewish eating places recapture the essence of the immigrant populations that contributed to the development of the city.

The children show an interest in the rollercoaster that is constructed above the New York-New York while sipping coffee in an Irish pub. "Why don't you take a ride while your mother and I visit the casino. I would like to shoot some dice at the craps table and your mother might give roulette a try."

* * *

Craps is one of the oldest games known to mankind. Dice have even been found in the pyramids and in the ruins of Pompey. The table on which the game is played is formidable, 18 x 5 feet, but the game itself is quite simple. Significant amounts of money can be won if chance favors the player long enough. The opposite, of course, also holds true. Whooping and hollering invariably occur as the game unfolds and particularly if a winning streak is in progress.

"It is my turn with the dice, Dominique. Blow on them to make me a winner."

With the 'point' established, Pierre tosses two 5 dollar chips to the attendant to be placed on the number 8. He wins the bet and the 6 to 5 odds earn him twelve dollars. He then rolls a 7 and loses his turn with the dice. After twenty minutes, he finds himself ahead by thirty dollars and he moves on with his wife; "It is my turn to watch you play, dear."

They walk slowly around the casino. Sights and sounds never fail to tempt the players who are enticed by the prospect of making a fortune, a wish which for the most part is nothing but a pipe dream. The gamblers gloat over the shiny red car on display on a revolving stage. The slots below are all occupied by those who hope to win it.

Dominique finds a chair at a roulette table. She is among four who are seated. Two other players remain standing.

"Place your bets… Place your bets." The attendant waves his hand palm down slowly. "No more bets."

Dominique plays the birthdates of the family and loses several five dollar bets. Number 19 finally pays her 35 to 1 and the attendant slides a stack of chips worth $175 in her direction. After another fifteen minutes at the table, she finds herself behind by $25. Pierre reminds her that she would have left the table a winner if she had stopped playing after her number 19 wager.

"Several of the players lost much more than I did."

"Small consolation, I would say."

Realizing that they come from the *Côte d'Azur*, they decide to have lunch at the Monte Carlo Hotel, not far from the New York-New York, and they are naturally drawn to the casino. "Does it resemble the real Monte Carlo Casino from back home, the one from Monaco? Will we see the adjoining *Café de Paris*, the Grand Prix raceway, the Palace of the Principality?"

They feel deceived by the difference in style, by the lack of elegance and at times even by the incivility. Where are reminders of the yachts in the bay, the elegant homes on the side of the mountain, the style of the *Belle Époque*?

This casino is like all the others on the Strip: too many gamblers in blue jeans and T-shirts. Where are the women in long gowns and the men in formal wear? There are simply none to be found.

The morning events are reviewed over a sandwich. Julie is pale as a ghost. "The rollercoaster ride was scary. Thankfully, Philippe protected me." Pierre gives an account of Dominique's roulette experience and launches into a lesson on the probabilities that favor the 'House'. Everyone agrees to a free afternoon. The family will gather at the Sports Bar at 5 p.m.

* * *

The Kentucky Derby takes place annually at 6:15 p.m. on the first Saturday of May. The race itself lasts only two minutes, but the preliminaries go on for a good 1½ hours. Churchill Downs in Louisville is the site of this most famous race. Kentucky, it is maliciously felt by many in the rest of the country, is the state where the people have two primary interests: basketball and horses. Horses, it turns out, seem to win out over humans. The tradition at the Kentucky Derby holds that the women dress well and that their wardrobes include striking, and even outrageous, hats. One is there for the spectacle to be sure, but more likely to be seen.

The winning horse achieves celebrity status, of course, and wins a small fortune and considerable acclaim for its owner and trainer. The best three-year olds compete in this six-furlong race and the amount of betting staggers the imagination. The jockey receives ten percent of the take.

The children enter the bar with their parents. They would ordinarily not be allowed to be present for this event because of their age, but the crowd is so overwhelming that nobody is there to notice. As it turns out, there is hardly space to move. Multiple television screens surround the semicircular room. The announcer offers a volume of statistics on the eighteen horses, their owners and jockeys that should allow any intelligent bettor to predict the exact order of finish. The cameras are fixed alternately on the horses and the spectators, particularly on the ladies and their hats.

Dominique and Pierre bet $10 each on the favorite. Philippe gives his father $2 to play a long shot to place.

The parents lose and Philippe wins. His $2 on *Funny Cide* earns him $12.40.

The bar quickly empties. The favorite has lost and most of the bettors are disappointed, many are despondent. For Dominique and Pierre, the loss is of little consequence, but they are effusive in their comments to Philippe. Dominique tears up her ticket. "The important thing is to have witnessed the most important race of the year. The next time, I will wear a hat."

"You will be ravishing, as usual."

* * *

"We will cross the boulevard and dine at the *Hôtel de Paris*. It is only fitting that we should make our way to the base of the Eiffel Tower."

Knowing what his father's response will be, Philippe nonetheless poses the question. "Papa, what do you think?"

"The Tower in Las Vegas? There is no longer anything sacred."

After the Tower, there is a replica of the *Arc de Triomphe* near the entrance to the hotel. "We are almost back in our country."

There is a shopping area in the vestibule. Dominique purchases four croissants for tomorrow's breakfast in a patisserie *à la française*. Pierre is more interested in *La Cave* which stocks the best French wines. He buys a *Châteauneuf-du-Pape* before rejoining the women at a boutique where Julie is persuading her mother to buy a dress for a special occasion. He gulps upon seeing the price but refrains from commenting.

Thc *Mon Ami, Gabi* terrace restaurant attracts Philippe's attention. "It is the perfect place from which to watch the girls go by and I am famished." They inspect the menu and engage the waiter. His French is impeccable. Two accordionists pass from table to table. “Could you play ‘*La vie en rose*’ for us please?” Dominique feels nostalgic. “It will remind me of Edith Piaf and Montmartre, *la Butte*. It brings tears to my eyes just thinking of her.”

Considering his Kentucky Derby winnings, Philippe announces that he might like to be a jockey. “Not if you continue to pack away the food the way you do.”

Dominique offers her opinion at the end of the meal. “The ambiance is great, but the cuisine is ordinary. It does not rival that of the Jules Verne Restaurant in our Eiffel Tower.”

“Your judgment is by our *cordon-bleu* standard,” shoots back her husband. “That sets the bar very high.”

* * *

Dominique and Pierre see a last opportunity to try their luck as the children make their way to the observation deck of the hotel. The ‘Club Slot’ is the ideal place to be swindled amidst its sights and sounds. The slots are the most profitable game for the casinos. Studies have shown that, on average, a player who sits down with one hundred dollars ends by standing up having lost sixty dollars. Considering that thirty-three million gamblers pass this way each year, one can only gasp at the staggering arithmetic!

Everything is designed to *stick it* to the slot player by having the machines accept indiscriminately paper money of different denominations and granting credits accordingly. It is no longer necessary to pull the handle of the one-armed bandit. It suffices to press a button and the credit increases or decreases according to the results. The individual encounters thereby succeed themselves at great speed.

Pierre wonders what attracts all these people to sit before these games. Obviously, there is the hope of winning! But there is also the anesthetizing effect of the pulsating music and the flashing lights. He observes the absence of clocks and windows that make one unaware of time. Moreover, the game has become dehumanized since the player need no longer be reimbursed at the cashier's counter but need only to insert his or her coupon into an automatic money distributor. The winnings or losses are dispensed with no human interaction.

Pierre approaches one of these slots, which 'swallows' his twenty dollar bill and records 80 credits of 25 cents. He succeeds in aligning enough peaches, cherries and pears to salvage the majority of his credits and he moves on after twenty minutes having lost six dollars. "Now it is your turn, Dominique."

She sits down in front of a slot called 'Little Green Men'. For her twenty dollar bill, she receives 400 five cent credits. After a few losing plays, she succeeds in placing three 'Martians' on the payline. The machine goes crazy. She has won the jackpot. The 2000 credits add up to one hundred dollars. Dominique is ecstatic. She has more than recovered her losses from the previous evening.

Pierre reminds her: "You did not know when to leave the roulette table. Maybe you should quit while you are ahead."

"You are absolutely right. Let us hurry before the 'House' takes away all my winnings."

From the top of the Eiffel Tower, Philippe and Julie have been able to count the hotels in both directions, twenty-three in all. The neon lights of each hotel illuminate the night-time sky. Philippe remarks, "Look at all the glitz of Treasure Island and the Sahara."

The Bar Napoleon is the meeting place before returning to Caesar's Palace. "Mama, you will go home a winner, thanks to the 'Little Green Men'," offers Julie.

"Keep me away from the casinos now. I could easily develop a gambling problem."

* * *

The morning of departure has arrived. Suitcases are left at the reception desk while they walk along the Strip a last time. The Hotel Venetian beckons. "Julie, I would prefer to see the Pirates of Buccaneer Bay. Will you come with me?" begs Philippe.

The parents enter the lobby as the children run off in the opposite direction. Pierre and Dominique agree that they could easily be in the *Piazza San Marco* as they ease into a gondola along the Grand Canal. They can simultaneously window shop during the leisurely ride. It is a winding-down time for them after the commotion of the previous three days.

Rejoining her parents, a thrilled Julie shows her mother Céline Dion's autograph. "I saw her in the lobby of our hotel this morning. She was very gracious. Her French is excellent… with a Canadian accent. I can't wait to show my friends."

* * *

A last gambling opportunity presents itself at the McCarron Airport. "Even here," mentions Philippe, "there are all these slot machines. Let me try to build on my Kentucky Derby success."

His father winces. "Play no more than $5. You should go home with at least some of your winnings."

Predictably, Philippe loses his bet. "So long, Las Vegas. We had a great time. This is really an unbelievable place. The next time, we will go to Monte Carlo, twenty-five minutes from home, but we will always remember what we did here."

Chapter 29.
June 2002 – Washington, D.C.

Pomp and Circumstances

The administration of the Woodrow Wilson High School has selected Julie to make the opening student remarks at the graduation ceremony that takes place annually on the first Friday of June at 6:30 p.m. The gymnasium is transformed into a festive hall for this event. A stage has been set where the basketball hoop would ordinarily be found and it is decorated with flowers and flags of the country, the school and the city. On the wall behind the stage hang pictures of class activities and sporting events.

The Secretary of Education and the mayor of Washington have been enlisted to preside over the ceremony. The chairman of the school committee, the school principal, three teachers and two students also occupy places onstage. Padded folding-chairs are arranged for the graduates, their families, the faculty, the school band and friends: fifteen hundred people in all.

The band played the traditional *Pomp and Circumstance* during the entry march of the teachers and students. All are dressed in caps and gowns. Among the graduates, red gowns are worn by the boys, white gowns by the girls. The caps of course are the traditional mortar boards, several of which carry messages: *Thanks Mom and Dad. Hi Sis*.

Digital and video cameras of parents and grandparents immortalize the occasion. A minister[34] offers the benediction. The principal and the mayor welcome the crowd. Dr. Higgins then introduces Julie, who holds the title of salutatorian and asks her at the end of his own remarks if she feels a bit Americanized.

"If I had been told upon my arrival in this country that I would be delivering a speech before this audience, I would never have believed it. But do I feel Americanized? No, not really. What I can say though is that I know this country and its people so much better now. I will always remember my stay here and I will happily recall the places that I have been privileged to visit, the people whom I have met and the friendships that I have made. I will not forget the welcome that I received from the students and teachers upon my arrival and all the help that I received along the way."

Julie looks at the crowd and notices Philippe who has approached the stage to take a picture of his sister.

"This said, I am greatly honored to be speaking to you and it is my turn to welcome you in the name of my 346 classmates. We are grateful to you, parents and teachers, for all that you have done for us. You are here to share in our joy on this wonderful occasion."

Julie receives a generous applause from the audience. She is followed at the podium by the Secretary of Education who

---

[34] Ministers, priests and rabbis take turns from year to year in this capacity.

offers her brief congratulatory remarks. The three brightest students are recognized and awarded scholarships to pursue their studies. The valedictorian is introduced and he addresses his remarks more specifically to his classmates. He recalls a number of special events over the course of the past four years: the basketball title of two years ago, the success of the debating team, the triumphs of the theater group, the domination of the mathematics club highlighted by the visit of Dr. Holmgren from MIT. "Let us not forget these precious moments which we have shared and may we be proud of the diploma which we are about to receive."

Derek receives a prolonged ovation. Then comes the conferring of diplomas by the chairman of the school committee, the students marching alphabetically across the stage, thereby mixing red and white gowns. The school band runs through an impressive repertoire during this twenty-minute segment. Flashbulbs capture every smile.

Julie receives her diploma with honors and, returning to her seat, thinks, "I will have it framed and will put it in a special place at home."

The last handshake is given to Walter Ziegler. While receiving his diploma, he jokingly mentions, "Why am I always last in line?"

The graduates all stand to sing the school anthem. Dr. Higgins makes his final remarks and the band strikes up *Pomp and Circumstance* once again as the students and teachers file out of the gymnasium to the applause of the crowd.

Caps and gowns are deposited in a nearby classroom and the graduates rejoin their families in the schoolyard. They gather in small groups of three or four students with family members and friends, congratulating each other, hugging, embracing and laughing. Julie, Philippe and their parents mix in among the crowd. Pierre has a chat with Julie's English teacher. Dominique meets Mrs. Farley, the Secretary of Education. Philippe prefers to speak to Julie's girl friends.

As dusk sets in, a dozen yellow school buses appear to transport the graduates to the vestibule of the Kennedy Center for the Performing Arts, transformed for the occasion into a discotheque. There they will play games and dance the night away under the discreet chaperoning of parents from the junior class. The party lasts until 5 a.m. and the graduates then find themselves on the banks of the Potomac to witness the rising of the sun. Many realize that they may be seeing each other for the last time.

Exhausted from their all night party, they are brought back to their school, again by bus, where they are met by their parents who bring them home and put them to bed.

* * *

The Benoits are touched by the events that have been organized in their honor. Pierre received a plaque in the amphitheater of the NIH in recognition of his services over the past two years. Karen Miller, always attentive to details, had invited the Secretary of Health and Human Services, Thomas Regan, and the Ambassador of France. Several members of Congress were also in attendance. Herbert Longval, Senator from Louisiana, presented Pierre with a painting of *Mardi Gras in New Orleans*. The final toast had been followed by a dinner in town, bringing together the members of the team, Drs. Murphy, Cousins, Winship and Kantrowicz and their spouses.

On her part, Dominique was acknowledged by the Duke Ellington personnel. Dr. Clark spoke eloquently of her significant foreign-language contributions to the school at a reception organized by her colleagues in the library. Her students gathered around her for a group photo and they presented her with a school banner.

Phil was saluted by his Jaguar teammates who in turn gave him his soccer shirt with his favorite number 10, that of his French hero Zidane. "Because of you, we will retire this number," said Ross Appleton. Philippe had even been complimented for the progress that he showed on the baseball diamond to which he had responded, "You are very kind, but, as I return to my country, I believe that my baseball career is over. As you may know, the game is just not played in my country."

* * *

The next door neighbors, Carl and Marion Lindsay, hosted a barbecue two evenings before the family's departure. Acquaintances were brought together to share many of the highlights of the past two years. The women delighted in acknowledging some of Dominique's culinary hits: bouillabaise, cassoulet, boeuf bourguignon. Pierre could not restrain himself from mentioning the time when one of the men had wanted a Coca Cola to drink with his meal. Pierre had been adamant. "No, no; Coca Cola is not allowed with this French cooking. You may only drink wine to truly appreciate what my wife has prepared, even if it must be a California variety." Bill had been taken completely by surprise by his *faux pas* and everyone laughed.

Dominique indicated the time when Julie gave a lesson to the supermarket baker on the proper way of preparing croissants. "You should really make them *à la française*. Yours are not flaky enough."

A friend employed at the French Embassy had recruited Dominique last year to help organize a reception on the occasion of July 14, the *Fête de la Bastille*. This gathering for ambassadors and dignitaries had been a huge success. "You are leaving a bit too soon this year. We could use you as our hostess."

The men too had taught Pierre much about American sports, making him aware of the likes of Tiger Woods, Alex Rodriguez and Cal Ripken, Jr. The Redskins were a favorite topic of conversation in season even though they generally were a lackluster team on the field. RFK Stadium was nonetheless filled to capacity every Sunday from September through December.

Politics inevitably entered into the conversation. The Bush administration was the subject of intense debate, particularly as the topic revolved around the possible invasion of Iraq. Colin Powell's stance and those in other positions of responsibility were assessed critically by the majority.

John Morrison, a member of the CIA, was prudently silent on the subject, but expressed concerns more openly on North Korea and Iran.

* * *

The next morning, the last-minute details need to be addressed: some house cleaning, stopping of mail, passports, suitcases. "Okay, we are leaving for New York tomorrow. You could at least help me a bit. Julie, you will be responsible for breakfast. Philippe, go pick up your room and start packing.

Philippe hits the off-button on the TV remote. "Maman, you are repeating yourself. We are no longer little children. This is not our departure from Nice. We are grown-ups now and we know what needs to be done."

Dominique simulates a frown. "Everyone to his or her chores and no further discussion."

Chapter 30.
July 2002 – New York

Auld Lang Syne.

This time, Melanie and Larry Winship are kind enough to accompany the Benoits to the 'Big Apple'. They arrived yesterday evening by plane and stayed at the Stanhope Park Hyatt Hotel, across from the Metropolitan Museum of Art.

The reception desk will store everyone's luggage during this brief visit before the family's scheduled flight this evening.

After a light breakfast near Central Park and last-minute gift purchases for the grandparents, the departing family would like to visit Ground Zero. They all recall having followed the events of last September 11th in this city on television and Pierre can almost still hear the Pentagon crash that he witnessed from afar that day. "We have two hours to see that about which we have talked so often."

In agreement with the Winships, they take cabs by way of Wall Street and get off on Vesey Street. They pause before photos of many of the nearly three thousand victims. Included as well are those of the sixty policemen, twenty-three from the city itself and thirty-seven from the port, and those of the 343 firemen who heroically died in the line of duty. Some are pictured in uniform, others in civilian clothes.

How can one ever forget the horror of the planes flying into the Twin Towers and the imploding of these enormous buildings of which New York had been so proud? They revisit the television images that were replayed so frequently, people throwing themselves into space to their deaths and the thick cloud created by the crumbling structures. Nearly all the families of the NIH, the National Gallery and the children's school had been touched by the catastrophes of this city or of the Capital. One of Philippe's friends lost his father in the Pentagon crash. Julie can recall her chemistry teacher telling the story of a cousin who scrambled down forty-seven flights of stairs to safety not more than five minutes before the implosion of the North Tower. She ran along Vesey Street as fast as she could and turned in horror when she heard the deafening noise of falling steel and concrete. The tale is again told of the blind man who was guided to safety by his seeing-eye dog. The flight of Melanie's supervisor was diverted to Canada as she was returning from an art exhibit in Dallas, Texas. She finally made it home three days later. Pierre remembers, as they stand facing where the South Tower had stood, his meeting last year with Dr. Abraham Schwartz on the eighty-third floor. He too had been counted among the victims. They remain there for a time without speaking, observing this enormous crater that defines Ground Zero and they walk the periphery slowly in honor of those who lost their lives in this terrorist attack.

"To think that we had a cup of coffee in this very place," mentions Julie. "From Ellis Island," adds Dominique, "we had a great view of the city skyline. How different it must be now."

A hard-hatted worker confirms this statement. "I ride the ferry every day. It chokes me up every time I look in this direction and fail to see that skyline as it had been and to which you refer."

Before leaving the scene, Dominique inwardly recites a brief prayer. Each person, teary-eyed, realizes that the world has changed since September 11, 2001.

Together they ponder over lunch the pilgrimage that they have just taken to this place that they will never forget. They then retrieve the suitcases that they had earlier left at the hotel.

* * *

The departure from JFK Airport to Paris is set for 7:50 p.m. Pierre, always anxious before trips of this kind, is insistent on checking in by five o'clock in order to go through security at a leisurely pace. "After 9/11, there is bound to be much greater scrutiny of passengers than there had been two years ago and the lines will be long."

Julie is already nostalgic. "What memories! What stories to tell. But, for the moment, I should buy my last issue of *Seventeen* in order to have reading material during the flight."

Larry helps Dominique with her luggage. "Let us hear from you when you arrive back home."

Melanie insists that they stay in touch. "As you have suggested, we promise to visit you next year. It will be your turn to show us around."

"Thanks for all your help in assisting my students at the National Gallery."

Larry teases Philippe one last time. "Don't forget the soccer moves that you learned here."

"I will be happy to wear my Jaguar shirt. From now on, it will be football and not soccer. Check the newspapers for my name when France competes in the World Cup in 2004!"

* * *

"So long, USA! Auld Lang Syne! Until we meet again!"

Chapter 31.
July 2002 – Paris-Nice
The Return

To see Paris and Nice
once again.
To finally be back home.

With an on-time departure the previous evening, the family arrives at Charles de Gaulle Airport at 7:55 a.m. Dominique's parents, Alma and Gérard, are there to greet them and to bring them to their home in Vésinet on the outskirts of Paris. Everyone is tired as the time zone changes in this direction are particularly difficult to negotiate.

A substantial breakfast has been prepared by the children's grandmother. "You will finally have something decent to eat."

"But, Grand-mère, do we look malnourished?" intones Philippe.

The newly-arrived sleep until mid-afternoon and they re-group around the table once again for finger foods and pastries. A barrage of questions inevitably follows. "Did you really eat well?"

Dominique senses her mother's concern over food. "You must realize that I still did most of the cooking and so our family was protected. In the circles in which we traveled, there were a few hefty teachers and researchers, but most managed to keep their weight in line."

"So," asks Dominique's mother, "is Washington nicer than Paris?"

Pierre is first to answer. "I became very familiar with the city. The administrative center is very well-designed. The Metro system is superb. The cherry blossoms seem to explode throughout the city and along the Potomac River in the spring and, much like Paris, winters can be raw and cold. An inch or two of snow can be especially disagreeable and can paralyze traffic everywhere. Fortunately, that does not occur often."

"But you have not answered my question."

"Well then, in my opinion, Paris is still nicer than Washington."

Gérard looks at Philippe. "What impressed you the most?"

"Montana was my best experience. Being a real cowboy for those three weeks was such a thrill."

Dominique weighs in. "Pierre and I especially liked New Orleans: its jazz, its French history. *Mardi Gras* was exciting. Quebec and *La Gaspésie* obviously also had a strong French connection, but the Canadian accent was always a challenge. There were times when we could barely make out what people were saying."

Pierre continues. "We were touched yesterday in New York by Ground Zero. We spoke to you of course about our own day on September 11th at the time itself. We lived the

Washington event, the plane launching itself into the Pentagon. We were all frightened to say the least. We had no idea how this would be resolved."

His father-in-law pursues. "And your work?"

"We were well-accepted and treated. Dominique will tell you more about her students. My colleagues were most welcoming. To think that they sent me to deal with members of Congress at the Capitol where once again everyone was most cordial. These elected officials had warm feelings toward our country and people. Your daughter was also one of my most important assets with her personality and her French cooking. 'Dom's dinners', as they were called, were a success."

His wife is more emphatic. "An unrivaled triumph, my dear. No need to hold back on the compliments."

Julie is questioned in turn. "Boston was a very interesting city, but my best memory is of having delivered an address at my graduation ceremony, proof that my English had become very understandable. We don't have graduations like those here in France, but they are rather important events over there and I spoke in front of fifteen hundred people."

"Congratulations; we are very proud of you. On a separate subject, you told us about the San Antonio dousing and we were amused."

"Yes, we were amused as well but not right away," adds Pierre. "Some spectators were reimbursed for what was for them more than an inconvenience, but Philippe would not consider leaving. We concluded by turning this initial awkward drenching into a comical event. There was much laughter when the workmen appeared to dry the playing surface with their buckets and kitchen mops."

"Well," says Gérard to his grandson, "football fan that you are, you may have read how miserably we played against Korea."

“The Americans call it soccer. I followed a few of the matches. I had excellent teammates on the Jaguars and the Woodrow Wilson team was quite successful as well.”

Julie gives an account of some of her American holiday experiences: January, Martin Luther King Day in Chicago; May, Memorial Day in Phoenix; and November, Thanksgiving Day in West Virginia.

Philippe tells the Lieutenant Schaeffer story. “He parachuted behind the German lines at Sainte-Mère-Eglise. He spent a year in France and made friends among those who participated in the Resistance movement as you had, Grand-père.”

“I met some Americans. They liked our cognac and some even learned to speak French quite well. We were fighting of course for the same cause.”

Julie intervenes. “Philippe and I really liked Phoenix and we will tell you the story of the Superstition Mountains at some point.”

“We received the photo of your Chicago *afro*, Julie,” says her grandmother with a chuckle. “What did you think of your sister, Philippe?”

“Actually, she was rather cute.”

Julie adds, “I had a wonderful time in Chicago and, after that trip, I sent Aunt Georgina and Sophie a letter in which I thanked them profusely. I included a note for my phenomenal dance partner, Antwain, who was very nice to me.”

The discussion goes on for more than two hours. Dominique finds herself suppressing her yawns. “We really need to turn in. There will be details to tend to tomorrow. So we will pick the story up then.”

* * *

Pierre cannot help recalling his trips to San Francisco, Vancouver, New Orleans and Toronto before making his way to the Pasteur Institute. The anxiety that he had experienced during his San Francisco trip, while normal, had not been necessary. The command that he possessed of his subject matter had served him well. His travels to the other places had been easier.

He had communicated regularly with the Institute and today's reunion is to be a mere formality. His colleagues, some of whom might follow in his footsteps, are particularly interested in his day-to-day life. Many questions are directed toward Pierre: the working conditions at the laboratory facility, the other researchers, the stipend. In every instance, he is most reassuring.

While meeting with the Director, a few work projects that might be considered after settling back in France are proposed. "From your letters and emails, it is obvious that you were happy in the United States. You can pick up your research and courses at your leisure. In the meantime, take advantage of this vacation period to catch your breath."

The formalities are as expeditiously handled at the Ministry and Pierre rejoins the family on the Champs Elysées. The others have used this time to visit the Marmottan Museum. Julie told her grandmother the Boston Museum of Fine Arts story loudly enough to attract the envious attention of other patrons. "Monet, Monet; I am now an expert on Monet."

Philippe has stayed behind to chat with his grandfather who has shown a keen interest in his grandson's sporting accomplishments. He has not failed to bring up his own boyhood football exploits, tales that seem to be somewhat exaggerated but are nonetheless interesting.

"Soccer, Grand-père!"

"Now I watch all these rivalries on television and I fall asleep halfway through the matches."

That evening, following another substantial meal served with a bottle of champagne, photos are reviewed and more stories are told.

The family is left to contemplate tomorrow's trip to Nice. It will be at least another few days before bodies are fully adjusted to local time.

* * *

It is Pierre's parents' turn to welcome them back home. The TGV left the Gare de Lyon in Paris at 9:45 a.m. and arrived at the Nice train station at 3:20 p.m. Germaine and Frédéric drove two vehicles to accommodate all the baggage and passengers. The plan was to quickly drop everything off at their now vacated home. The American travelers inevitably met some of the neighbors and questions were given abbreviated answers with the intent of managing longer ones later. "Is life expensive in Washington? Did you like the city? Did you see the White House and the president? Did you visit Niagara Falls?"

The meal at the home of Pierre's folks is taken leisurely. Germaine puts a paté on the table. "Your letters were always received with great interest but, now that we have you in front of us, give us some of the details."

Pierre offers a few remarks. "As we have said repeatedly, we were well-received. I was a member of a team that benefited from a very modern laboratory on a college-like campus. I liked San Francisco, the first city that I visited and one to which I returned. Signs as one leaves the airport are bilingual, English and Spanish. The Latinos now form the majority in California. You saw *The Streets of San Francisco* on television: the cable cars, the hills, the bridge. It is a city with a great deal of charm."

"And the California wines?"

"I sent you a map of Napa Valley. Dr. Kantrowicz and I became good friends in the course of that trip. You will be able to try a few samples shortly."

Dominique comments on her courses. "For the most part, my students were delightful. I had no trouble with them even though some of them did not have much of a work ethic.

"Leaving aside the large cities, the small towns tend to resemble one another. The centers very often revolve around a town hall, a church, a bank."

Pierre's father mentions the likely increased police presence. "We sensed that to be the case while watching events there on television after last September 11th."

The son agrees. "I became constantly aware of more security after that day. It was a dominant feature of daily life at work and elsewhere. It was of course obvious at the airport when we left New York the other day."

"Papa," says Philippe, "tell them the customs story."

Pierre grins. "A friend from Washington was returning from Paris and he was asked to open his luggage by the customs officer. A packet of white powder tucked among his clothing was picked up and suspected of being some type of illicit drug. My friend could not contain himself with laughter. It was a kilo of the particular salt for which our Island of Noirmoutier is noted. We have since jokingly reminded Albert that, with just a little practice, he could pass as some kind of drug dealer."

Julie helps her grandmother with the *Poulet cordon bleu.* Again, inquiries are made concerning the treatment that they received from the Americans.

Dominique responds, "We were struck by everyone's kindness, whether it be in stores, in hotels, in restaurants. We encountered few French-speaking people and most Americans whom we met made a real effort to understand our

English at a time before we became more fluent. Pierre's English skills were always better than ours. The children and I were not always understandable at the outset.

"The children were quickly adopted by the neighbors and by their classmates. We were surprised by the almost immediate recruitment of Philippe into the local soccer program. Julie befriended Juanita of whom you heard from the very first week. One might say that, from the American standpoint, there was a certain appeal, almost envy, to having a French companion."

"We have heard a good deal about the obesity problem in America," comments Frédéric. "Were you aware of it as much as it is described in our reading material?"

Dominique agrees that it is a major problem. "The statistics are appalling. There are more and more people who are even morbidly overweight and that includes a significant number of children. One evening at a nearby table in a restaurant, we saw this enormous lady eat a bowl of chowder, a substantial salad followed by a heaping pasta dish and topped off by a three-scoop ice cream sundae piled high with whipped cream and dripping with chocolate syrup. We immediately recognized her problem. The portions when eating out tend to be frighteningly large. We always benefited from a second meal by requesting what they call *doggie bags* that we would bring home with us."

"And, Philippe, you have grown taller," comments his grandmother.

"It is probably the Montana air that is responsible," says Dominique. "He was given many tasks there and he returned home with much more self-confidence than he had had before he left."

Phillipe blushes and changes the subject. "I enjoyed skiing in Colorado, but I could have done without my appendicitis."

Pierre adds. “That surgical event allowed us to test the American medical system. You were well-treated, my son, but those HMOs are certainly complicated compared to our payment system here.”

“And you have said nothing about Canada,” comments Germaine.

Pierre sings Vancouver’s praises. “It is a beautiful city and we were never far away from the mountains or the Pacific Ocean. The mountains reminded me of Grenoble. I was surprised by the large Asian population. The pace of life is much less frantic there, certainly calmer than in Washington.”

Dominique speaks of *La Gaspésie* on the Atlantic side of the country. “We visited that charming part of the Quebec Province with one of Pierre’s colleagues and his wife, both of whom we came to know well. He is from Maine. By car, we covered half of the peninsula and we followed the coast to the city of Gaspé at its far-end.”

“So the people spoke French there.”

“Yes, although by then we had become quite fluent in English. We took advantage of our French nonetheless and the people did not fail to comment on our accent. ‘Ah, French from France,’ as they would say in their own Quebec accent.”

Philippe shows off his own English proficiency. “*But Grand-mère, we speak English now*.”

Julie recalls the early-morning awakenings. “The alarm went off at 6:15 and Philippe and I left the house at 7:10 to catch the school bus. It took 25 minutes to arrive at the Woodrow Wilson High School with stops along the way at almost every intersection to pick up more students. The trip took place in silence except when Philippe and his friends argued with one another or chose to tease the girls.”

Philippe adds his comments. “Yes, girls and boys sat separately, girls in front and boys out back. The lady driver would yell at us when she became annoyed by our mischief. She would say to us at least once a day, '*I will make you walk to school if you don't settle down.*' We boys would all laugh."

"Our first class," adds Julie, "started at 7:50 and our last class ended at 2:45. Our after-school activities extended until 5:15 and might include any number of sports or, as in my case, play rehearsals. Our early evenings were spent doing homework."

Dominique returns to her teaching obligations. "My homework consisted in preparing my classes. I left the house at the same time as the children the three days a week that I taught. Thankfully, I did not ride on a yellow school bus.

"This past year, as I mentioned to you in some of my communications, I also taught a class of graduate students at Georgetown University. I particularly enjoyed that assignment. It was a very diverse group of students from several different countries. While identified as a literature course, we discussed many issues relating to serious topics: war and peace, faith and reason, existence or non-existence of God. Camus was one of the principal authors that we studied. We covered *La Peste*, *The Plague*, in considerable detail."

"And you, Pierre?" asks his father.

"My schedule was not as rigidly fixed. I traveled a good deal. I met often enough with high-ranking officials and members of Congress. I was a member of two committees at the Capitol."

"In honor of French scientific knowledge, no doubt."

"One committee dealt with a study of the West Nile epidemic; the other related to Mad Cow Disease.

"Of course, I still spent much of my time in the laboratory tending to my research. I came to familiarize myself with the city and I circulated easily around the Mall and the Washington, Lincoln and Jefferson Memorials."

"And what about your weekends?"

Dominique picks up the conversation. "We visited within the city. Museums are free to the public and, without exception, are superb. I was even able to do a study of some of Picasso's works that are scattered here and there. We attended a number of theater productions at the spectacular Kennedy Center for the Performing Arts."

"Like us," adds Pierre, "the Americans are very much into sports. I played some golf with my laboratory colleagues and there was a gym with a pool that we joined. There was never a lack of activities and, lest I forget, there were frequent enough dinner engagements Saturday evenings at our or somebody else's home. My wife obviously excelled."

"Thank you."

"I must add, however, that her pork-tongue recipe did not go over well with everybody. One of our guests nearly choked when she discovered what she was eating. Dominique was obliged to open a can of spaghetti to help her through the meal.

"I almost forgot. We went to the French Embassy for our Bastille Day celebration on July 14 of last year. We helped provide finger foods and champagne for the assembled guests. Our French diplomats and those from other countries really know how to live."

Julie shows her grandparents photos of her graduation. "See, Grand-père, I have my high-school diploma."

"But it is not the baccalaureate."

"It is not the baccalaureate, but it is the American equivalent. I doubt that my education has suffered in any way."

"Still, equivalent or not, you will need to present yourself for your *bac*."

Julie looks to her parents for help. Pierre smiles and remains silent. Dominique shrugs her shoulders. "We have foreseen all of the baccalaureate requirements. The children did some extra studying most weekends and last summer to not fall behind in that regard. The internet was very helpful."

"We shall see if she will succeed."

"If you insist, Grand-père," concludes Julie with a grimace, "I will take the exam."

The discussion continues late into the evening. The recent travelers are critical of the eating habits of many Americans, meals taken too rapidly and all that snacking in front of the television.

On an unrelated subject, homes and rooms in hotels are much larger than in France.

Julie cannot help commenting on some of the accents. "The Downeasters of Maine and the Hillbillies of West Virginia, for example, speak almost totally different languages with their particular accents."

Pierre suggests plans for the future. "We certainly will return to the United States and Canada. The NIH would like me to consult at the laboratory for short periods of time once or twice a year. The University of Toronto has also requested that I give my course there again. These are offers to consider after I get reacquainted with my work here in this country."

Dominique adds: "The children will resume their studies soon, Philippe at the lycée and Julie at the university… after the *bac* exams. At some future date, Julie might find it possible to return to the States for further studies at the graduate level at Boston College or Georgetown University. Scholarship help would no doubt be available."

"Not completely a surprise," adds Pierre, "Philippe is showing some talent in physical and natural sciences and, while early, he seems to be gravitating toward a career in engineering like you, Papa. Your daughter-in-law will remain at home for the time being, but she may resume her teaching at some later time."

* * *

Frédéric feels that it is time to summarize everyone's thoughts. Germaine presents a platter of three cheeses and an assortment of fruit as her next course.

Frédéric opens another bottle of wine. "Well, what are your final impressions?"

Pierre pauses before answering. "Great contrasts ranging from the ultimate luxury of Las Vegas to the extreme poverty of Appalachia and just about everything in between. We were not often exposed to the countryside. We associated mostly with a highly educated segment of the population. Politically, it appeared to us to be a polarized country, the one that supported Bush and the other that favored Gore. You can imagine the differences that those two candidates represented."

Julie takes a turn. "It was a very enriching experience for us, well beyond the language. I believe like Papa that the terrorist attacks of September 11th have had important consequences throughout the country. We have witnessed those effects in the newspapers, on television, in train stations and airports, everywhere. Security has become an obsession and a daily reality."

Pierre describes the situation in Washington. "We were obliged to go through a security check in each government building. Americans now feel threatened and it was apparent to us that life in the United States would never be the same again. Americans work, business as usual, but remain suspicious and fretful."

"Still," adds Dominique, "they remain proud and we have sensed a certain patriotic fervor that might have been lost at some point."

"Is there anything to add?"

Dominique gathers her thoughts. "I have already commented on the cordiality directed toward us. Americans, particularly among the young, tend to be very informal and to pay little attention to appearances. They are persuaded that they can realize all their desires if they work hard. They are impatient when things don't go well or work right. They are consumers to excess. They drive big automobiles, although that tendency may be changing a bit. Still, one-third of their vehicles are SUVs. Gasoline, while expensive by their standards, is much cheaper than it is here. Households often are heavily indebted."

Pierre follows with his comments. "I appreciated the freedom of their press which can be very critical, oftentimes severely so. You may recall Watergate and the role that the press played in that scandal. A detail that I would add is that, if Canada is very neat and clean, the U.S. often is not. The cities and the highways in the States are often littered more than they should be."

Philippe chips in, "Julie and I were always well-accepted at school and on the playing fields."

Julie agrees, "On occasion, I found the Americans to be very reserved, almost cold. This reserve tended to dissipate quickly enough, at which point they could become quite warm."

Pierre finds that Americans are generous with their time and money. "They are part of the human family and they have the same aspirations that we have. There is more that unites us than there is that separates us."

Dominique comes back with a few gentle criticisms. "At the risk of whitewashing everything, I would add that poverty does exist in the United States; there certainly are the working poor among them. Homelessness in the major cities is not uncommon. We actually saw people sleeping in the streets in New York."

"Forty-five million Americans," adds Pierre, "have no health insurance, which for us in our country seems so strange. Our system never failed to surprise my research colleagues and the physicians that I came to know. It is like everywhere else, life is difficult for those who find themselves at the bottom of the economic ladder."

Before the end of the meal, Pierre ceremoniously presents four bottles of wine to his father. "A gift to you from California. They are quite good. You will need to taste them."

"That is very kind of you." Frédéric raises his glass, "Let us drink to the Americans and to the French, but let us not forget our own wines in the process!"

"Always so nationalistic, Papa," replies Pierre.

The grandmother is happy to see the family once again. "Don't go back too soon. We would like to see our grandchildren grow up and get married."

* * *

The family has finally returned home. The children have regained their rooms. Julie immediately sees where she will place her American treasures. Philippe finds a place for his soccer trophy from the Woodrow Wilson on top of his bookcase. The *Camden Yards* poster is sure to impress his friends. He will be happy to see them and will have many stories to relate.

The following morning, while Philippe and Julie are still sleeping, Dominique and Pierre find themselves on their sixth-floor balcony overlooking the bay. "After all our experiences in the United States," comments Dominique, "I must say that everything has seemed so much smaller over these past three days. I am certainly thrilled to be back home. It will take some time for us to process the meaning of these past two years that have unquestionably been worthwhile for us. To be sure, the children have been enriched and have grown up as well." Pierre points to the hordes of people strolling below them on the *Promenade des États-Unis*. Even at this early hour, many sun worshipers have staked their spots on the adjoining beach along the *Promenade des Anglais*. Bathers and surfers are enjoying their traditional vacations away from the cares of work.

The husband and wife delight in sipping a strong cup of coffee. They feel a gentle breeze; they see a cloudless sky; they note the aroma of the abundant bougainvilleas; they hear the slap of incoming waves.

A sense of contentment wells up in Pierre. "It is a delight to be back on our French Riviera, our *Côte d'Azur*. Look at the water, its distinct shades of blue and turquoise. I had almost forgotten how beautiful a view we have from here. Is it any wonder that so many people come to vacation in Nice?"

"It is fair to say," adds Dominique, "that we accounted well for ourselves and so, in returning, we can sing in unison:

Sweet France,
Dear country of our youth!"

Pierre expresses their mutual sentiments. "While grateful for our time in America, we are indeed happy to be back home."

Bibliography

Chapter 1

Fallon, Steve; Robinson, Daniel; and Wheeler, Tony; *Paris*, Lonely Planet Publications, 2001.

Chapters 2 and 3

Jones, Stuart E., *Washington, D.C., History, Site Selection and Planning*, Encyclopedia Americana International Edition, Grolier Publishing, Danbury, CT 06816, 2001, Vol. 28, pages 415-416.

Spencer, Jean E., *District of Columbia*, Encyclopedia Americana International Edition, Grolier Publishing, Danbury, CT 06816, 2003, Vol. 9, Page 192.

Chapter 4

Andrew Wyeth, Autobiography, Introduction by Thomas Hoving, Bulfinch Press, Little, Brown and Company, 1998.

Banks, Ronald F., *Maine Becomes a State*, Wesleyan University Press, Middletown CT, 1970.

Clark, Charles E., *Maine, a History*, W.W.Norton and Company, Inc., 560 5th Ave., New York, NY 10036, pages 185-186.

Conkling, Philip and Hayden, Anne, *Lobsters Great and Small, How Scientists and Fishermen are Changing our Understanding of a Maine Icon*, Island Institute, Rockland, ME, 2002.

Farnsworth Art Museum and Wyeth Center brochure, Rockland, ME.

Internet, *llbean.com/customerservice/aboutLLBean/timeline.html*, 07/12/2002.

Internet, http://www.manchesterhistorical.org/masco.html, *Masconomo: Sachem of the Agawam Tribe.*

Maine Potato Board, *Maine Potatoes*, Presque Isle, ME.

McClatchy, J.D., editor, *Longfellow, Poems and Other Writings*, Literary Classics of the United States, Inc., Penguin Putnam, Inc. New York, 2000, page131.

New England Outdoor Center, 2002-2003, pages 2-4.

Chapter 5

Feigin, M.D., Ralph D. and Cherry, M.D., John D., *Textbook of Pediatric Infectious Diseases*, Vol.II, W.B. Saunders Co., Philadelphia, 1981, page 1298 to 1311.

Goodwin, Bill, editor, *Frommer's USA*, Simon et Schuster Macmillan Co., New York, 1998, page 678 to 699.

Husson, M.D., Robert N., *Tuberculosis Update: What's New in 2002*, presentation given at Burlington, Mass., symposium in Pediatrics, May 15, 2002.

Internet, http://www.*goldengate*.com.

Internet, http://www.*halfwaytohellclub.com.*

Palmer, Phil and Mike, *The Cable Cars of San Francisco,* Howell-North Books, Berkeley, CA, 1959.

Soulé, Frank, et al., *San Francisco During and After the Gold Rush*, The Annals of America, 1841-1849, Vol. 7, Encyclopedia Britannica, Inc., Chicago, London, 2003, page 492.

Chapter 6

Crimson Key Society, *Guidebook to Harvard University*, pages 42 and 43.

Frost, Jack; Booth, Robert; Blotnick, Shirley, *Boston's Freedom Trail*, Third edition, The Globe Pequot Press, Old Saybrook, CT, 1994, pages 13 to 19.

Internet, *Le Marquis de Lafayette*, http://www.lafayette.com.

John F. Kennedy Library, visit in April, 2002. Film without title on the biography of Kennedy. Film of the *Cuban Missile Crisis*.

Langguth, A.J., *Patriots, The Men Who Started the American Revolution*, Simon and Schuster Paperbacks, 1230 Avenue of the Americas, New York, NY 10020, 1988.

The McGraw-Hill Encyclopedia of World Biography, pages 59 and 60, *Faneuil Hall*, 1973.

Tucker, Paul Hayes with Schackelford, George T.M. and Stevens, Mary-Anne, *Monet in the 20th Century*, Royal Academy of Arts, London; Museum of Fine Arts, Boston; Yale University Press, New Haven and London, 1998.

Wood, Gordon S., *The American Revolution, a History*, A Modern Library Chronicles Book, The Modern Library, New York, 2002.

Chapter 7

Internet, http://wwwskeptictank.org/barry.htm, *Actual Quotes Taken from Mayor Marion Barry.*

Internet, http://en.wikipedia.org/wiki/Marion Barry, *Marion Barry, Washington, D.C. political career.*

Chapter 8

Vail Valley Chamber of Commerce, *Vail-Beaver Creek*, Winter, 2002.

Vail Valley Chamber of Commerce, *The Vail Guide*, Summer, 2003.

Chapter 9

Adler, Jerry, *Mad Cow: What's Safe Now*, Newsweek, 12 January, 2004, pages 43 to 48.

Davis, Chuck, editor, *The Greater Vancouver Book*, The Linkman Press, 15032 – 97th Avenue, Surrey B.C. V3R 8K2. 1997, pages 48, 52 and 817.

Internet, http://www.vancouverchinesegarden.com, *Dans le jardin d'un érudit.*

Swiac, Chris, writer, and Kelly, Shannon, editor, *Fodor's Canada*, 26th edition, Fodor's Travel Publications, New York, Toronto, London, Sydney, Auckland, 2002, pages 17 to 130.

Chapter 10

Barry, John M., *Rising Tide, The Great Mississippi Flood of 1927 and How It Changed America*, Simon and Schuster, New York, NY, 1997.

Cirigliano, Rosanna, *La Nouvelle-Orléans*, French edition, Casa Editrice Bonechi, Via Cairoli 18/b, Florence, Italy, 2001.

Corrick, James A., *The Louisiana Purchase*, World History Series, Lucent Books, San Diego, CA 92198, 2001, pages 499 and 503.

Cox, Isaac Joslin, Ph.D., editor, *The Journeys of René Robert Cavelier Sieur de LaSalle*, AMS Press, Inc., New York, NY 10003, 1973.

Feigin, M.D., Ralph D. and Cherry, M.D., John D., *Textbook of Pediatric Infectious Diseases*, Vol.II, W.B.Saunders Co., Philadelphia, 1981, pages 1104 and 1121 to 1126.

Finley, John, *The French in the Heart of America*, Charles Scribner's Sons, New York, 1915.

Goodwin, Bill, editor, *Frommer's USA,* Simon and Schuster Macmillan Co., New Orleans, 1998, pages 381 to 404.

Jones, Max and Chilton, John, *Louis, The Louis Armstrong Story*, Little, Brown and Company, Boston, Toronto, 1971.

MGM, *Gone With the Wind* (*Autant en Emporte le Vent)* with Clark Gable and Vivien Leigh, Turner Entertainment Co., a Time Warner Co., 1939.

New Orleans, Official Visitors Guide 2002, New Orleans Metropolitan Convention and Visitors Bureau.

Osborne, Mitchell, *Mardi Gras in New Orleans*, Video by Mardi Gras Records, Inc. 1997.

Petersen, M.D., M.P.H., Lyle R., et. al., *West Nile Virus Encephalitis Outlook*, New England Journal of Medicine, Vol. 347, No. 16, 17 Oct., 2002, pages 1225 and 1226.

Teacher, Lawrence, editor, *The Unabridged Mark Twain*, Courage Books, The Running Press, Philadelphia, PA, 1976, pp. 77 and 78.

Terkel, Studs, *Giants of Jazz*, The New Press, 450 West 41st St., New York, NY 10036, 1975.

The World Book Encyclopedia, World Book Inc., 1999, pages 478 to 503.

Chapter 11

Boston Globe, *Counting the Homeless*, December 14, 2002.

Crossette, Barbara, *United Nations*, New York Times, March 25, 2001.

French, Howard W., *Seoul, South Korea*, New York Times, March 25, 2001.

Hillenbrand, Laura, *Unbroken*, Random House, Inc., New York, 2010.

Internet, *Ellis Island History*, http://www.ellisisland.com/history.html.

Internet, *Ellis Island Restored*, http://www.*ellisisland.com/restored*.html.

Internet, *Empire State Building*, Wikipedia, the free encyclopedia.

Internet, *The Statue of Liberty*, http:/www.*statueofliberty.org/default*.sol.html.

Internet, *Twin Towers New York*, Wikipedia, the free encyclopedia.

Visalli, Santi, photographs by, *New York*, Universe Publishing, a Division of Rizzoli International Publications, Inc., New York, 1995.

Chapter 12

Ben Cramer, Richard, *Joe Di Maggio, The Hero's Life*, Simon & Schuster, Rockefeller Center, 1230 Avenue of the Americas, New York, NY 10020, 2000.

Internet, http://www.*The Origins of the National Hall of Fame and Museum*, Baseball History.

O'Donnell, Edward T., *1845 The Ultimate American Game-Baseball*, Turning Points in American History, The Great Courses, page 293.

Chapter 13

Astor, Gerald, *The Greatest War, Americans in Combat, 1941-1945*, Presidio Press, Inc., Novato, CA 94945-1340, 1999.

Bernage, Georges, *Les Plages du Débarquement*, le guide, Editions Heimdal, 14406 Bayeux, 2001.

CBS Fox, *The Longest Day* (*Le jour le plus long)* with John Wayne, Robert Mitchum and Henry Fonda, 1962.

Glover, T.E., PhD., *The Lost Dutchman Mine of Jacob Waltz, Part 1: The Golden Dream*, Cowboy-Minor Productions, Phoenix, AZ 85068, 1998.

Internet, http://www.linternaute.com/citation/3959/les-sanglots-longs-des-viol…

Lazaroff, David Wentworth, *Arizona-Sonora Desert Museum Book of Answers*, Arizona-Sonora Desert Museum Press, Tuscon, AZ 85743, pages 18 to 28.

Maule, Henry, *The Great Battles of World War II,* Henry Regneri Co., Chicago, IL 60610, 1973.

MGM/UA, *Casablanca* with Humphrey Bogart and Ingrid Bergman, 1943.

Chapter 14

Columbia Pictures Industries, *A River Runs Through It*, (Fly Fishing), with Robert Redford, 1992.

Goodwin, Bill, editor, *Frommer's USA*, 5th edition, Simon and Schuster MacMillan Co., New York, page 849 to 863.

Jackson, Elmer M;, USN, Speech delivered before the *Jackson Hole Chamber of Commerce* on September 11, 1992.

Jackson Hole Chamber of Commerce, *Wyoming Facts*, *History of Jackson Hole*, *Geology of Jackson Hole*, *Yellowstone National Park*, *geology fieldnotes*, P.O.Box 550, Jackson, WY 83001.

Chapter 15

Internet, http://www.waltdisney.org, *The Walt Disney Family Museum*, *Walt's Masterworks.*

Chapter 16

O'Connor, Sandra Day and Day, H. Alan, *Lazy B*, *Growing Up on a Cattle Ranch in the American Southwest*, Random Press, New York, NY, 2002.

Raban, Jonathan, *Bad Land, An American Romance*, Pantheon Books, New York, NY,1995.

Steinbeck, John, *The Grapes of Wrath* (*Les raisins de la colère)*, Published by The Viking Press in 1939, Penguin Books, 375 Hudson St., New York, NY 10014, 1976.

Tirrell, Norma, *Montana*, Compass American Guides, Inc., Oakland, CA, 1991.

Chapter 17

Dickinson, John A. and Young, Brian, *A Short History of Quebec*, 2nd ed., Copp Clark Pitman Ltd., Toronto, 1993.

Hémon, Louis, *Maria Chapdelaine, Récit du Canada Français*, les éditions du Boréal, Montréal, Bibliothèque nationale du Québec, 1988.

Wood, Gordon S., *The American Revolution, a History*, A Modern Library Chronicles Book, The Modern Library, New York, 2002.

Chapter 18

Internet, *American Airlines Flight 77*, http://en.wikipedia.org/wiki/American_Airlines_Flight_77.

Internet, Morin, Terry, *Eyewitness Account of Pentagon Attack* http://www.coping.org/911/survivor/pentagon.htm.

Internet, *September 11, 2001 Attacks*, http://en.wikipedia.org/wiki/September_11%2C_2001_attacks.

Internet, *Lloyd, Survivors' Fund Project Survivor Story*, http://www.survivorsfundproject.org/SFPFinal/survivors_fund_project_clients/lloyd.asp.

Chapter 19

Fluchère, Henri, *Wines*, Golden Press, New York, 1974.

Internet, Mumm Cuvée Napa, *Is Sparkling Wine Champagne, Méthode champenoise*, http://www.mummcuveenapa.com.

Joseph, Robert, *French Wines, The Essential Guide to the Wines and Wine-growing Regions of France*, DK Publishing, Inc., 95 Madison Ave., New York, 1999.

Chapter 20

Internet, *Habitat for Humanity*, http://www.habitatforhumanity.com.

Internet, *Pilgrim Plantation*, http://www.pilgrimplantation.com.

Internet, *Wampanoag Homesite*, http://www.plimoth.org.

Internet, *umwa*.org/history/hallpres.shtml.

Chapters 21 and 23

Camus, Albert, *la Peste*, Collection Folio Plus, Editions Gallimard, 1947.

Camus, Albert, *l'Etranger*, Collection Folio, Editions Gallimard, 1942.

Lévi-Valensi, Jacqueline, *La Peste d'Albert Camus*, Collection Folio, Editions Gallimard, 1991.

Lottman, Herbert R., *Albert Camus, Biographie*, translated by Mariann Véron, Editions du Seuil, 1978.

Mérimée, Prosper, *Colomba*, Folio classique, Editions Gallimard, 1999.

Chapter 22

Beck, Simone, Berthole, Louisette, Child, Julia, *Mastering the Art of French Cooking*, Alfred A. Knopf, Inc., New York, 1964.

Devoto, Bernard, *The Year of Decision, 1846*, Little Brown and Co., Boston, 1943, page 13.

Harmon, Daniel E., *Davey Crockett, Famous Figures of the American Frontier*, Chelsea House Publishers, Philadelphia, 2002.

Internet, *Texas Annexation*, http://en.wikipedia.org/wiki/Texas_Annexation.

Internet, *Welcome to San Antonio*, http://.wwwsanantoniovisit.com.

MGM, Western Collection, *Alamo* with John Wayne, Richard Widmark, Lawrence Harvey and Richard Boone, 1960.

San Antonio Convention and Visitors Bureau, P.O. Box 2277, San Antonio, TX 78298, *San Antonio Visitor Guide and Map.* 2002.

Tinkle, Lon, *13 Days to Glory*, McGraw-Hill Book Co., Inc., New York, 1958.

Chapter 24

Bliss, Philip P., *Ville du Havre, It Is Well with My Soul*, Beckenhorst Press, Inc., 1981.

Bray, Rosemary L. and Zeldis, Malcah, *Martin Luther King*, Greenwillow Books, New York, 1995.

Encyclopedia Americana, *The Great Lakes*, International Edition, Grolier School Publications, Danbury, CT, 2003,Vol. 13, pp. 348-349.

Gordon, Devin, *The Power of P. Diddy*, USA Weekend, 25-27 October, 2002.

Smalley, Suzanne, *The New Age of Rave*, Newsweek, July 7, 2003.

Chapter 25

California State Parks, Sacramento CA 94296, *Old Town San Diego, State Historic Park*, 2002.

Encyclopedia Americana, International edition, Vol. III, *Balboa, 1475-1519*, Grolier Publishing Co., Danbury CT 06816, pages 79-80.

Goodwin, Bill, Editor, *Frommer's USA*, 5th edition, Simon and Schuster Macmillan Co., New York, 1998, pages 755 to 771.

Internet, http://en.wikipedia.org/wiki/Pete_Wilson.

Underhill, William, *Fill'er Up, But Not With Gas*, Newsweek, 16 Dec. 16, 2002, page E14.

Chapter 26

Albert, Thomas, *The History of Madawaska*, translated by Sœur Thérèse Doucette and Dr. Francis Doucette, Madawaska Historical Society, Madawaska, Maine, 2nd edition, 1990.

Développement économique Canada, *Gaspésie, le Québec Maritime*, Guide Officiel, 2002-2003.

McClatchy, J.D., Editor, *Longfellow, Poems and Other Writings*, Literary Classics of the United States, Inc., Penguin Putnam, Inc., 2002.

Chapter 27

Feigin, M.D., Ralph D., and Cherry, M.D., John D., *Textbook of Pediatric Infectious Diseases*, Vol. II, W.B. Saunders Co., Philadelphia, 1981, page 911.

Ksiazek, T.G., et al, *A Novel Coronavirus Associated with Severe Acute Respiratory Syndrome,* N Engl J Med 2003; 348: 1953-66.

Lee, N. et al, *A Major Outbreak of Severe Acute Respiratory Syndrome in Hong Kong*, N Engl J Med 2003; 348: 1986-94.

Low, D.E. and McGeer, A., *SARS—One Year Later*, N Engl J Med 2003; 349: 2381-82.

Olsen, S.J., et al, *Transmission of Severe Acute Respiratory Syndrome on Aircraft*, N Engl J Med 2003; 349: 2416-22.

Peiris, J.S.M., et al, *Current Concepts: Severe Acute Respiratory Syndrome*, N Engl J Med 2003; 349: 2431-41.

Poutanen, S.M., et al, *Identification of Severe Acute Respiratory Syndrome in Canada*, N Eng J Med 2003; 348: 1995-2005.

Reilley, B., et al, *SARS and Carlo Urbani*, N Engl J Med 2003; 348: 1951-52.

Tappero, J.W., et al, *Reduction in incidence of human listeriosis in the U.S.: effectiveness of prevention efforts*. JAMA 273: 1118-1122, 1995, Yearbook of Pediatrics, 1996.

Tsang, K.W., et al, *A Cluster of Cases of Severe Acute Respiratory Syndrome in Hong Kong*, N Engl J Med 2003; 348: 1967-1976.

Chapter 28

Goodwin, Bill, Editor, *Frommer's USA*, Simon and Schuster MacMillan Co., New York, 1998, pages 771 to 783.

Internet, Photo « *The City of Lights* » http://www.alexanderchen.com.

Mezrich, Ben, *Bringing Down the House*, The Free Press, New York, London, Toronto, Sydney, Singapore, 2002.

Patterson, Jerry L. and Jaye, Walter, *Casino Gambling*, A Perigree Book, the Berkeley Publishing Group, New York, NY 10016, 1982, pages 39-54.

Chapter 29

Internet, http://www.elgar.org/2english.htm.

Internet, http://en.wikipedia.org/wiki/Pomp_and_Circumstance_Marches.

Table of Contents

Cet ouvrage a été édité par la
Société des Écrivains,
14, rue des Volontaires – 75015 Paris
Tél: 01 53 69 65 33 – Fax: 01 53 69 65 27
www.societedesecrivains.com
info@societedesecrivains.com

Imprimé en France